Basket
Case

∫

SCEPTRE

Basket Case

DOUGLAS CHIRNSIDE

SCEPTRE

First published in 1996 by Hodder and Stoughton
A division of Hodder Headline PLC
A Sceptre Book

10 9 8 7 6 5 4 3 2 1

Basket Case is fiction, a novel set in the worlds of television
and advertising. In order to make it as true to life as possible
the author has occasionally mentioned real people, but all the
main characters and events are completely imaginary and no
reference is intended to people or companies in either industry.

British Library Cataloguing in Publication Data

Chirnside, Douglas
  Basket case
  1. English fiction – 20th century
  I. Title
  823.9'14 [F]

  ISBN 0 340 68060 1

Typeset by Palimpsest Book Production Limited,
Polmont, Stirlingshire
Printed and bound in Great Britain by
Mackays of Chatham PLC, Chatham, Kent

Hodder and Stoughton
A division of Hodder Headline PLC
338 Euston Road
London NW1 3BH

For Michael Attwell

BASKET CASE ∫

Thursday, 3 May 1979. On the day it looked as if Britain would elect its first woman Prime Minister, Paul McCarthy was still the only male secretary he knew of.

It was a mistake, he had decided, to think that this was an easy way to get into television. He should have used his degree properly and applied for a production traineeship or something. He should not have gone to work for the notoriously high-profile Karen Myhill, The Most Difficult Woman In Television. She had not, alas, turned round on day one and announced that he was to be her next executive producer on *Alive at Five*. In fact, she had not even made eye contact. She rarely did with anyone.

Instead, Paul had discovered too late that as her first male secretary he was some sort of Amazonian trophy for Karen to brandish at Trafalgar Television board meetings and generally throughout the entire ITV network. He was even mentioned in the profile *Broadcast* had run on her, not tucked away on the 'continued' page, but right in the opening paragraph in Century Bold.

No. Rather than a subtle way of getting a foot in the proverbial door, this job had quickly turned out to be an indelible stamp on his c.v.: SECRETARY. MALE. DO NOT TAKE SERIOUSLY. DO NOT RECRUIT INTO PRODUCTION. Within just six weeks of finishing his typing course he had entered into telly lore and the mythologising of Karen Myhill.

It was 5.35 p.m. Paul could go home as soon as he had filed this videotape in the security film library on the seventh floor. This was Karen's idea of what a secretary did. File a tape. Make a cup of coffee. Hand a piece of paper to Bob Dresler's secretary. Sit in front of her office door and make She Who Must Be Obeyed look important. She never wrote anything.

'Don't ever write anything down,' he had heard her tell her Ethnic Minority Advancement Scheme intake graduate, 'then they can't trap you with it later.'

What was a poor twenty-one-year-old on her first day meant to make of that? Other than that the woman was neurotic. 'Trap you with it later.' That was how the preying Myhill mind thought.

He scuffed his feet on the linoleum floor of the lift. He should have made this trip earlier in the day when he was asked to, rather than leaving it to the last minute. It was a largely ignored rule that tapes without clearance were not to be left lying around on secretaries' desks. He had filed so-called secret tapes so often before there was no longer any thrill in wondering what they might contain – which politician's gaffe would never be broadcast, which geriatric American star's embarrassing swansong would be snipped in editing.

He got out at the seventh floor and turned left into the long corridor. The strip lighting reminded him of the hospital where his grandmother had died. Luridly coloured blown-up portrait photographs of celebrities lined either wall. Petula Clark. Dick Emery. Gracie Fields. Anita Harris. Charlie Drake. Paul couldn't think when he had last seen any of them on Trafalgar Television, if at all, but then, like most of the younger ones in the office, he rarely watched TV and never light entertainment. Or LE as he knew to call it now.

He hated his suede brothel-creepers – they were all he could afford – but they did not betray his footsteps as he approached the security film library. As it was past 5.30 there would be no staff on duty. That was the difference between the junior staff in Administration and the junior staff in Production. Nine till five. They didn't hang about. He hadn't needed to memorise the four-digit code required to release the door. It was unforgettable. Six, two, zero, seven – the first three numbers of the Trafalgar telephone number followed by the number of the floor. With imagination like that, thought Paul, no wonder this was the leading LE company in the network.

He pressed the four numbers and pushed open the door. He

felt for the light switch. By the time the fluorescent ceiling lights had flickered fully on, he was too far into the room to withdraw without being identified. It was all over in a split second.

As Paul was gay he had no real-life experience of heterosexual lovemaking. But he had seen enough straight porn to immediately realise he was seeing The Most Difficult Woman In Television in The Most Compromising Position Of Her Life. Karen Myhill was lying on her back, her peroxided hair spilling on the linoleum, her trademark bejewelled glasses fallen from her face and lying to the side of an empty cane wastepaper basket. Her straight skirt was pushed up over her hips and her horribly white legs spread outward. A giant cock stuttered into her like a pneumatic drill. Whoever the guy was, the man on top of her appeared to have taken her there and then. He had barely got his trousers and pants down below the back of his knees. Paul blinked in the spectacle like a mole surfacing into sunlight. God, she really was grotesque, this crazed, ugly, fascinating media harpy. That was all that impinged on his consciousness.

It was a matchless combination of presence of mind and sheer nerve which had allowed Karen Myhill to launch herself from a semi-detatched in Bedford to her place at the top of British commercial television. Now her subliminal survival instinct soared into overdrive. Her feckless personal assistant was so fixated on the splayed arse and balls of the man fucking her that he had failed to register who he was. All was not lost. She flung her arms behind her head and frantically felt around the floor. In one decisive sweep, she grasped the wastepaper basket in both hands and propelled it upside down over the head of her oblivious lover.

Triumphantly, she thrust it downward as far as it would go and held it there hard. This novel sexual practice rendered the grunting mystery man utterly soundless and Karen now strained her neck towards Paul. Her face was a sublime concoction of power, sex, fury and victory as she looked up.

'You're fired,' she said, then added, 'I was going to do it anyway.'

It was the casual confidence of this afterthought that destroyed Paul. For a humiliating instant he thought he might burst into tears. This should have been *his* moment, a heaven-sent weapon with which to strike back. For whatever reason, he had blown it. But he had enough spirit left to retort. He drew himself up to his full five feet eleven inches and tried to summon up the most apt vocabulary with which three years at Warwick had provided him.

'You slag,' he said.

He spun round, pulled back the door and fled down the corridor, unaware that Ms Myhill's peachy satin Janet Reger knickers had somehow become attached to the heel of his suede shoe.

Karen's mind was a turmoil as she went into the polling booth. It wasn't the election and the future of Britain which concerned her, but the earlier events of the day. It was 8.55 p.m. and she had only just made it before polling ended at nine o'clock. She took her mind off her own problems for just a minute to take part in the most important election since the war. Supposedly.

She had decided to vote for Margaret Thatcher long before the party political broadcasts had shown the new-look, floppy-bowed blonde sitting demurely on a lichen-covered stone balcony with England's green and pleasant land falling away behind her. Admittedly, it seemed a bit of a volte-face after voting Labour and then Communist in the two '74 elections, and Karen had taken some stick in the boardroom for 'coming round'. But she had been five years younger back then and five years further behind in her career, and now a new decade beckoned. Karen identified with Thatcher's small-town-to-world-power surge to glory. She wanted business, *her* business of television, freed up and the sodding TV trade unions told to piss off and leave her programmes be. She wanted women like herself to gain the chance of power and to learn how to wield it. And she wanted to earn her rewards and keep them, because money was power too. Thatcher probably would go the way of all the others, but at least if she won, for a while Karen could tell all the fat bastards on the board to fuck off. She would watch them squirm at the success of The Female.

Unfortunately, her idea of keeping her main residence near her parents and clear of Trafalgar had led her to a rock-solid Tory stronghold, so her vote would be more a gesture of principle than a crucial rung in Margaret Thatcher's climb to power. In

Huntingdon the previous Member of Parliament had just retired so there would be a new MP. She had seen his face on the posters, a weedy young accountant type with big glasses and a cheesy grin to match.

Although Karen would have preferred to have voted for a woman candidate, when she had read the literature she was pleasantly surprised to see that this new breed of Tory had formerly sat on the local council where Trafalgar had its stumpy tower block – Lambeth. Apparently he had stood up against the waste and squander of the Loony Left there and protested on Trafalgar's behalf about the level of business rates and the like. So she could personally thank him with her vote here, one hundred miles away, and at the same time send Mrs Thatcher a nice little smiley councillor to sit behind her and dutifully support her every whim. She took the half-pencil and marked her 'X' beside his name: Major, John (Conservative Party).

She drove the last half-mile to her house. She still couldn't get the sound of the library door opening out of her head. That stupid boy had just stood there. She wasn't prejudiced against homosexuals but the really feckless, faggy ones like him irritated the tits off her. Just like those bone-headed Huntingdon hags in hats who would vote for nice Mr Major without a thought. They had never voted Communist, nor held their own in an ACTT meeting. They hadn't been forced to stand up for the whole of womankind and take the innuendo of dirty after-work sexist jokes in the bar. They hadn't been invited to join the board, however reluctant the offer was, nor run the gauntlet of the press for going tabloid on current affairs programming. God. Was all of that at risk now? Her entire career? Her London flat and Huntingdon house? Her company Granada? The dinners at Langan's? Paul was such a gossipy little queen at the best of times. Now he had the story to cap the seventies. Through habit only, she managed to stop herself driving through the red light at the crossroads.

Still, it could be twice as bad. He could have *seen* who her mad fuck was. Once they all knew *that* she would not just be a laughing-stock but a source of complete derision. She could never show her face in public again. She smiled suddenly at the mental picture of herself and her five-minute lover dining out, each wearing a matching cane wastepaper basket over their heads. Her smile became a chuckle. She felt herself relax. Come on. She could ride this one out. It was her against her ex-secretary, for God's sake. She had reached the driveway of the mock cottage and pulled the handbrake up sharply. Poofter Paul was a standing joke in the company. She'd already seen to that. Unintentionally, of course, but just as well bearing this afternoon in mind. No one would believe *him* against *her*.

But everyone did, because everyone believed everything about Karen Myhill, The Most Difficult Woman In Television. And when Max was born exactly nine months later, the rumours got worse. As Max grew both wide and tall, and his eyes changed from blue to brown, his hair from fair to dark and his face from round to square, the myth flourished and spread. And when Max grew to teenagehood and began to counsel, critique and control his manic mother and everything she did in television, the speculation as to the identity of his father got completely out of hand. Woe betide the man who asked for Karen Myhill on reception, or who invited her out to lunch or who paused at the door of her ever-larger office. Because then the tongues would start to wag and the index fingers point and television folk would be heard to say:

'I reckon that's Max's father. I reckon that's Basket Case.'

Major, John (Conservative Party) was Prime Minister now and not quite so smiley. He was struggling almost as much with John Humphrys' questions as he was with the country at large.

As Duncan stirred and turned down the alarm clock radio, he nudged his sleeping partner. She moaned a bit from under the duvet and stretched. Duncan always set the radio this loud to guarantee he would actually wake up. In the years when Brian Redhead had presented BBC Radio 4's *Today* programme he could keep the volume constant. Since Redhead's death, John Humphrys seemed to have become more bad-tempered and louder with the politicians who lined up each morning to set the day's agenda. Duncan reached for his contact lenses – he had dispensed with glasses entirely – and launched himself out of bed and towards the bathroom to pee away his erection.

'Come on, baby. Time to get up.'

He sped out of the room. Why it should embarrass him to sport a hard-on in front of her he didn't know, but it did.

When he came back twenty minutes later she was awake and he was a different man. He could see, for a start. His lenses made his grey eyes liquidy. He had showered, shampooed and shaved. His fairish hair was sparkling with L'Oréal Studio Line Design Gel, short, with just a few spiky bits on top. His slight sideburns were neatly trimmed and his finger- and toenails freshly clipped. His armpits glistened with fragrance-free roll-on, so as not to clash with the scent of the Antigua fragrance bodyspray he had applied across his upper torso. And, because he was thirty-two and age had just begun to draw fine lines around his eyes and dry out his skin, his face was lightly moisturised and aglow.

He leant over the bed and kissed the line of soft blonde down on her belly. This was her favourite start to the day, when Duncan was alert and playful. She loved the tingle in her nostrils of his Armand Hammer Baking Soda toothpaste – Wow! – or the medicated smack of Listerine. Playful or not, Duncan had a strict morning regime. Like absolutely everything in his life – his flat, his friends, his career, his car, his sex – it was meticulously organised and immaculately executed. Duncan was supremely anally retentive and proud of it.

He stepped across the cream carpet to the antiqued pine chest of drawers. From the second top drawer he selected a pair of white Calvin Klein trunks he had bought in New York. He slipped them on in front of the mirror. He was quite pleased with the way he looked, although he thought he could lose half a stone. His stomach was still flat although not quite as firm as when he was twenty-five. However, the trunks drew the eye away from his waistline and down to his crotch and the top of his smooth thighs.

Now he pulled open the sock drawer and brought out a pair of navy blue cotton ones. He didn't need to see into the drawer to know exactly where they were. From the wardrobe filing system came a Ralph Lauren pale blue Oxford button-down, followed by a plain navy, softly tailored suit in light wool. Single-breasted, four buttons, the buttons being dark brown. It was really an Armani rip-off, of course, but neither Marks & Spencer nor Duncan would admit to this. In the winter he might wear a little coloured waistcoat, but with the May sun beating into the bedroom that was not necessary today.

Duncan was a past master at buying expensive-looking designer clothes from the likes of the M&S Marble Arch store and passing them off. This he did by wearing genuine accessories. A pale gold and blue Dolce and Gabbana tie, a steel and gold Santos de Cartier watch, a decent dark burgundy belt and matching loafers by Patrick Cox. His style, he would say, was relaxed formal. Colleagues, however, had once dubbed him Wingco for the way he would present himself on the dot each morning as if for military inspection.

Duncan never ate breakfast on weekdays. Timed to the last

minute, that was his routine. Wake. Wash. Dress. And feed Pushkin.

'Come on, baby,' he signalled to his bedtime companion, a sorrel-coloured Somali cat lying on the bed. 'Foody-woody!'

She jumped down and raced through to the tiny kitchen, anticipating the moistest Select Cuts imaginable.

Duncan's car purred too. A year-old navy blue BMW 3.25 convertible. This was why he worked in advertising. For the perks. Duncan liked Nice Things. The roof peeled away automatically and let in the morning sun. Despite his car's being open to the air, Duncan flicked down the central locking button and secured himself in the luxuriously lined and trimmed interior. And despite being Mr Attention To Detail, he had still not remembered to put his Ray Bans into the glove compartment. Shame on you, Dunky, he admonished himself. Cherry blossom fluttered past on the breeze. Into the never-used cigarette lighter socket he slipped the connector for his Nokia Orange digital mobile phone and watched it light up on stand-by. He slotted the removable panel of the Panasonic RDS radio into place and turned on more of the *Today* programme. He pulled sharply out of residents' parking on to Sutherland Avenue. Maida Vale to Soho in twenty minutes. And an unsolicited phone call from The Most Difficult Woman In Television.

2

Duncan enjoyed the drive to work but had only done so since he joined the board eighteen months before and gained a reserved parking space in the NCP in Wardour Street. He didn't know it, but it cost more per annum than his first advertising agency had paid him ten years before. This morning he was thinking about his time there, as he always did when he had to interview someone making their first move. What had been in his mind when he had left his own first agency, O&M? He couldn't remember. Anyway, this girl was different from him. She had Hampshire, Bedales and Exeter behind her. She had once been a chalet girl in Val d'Isère. And she had sounded frightfully cut-glass on the phone. Being a Scot, Duncan was still a sucker for English upper-middle-class credentials and this lady's c.v. had the lot. Audrey Goldberg, the headhunter, wouldn't be sending her in if she wasn't right. He was leaving the white stucco of Regent's Park when he drew up alongside a determined young road hog on a contemporary classic motor bike, distinctively a Ducati. Without a sideways glance Duncan put his foot down on amber. He may have matured from an XR3i with Go Faster Stripes but, like all admen, he was still a Boy Racer at heart.

Duncan was first in. No one else ever got in this early. He sat down at his black ash veneered desk and proudly surveyed the gleaming surface of his personal domain. Lined up along the back of it a row of executive accessories stood to attention, each item accurately squared up with the right-angled edges of the desk. A matt-black calculator with Bauhaus coloured buttons. A matt-black plastic desk tidy containing rollerball pens and needle-sharp company pencils. A steel magnetic block for black paper clips and black-headed drawing pins. A matt-black plastic and steel stapler and a matching hole punch. A flat chrome Sony Walkman pocket memo speech recorder. A matt-black Panasonic telephone answering machine with voicemail facility. A matt-black plastic and steel in-tray. A matt-black sexily Italian weighted and sprung desk lamp with halogen spot, clamped securely to the desktop and bringing the row of accessories to a neat end, anchoring them in line. Each object was perfectly positioned in parallel, each precisely in its place, just as Duncan always insisted everything should be. It had taken him months to collect the set. The stationery department had him down as a troublemaker. Other people made do with whatever colour or whatever style was in stock or was easily obtained. But as his colleagues knew to their cost, Duncan Cairns did not make do. He placed his matt-black mobile phone adjacent to the table telephone, it being no extra effort at all to set it properly in line. Just in front of it was a neatly ordered pile of messages from yesterday afternoon, when he had been out filming at Shepperton Studios. A yellow Post-it note was stuck to an audio cassette tape.

'Duncan. This is the revised jingle for the end of The Station commercials. Please approve a.s.a.p.' Duncan swivelled round and popped the cassette into the stereo system.

'The Sta-a-a-a-tion. The Sta-a-a-a-tion. The Sta-hey-hey-hey-hey-hey-hey-shun. Do let it pass you by.'

Duncan had to think for a minute whether or not he could get this version through his biggest client. It was better than the previous one. At least you could understand what the hell they were singing this time. He loathed and detested that line, 'Do let it pass you by.' What silly fucker had thought that up? No one knew. It was an imposition from The Station's American parent company which they all had to live with.

He searched out a compliment slip from his drawer and swiftly wrote a note to his client to listen to the cassette and approve the jingle by lunchtime. He popped the note and the cassette into a manila envelope. It would have to go round to The Station on a bike. There was no one free this morning to take it round and present it. This was an irritation to Duncan, who had been schooled only ever to present creative work for approval to clients in person.

Next, there was a Sony Umatic videotape which a typed message told him to look at.

'Girl number five is a natural blonde. Her legs are right for this and she can do getting out of a car in under three seconds. She's done a Tampax film. Is that a prob?'

Duncan didn't have a video player in his office and didn't want to leave his desk so he put it aside for viewing later.

Underneath was one of the TV producer's expenses. 'Sign this. Ta.' was written on another Post-it note which was stuck on top. Duncan wrinkled his nose at the use of the word 'Ta'. Not something he would ever allow himself to say, let alone write down. He peeked at the bottom line.

'Jesus. How do they get through so much money, those guys?'

He initialled the forms and put them in the Out post tray.

Then there were a couple of internal memos. One announced that the agency was pitching for a condom account and, in the interests of research, would you please fill in anonymous details about your sex life and return to Rachel Hudson in Planning.

'That has to be a ruse.'

Duncan laughed. Yeah. The multiple-choice answers to 'What size of condom do you find most comfortable?' were 'Slimfit', 'Supershag' and 'Salami'. Like probably at least thirty other people, he toyed with the idea of filling it in with someone else's details, then couldn't be bothered and crumpled the memo into the bin. These anonymous things, so-called. They could always work out who they'd come back from.

At the bottom of the heap was a Chromalin proof of the cover for the latest Station brochure.

'Duncan. This is what is going out unless you stop it NOW!' read its Post-it note.

'The Station. The World's First Fully Interactive Cable Television Channel.' In smaller type below: 'You've heard about the information superhighway. Now it's coming to your street. The Station. Do let it pass you by.'

That fucking endline. Duncan wished they could drop it and have done with it.

He noticed that the post boy had left the press cuttings from the previous day in the filing tray at the back of his desk. He ought to go through them now, and catch up while he had a minute.

'BBC Set to Decline Further as Rival Launches,' said *The Times*.

Good, thought Duncan.

'Sky Dished by Switch to Cable,' said the *Daily Mirror*. Without bothering to mention their own stake in the Live TV cable channel, the article pointed out that The Station's sophisticated interactivity was not possible on satellite television and Sky viewers would not want to get left behind with outdated technology. Would British Sky Broadcasting abandon its dishes and switch underground to join The Station?

I hope not, thought Duncan. What was in the *Guardian*? Hmm. Similar to *The Times*, but with a sub-head:

'C4 Remit Safe With Me Says Grade. Michael Grade, Chief Executive of Channel Four Television, yesterday repeated his oft-made remark that Channel 4's targeted minority appeal is its greatest asset in the ratings war. "Channel 4 welcomes new broadcasters such as The Station and is itself at the forefront of new developments with wide-screen technology."'

He seems to be the only one with a strategy, thought Duncan. What's this? He sniggered.

The *Sun* was not the world's biggest-selling daily newspaper for nothing. It had run a Page Seven Fella photo-story on one of The Station's sub-contractors' workmen. There he was, a good-looking guy stripped to the waist, suggestively holding a foot-long chunk of black cable down by his crotch.

'Can I Slip You A Length, Mrs?' ran the headline. It continued underneath: 'Big Boy Bernie offers to do a spot of laying down your way.'

The telephone rang.

'Your eight o'clock appointment is here.'

Duncan replaced the receiver and checked his steel and gold Santos de Cartier watch. It was eight o'clock exactly.

'That's my girl,' he said, rising. In advertising first impressions are the only ones that count.

The telephone rang again. Duncan was already heading for the lift to greet his interviewee. He could take no calls now. On the other hand, perhaps it was reception telling him to hold on or something. He sprang back and lifted the receiver.

'Duncan Cairns.'

'Hello, Duncan. You were recommended to me by the head of programmes at The Station. This is Karen Myhill. I'm an independent television producer with my own company and I would like to meet you.'

3

'Duncan Cairns?'

Although she put them as a question, she took the words out of his mouth. She stepped forward and the lift doors shut behind her. She extended both her white-light smile and her right hand. Duncan had noticed that at this stage the poorer interviewees always seemed to find their briefcase on the how-do-you-do side. Charlotte Reith had only a strappy shoulder purse.

'My God,' said Duncan. 'Where's your whip?'

Charlotte laughed at his reference to her outfit and pushed her flighty blonde hair back from her face. In her fitted red blazer, jodhpur leggings and riding boots, she looked like a Grace Kelly about to join the hunt. Or she looked liked a blonde Audrey Hepburn, girly, gamine and all gold buttons. Well, whoever she looked like, she looked gorgeous. Absolutely gorgeous.

'I came on my bike. It's such a beautiful morning.'

This to explain her interview outfit.

'You cycled here?'

'Not exactly. I came on my Ducati. I left my helmet on reception.' She pushed back her hair again. 'At least I wasn't mistaken for a courier and sent round to Dispatch!'

'I hardly think that's likely.'

'It's happened to me before. I hope you've got coffee. Most agencies don't before nine thirty a.m.'

'We're not most agencies.'

'Sales pitch!'

'OK, we're pretty much the same as most agencies, but I'm not like most account men. I run my business properly. And that includes preparation, meeting rooms and lots of coffee for interviews. Follow me.'

'You've actually read my c.v.' This guy was more polished than the others. She knew that, so far, she hadn't put a foot wrong. 'How refreshing.'

'What do you think the most essential quality of a good account manager is?'

'God. I suppose what you're meant to say is good creative judgment and the ability to sell good creative work to clients. And what you're not meant to say is keep the client happy.'

'Is that it?'

'Well, what I think I do well is recognise whether the creative work actually embodies the advertising strategy and is the most effective way of communicating it. My job is to make sure it does, before I try to persuade the client to buy it.'

'Sounds good to me.' She was footsure for a twenty-five-year-old. 'What's your favourite commercial at the moment?'

'That Levi's one from Bartle Bogle Hegarty.'

'And what d'you think it's trying to say?'

'Well, *he* says "Shag me, shag me" to me! Forget the product points. It's all about sex. I don't know why everyone goes on about creative strategy and art direction. Just stick in a washboard stomach or a big pair of tits. Sex sells.'

'Yes. I can see you understand that.'

She giggled. She wasn't quite sure how she was meant to take that one. Duncan didn't send out the vibes of the legover merchants she had had to put up with at Saatchi's. But he didn't progress with that line.

'What made you first come into advertising?'

'I suppose I always wanted to work in the media somewhere, do something creative. Advertising seemed the most business-like, the most professional.'

'I suppose it is.'

'And, if this doesn't sound too ghastly, I wanted to work with people like me.'

'People like you?'

'I mean like-minded people. You know. Self-starters. Achievers. What about you?'

'What about me?'

'Why did you come into advertising?'

'God, I can't remember now, it's so long ago. I know why I stay in it.'

'Why?'

'Hey, I'm asking the questions round here.'

'I'm just curious. It's only fair I should get the chance to learn as much about you as you do about me, isn't it?'

Duncan chuckled at her naïve audacity and answered her question. 'You know on those omnibus market research surveys they always ask consumers to agree with either "I think it's better to buy lots of cheaper things than just a few dearer ones" or "I prefer to buy few things of quality rather than lots of cheaper items"? Well, I'm the second kind of person. But you can't buy any decent stuff without the earning power. That's what makes me stay. The lifestyle.'

'Personally I prefer to buy *lots* of incredibly expensive things and bugger the consequences.'

From the conspiratorial way Duncan laughed with her – as only the comfortably-off can about money – Charlotte knew that they had hit it off. His next question, though, arrived faster than she expected.

'How soon can you get out of Saatchi's?'

'Immediately, if you put me on The Station account.' She hoped that didn't sound desperate. 'Saatchi's would regard it as competitive business. I'd be chucked out in minutes.'

'You know I have an account manager on The Station account already. There's no vacancy – at the moment. But I do need to bring someone good in on the other smaller accounts which need more attention than I currently have time for.'

'Well, I'm very keen. Everyone is talking about The Station launch. It'll be bigger than Sky and Channel 4 put together, won't it? The implications for advertising are tremendous. I really want to learn more about interactive TV.' Now that did sound desperate. She backtracked. 'Of course, I'm still equally enthusiastic about the other accounts.'

'They're all good clients. Is there anything you would like to ask me?'

'Absolutely.' From her strappy shoulder purse Charlotte pulled out a compact, mottled-blue notebook. Duncan spotted the word Challenge on its cover, glittering in gold under the meeting room's recessed halogen lights. She flicked through its pages and then snapped it shut again. Duncan, a stickler for detail himself, was impressed.

Charlotte smiled at him. 'You've answered most of my questions already, actually. Audrey Goldberg wasn't able to say exactly what accounts you were recruiting for.'

'That's because I wasn't specific with her. Our general work-load seems to be increasing so I need to bring in someone who can work across a range of business. I'll mix and match it to whomever gets the job. Probably it'll be the Carpets Company and Bencelor. I'll start the new person off with those two and then see what more I think they can manage.'

'Not The Station?'

'Not right now.'

'OK. It's important to me that – if I should move – I go somewhere stable. What's the staff turnaround like here?'

'Average, I suppose. No one's left lately. This is a new position we're creating. It's not a vacancy.'

'I'd be reporting to you and you alone, Duncan?'

'Yes. You'd work alongside the other account manager in my group.'

'And what are your own plans? How long have you been here?'

'Two years.'

'And you intend to stay here long-term? When I joined Saatchi's I started with somebody who left within two weeks. All the shit, if you'll excuse the expression, got dumped on me.'

'Don't worry. I'm not going anywhere. I have a very cushy position here. There isn't a better job out there in adland for me.'

He paused to see how she would progress the conversation. Charlotte handed him the hot potato.

'You must know that people say that Clancey and Bennett is not a proper agency since the takeover. Not now it's inside MCN International?'

'They're wrong. It is. The strength of the Clancey and Bennett name is evident in the fact that it didn't disappear in the takeover. Think of it as an agency within an agency. Out of the three hundred MCN people in this building, we've got sixteen people working solely for us in C&B. The buying departments, like media, print and TV production and art buying, are part of MCN and we share them equally.'

'And do you actually run Clancey and Bennett?'

This was the bit Duncan hated.

'No, I run the accounts but not the agency. You'll have to come back and meet Nigel and Serena. They work as a partnership. It'll be a double interview. It's not a rubber stamp, but they go with me normally.'

The fuck they did.

'So, have I got the job, then?'

She was mischievous as she turned into the lift.

'Don't push your luck, young lady. Wait to hear from Audrey Goldberg. She's your headhunter, isn't she?' He glanced towards her riding boots. 'Give my love to Dobbin.'

'It's a Throbbin' Dobbin, actually.' The doors cut in on her laughter.

4

Breakfast wasn't going too well.

'It looks like a jar of shit.'

Max Myhill was referring to the Nutella Hazelnut Chocolate Spread on the kitchen table.

'Max! I won't tell you again. You mustn't use language like that.'

'You swear all the time.'

'I'm an adult,' said Karen.

'Jesus, Mum! That's hardly a rational response.'

'I don't have to be rational. I'm the mother round here. You're the child. You do as I say, not as I do. You mustn't use four-letter words.'

'I'm a teenager, actually, not to be too technical about it. Not a child.'

Karen sighed in exasperation. Max laughed at her sad attempt at discipline.

'OK, then. It looks like a jar of whipped-up jobbies. No four-letter words there.'

Karen was pushed to her limit. 'Max, I could hit you sometimes.'

'Uh, uh. Not allowed.'

'I know it's not allowed. But you mustn't use bad language. It's beneath someone of your intelligence.' Max was always appealing to her to be logical. The most logical person she could think of came to mind. 'You don't catch Professor Stephen Hawking saying expressions like "whipped-up jobbies".' There.

'That's because he talks through a machine. It's probably not been programmed to handle that sort of vocabulary.'

'Don't be nasty, Max. You must never make fun of those less able than yourself.'

Max smiled wryly to himself. How could his mother consider the author of *A Brief History of Time* to be one of the less able? He remembered something. 'Did you call that man?'

'I did. A little while ago. I got through this time. He obviously starts very early.'

'Who is he again?'

'He works for The Station's advertising agency.'

'How d'you know him?'

'I've never met him, Max. But the head of programmes at The Station said very good things about him. I'm going to meet him tonight.'

Max looked suspiciously at his mother. 'What would he do?'

'Max, I'm only having a drink with him. I probably won't even like him. He might not like me. He might not be interested anyway. Advertising is so much more glamorous than boring old television.'

'Boring old television!' Max scoffed and laughed again. 'Myhill Productions is dead exciting and you know it. Time to go! You're holding me back.' He leapt off his chair and scrammed out of the kitchen. Karen called after him.

'You've not eaten anything! You can't go to school on an empty stomach!'

He reappeared and pecked his mother on the cheek. Sweet, she thought.

'I'll be OK. Have a good day at the office. Don't sign that BBC thing without us getting the secondary rights or at least unless they alter it so the rights return to us in five years. No. Three years.'

'I won't.'

'And don't pay over the odds to get John Leslie on the other thing. We can create our own star ourselves. Point out our track record.'

'You're right, Max. I'm so lucky I've got you. I'm spending most of today with the accountant, anyway. It's not a creative day. You realise we could have an income crisis looming?'

'Who? Us? No way. We're gonna be huge.'

'I wish I had your faith.'

Max zoomed past his mother down the hall and almost out through the wide open front door. Karen was suddenly seized by impulse.

'Max!'

Her son stopped, framed in the doorway.

'C'mon, Mum. I'm late as it is. You may have forgotten but school is not like the office. They have this bell thing that rings at nine on the dot and if you're not there, then— ' He slit his throat with his finger.

She hesitated. 'Bigger issues, Max.'

Something in the tight tone of her quiet voice signalled to Max to hold on. He played it as cool as he could manage.

Karen couldn't quite look him in the eye. 'I've been thinking . . .'

'Are you going to tell me?'

'Not right here and now on the doorstep, Max. Now is not the time nor the place. But . . .' Karen was stalled by the imploring look of sheer expectancy on her son's face. Always articulate, she was unexpectedly drowning for lack of choice words. 'Max, lately you've been such a source of help and inspiration with the company and everything . . . and acting so mature . . . that

I don't think we need to wait until you're sixteen. You're much further ahead than I had ever hoped or imagined you would be by now. You're a grown-up now, really. I rely on you. God knows, Myhill Productions relies on you. Perhaps we can go out at the weekend and sit down somewhere away from everything, somewhere really discreet, and I can tell you the whole story. There are lots of implications and things, so it has to be right for me as well as right for you. That's only fair, darling, isn't it? It'll be a very difficult conversation for Mummy.'

'Naming names?'

'Yes.'

'You really mean it?'

'Yes, Max.' There was a detectable break in her voice. 'It's time for me to tell you who your father is.'

'Really?'

'Really.'

'Promise?'

'I promise, darling.'

Max stood and faced her square. He looked younger again now, equipped as he was for school. He began to say something and stopped. 'Tell me now.'

Karen tutted on reflex. 'Not right now, Max.'

'Clue, then.'

'No clues.'

Max was disappointed. 'I don't believe you. You won't bring yourself to tell me. Not yet. I know you.'

'I don't think anyone knows me, not even me. I will tell you, Max. I promise.' And she said it with conviction.

'Yo!' shouted Max, and punched the air with his head. He whirled round and sped out and off.

Oh, thought Karen, aware of wet, watery eyes. My precious baby.

5

Duncan had no chance to discuss Charlotte Reith's interview with his superiors for the rest of the morning. However, he was convinced she was way ahead of the other candidates that headhunter Audrey Goldberg had picked out for him.

'Isn't she gorgeous, Duncan?'

Audrey's calls always managed to catch him between meetings.

'She turned up here in leathers and all that blonde hair just tumbled out from her crash helmet. I knew I couldn't lose with her. She's Cathy Gale. You know, Honor Blackman in *The Avengers*.'

'Audrey, you're giving your age away. I don't recruit on looks. That would be unprofessional.'

'Of course not, Duncan. I know you don't. I did fax you her c.v., didn't I? She's got everything you briefed me on. But we both understand the value a young attractive woman can have to business. Clients like it . . . By the way, *The Avengers* is on UK Gold in the afternoons. I have it on sometimes in the office.'

She was obviously touchy about the reference to her age.

'I need to speak to Nigel and Serena first and get her in their diaries.' He needed to ease Charlotte in at the right time if she was to avoid a mauling from those two. 'Actually, Audrey, can you find out if she could pop back this evening, say five thirty? They might be able to do it then. My secretary will call you to confirm.'

'So has she got big tits, then? Alan always says he recruits on that basis.'

'Why did he once give *you* a job then?' Duncan joked.

'Piss off,' retorted his lunch partner.

'She was wearing a jacket. I couldn't tell. She looked lithe all over, actually.'

'Small pointy ones, then.' Cindy Barratt peeked over the top of her menu and gave Duncan one of her naughty looks. They were in Pizza on the Park, at the top end of Knightsbridge. Excellent budget pizzas in smart modern surroundings. Since it was so sunny, if the service was quick, they'd risk crossing the road and stroll through the formal flower beds in Hyde Park after lunch. Duncan could still be back in Soho by three.

'Dunky!' She squealed. 'Guess who I saw in Harabs on the way here?'

'Since when was Harrods on the way here from Haringey?'

'Let's face it,' said Cindy, 'nowhere is on the way from Haringey. I hate Haringey. That's why I popped into Harabs on the way here. To cheer me up. Anyway, I'm having a cash flow crisis. No money.' She spotted her best friend was not catching her drift. 'I can shop in the Food Halls on my card. I don't have to pay for two months. You know, like Marie Antoinette said, "Let them eat cake." I bought this really delicious focaccia and some Greek bread with olives in it and some taramasalata. And the smallest tin of red caviar they do, which is actually quite big—'

'You must stop penny pinching,' said Duncan dryly.

'—and lovely lemons and a few Godiva chocolates for when I'm lying in bed on Sunday. Well, I have to have something to do while Alan is writhing on top of me.'

That naughty look flitted across her face again.

'No one eats chocolates during intercourse. Not even you.'

'Stop interrupting. Going up the escalator as I was coming out was Joanie.'

'Joanie?' Now she probably did go through a quick assortment while in between the satin sheets. 'I hadn't heard she was in London.'

'It was in last night's *Standard*. She's presenting some old ballet queen with an award for still standing up at seventy-five or something. Anyway, she looked incredible. Everyone was looking at her, and Whatsisface Fayed was slimeballing her, needless to say. If I look like her at sixty . . . ! She had on the most fantastic wig. She just stops short of caricaturing herself.'

'Obviously your role model.'

'Piss off. And we thought she was wearing arm make-up!'

'Who's "we"?'

'Me and this woman next to me. Now *she* obviously hadn't been reading *Joan Collins's Secrets*. She was dead British. She had boobs like the Queen Mother's. Honestly, before *Dynasty*, I thought that was how you had to end up looking. I wish they'd bring it back.'

'It's on UK Gold. You'll have to get cable. It's much more upmarket than people realise. Don't most women hate Joan Collins?'

'Only the ones with moustaches. All the British ones.'

'She's British too. Go back to Australia if you don't like it here.'

'What? After fifteen years? Australian women are even worse. Anyway, what else were you going to tell me?'

'Well, it's been funny me trying to recruit for Clancey and Bennett. I had a call myself this morning. I think someone was making overtures.'

'Brilliant. But the opera isn't over until the fat lady sings. Or Jessye Normous, as we opera buffs like to say! Don't do anything until you've got a contract.'

'I'm not going to, stupid. I'm not sure if I was reading between the lines properly. It might not mean a job offer. If it does it would mean a career change.'

'It's not in advertising? Even better. Get out of advertising, Dunky. It stinks. Alan says it's had its day. Look at me. D'you realise it's two years since I left advertising and turned self-employed? I'm so much happier since I set up on my own. Alan's only stuck in advertising now because of his age and the partnership and everything.'

The Portuguese waiter interrupted them and they chose their pizzas.

'What is it, then?' asked Cindy after a while. 'Marketing?'

'Television,' replied Duncan. 'Helping with development for an independent production company.'

'Really? That's fantastic.'

'I thought so too.'

'And what's Pointy Tits going to say about that, then, when she finds out? I'll bet she'll be dead chuffed to turn up to work for you and have you piss off on her, you bastard.'

'I've not been offered anything yet,' protested Duncan. 'I've not even had the first meeting. And Miss Pointy Tits, as you call her, hasn't been offered her job yet either, so it's nothing to do with her.'

'*Miss* Pointy Tits.' Cindy laughed. 'That's rather a lot of respect for an account manager. She *must* be good. Anyway, I think it's exciting. You'd be brilliant in TV. You've got great ideas. Much better than all that crap they usually put on. Did you see that TV movie the other night?'

'Which one?'

'It had Jaclyn Smith – remember her in *Charlie's Angels*? – Jaclyn Smith as *a brain surgeon*!' Cindy dissolved into sniggers. 'Great casting, eh?'

'It sounds like what passes for art in Hollywood. Anyway, I wouldn't be doing drama.'

'Your play was fantastic.'

'You're the only one who ever got to read any of it.'

'That's your own fault. You should have sent it to someone. Who's this job with? Are you allowed to say?'

'It's just a small production company. I checked it out with The Station. Discreetly, of course. It's quite new, but it's run by a woman who used to be top banana at Trafalgar TV. Apparently she's the most difficult woman in television.'

6

Looking less than frankly fabulous at fifty, and feeling more than just a bit down, Karen Myhill stumbled through the revolving doors and into the brown library gloom of the Groucho Club, that fabled haunt of London's glittering and chattering media fraternity which stood not only at the centre of Soho but also a short walk down the street from the MCN International building, further up on the other side of Dean Street.

Karen disliked the density of Soho. She inclined to be at the edge of where things were at rather than at their heart. She had a paradoxical preference for the anonymous, wide modern deserts that make up peripheral central London and that are devoid of society. Windy Waterloo with its bomb-site bleakness on the soulless South Bank where she had once worked at Trafalgar Television. Or empty northern Paddington, an area cruelly sliced up by concrete abattoir buildings and scarring flyovers and left dissected and lifeless. There, where there were no ideas people and no other people with ideas, Karen had established Myhill Productions in an old post office annexe backing on to rusting railway lines. There nothing mattered. There no one knew her. There she felt comfortable.

But here in Soho, she felt threatened. Threatened by the jostle of tightly built, lively streets of packed Georgian houses which squeezed inwards on both sides of every road. Threatened by the cliquey culture of *avant-garde* shops too small to make money anywhere else but big in Soho where they could feed off the designer eating and clothing and listening and reading tastes of the twenty-four-hour metropolitan set. Threatened by the close concentration of noisy media men who could be found gorging greedily in every chic eaterie and propped up pompously at every lubricant watering hole. For Karen, these were the men who knew her and who talked about her and who loud-mouthed her story. The tightness of Soho forced her into streets too narrow to turn in and escape, doorways where passing shoulders would have to rub, public rooms where eyes might meet privately. For Karen, Soho's silken web would always be a trap.

So she slipped uneasily into the Groucho Club, itself the beat of the heart of the body of broadcasting. She stepped forward unsurely, having trouble seeing where she was going, not just because her eyes were taking time to readjust from the late afternoon sunshine outside, nor because she could only shuffle forward feebly in her long, tight, dark, unflattering hobble skirt, but mainly because one of the lenses in her trademark bejewelled spectacles had smashed when she had knocked them on to the floor at the hairdresser's just an hour or so before. This constituted a crisis. The broken glass remained there, suspended delicately but dangerously in its frame, her left eye peering out furtively from behind its cracked cobweb pattern. It was not the impression Karen wished to create at all, not least at the Groucho Club of all places. But La Myhill was always a formidable and feared figure, however she might present herself and however ill at ease and down at heel she might feel inside. An infamous if misunderstood member of her community, to the florid-faced boozers at the bar Karen was immediately recognisable and immediately recognised.

'Look at that,' nodded one underhand wag to his companion, pointing to Karen's shattered eye. 'Mad Max has gone and socked her one. Not before time.' *Sotto voce*, he began to explain to his guest who Karen Myhill was.

The bartender smirked.

'Good evening, Ms Myhill,' he said. In London clubs it is definitely evening at 5.45 p.m. 'What can I get you?'

'A Bloody Mary,' said Karen.

'A Bloody Myhill,' said the underhand wag out of earshot. 'That's what we call it. She always has that. Only so as when she throws it at you it leaves a mark.'

Karen, conspicuously aware of the sideways looks, stared starkly forward through her crazy-paving eyewear. When it came, she snatched her drink, found the money in the pocket of her hang-loose waistcoat and, in the tiny geisha steps dictated by her skirt, removed herself to a small out-of-the-way table for two. She sat there, alone, her body language too crumpled and uncalculated to be judged by any passer-by to be that of one

of the most powerful women in the moving media. But that is
what she was and desperately wished to continue to be.

Only it didn't look that way to Karen at the moment. Not
after a day of grim reckoning with her financial adviser. In his
opinion, and now increasingly her own, the future for Myhill
Productions was at best shaky and at worst short-term and final.
Since leaving Trafalgar Television and setting up on her own,
Karen's fortunes had climbed and climbed up the steeply rising
slope of a financial rollercoaster. But now she had reached the
top and, for the first time, she could see the dreadful plunge
and the hurtling way down. Nauseous at the prospect, Karen
slumped lower in her seat, feeling unattractive and depressed,
her wine-bottle shoulders falling away from her thin neck even
more so than usual.

This meeting was taking on new implications for her. How
candid should she be with this Duncan Cairns? How loyal was
he to his television client? If she told him things, how sure
could she be that it would not travel back to The Station?
What on earth was she seeing someone from his background
for anyway? Why the hell was she seeing anyone at all? Why
did she not just give up? Because there was no alternative,
was there? And Duncan Cairns was just one of her whims.
Someone had fleetingly mentioned his name and his talents
and she had had one of her ideas. What would he think of
her? He was a senior-ranking executive in a huge international
organisation. He was a board director in charge of millions of
pounds' worth of business. He had a sterling-silver career and
no doubt a gold-plated salary to go with it. He was probably
merely humouring her. If you're someone in telly everyone
always agrees to meet you. She had known some advertising
types in the past. Television had all the content but advertising
had all the style. What *would* he think of her? Apart from
everything else, she was wearing all the wrong things and
people in advertising were likely to judge you completely just
by what you had on. And what she had on was smashed-up
specs and a stupid sack that was a strait-jacket for her legs.
On the other hand, her peroxided hair, a model of controlled
cutting and colouring, was at least one small triumph she could
sport over the unkindness of a Nature that had given her a great

mind if not a great face and body. She was reassuring herself with this thought when his voice interrupted her.

'Karen Myhill?'

She looked up, squinting through the kaleidoscope shapes obscuring her left eye.

'I'm Duncan. How do you do.' He shook her hand quite firmly, but not too firmly. 'I brought you a refill.' He placed a fresh Bloody Mary on the table and sat down opposite Karen and behind his own drink of mineral water.

'How did you know it was me?' she asked.

'I asked the barman. He said you were the woman with the cracked glasses.'

'Little fucker!'

'Me or him?' asked Duncan, taken aback.

'Him, him, him. Oh, not you. Of course not.' Karen was horrified that they might start off on the wrong foot. 'Sorry. I'm a bit low this evening. I've had a hard day and breaking my glasses and having everyone looking at me hasn't helped.'

'D'you want to call it off?'

'Of course not. Don't be silly.' Karen pulled her new Bloody Mary towards her. 'Thank you for the drink. Should I not have got one for you?'

'No. I asked him what you were having. I hope you don't mind.'

'Of course not. It's encouraging to see you're a man who can spot a much-needed refill at fifty yards.'

'That's advertising for you.' Duncan smiled.

Karen did not personally know any men who were quite this polished, this well dressed. Duncan was immaculate in his navy wool suit, uncrushed and unrumpled by a careful day in the office. He was good-looking with an air of benign authority, something she had never managed to cultivate herself. His attention to personal detail made poor Karen only more self-conscious of her own image, as did his next question.

'How did you break your glasses?'

'Don't ask. I dropped them at the hairdresser's. I didn't have time to go home and change them.'

'I wear contact lenses.'

'Do you? I couldn't bear sticking something in my eye.'

'Mine are disposable. You should try this sort. They're very comfortable.' Karen Myhill did not seem like the small-talk type so Duncan moved on. 'I hope this isn't rude, Karen, but as I told you, I'm afraid I haven't got much time. I have another appointment after this. Would you mind if we cut to the quick? Also, this place is just down the road from my agency. I don't want to be overheard by any stray colleagues.'

'I only suggested the Groucho because you work up the street.'

'I know. It was a good idea.'

'Are you sure? D'you want to go somewhere else?'

'No. This is fine. It doesn't matter if we're spotted together. We could be talking about something you're doing for The Station. But when it gets busier I could do without eavesdroppers.' He looked up expectantly and Karen took her cue.

'Well . . . how shall I put this? I've had a really interesting day today, Duncan, sitting down with my company accountant. That's sort of put this little meeting we're having into focus, really. I've reached a crossroads. I'm under huge pressure. This year is absolute make or break for Myhill Productions. And for me. We could become one of the really big players in independent TV production or . . . we could go bust and I'll be finished.'

'I should have got you a double,' joked Duncan, eyeing her glass, but Karen did not laugh. Her confession was an honest one. 'Why? What's the problem?'

'I used to be on the board of Trafalgar Television. I knew everything there was to know about corporate TV. Then a few years ago I set up my own independent production company to make light factual and entertainment programmes. But it's very tough out there. I've found it much more difficult than I had expected. I've made mistakes.'

'I'm sure everyone else has too. It's an immature market.'

'The truth is there *is* no market and the competition is intense. My problem is that although Myhill Productions is quite big as production companies go, that ain't big, and it hasn't reached the critical mass to be self-sustaining.'

'It's a cottage industry.'

'You bet. All my series are coming to an end this year. And that's that. Finished. New commissioning editors are coming into the business and they always want new companies with younger producers than me. I'm concerned that with no new substantial product, the company is going to evaporate into thin air.'

'Surely it's just a case of coming up with something new and getting that commissioned?'

'Of course. But you spend all year getting one measly six-part series. It's ball-breaking for very little gain. Ninety-five per cent of every company's ideas get rejected, irrespective of how good they are. But I'm really talking about creating and owning a *Wheel of Fortune* or a *Baywatch* – something that runs year in and year out, five days a week if possible, with programme or format sales all over the world.'

'The Coca-Cola of TV.'

'The Holy Grail. But no one in myopic Britain is really looking for anything that big, not from the independent sector anyway. There is nothing long-term and on-going that guarantees my company's survival. I need to crack that problem fast.'

'The Station is looking for a breakfast show. It's meant to be worth twenty-two million per annum. That's hardly small pickings.'

'And don't we all know it. I think it's the biggest single independent commission ever in the UK. Whoever gets it will be bankrolled for the next five years at least. I *have* tendered for it. So have literally hundreds of others. We'll just have to wait and see.'

'I hope you get it.'

'So do I. I'm pinning my hopes on it. If I don't get it I don't know what will happen. To go out of business will be a disaster, not to say a humiliation.'

'Would you really go out of business? Can't you borrow from the bank?'

'There's so little profit in UK TV, Duncan, and such huge risks that the banks won't stump up.'

'How about a private backer? Sell shares in your company.'

'What would they be backing? There's nothing there. Everything we do relies on me to think it up, Duncan. I'm fifty. That's an old woman in TV terms. If I fall under a bus, or, more likely, get pushed under one, the company would fold overnight. We have no assets. We don't own the secondary rights to the shows we've done because the broadcasters keep those. We have no artistes or staff under anything other than short-term contracts.'

'Why not? We do in advertising.'

'Advertising is commercial. You advertise something, it sells, you make a lot of money. You have ten times the budget. In television you beg the broadcaster pathetically to give you a measly commission on half the budget you need because there are nine hundred other companies out there who'll kill you for it, and no other broadcasters to sell it to. And in your business you have strategic thinking and forward planning. Advertising is a business, TV is a lifestyle, Duncan. That's what the head of programmes at The Station pointed out to me. And it got me into thinking that what I need is someone to help me devise a long-term competitive strategy and the new programmes that fit it and will make money, and I don't think people in television think like that. It was the head of programmes at The Station who suggested someone like you.'

Duncan laughed. 'You've painted such a grim picture. You've kind of put me off.'

'It's a challenge.'

'It sounds more like an ordeal.'

'If we pick up The Station breakfast show things will be absolutely fine. Otherwise it will be tough. But if I can work out the figures, I'd like to talk to you some more. Think about what I've said and then we can meet again. I'll take you to lunch at Le Caprice, how about that? It's an incentive to turn up.'

'Le Caprice? You can't be that close to going out of business, then! I'm not really sure what you'd want me to do.'

'That's because I'm not, either. I rely on organic thinking. It will emerge from the ether somehow like all my best ideas.'

'I have no real TV experience.'

'So? You've studied the whole TV market in depth for The Station launch, haven't you?'

'I suppose so. We haven't launched it yet.'

'Well, it's still more than any TV producer has done, I can tell you.' Karen sighed. 'I'll let you get away for your appointment.'

'Thank you.' Duncan felt that this was all rather weird. If this was an interview, Karen Myhill knew no more about him than when he had first sat down. She had hardly looked him in the eye. Perhaps that was down to her splintered specs. She had asked him not one thing about himself. Nor had he pushed. Perhaps he should have done. Perhaps that was what he was meant to do, refute her negativeness.

'I've really enjoyed meeting you,' he said.

'Have you? You don't think I'm a depressed middle-aged woman with broken glasses she can't even see out of and who has no idea of what she's doing?'

'I don't think that at all.'

'I know exactly what I'm doing, Duncan. This year it's boom or bust for me and I have to take a few risks and call in all the debts I'm owed.'

'People owe you debts?'

'Of course. I've been in television for twenty-five years, Duncan. There are definitely people who owe me a favour or two. Now is the time to collect with interest.'

'Shit!'

On the windscreen of Karen's car was a parking ticket and the prospect of a thirty-pound fine.

'I put money in the fucking meter, for fuck's sake.' She ripped the ticket from under the windscreen wiper, pressed the infra-red beam on the central locking gadget for the car and threw the ticket inside along with her bag. She walked around to the other side of the parking meter and tried to read the parking times. It was easier with her left hand held over her glasses. 'The fuckers have extended the time! Eight thirty p.m! It used to be six thirty. It was last week, I'm sure it was. Fucking council. People want to drive cars. They vote with their wheels, don't they know that? How do they expect us ever to do any business in this dump of a city?'

Karen realised she was talking out loud and shut up. From the glove compartment she heard the high-pitched tone of her mobile phone. She jumped into the car and got it out. She checked the caller ID facility but the number meant nothing to her.

'Karen Myhill.'

'Hello, Ms Myhill. This is Tim Lutyens speaking.'

'Who? Do I know you?'

'I am a partner in Lutyens Kleiner.'

'Is that a production company?'

'I am your son Maximilian's father's solicitor.'

The phone slipped slightly within Karen's grip.

'His solicitor? Why are you calling me? Where did you get this number?'

'Your secretary gave it to me when I told her I needed to speak to you quite urgently.'

Karen wondered if the day could hold still worse news. 'What about?'

'I have information of some consequence for your son. I would be most grateful if you would come to my office in the next day or so and we can discuss it. We're in Piccadilly.'

'What sort of information?'

'I think it would be inappropriate to say over the telephone. If you could suggest a day and time—'

'Couldn't you at least give me some idea. I could prepare for the meeting—'

'Ms Myhill, I can assure you there is nothing you can do. Shall we say tomorrow afternoon at five o'clock?'

'Yes. Whatever.'

Karen pressed the clear button on the phone. At last, a pointed triangle of glass fell from her spectacle lens and dropped downwards, catching on her waistcoat, a little dagger near her heart. But Karen failed to notice. Her mind was awhirl with thoughts of the solicitor, Max's father and her son. Oh, she thought. My precious baby.

7

'Hey. Over here. What d'you think? Arm make-up!'

Cindy Barratt got up from the ground to kiss Duncan hello. She held out her bare arms.

'Clarins Bronzing Powder! Copying Joan Collins's techniques at thirty-six! I must be off my head! But I'm not exactly Elle Macpherson, either. I got this lot at Harvey Nicks after you abandoned me.'

She had been sitting in the crowd on the cobbles of Covent Garden Piazza outside Tuttons, with a clutch of Harvey Nichols and Harrods carrier bags. The Royal Opera House was bringing opera to the masses with one of its live open-air broadcasts.

'You're cutting it a bit fine, aren't you?'

'Cindy, not everyone is self-employed and can piddle around in Knightsbridge all afternoon just because the sun is out.'

'Well, they ought to. You don't get much chance in Britain.'

'Anyway, I'm exactly on time. Look.' Duncan pulled back his cuff and showed Cindy his watch.

'You don't have to prove it, Dunky. I know you. You're always right. That's the screen over there.'

'What? That thing? It's not very impressive. Can you see it from the ground?'

'You can at the moment. No doubt some ghastly old-age pensioners will come along with folding seats and white bread sandwiches and plonk themselves down in front of us. Glyndebourne for the plebs. And to think this is supposed to be where Henry Higgins met Mary Poppins.'

Duncan raised an eyebrow. 'I beg your pardon?'

'You know. In the movie.' She sang. '"All I want is a room somewhere."' Her cockney accent was only marginally more realistic than Dick Van Dyke's. 'She did that big song and dance number right here.'

'Right here in Hollywood, I think you'll find. It was a set. They reconstructed it.'

'Did they?'

'And it was Eliza Doolittle he met, not Mary Poppins, stupid. You're mixing up your Julie Andrews characters.'

'Oh yeah? Well it's easily done. I can't say she ever did much for me. Anyway, the impression of London you get from those movies, if you're a foreigner like me – well, Covent Garden is the only place *in* London where London is actually like that. All columns and chimney pots.'

'And tourists. Look at them.'

'Yeah. Why do people always take their worst clothes with them on holiday? I don't suppose you brought anything?'

'I didn't have time. The idea was to get an outside table at Tuttons.'

'Well, I'm sorry. Mandy fucked up. She didn't get as many seats for *Fedora* as *Carmen*. She said she'd chuck us some crumbs from her table, South African bitch. What does she know about opera anyway? She's supposed to be over there at the back.'

'You can see better from here. And this is free.'

'You should've brought a cushion. Your bum'll get sore, but you can always leave at the end of Act One.'

He sat down on the warm stone surface. His suit was due for cleaning so he felt that it was all right.

'You know it's José and Mirella tonight, don't you?'

Duncan pretended he did.

'Apparently he's not on top form, but we don't care, do we? You don't get many chances to see *Fedora*. Look!'

She opened her Harrods bag to reveal the focaccia, Greek bread and other treats she had bought earlier in the day.

'I've eaten all the chocolates first, I'm afraid. That's what I love about the opera. The food! Not that this outside crap is opera, you understand. Kenwood beats it hands down. But we can pretend we've been to Covent Garden one extra time.'

The giant video screen suddenly flickered into life with a shot of the red and gold interior of the stalls.

'It'll be stifling in there tonight,' Cindy continued. 'It looks better on the screen, doesn't it? You can't see just how run-down it is. They ought to do something about that wiring. I couldn't believe it when I first went.'

A matronly lady standing to their rear announced to her friend that her husband had once been to Bayreuth. Her clipped accent carried and one or two of the casual crowd looked round, impressed.

'Yeah.' Cindy could be loud. She was being naughty again. 'And *I* once overheard the name of Maria Callas mentioned in the crush bar of Covent Garden!' She laughed at her own joke which was lost on anyone but her friend.

Duncan looked at her fondly in the evening light. Here was a genuinely beautiful woman. Impeccable bone structure softened by olive skin, only the little extra weight beneath the chin hinting at her age. Her brown hair lightened with hazel to cover the traces of grey. Her bodyline fluid and feline beneath natural-fibre clothes – a linen halterneck top, putty-coloured palazzo pants, canvas shoes. Her whole look was low-key and yet sensual. Except for this evening's arm make-up, one of the many self-parodying jokes she indulged in with Duncan, her discreet image contrasted with the louder person beneath. Duncan put this down to her not being English. While little Cindy had dreamt of European chic in the outback of her mother's farm on the edge of the Blue Mountains of New South Wales, by the time the woman presented herself in London, her personality was formed in a less subtle mould. She would always be *arriviste*.

'So, has Pointy Tits got the job, then?'

'She was in with Godzilla and Dracula when I left. She stands a good chance. I did mention a new point in her favour.'

'What's that?'

'Apparently she once had dinner with Prince Edward at Buckingham Palace.'

'How did she swing that?' Cindy was impressed. 'We liked Buck House, didn't we, Dunky? I seem to remember you made me do all the queuing 'cause you didn't want to be seen being a tourist. Shame about him, though, Prince Edward.'

'What? That he's meant to be getting married?'

'No, that he's so unattractive. Runs in the family, I guess.'

'Nigel and Serena are easily impressed by name-droppers.'

'Pointy Tits obviously thinks you are, too.'

'*She* didn't tell me. Audrey Goldberg mentioned it.'

'God, is she still going? She must be on her second facelift by now. Don't ever tell *her* anything about yourself unless you want to hear it later on *News at Ten*. She's got a mouth on her bigger than Fergie's backside.'

'And you're a model of discretion yourself, of course.'

'Look who's talking!'

'Well, sometimes you have to trade information. I went to the Groucho Club on the way here.'

'You went to the Groucho Club and didn't take me?' said Cindy with mock annoyance. 'No wonder you were late.'

'I had to meet that TV woman.'

'What was she like? Dead glamorous?'

'Huh. Anything but. She's one of the strangest people I've ever met. She's very intelligent, though. Just a bit unhinged.'

'And?'

'And what?'

'Like "and did she offer you the job?"'

'She wants to meet me again.'

'That sounds promising.'

'It's a big decision for her. I suppose I'm hardly likely to get a career in TV off the back of only one interview. She wants me to have lunch with her. At Le Caprice, no less.'

'So? You've been there a million times.'

'It's not like advertising,' explained Duncan. 'Telly people only do lunch when they're ready to put their cards on the table.'

'What? No lunches?' said Cindy, picking at the focaccia. 'Sounds like completely the wrong business to me, Dunky!'

8

London days come in pairs. Again the sunshine found its way with difficulty into the bricky alleyways of Soho. For the second day running, Charlotte Reith also found her way there with difficulty. As a sleek, classic, shapely girl on a sleek, classic, shapely bike, her problems were largely of her own making. As she threaded her way recklessly at speed through the boring, belching morning traffic, to the London cabbies who owned the roads and who wound down windows to call out clever quips ending in 'darlin'', this seemed to be an astonishingly arrogant if astonishingly nubile young woman who was needlessly risking both her life and their paintwork for precious little advantage. For Charlotte, it was less a matter of progress and more a matter of point-scoring that she got where she was going and got there first, even if it was just to the next red light. Lucky for her that her black crash helmet protected her not just from any collision with the four-wheeled competition but also from any collision with the four-lettered insults lobbed her way.

Once again she left her Ducati in St Anne's Court, the pedestrian lane beside the modern grey steel building housing the agency. She was unsure if she was allowed to park here, but she could pop back and move her motor bike at a moment's notice. She would ask Duncan. Would he know? Probably not. Charlotte plucked her helmet from her head and her blonde hair tumbled out in a scene that any haircare commercial would be privileged to capture. She went to check the line of her lycra leggings in the ground-floor mirror windows of the agency and then thought better of it. God knows who could be on the other side, ogling her.

The agency ground floor was slightly dated, all brushed-steel panels and low-slung black leather settees. On the reception desk was a sculpted vase containing an abstract arrangement of orange and lilac South African strelitzias and palm leaves at least four feet high. Behind it, the client list of MCN International and its subsidiaries. Charlotte speed-read it. The Clancey and Bennett name itself did not appear. In her mind an alarm bell rang. Why hadn't she noticed that before? The whole of the left-hand wall was taken up by a forty-foot-long '96 sheet' poster, printed in gold and silver metallic ink. Wow, thought Charlotte.

'The Station. Live it. Love it. Feel it. Breathe it. Eat it. Sleep it. Do let it pass you by. Takes off September 1.' Well. At least MCN International had given pride of place to a Clancey and Bennett poster.

The young black receptionist let her through unannounced. A nice touch, Charlotte thought. There were hardly any blacks in advertising. Charlotte had had reason to be thankful for her own pedigree the previous evening. Honestly. All Nigel Gainsborough had asked her was who she knew at school, because they might know his daughter. He was a classic duffer of the old school. While his bonhomie was appealing, she might have been concerned about his business competence, but for Serena. Serena was a revelation, the most acidly intelligent woman Charlotte had had occasion to meet. Her brilliant searchlight technique illuminated each of Charlotte's strengths and weaknesses until they were blindingly obvious. Nigel and Serena worked as a team. The Charm and The Harm.

They had offered Charlotte the job on the spot, flattering her into accepting it immediately. Getting allocated to The Station account, despite Duncan's dismissal of the idea, was an unexpected bonus, and had allowed her to resign from Saatchi's at 9.30 a.m. So, here she was, two hours later.

She entered the lift and pressed the button for the third floor, but it took her only as far as the first before it stopped and the doors opened to reveal the silhouette of a man. Another black, she thought. How unexpectedly progressive. He must be Dispatch from the way he was dressed. Why was it that service staff always filled up the client lifts just to go one floor? MCN was just the same as Saatchi's. No doubt he would want to take the lift back to where she had just come from.

'Going down?' she asked unenthusiastically.

'I normally wait for an introduction before I go *that* far.' His jaw widened into a grin and he gave her the once-over. 'Let's meet for a drink first.'

This was par for the course in any big agency, but it infuriated Charlotte.

'I happen to be going up. It's just as well for you that I'm not a client, you know.'

'You wouldn't be on your own if you were. Are you a temp?'

'No I'm bloody well not. I'm the new account manager in Clancey and Bennett, actually.'

'C&B? Couldn't get a job in a proper agency, then? Like MCN, for example?'

Just what Charlotte didn't need to hear after her concerns. She noticed his hand on the door, holding back the lift. She raised her finger to press the button again, but he stepped forward into the lift first and did it for her, then pressed for the fourth floor.

Close up he was massive. He had the shiny, muscled body of a Chippendale, barely contained in cycling trunks and lycra singlet, which wrapped him like clingfilm. He appeared to have been for a run, and he pushed the sweat off his face, back into his shoulder-length mane. He wasn't nearly so black now, under the ceiling spot, and he had the wrong sort of hair to be a West Indian. Perhaps he was half-caste or even an Indian Indian. Ethnicky types were not Charlotte's strongest point. He was standing too close, loose-limbed and panting like an animal in Charlotte's body space. She involuntarily glanced down at the huge presence constained in his trunks. She thought she could smell him and he smelled of sex.

The lift ascended in slo-mo. They made flitting, silent eye contact. This was a new experience for Charlotte, chemistry that felt intensely physical. Suddenly the doors sprang open and she escaped backwards. His hand was raised once more to hold the door.

'Let's do lunch. Say one o'clock?'

God, he was a cheeky bastard.

'I don't think so.' Her eyes ran to his prominent bulge. 'Anyway,' she said, 'it looks like yours is a packed one today.'

She didn't hang around for an answer.

9

'You look lost. Can I help you?'

The accent was Australian.

'I got out of the lift at the wrong floor, I'm afraid.' Charlotte wondered if this was the other account manager. 'Someone made the nearest thing to a pass at me, so I jumped out at the first opportunity.'

'Yeah, well, you can get gang-raped in there if you hang around long enough.'

She gave Charlotte a broad-beamed smile. She could be twenty-five. She could be thirty-five. She was too much in charge to be the secretary. A phone went off on the counter by the double doors.

She went over and put down a press advertisement in the form of a piece of production artwork that she was holding.

'Where is everybody in this place? Yeah, I'm coming.' She kept up the smile and took the call. 'Oh, hi, Stella. Yeah, that's OK. Say three o'clock? No, we'll just have a longer lunch. You know us.' She laughed. 'D'you want parking underneath? OK. See you later. Bye.' She put the phone down.

'I'm Charlotte Reith, the new account manager.' Charlotte saw that her announcement immediately wiped the smile off the woman's face.

'Oh, that's nice. That's very nice,' said the woman angrily. 'That's par for the course.'

Charlotte waited. She wasn't following.

'Nobody tells me anything round here,' explained the other woman. 'I didn't know you were coming.'

'I only got the job last night,' said Charlotte. 'I was able to start right away. I expect they didn't have time to tell you.'

'I expect that, frankly, my dear, they couldn't give a shit. So, able to start right away? Nigel loves that. Who did you get made redundant from?'

That annoyed Charlotte.

'Actually,' she said defensively, 'I was at Saatchi's until this morning on competitive business. So I left immediately.'

'Saatchi's, eh? What carpet business have they got?'

'It wasn't the Carpets Company that was the problem. I'm also going to be joining The Station account team. Nigel and Serena have put me on it.'

'Fucking hell!' The girl was obviously not angry with Charlotte herself, but with Nigel and Serena. 'That's my account! Honestly, those two are such bastards. I wonder if Duncan knows about this?'

Another phone went off.

'Knows about what?'

It was Duncan. At last, a familiar voice. Thank God, thought Charlotte. So far they hadn't exactly rolled out the red carpet. Duncan came round the corner and through the double doors with an older woman and a suntanned man, probably a creative. While Duncan concluded his conversation with him, the suntanned man assessed Charlotte out of the corner of his eye.

At least, that's what it felt like to her, the new girl on her first day, on display and up for tacit inspection.

'See you later, Orlando,' said Duncan.

The man turned to leave and then turned back, said something to Duncan and left. Charlotte wondered if it was a comment about her, then reassured herself with the thought that she was just acutely self-aware because of the unfamiliarity of everything. Soon these people would be her friends. Well, she hoped they would be.

The older woman came through and sat behind the counter-top. She appeared to be the C&B secretary. She ignored Charlotte and busied herself answering the phones. Duncan smiled and moved forward to shake hands.

'Back again already, Charlotte? I hope Hazel hasn't been stirring it?'

'Too right,' said Hazel. 'God! I forgot to introduce myself. I'm so crap at my job – I thought I'd tell you that before anyone else does.' She turned to Duncan. 'Did you know she was joining today?'

Duncan's eyes blinked. He was thrown for only a second.

'Er, sort of. Nigel and Serena just had to rubber-stamp it, really.'

'Oh yeah,' joked Hazel. 'Which planet are you on, Cairns?' She turned to Charlotte with her big smile again. 'He didn't know either. Hah!'

'Hazel, go and do some work.'

'I will, if you'll sign off this artwork. It's the little retail ad for Bencelor.'

She pulled the artwork across the counter-top and opened up its grey cover and tracing-paper protector to show him the ad beneath. She went to lift it, but Duncan held Hazel's wrist until he had read every word. Duncan was one of the world's great readers of copy and could spot any typo at fifty yards. Hazel, who couldn't, turned the artwork over and Duncan signed the stamped panel on its hardboard back.

'He doesn't trust me,' Hazel said to Charlotte. 'Bencelor is our worst client, and that's saying something. But what can you expect from a Viennese company that began life making industrial widgets?'

'I thought they made household gadgety things?'

'They do, sort of. They're still painfully industrial, I'm afraid. That's their core business. We just promote the sidelines. They can just about afford classified advertising space.'

'Don't lie, Hazel,' said Duncan crossly. 'We're doing TV this year.'

'If it happens.' Hazel flapped her wrist dismissively towards Charlotte. 'I'll be in my office over there. Come and say hi and I'll talk you through some things. What are we doing for lunch, Cairns?'

'What makes you think you're included?'

'Oh, come on.'

'You're invited, stupid. We'll have to go to Pizza Express. Stella's coming in at two. You can blame yourself, Hazel. Don't arrange two o'clock meetings.'

'Actually, she's coming at three now. So we can go somewhere else. We haven't been to Soho Soho for ages.'

'You mean not since last week. OK. The brasserie, not the restaurant. And you'll have to lose it on a job somewhere.'

'This Bencelor crap is one hundred and fifty pounds under budget. We'll shove it on there. I'll book it.'

She beamed at Charlotte again.

'Come and say hi. I'll give you the lowdown on him before lunch. He squeezes the toothpaste from the bottom of the tube, does old Cairns here.'

'I use a pump, actually. It's more efficient.'

'See? He won't rape you in the lift but he will work you into the ground until you're reduced to pulverised dust.'

She jabbed a chunky finger at Duncan and stomped off.

10

Duncan narrowed his eyes and zeroed in on Hazel's glass. She had refilled it again, almost to the brim. Hazel felt the burn of his X-ray vision.

'Keep your hair on, Cairns. I can hold my drink.'

'Vast quantities of it, obviously.'

'What is this wine?' asked Charlotte. 'It's lovely.'

'Penfold's Semillon Chardonnay. Australian, naturally.' Hazel's eyes shot to Duncan. 'He's such a Presbyterian.'

'I'm not a Presbyterian. My family are Episcopalians and I'm not anything. And you'll have a drink problem soon if you don't watch out.'

'I *don't* think! Unless I can't get enough of it!'

Charlotte laughed, and laughed some more when she realised Duncan was giving her a look to say 'Don't encourage her'. The maître d' approached.

'Are you Mr Cairns?'

Duncan looked surprised.

'There's a phone call for you.'

Concerned, Duncan stood up to go to the phone, then caught Hazel's eye.

'Maybe Nigel and Serena have been killed in a car crash,' she said, beaming.

'You wish,' said Duncan, and left with the maître d'.

'Yeah, well I live in hope.' Hazel took several large swigs from her glass and then refilled it quickly. She topped up Charlotte's too, by a tiny amount. Charlotte smiled.

'They must make a fortune in here. It's so incredibly busy.'

'It's always packed,' said Hazel. 'And it's so noisy. It's even worse at night. They have some woman sing at a piano. I don't know why she bothers because you can never hear her. Probably an advantage. Have you been upstairs?'

'No. I've never been in here before. Don't know why. It's not a Saatchi's place.'

'There's a restaurant upstairs. It's good. And there's a private room, modern, sort of Italian. It's very stylish. My flatmate is in PR. She tells me about all the best places. Where d'you live?'

'St John's Wood,' said Charlotte. 'I bought my own flat recently. The prices there are a bit lower than you'd think,' she added defensively. 'At the moment anyway. I was just lucky with my timing. I love the white swirly bits on the blue wall over there. It's meant to be Mediterranean, I suppose.'

'Yeah, like if Matisse were an interior decorator. Your own flat in St John's Wood? You're a lucky girl.'

'I know. It's very small, really. Come round one evening after work.'

'I'd love to. You know, the whole agency is already talking about you and your bike?' Hazel smiled warmly.

'God,' groaned Charlotte, who knew only too well what the comments would be.

'What sort is it? I don't know much about bikes.'

'It's a Ducati. They're considered classics. Italian. For the cognoscenti, I suppose. I get a huge number of comments about it. I have it for convenience, really. I mean, how are you meant to get round London by car, for God's sake?'

'I use the tube and take taxis. But that doesn't get a girl a reputation. You could always go round on a moped.'

'Oh, do me a favour, please! My father bought it for me. That's why I have that particular model. And, yes, it is very expensive and there's no way I could afford it myself and he pays for the upkeep. But if I didn't have that I'd have a Yamaha or something and I certainly wouldn't be seen dead on a moped in a hundred million years. I'd rather be spotted with one of those shopping baskets on wheels old ladies have.'

'Yeah? But that's just so you! They're not quite so sexy, though, are they?'

Charlotte laughed. 'That's men for you. They mix up the huge c.c. throbbing between their legs with the size of their willy. Big joke. And somehow a girl on a motor bike becomes a tart. It's a double standard. It's pathetic.'

'Tell me about it. I wonder who Cairns can be talking to all this time? Why did you leave Saatchi's? I mean, whatever's happened to that place, it's still world famous. And C&B is – eh – not!'

'It was my first job and I'd done four years. That's quite a long time in any one agency. Saatchi's is enormous. My leaving had nothing to do with anything there. I just thought I'd try being a bigger fish in a smaller pool.'

'Yeah, well it's not a pool, it's a goldfish bowl! Hope you like going round in circles.'

'Hazel, don't put me off on my first day! The whole world is talking about The Station. That was a pretty persuasive carrot. I also came because I really liked Duncan, and Serena's very impressive.'

'She is indeed. Shame she's such an old witch, really! You're right about Cairns, though. You couldn't work for a nicer guy. He's very good at his job. He'll go places, that one.'

Charlotte looked alarmed. 'Not too soon I hope. He's the principal reason I've joined C&B.'

'Well, it couldn't be to work for old fat-arse Gainsborough, that's for sure.'

Duncan returned. Hazel leapt in.

'So are Nigel and Serena splattered all over the road in a pile of metal somewhere, their dismembered hands still joined in a loving clinch? Say yes!'

'I'd love to see your face if I did. Hazel, it's Charlotte's first day. Try and behave, for God's sake. That was Margaret on the phone. Stella is here now.'

'Christ. It's only two o'clock.' Hazel fought her cuff to find her watch. 'She said three. She did!'

'Well, I've said come over and join us for dessert.'

Charlotte's face clouded. She had had an excellent but rudimentary briefing from Duncan that morning. And she had left her files back at the agency. Now she had to face her new client.

'Don't worry,' said Duncan. 'Stella is lovely. Hazel, you can put lunch on one of Stella's jobs, now it's legit.'

'Yeah, well I hope the kitchen's well stocked.' Hazel certainly had her opinions about people. 'I mean, I know I'm built like a brick shithouse, but she is one big lady. If she can actually squeeze her thunder thighs under this table she'll clear the whole sweet trolley.'

'What choice does she have?' said Duncan. 'You've already emptied the wine cellar.'

Charlotte laughed again.

'Touché,' she said.

Stella Boddington was big and bosomy and bursting out of her berry-brown suit. She dabbed the very last trace of crème fraîche from her lips with her paper napkin.

'Delish,' she said. 'Now, if you lot weren't here, I'd pick up that plate and lick it clean.'

Charlotte let out a semi-shocked laugh. Stella went on.

'Just space to squeeze in a cappuccino. Coffee, everyone? Or do we have to go back to the agency?'

'No,' said Duncan. 'We can do most of the meeting here.'

They ordered their coffees, the agency team going for espressos.

'I'm sorry I got here early having said I'd be late,' said Stella. 'I'm in London now until Monday. I rather fancy doing Covent Garden – the Neal Street bit. How are you getting on with The Station, Duncan?' Stella was interested but she also had a point to make.

'Fine.'

'I'm sure you'll find working on a TV account much more glamorous than my boring old carpet shops.'

Charlotte realised the comment was addressed to her, but Duncan stepped in to save her.

'It's not any more interesting once you have to work on it. All the manufacturing and design element of your stuff is fascinating. And we get the opportunity to do really varied creative work for you.'

'Do you think you really have the time and resource to put into my business as well as the launch of The Station? I want my campaign to run at the same time.'

'I know,' replied Duncan. 'I knew you were going to ask that. To be honest, Stella, you're right to be concerned. We'll have to work extremely hard. But we won't get sidetracked by The Station campaign. In terms of our creative resource, it's very likely that we'll bring in at least one creative team from MCN to help Orlando.'

This was news to Charlotte. Couldn't Orlando, C&B's creative director, produce the top campaign of the year himself without the aid of MCN?

'Second, we're almost certainly looking at press for you. The Station is using TV, radio, which we've almost completed, and posters. The lead times are different, so we won't be in production on both campaigns at the same time.'

'I'm not questioning the production resources, Duncan. The MCN departments can handle all that. I'm more concerned about the thinking, the planning, the attention to detail from the team round the table now. C&B's got to manage my campaign and run it like it's the only thing you have to do this year. The launch of these new carpets with the new fibre is very important to the Carpets Company, not to say to Fibrella.' She explained to Charlotte: 'Fibrella is the manufacturer of the fibre that this new range is based on. They're putting up half the money for the launch.' She turned back to Duncan. 'This is the biggest revolution in British domestic carpeting for ten years. It's of crucial importance to the Carpets Company. It's very important to me personally. If it gets screwed up I can say goodbye to my job and you can say goodbye to the account.'

Duncan looked straight into Stella's eyes. This was the perennial problem of all number-two clients. The obvious fact that their business came second. But she was right. Without ever admitting it, they'd plan all the Station work carefully and then fit Carpets in around it and pretend they hadn't. The best thing to do was to play the Integrity and Trust card. He spoke slowly and apparently thoughtfully.

'Stella, you know we won't let you down. You aren't our biggest client but the company has worked with you longer than almost anyone else. It's the most important relationship we have. The Station will cut its spending next year, but you're a consistent spender. In the long term, your account is the goose that will lay the golden eggs. It's the reason we brought Charlotte in. She's come from one of the best agencies in town specifically to work for you. No doubt, as we go along, we'll have our differences on the creative work and media and so on, but we'll get the campaign out. I promise you. We won't let you down.'

Stella liked Duncan and always found his plain Scottish tone reassuring. She just needed to hear it.

'Anyway, Stella,' he laughed, 'Nigel Gainsborough can't stand Yoof TV. But he does need a free carpet for his cottage on the

South Coast. So guess what we'll be instructed to make our priority?'

Stella smiled. Duncan wished it wasn't so true. Integrity and Trust always worked better when spiked with irreverent humour. It showed clients it was the real you that was talking and that you were on their side.

Stella turned to the new team member.

'Do you know much about the Carpets Company yet, Charlotte?'

'No. Other than that I bought my living-room carpet from one of your stores.'

'Good for you.'

'I'll pick it up quickly.'

'I'm sure you will.'

Charlotte slipped her little blue Challenger notebook out of her shoulder purse. She flicked it open and propped it on the table. With one eye on it and the other on Stella she spoke hesitantly, remembering Duncan's précis. 'You're aiming to launch a range of carpets made from a new type of nylon fibre. It combines the duller, natural look of wool with the hard-wearing properties of nylon.'

'Very good!' Stella had expected the new girl to say nothing at all. 'I have a fourteen-volume design manual which says just that in several million words. I love the way you agency people can say it in only one line.'

'Is it environmentally friendly?' asked Charlotte.

'Not compared to the International Wool Secretariat, dear. They don't emit sulphur all over North Yorkshire, do they?'

'Just sheep shit.' Hazel squinted. 'Is there any wine left in that bottle?'

11

'Hey, guess what?'

'What? Cindy, you'll have to be quick. Serena's hovering outside my door.'

'Relax, Duncan. Pretend it's a business call. Alan and I are going to be staying at Blakes tonight.'

'Really. Remind me what that is again?'

'The hotel run by Anouska Hempel. She was brought up in Australia, you know.'

'Must be brilliant, then.'

'It is, actually. It's like a private home with every room designed by her to be completely different and fantastically luxurious. We've got moiré silk walls, antique prints and an ebony Empire bed. Not to mention a marble bathroom. Jealous?'

'Just a bit. So what brought this on? D'you have to go to those lengths just for a hot nobbing session?'

'Dunky! God, you're in a snappy mood this afternoon.'

'I'm just very busy. That new girl started this morning and I lost quite a bit of time bringing her on board.'

'Pointy Tits? She's a fast worker.'

'You mean Serena's a fast worker. I'm just going to have words with her now about hiring behind my back.'

'Words, eh? Sounds nasty.'

'Yeah, well, I'm really irritated. So what's the celebration at Blakes for?'

'Nothing. But one of Alan's clients was meant to be staying in London tonight and he's not coming now. So, since Alan's company's paid for the room, we might as well use it. Charge a few yummies up to expenses.'

'Well, at least save the bathroom freebies for me. I've got to go. Have a nice time.'

'Bye. Oh, Dunky—'

'Yeah?'

'Give her hell!'

*   *   *

'How was Stella at lunch?'

Duncan winced. Serena Sark was a first-class fault-finder and her shrill voice could intone the simplest question with implied criticism. She had sat down in Nigel Gainsborough's office at his table and was scribbling with her Tiffany pen on a pad. She was doing Nigel's budgets for him. He was on the phone at his desk, holding for his garage.

'Fine, basically,' said Duncan.

'Did she understand what I was saying the other day? Has she read my paper?'

'Yes, but—'

'But she doesn't understand it, no need to tell me. She's not really very intelligent is Stella. I've simplified the strategy as much as is humanly possible.'

'I know.'

Duncan also knew that Serena would now launch into a long lecture. Word perfect, Serena repeated her presentation mantra-like, as if instilling the will to believe it into herself and Duncan yet once more would somehow help persuade their client.

'Shoppers are carpet-illiterate. They haven't heard of any brands. They have no criteria by which to judge carpets. They don't understand anything about the different fibres. They cannot analyse carpet construction. Retailers concentrate too much on cost and tend to sell down to a price to close the sale. All these problems can be overcome by advertising.'

Duncan listened politely but he really didn't need to hear this.

'Advertising can create brands with emotional values. In a market where people don't know much about the *product* they will buy a *brand* because they've heard of it, they trust it, they like it. We can communicate a list of rational fibre end-user benefits. We can educate the consumer about what to look for in construction. By adopting a quality positioning we can reduce the importance of price in the equation. Marks & Spencer sells on the ratio of quality to value, not on absolute price. That's what makes it so profitable.'

Serena emerged out of presentation mode.

'Why don't our clients just do as I tell them? That whole market is a complete mess and yet the solution is staring them all in the face. They don't have to be as bright as me to see it.' In disgust, she jabbed the notepad with her Tiffany pen. 'Her trouble is she just wants us to list where her stores are and flash cheap prices all over the place to attract more store traffic, what she calls the punter. I do wish she wouldn't use that expression. It's so ghastly. But lack of store traffic isn't the problem, it's the low sales-to-store-visits ratio. You know, Duncan, if you're very intelligent it's so frustrating dealing with stupid people all the time.'

Obviously Duncan wasn't meant to know that. He saw a chink of light and made his move.

'She's concerned that we don't have the resources to handle her business properly. Because of The Station. She's well aware she's number two.'

'Well, Duncan, she must have got that from you, because Nigel and I always make her feel she's number one. You know that's Nigel's strength. You should observe from him how to get really close to your clients.'

Nigel pointed at the telephone mouthpiece. He'd let Serena do this meeting.

'No, she hasn't got that from me,' retorted Duncan. 'She can read in the papers how big The Station is going to be and draw her own conclusions. We've only got three creative teams. Not to mention eight other clients. It's only natural for her to be worried. I reassured her. And Charlotte made a good first impression.'

'Better than Hazel? Not that that is saying much. We *will* have to do something about that girl. She answered Nigel back in a Bencelor meeting in front of the client. I really think that's unforgivable.'

'She just speaks her mind. She's an Australian. Anyway, I wouldn't do anything about her at the moment. We need to keep her motivated. There's going to be so much work over the next three months.'

'Duncan, it's not for you to say how we handle the staff.'

'I didn't mean to suggest it was. But obviously, since I'm working closely with the girls day to day, I can fill you in on what they need to do.'

'Well, leave Hazel to our better judgment. Is Charlotte all right? Is she going to dress like that every day? She was very smart for the interview. I didn't expect a lycra top and leggings on her first day. She needs to keep her jacket on and her bottom covered or it's a bit revealing.'

'I'll say.' Nigel smirked and put the receiver down. He was a bit flummoxed. 'I'm not sure if I was meant to be holding or not. Perhaps he'll call me back. Jaguar aren't nearly as good as they were since Fords took them over. What would your bum look like in that outfit, eh?'

Serena pointedly put down her pen and shot a furious 'not in front of the children' look at Nigel.

'Nigel,' she said. 'I'm just finishing this income forecast for the MCN executive meeting. What was the last conversation you had with Stella?'

'Oh, I can't remember. What did I agree, Duncan?'

'Fifteen per cent on the first million pounds, thirteen per cent on the second and ten on everything else.'

Serena screwed up her face. 'Should have gone for eleven and a half on everything else. Duncan, what are the latest figures?'

'I've sent you a copy today following the meeting. We're aiming to bill three point three million pounds. All in quarter four.'

'It had better be. It mustn't fall into next year. Pre-bill if you have to.'

Serena picked up Nigel's desk calculator. After a lot of button-tapping she pronouced: 'That gives us four hundred and ten thousand pounds. Clancey and Bennett needs it all desperately if we're going to meet the MCN targets. Stella's our only hope. Our income from The Station is fixed in stone and none of the others have really got any money. Nigel, we must get a cash cow. We need more money to invest in ourselves. How can we hope to recruit any more talent like Charlotte?'

Duncan jumped in.

'Charlotte was something I wanted to talk to you about.'

'Yes?' Serena's voice was sharp enough to lift paint at thirty yards.

'I hadn't expected to see her quite so quickly after her interview yesterday. You didn't tell me she was coming.'

'You liked her, didn't you?'

'That's not the point I'm trying to make. It undermined my

authority both with her and with Hazel. It made me look as if I was one step behind.'

'Well, you normally are!' scoffed Serena. Her voice was irritatingly shrill. 'Really, Duncan, if we waited we wouldn't have got her. You yourself got her back in on the same day so we could see her. Honestly, you mustn't act as if there's a conspiracy. We agreed with *you*. Anyway, you left early last night and we couldn't tell you this morning because we weren't here. I would have thought that awful Audrey Goldberg woman you're so chummy with might have told you. How much is she getting for doing virtually nothing?'

There was no point in taking on that last comment.

'Serena, you could have left a note on my desk. Anyway, it doesn't matter now. I'm pleased she's joined. However, I thought we agreed she wouldn't work on The Station. She was promised solus to Stella.'

'If we didn't put her on The Station she wouldn't have come.' Serena was laughing now, as if Duncan were an idiot. 'Sometimes, Duncan, you can be such a stupid boy. We did the right thing and just because you didn't hear about it first you're having a sulk. The point is, Duncan, that as a junior board director you work for Nigel and me, not for Stella Boddington. Your first loyalty is to us. Actually, we were meaning to have a talk with you. You're much too friendly with some clients. *We* don't get that close to them, do we, Nigel? You need to keep a professional distance. And you must represent our viewpoint at all times. Your job is not just to run back to the agency and do the client's bidding.'

Duncan seethed and switched off. God, she annoyed him. Just a minute ago she had told him to get closer to his client, now she was flatly contradicting herself. They just made it up as they went along, these two old-timers. He had virtually run their company for them single-handed, covered their mistakes, improved the creative work out of all recognition, and all she could do was nag like an old shrew. The only words missing from her voluminous vocabulary were 'Thank you'. She was The Most Difficult Woman In Advertising. He had long resolved never to work for such a woman again. He looked critically at her blue and orange chiffon dress and her helmet of dyed jet-black hair and her bright turquoise eye shadow. And her roly-poly lover. Rumoured.

'You know she's right, old boy,' chortled Nigel.

12

'There are obvious implications for your son one way or the other. Whether you choose to tell him or whether you choose not to tell him – that, I'm afraid, is up to you.'

There was a very, very long pause before the solicitor got a stunned, albeit soft, response.

'Jesus.'

On her way to Lutyens Kleiner's stately offices in Piccadilly, Karen Myhill had been trying to imagine what more this week could have in store for her. The business consequences of her meeting the previous day with her financial adviser had sunk in quickly. It was only when she had got home after her meeting with Duncan Cairns the previous evening that she had registered the domestic implications too. As she had stood outside her front gate she had realised she soon might not be able to afford her home, her car, her way of life. What would happen to her? What would happen to Max? Financial disaster was looming, dark clouds, the works. And, as if that were not bad enough, now, on top of it, there was this: the unexpected bolt from the blue that Tim Lutyens had just fired at her. Unbelievably, it came the very week when she had only just come to the conclusion that she could reveal to Max the true story of her and his father and clear the air. She had been convinced her timing was right. But no longer. With a sense of crushing lack of certitude, she realised that the extraordinary news the solicitor had just communicated to her was a double-edged sword. It would create a cruel dilemma for Max were he to hear it. It was already an equally cruel one for Karen to have to choose whether to tell it to him or not. Her flickering, unfocusing eyes, now peeking through stretched-oval leopardskin-effect replacement spectacle frames, tried to follow the reassuring strong architectonic lines of the heavily moulded dado around the room.

'Are you related to Lutyens the architect?'

'I beg your pardon?' Tim Lutyens raised one fine eyebrow. 'I must say, Ms Myhill, I hadn't expected that to be your first question.'

'I just wondered. On the way here I walked past those buildings, you know, there's one with a big copper dome and huge stone bits and another with columns and pillars, and all along Piccadilly there are engraved brass plaques and things. I suppose I noticed them because I was frantically thinking about what you might have to tell me about Max's father and my mind was wondering what with your name and everything—'

'You realise now why I was reluctant to tell you down the telephone.'

'I do. Yes, I do. I'm glad you didn't,' said Karen. Her mind was in turmoil.' Your offices seemed to live up to it – being in Piccadilly, with the huge staircase and all this plain panelling and cornicing on such a scale. It's designed to make people feel small and insignificant, isn't it, all this British Empire stuff? This bombshell of yours certainly makes me feel small and insignificant. You plan your future and you have all these great ideas and then Life lets you have no control over it . . .' She shut up.

'It's obviously come as something of a shock to you. And no, I'm not aware that I am related to Lutyens.'

'It's just that only this week I promised Max I would tell him who his father was. I have no idea what to do now. If I don't tell him he's going to be devastated. He'll hate me. If I do tell him he might be equally devastated. He might hate me more. Either way Max is going to hate me. What do you recommend?'

'I really could not make a recommendation, Ms Myhill. Not least because I do not represent you. I represent the other party. I was instructed only to pass on this information at this time.'

'How long have you known?'

'Me, personally, months. But it has obviously been known for some years.'

'Jesus.' Karen looked up at the moulded ceiling. 'I realise now why they have all this architecture in these places. It's supposed to stop you from swearing. Well, fuck you!' She pointed into the air.

'Are you religious, Ms Myhill?' asked Tim Lutyens, fine eyebrow raised once more. Lutyens Kleiner was not a place in which swearing was approved.

'I'm an atheist. If there was a God in heaven he wouldn't have waited two thousand years to create television and then let it be so fucking crap. Let alone land me in the mess I'm in now. Why do you ask?'

'Just interested. I am unable to advise you, Ms Myhill.'

'I got the message.'

'But what you might consider thinking of, and of course this really could not constitute advice on my part at all—'

'No, no. But you're going to say it anyway, so get a move on.'

'Really, Ms Myhill, you don't have to be so unpleasant. I merely wish to point out the option that it would be possible to reveal Maximilian's father's identity to him without telling him this . . . development.'

Karen shook her head. 'I don't think so at all. I think that would open up a real can of worms. I know my son. I have to tell Max all or nothing. There is no in-between ground. God, how am I going to make up my mind?' She rose, picked up her things and started for the door, more round-shouldered than ever, to the point of hunchbackedness. 'I suppose I should say thank you.'

'Ms Myhill.' Tim Lutyens stood up behind his desk of honest English oak. 'That was only the first point I have to communicate.'

Karen stopped dead in her tracks. She looked desperate. 'There can't be more? Jesus.'

'I'm afraid there is, but I'm sure this will be more to your liking.'

Tim Lutyens gestured for her to return to her seat and, after she had done so, sat down once more himself.

'What?'

'Would you like another cup of tea?'

'No. Just tell me what it is you've got to tell me.'

The solicitor looked disappointed that no more tea was to be ordered. It was obviously his convention that if his guest refused he could not indulge himself.

'It also constituted part of my instructions that whenever this meeting between us came about I was to reveal to you that a trust fund was established in Maximilian's name.'

'A trust fund?' Karen was surprised. She was flabbergasted. She was intrigued. 'Since when?'

'Maximilian's father created it at the time of his birth. It was reasonably generously endowed and has performed well, particularly in the nineteen eighties. Your son is to come into a not inconsiderable amount of money.'

'How much is not inconsiderable?'

'I'm not at liberty to reveal that.'

'Oh, for fuck's sake!' Karen's simmer boiled over. 'This is all worse than some fucking stupid game show. This is my son's life – and mine – at a crossroads. I should be told.'

'I'm simply not allowed to mention specific figures.' But Tim Lutyens's fine eyebrows implied that Karen could have a stab at a number.

'Is it thousands or . . .' She nearly didn't dare say it. '. . . tens of thousands?'

'Oh, more than that.' He seemed quite dismissive of her guess.

'*Hundreds* of thousands?'

The fine eyebrows rose subtly upwards.

Karen could barely get the word out. '*Millions?*'

Now the fine eyebrows descended and Tim Lutyens looked disapproving.

'Please don't get carried away. It's round about one.'

'Max is a millionaire?'

'Only just.'

'Jesus. That's a fucking fortune. I had no idea his father had that sort of money.'

The solicitor gave her a wilting look which could only suggest that unless big money figured in the picture this classy legal practice would not be wasting its time with her.

'The fund has been lucky, actually. His father put nothing like that much into it in the first place. But I wouldn't get too excited. That would barely buy you a six-month lease on a small place in Eaton Square. A million pounds goes nowhere these days. I can't understand why they make all that fuss about the National Lottery.'

'Who wants to live in Eaton Square? Jesus.'

And then it just struck Karen smack on. A warm wave of complete relief washed over her. She became tangibly ecstatic.

'This is just what we need!' she gushed. 'Max is right at the heart of everything Myhill Productions is about and this will let him invest in his future. This money can insure our cash flow for years and guarantee his inheritance and a career when he gets out of university. It's the solution to all our problems. We're saved! It's brilliant! It couldn't have come at a better time!'

'I'd stop right there if I were you, Ms Myhill. It's his money to do with as he pleases. Not yours.'

'Aha. Max and I agree about everything. Max will put the money into the company just as I have said. Anyway, whatever he does with it, it is none of your business.'

'As one of the trustees, I think you'll find it is rather more my business than it is yours.'

'What d'you mean, "I think you'll find . . ."? I'm his fucking mother!'

'Of course. But his father planned for this.'

'Planned for what?'

'A single mother with a single son . . . well . . .'

'If you're going to trot out some moral lecture you can fuck off.'

Tim Lutyens had no intention of fucking off and changed his tone.

'I deal in the law, Ms Myhill, and the law alone. You must wallow in your own morality. In cases such as this there is clearly the factor of parental influence to be taken into account when assessing the best path to take with a trust fund set up in a minor's name. Maximilian's father clearly did not want you to know this fund existed when he set it up and so you were not named as one of the trustees.'

'You mean he was worried I'd get my hands on Max's money and use it for my own ends? That's ridiculous. What a stupid bastard.' But Karen was careful not to annoy the lawyer further and quickly added, 'Him, not you. Mr Lutyens, there is no one else in my life nor has there ever been. Max *is* my life. Max is my love. Everything I do, I do for my son.'

'I'm sure you have his best interests at heart. And so did his father when he created the conditions of the fund.'

'What conditions?'

'Maximilian will have no access to the money until he is twenty-five years old.'

'*Twenty-five years old?!* Jesus fucking Christ! That's well into the next century, for God's sake! The law is you get everything at eighteen in this country.'

'Allow *me* to tell *you* what the law is, Ms Myhill. One supposes the idea was that at twenty-five Maximilian would know his own mind and be mature enough to take the correct actions with such a substantial endowment.'

'The idea, no doubt,' said Karen, spitting venom, 'was that he would be free of me and my influence.'

'I think that's rather a dramatic interpretation of the fund's principles,' replied the solicitor calmly. 'It is quite the done thing not to hand over property and estate and so on before the recipient has attained the age of twenty-five. One has a certain maturity and responsibility by then and an idea of where one wants to go in life. One has completed one's education and perhaps one has married and has thoughts of children.'

'Oh, has *one*?' mocked Karen.

'It makes perfect sense to me.'

'No doubt. Well, I shall speak to Max about this. Max is actually exceptionally grown up for his age. He has a fantastic head for business. He will want to borrow against his future income and as it's guaranteed I would think in today's climate there should be no problem. How does *one* feel about that?'

'The fund bars Maximilian from borrowing against his future income, I'm afraid. Nor, specifically, is Maximilian allowed to buy shares or invest in any company owned or operated by you, I'm sorry to say.'

Karen was staggered. 'You've thought of everything, haven't you? I suppose Max gets a bonus if he creeps up on me in the dead of night and plunges a wooden stake through my heart and kills me!'

'That sort of silliness does you no credit, Ms Myhill. Goodness me, you do possess a fertile imagination, don't you? Although I'm sure that's most useful in your line of work. The trustees have decided you may tell Max about the fund now. However, if you think it unwise to, then we will not contact him yet. We'll leave that one to you. Sometimes it's better not to know. It can act as a disincentive to completing one's education if one realises one may not have to work for a living.'

Karen ignored him. 'Jesus! What sort of vindictive bastard thought all this up? How could his father do this to me?'

'I think you'll find it's all perfectly standard, Ms Myhill. I don't think his father thought of anything that's out of the ordinary at all.'

'He didn't, didn't he? Well, I'm not so sure. Is that it?'

'I believe so.'

'Well, you've given Bomber Harris a good run for his money this afternoon, haven't you?'

'I have no idea what you mean, Ms Myhill. If I can be of further help . . .'

'Don't worry. I won't be in touch. I'd rather stick red hot needles in my eyes.'

Karen slumped out of Lutyens Kleiner and down the mahogany processional staircase from days of Empire. What was she to tell Max about the money and the rules and the regulations, if anything? Twenty-five years old was an age away for him. They could not put the money into Myhill Productions. They could not borrow against it, either. Karen had had her hopes raised and then, somehow worse than dashed, thwarted. But right at this moment, as she left the solicitor's office, the trust fund was the lesser of her troubled questions. If the issue of the money had arrived as a surprise, it was the solicitor's first piece of information which had arrived as a shock. Its implications were far more serious in Karen's eyes and, whether she were to tell Max or not, there would be huge consequences for his life and huge reverberations in his relationship with her.

As she stopped outside the great monumental double doors of the building, and stood at the top of the black-dotted marble stairs leading back down into Piccadilly, her leopard-lined eyes spotted a brilliant brass plaque mounted on the entrance wall and bearing the name Lutyens Kleiner in Roman letters. Glinting in the sun, it was a proud plaque, pristine and perfectly polished. In frustration, Karen took the index finger of her left hand and, with a flourish, rubbed it ragged, right across the classic lettering, leaving a dirty great big messy swirling smudge.

'That sort of silliness does you no credit, Ms Myhill,' she said, and descended to the street.

13

Although Cindy Barratt had wanted to inspect the room in minute detail, she hadn't expected to have an hour and a half in which to do it on her own. She sighed and put the champagne flute back on the tray. Champagne didn't sparkle without company. She flicked through the copy of *Vogue* on the secretaire but it only threw her boredom back at her. She looked at her watch. She pulled one of the curtains away from the window and looked down into Roland Gardens No sign of the lovely, little, red TVR Griffith. Where was Alan? Why did he always do this?

She loved this black room at Blakes Hotel. It brought back a lecture she had gone to as a teenager in Sydney. The lecturer had been telling them about Symbolist painting and Puvis de Chavannes. Now there was an unforgettable name. Then he had read an extract from a French novel about a man – was he dying? – who had held a dinner party. All the guests had to wear black. The dining room was draped with cyprus leaves and black silk. All the plates were made of slate. The cutlery had ebony handles. They dined on black turtle soup, black Russian bread, black guinea fowl stuffed with prunes and black-eyed beans. Black-eyed beans? Surely not. That didn't sound very Parisienne. Perhaps he was in New Orleans. She couldn't remember now. It all seemed an awfully long time ago. Poorly educated Cindy had been too shy back then to ask what the novel was. She had never found out nor met anybody who knew it. But it was definitely her kind of book. Like Madame Bovary.

She toyed with the last olive and bit into it as she wandered into the bathroom. If she ran a bath and got into it Alan would turn up and expect to go down for dinner straight away. If she didn't run a bath he'd take another hour. The problem was that she could never predict what Alan would do. She turned the large plain handle of the tap and jumped backwards as a torrent of water gushed out with force. I wish I had plumbing like this, she thought. If I had marble in my bathroom I'd freeze to death. This, though, was a warm and reassuring beige marble, hand-cut into little diamonds and squares to give a Roman effect. Her face lit up with an idea.

As the foamy water fell still, she tested it with her toe. Mmm. Just right. The bath seemed enormous: deep and wide with straight, solid sides. She switched on the whirlpool spa mechanism and it chugged into life. She slipped out of her robe, letting it fall to the floor, and ceremoniously stepped in. With a theatrical flourish, she sprinkled the almost full forty-five-pound half-bottle of Moët et Chandon over her boobs and into the water. Who was she? Cleopatra? Marie Antoinette? Joan Collins? As she lay back in the warmth, her sparkling breasts bobbing above the foam, she spotted the white bakelite telephone. Fantastic. Who can I call? Before she had thought of Duncan's number, it rang.

She could hardly breathe. She pulled her head from under his and came up for air. Her face was suffocating in the silk bolster. She was worried about Alan. He was working far too hard and only doing this sort of thing for her. After the call to say he was on his way, it had taken him another three-quarters of an hour to arrive. She ran her fingers through his thinning hair and wiped the perspiration from his forehead. His face was florid, his breathing rapid, his heart racing. And his cock was whacking into her. To be honest, it was doing absolutely nothing for her, but if it kept him happy she was pleased. And having him thrashing away on top, while uncomfortable, was better than having to squat and suck him off.

She'd overdone the food and drink, enthused into a frenzy of overeating by the rich variety of black dishes on the menu. Black tagliatelle with ebonised mushrooms in a dark wine sauce. Claret. Ink-fish risotto with Beluga caviar and charcoal kelp. Baume de Venise. Liquorice and mascarpone ice-cream garnished with prunes. All served on huge black plates in the black basement dining room. Thank God Alan had suggested coffee in the room before she bloated up in size to rival Orca the Killer Whale. At least she could kick off her shoes and unhook her bodice.

Now she pushed his face into her hair and he found her ear with his hot tongue. She turned to the side to make it easier for him. It felt like a little wet animal burrowing underground. She pulled her trapped arm from under his thigh and, glancing sideways, let her hand flop over to the commode-style bedside table. Her fingers found the box on top and slipped inside. She found the small, dark prize and retrieved it. Imperceptibly she brought the chocolate to her lips and popped it in. The fresh cream champagne centre star-burst in her mouth. If confectionery could have an orgasm this was it. Bliss. Alan continued to thrust his groin into hers. There was no rhythm, no pattern, just the urgent search for release.

Alan and his tongue suddenly abandoned her ear. Startled, Cindy found herself caught, looking straight up into Alan's boiling, crimson face. He was about to penetrate her mouth in a mirror image of his insertion below. With all the sensuality and passion he could muster, and with all his powers of concentration centred on achieving climax, he straightened his ramrod tongue and dive-bombed it between her succulent lips.

He felt like a rider thrown from his mount, confused and betrayed.

'What the fuck?'

'It's a chocolate.'

He was dumbfounded.

'Joan Collins does it! At least, I'm sure she does.' She giggled at the gooey brown on his lips and tongue.

His cock subsided to uncooked sausage inside her. His face was no longer red with lust and passion. Instead it appeared blotchy with boozing and exhaustion. He didn't have the twenty minutes of determination it would take to get another erection.

'I'm sorry, darling,' said Cindy. 'I was being silly. We can try again in the morning.'

She was genuinely apologetic. She knew she had spoiled it for him. Alan rolled over on his side, flattening out his love handles as he did so. A short while later she spoke.

'Alan?'

'What?'

'Why don't you get a mobile phone?'

'I don't want one.'

'Why not? You've got everything else. A TVR. A Rolex. If you had a phone I could call you to find out where you are. I'll buy it for you as a gift.'

'I'd only have had it switched off because I was in a meeting. If I had a mobile phone I'd be on call twenty-four hours a day to my clients. I work long enough hours as it is. And I can't have one client ringing me when I'm with another.'

He'd obviously thought it through.

'I'm not complaining. I've had a lovely evening. Thank you.'

She pecked him on the cheek then suddenly eyeballed her watch. She lunged towards the TV remote control.

'We can catch the Doris Day late-night movie. Quick! The TV's inside that Chinese thing. Open the doors for me, Alan, will you?'

He climbed off the bed, opened the doors of the Japanese lacquer cabinet, then got back under the sheets and went soundly to sleep with the Eternal Virgin.

14

The pianist was slaughtering 'Send in the Clowns'. Nigel Gains-borough and Serena Sark, who had long ago learned how to survive a marathon Marketing Society dinner, were propping up the first-floor bar at the Lancaster Gate Hotel at the top of Hyde Park. There were not many of the original four hundred people left now, and Serena was the last woman. She was one of the few female managing directors on these bi-annual black-tie events, and she always glitzed up to stand out in the crowd. She had worn a simple black strappy dress tonight, but drawn maximum attention to herself with a glittering yellow sequined jacket embroidered on the back with a multi-coloured parakeet. Showing off paid off. Half the attendees tonight were from advertising, sniffing out the new business potential of the other half from marketing. It was quite the done thing to make eye contact across the tables and approach old comrades, old colleagues, old contacts, and exchange pleasantries and business cards. And give them the story about how well your own company was doing now you were running it yourself and how you had a gap on your client list in their field. It was all very kissy-kissy and Nigel and Serena excelled at such socialising. They were old-school and bred for it. They had both had a little too much to drink, but so had everyone else. One always did on these nights.

'I know I've said so a hundred times already this evening, but I really didn't think much of that speech.'

'That makes it a hundred and one, old girl.'

'No, but I mean the whole point of attending these things is to learn something.'

'The whole point is to schmooze, isn't it, and pick up some extra business?'

'Nigel, I do wish you wouldn't use words like that. It's so undignified. It sounds like booze, for God's sake.'

Nigel snorted and resisted the temptation to answer back. She was on a roll.

'Well, it does. It's déclassé.'

'You're a snob, Serena.'

'Well, someone has to be. The trouble is one feels one has nothing to learn from the Third Wave.'

Nigel, sozzled, stared back blankly.

'The Third Wave. All those new agencies run by the young Turks that took off in the late eighties. I mean, they're just all so . . . so young.'

'I know what the Third Wave is. But what does that make us, then, old girl? The First Wave? The Old Wave? The Permanent Wave?'

'We're the originals. We were important when British advertising was the best in the world. What we did was really talked about. *Campaign* is calling the seventies the golden age nowadays. We had the Midas touch. People look back at the old Clancey and Bennett and realise that it was the place to be. No one can emulate that now. None of this lot will ever achieve what we had.'

'I know what you're thinking. You're thinking we shouldn't have sold up.'

'Sold *out*, you mean. No, I'm not thinking that.' But she was. They had lost control. She drained her champagne glass and rolled its base back and forth on the counter of the bar. 'The industry has moved on completely and we've had to move with it, that's all. We did the right thing. It's just a disappointment, I suppose. It was better the way it was before, the way it used to be.'

'Well, it was more fun. It's a load of bloody hard work these days.' Nigel yawned.

'When we started in the business it would have been ridiculous to have had chairmen in their thirties. You don't know anything when you're thirty. Look at Duncan. He's reasonably intelligent but he's simply not able to mix with the top people yet.'

'No.'

'He's not developed or mature enough. Yet we've had to make him a board director, for God's sake. What can he tell our clients about anything? Virtually nothing. It's happening everywhere now. Look at MCN's head of TV media.'

'It's been a long day. Remind me who that is.'

'That stupid little girl aged twenty-eight. I wouldn't hire her as a secretary.'

'I would,' chuckled Nigel. He bulged his eyes.

Serena looked cross for a second. 'You know what I mean. Once you're over thirty-five nowadays you're stuck. You can't move anywhere else because you're too old. Tonight was almost embarrassing. We forked out a small fortune for our clients – prestigious people, I might point out – to come and see someone we've barely heard of, promoted far too soon, giving the keynote speech of the year. I could have done it much better.'

'Sounds like you're giving it now.' Nigel brought his arm up to his round face to check the time.

'Don't be rude. All that research we did under the last Labour government. D'you remember that? I think people would be interested in that. It's relevant with the swing back in politics. But they think they just know better, don't they, this next generation? Well, I for one learnt absolutely nothing from that chap tonight.'

Nigel rubbed his eyes blearily.

'No, old girl. You can't teach an old dog new tricks.'

Serena smarted.

'I hope that wasn't meant to be a reference to me.'

'What? No, of course not, old girl.'

Nigel smirked. Serena arched her back prissily.

'D'you think I could take my bow-tie off now, old girl?'

'No, you may not,' Serena snapped. 'Nigel, you really must get a new dinner jacket. If you expand one more inch that button'll come flying off and take my eye out.'

'You'd look terrific with an eye patch. You could have a diamanté one for these occasions.'

Serena smiled coquettishly. She enjoyed his teasing. 'Didn't you think our table worked well?' she asked.

'Yes. I thought it all went splendidly.'

'I thought so too. It was a bit of a challenge having ten clients and only us two, but I managed to talk to them all. And they were very good with each other.'

'Well, the only other person we could have invited was Orlando and he never says anything, so we saved there. Don't worry about it. We talked it over when we drew up the list. We couldn't have had anyone from MCN. It's too risky.'

'Perhaps someone from the media department could have come.'

'You don't mean that girl who heads up TV? There isn't anyone senior enough. It would look odd not to have Duncan then.'

'He really is a problem, isn't he? We'll have to do something about him, but I don't know what.'

'He'll overstep the mark sooner or later and we can fire him.'

'Oh, Nigel, that's impossible and you know it. Sometimes I think you've just given up, you know. We need a survival strategy.'

'We've got one. It's Keep Your Head Down.'

'That's completely the wrong thing to do. Nigel, we have to face up to it, when we were running the old C&B we could do what we liked, but since the takeover MCN have reduced it to a rump. It doesn't need two managing directors. We've only got sixteen direct employees, for God's sake. All the others really work for MCN.'

'And drag their feet on our business.'

'There's no way MCN will continue to pay for both of us, or even either of us, beyond the end of the year. Once the buyout contracts are up we have no security. We'll get unceremoniously dumped. Not unless we can win something really big that's ours.'

'Wouldn't our clients back us when it came down to it?'

'You always think they would. But look at everyone else of our generation. Unless they have a shareholding or a watertight contract, they go. When it does come down to it the clients just say, "Sorry, perhaps I could help you get a consultancy project." That's the business nowadays, Nigel. It's no fun any more.'

'C&B's too small to lose us. It would just fall apart. None of our clients would choose to go into MCN. That's our security.'

'No it's not. Duncan would run it. Badly, but no one would spot it for a year. Look at the bottom line. He earns a fraction of what we jointly make, so MCN would be happy. The clients who matter adore him. He's cut us right out of The Station and Carpets. Those two stupid women worship the ground he walks on. When did he last show us any work we really had any chance to comment on before it was whisked away? And he connives with Orlando against us. He's going to push us out. And what's worse, he probably doesn't even realise he's doing it.'

'We'll have to fire him.'

'We can't. He's very difficult but he does play by the rules.

We've been done for unfair dismissal twice already, remember. MCN won't let us get away with that again.'

'So? You're meant to be the great strategic thinker.'

'We need to encourage Duncan to leave of his own volition. We need to undermine his security in his job. Make him a bit miserable. Then he'll go of his own accord. He doesn't like not being in complete control.'

'Can we do that?'

'We could if we could find his Achilles heel. Everyone's got one, you know.'

15

Duncan was in the back extension. It was colder and damper than the rest of the flat at this time of night, when the temperature dropped like a stone. He had painted it British racing green to look like a study, but he really only used it as a store. He was annoyed – and hurt – that tonight yet another client contact opportunity was being monopolised by Godzilla and Dracula. Still, since they had spent an hour getting ready, it had given him time to run quite a few more files through the photocopier.

Duncan had always been methodical about keeping duplicate documents at home. It was part of his efficient approach. He could work on in the evenings with everything at his fingertips. He could catch clients at the weekend from his home office. He could feel secure that everything he ever needed was in its place where it should be in this, his personal retrieval system, and not left to chance in the sieve of disorganised public files in the agency. Lately, though, there had been more pressing reasons to loot the more critical and confidential records. Information was power and Duncan's gut survival instinct told him he needed to build a power base. Everyone knew that the MCN–C&B set-up had been a compromise skilfully negotiated at the time of the takeover by Serena Sark to preserve her own and Nigel Gainsborough's status, not to mention their huge incomes. The commercial reality was that, as time went on, MCN would have less and less need of a costly agency within an agency and one day, sooner or later, something would have to be done. MCN knew it. Duncan knew it. Godzilla and Dracula knew it better than any of them.

Nigel and Serena were performing a high-risk, high-wire, trapeze double act, but had every intention of ensuring that, if anyone was going to take the drop, it wasn't going to be them. Duncan felt it was only wise, therefore, that *he* should perform with a safety net. So he was. And his cache of hidden-away papers was one strand of it. Duncan's armoury of ill-gotten information was a secret weapon. There was no problem slipping out the heavy bundles past security in carrier bags. The agency was always full of those really robust ones from the TV facilities houses, made of strong plastic for transporting stacks of videotapes.

Duncan was still irritated at being excluded from the client do. To annoy him further, there had been the ritual Maida Vale residents' parking crisis. Duncan no longer expected to park right outside his flat but he did think he had a right to get parking somewhere in Sutherland Avenue. That was what he was paying seventy-one pounds a year for. Seventy-one pounds for the privilege of parking in his own street. Seventy-one pounds for the privilege of leaving his car languishing on a public road where, alarmed or not, it was a sitting target for break-ins. There were patently far fewer parking spaces than permits issued by Westminster City Council. Duncan had often wondered whether or not that was legal. Whether or not it was, the result was that Londoners who lived in Maida Vale, laid out in the 1850s, seemed to spend their evenings cruising the streets looking for somewhere to park. You didn't have to be mobile around here to succumb to road rage. You could get into a state of apoplexy just standing at the edge of the kerb.

After quarter of an hour driving up and down the road, Duncan had been obliged to park what felt like half a mile away in Randolph Avenue. As he stomped home he noticed the weather had turned. There was the beginning of rain in the air. Much later, after an hour in front of the television snarling back to the *Question Time* panel and their formulaic answers to the problems of the day, he had remembered than he still had to stack away the photocopied documents he had slipped out of the agency. Now he was struggling to shut the old chest of drawers.

'Pushkin! How did you get in there?'

Pushkin's fluffy face popped out of the bottom drawer as Duncan was about to squeeze it shut. She had imperceptibly tunnelled her way in there, via the back of the chest, after going in at the top drawer. She miaowed and rubbed herself on his calves.

'Oh, baby,' said Duncan sweetly. The day's problems could always be massaged away by Pushkin's touching presence. 'You're so thin, aren't you? Such a little girl. OK. Foody-woody.'

He tried to scoop her up but she poured like quicksilver through his arms and led him through the living room and into the kitchen. She jumped up onto the counter-top and rubbed her forehead on the light switch. She knew by heart the journey that led to dinner: light switch, cupboard, electric can opener, bowl.

Pushkin's face pressed into the plastic dish. Duncan went into the bathroom and ran the bath. He carefully measured out the heady vanilla oil bought in Florence and poured it on to the water. He wasn't wild about the way it didn't foam but he found the aroma seductive, almost hypnotically so. This oil left your skin strongly scented and feeling really ripe. He went to the bedroom to undress. Pushkin followed him in and jumped on to the chest of drawers to perform her post-prandial grooming routine. The phone by the bed rang. He let the answering machine take over. He ought to redo that tape, it was getting worn.

'You have called Duncan Cairns. I'm sorry I'm unable to come to the phone at the moment. Please leave a message after the tone and I'll call you back.'

His voice sounded too high and hideously Scottish. Or so he thought. Friends always said they thought they'd got through to the BBC. Then he heard who it was. He threw himself on the bed and cut in.

'Hello, stranger. I'm here really. I'm just about to get into the bath.'

'Are you, darling? Are you naked?'

'Yes I am, actually.'

'Mmm! My dream boy! I thought you might be out on the razzle.'

'Not tonight. I've been doing boring things like filing documents.'

'Yeah? How's Pushkin?'

'She's missing you. Nearly as much as me. She's on top of the chest of drawers licking her paw and washing her face. Hey, guess what?'

'What?'

'I've sort of been approached for a job in television.'

'Television! Really?'

'By a woman called Karen Myhill.'

'*Karen Myhill?!*'

'You know her?'

'She's The Most Difficult Woman In Television.'

'That's funny. Someone else said that, the exact same words.'

'Dunky, Karen Myhill and I . . . our paths have crossed in the past, not to say our swords. Don't do anything until I get back.'

'When *are* you coming back?'

'How about now? Shall I come round?'

'My God! Where are you?'

'I'm at Heathrow!'

'*Are you*! I thought you weren't coming back till the weekend. I assumed you were still in Jo'burg.'

'I couldn't take the family any longer. Nor their views on Mr Mandela. I'll tell you all about it. South Africa has changed beyond recognition. I wish I'd gone back at the time of the handover. The whole experience was so emotional. I've spent the last two weeks crying. The family's still petrified, needless to say. They're so funny. I wish you had come with me.'

'You know I didn't want to. It doesn't interest me very much. If we go to South Africa I want to lie on a beach, not hang out with your folks wringing their hands because more blacks have got into the Cabinet.'

'Shall I come round, then? Will you stay up? I'll be about an hour.'

'Well, hurry up. I'm frozen stiff standing here.'

'Stiff, eh? Have you got a hard-on?'

Duncan looked down.

'Yes, I have, actually. You know I always get one when we talk on the phone.'

'Do you, Dunky? I always get one too,' said Michael.

After the goodbyes, Duncan replaced the receiver, picked up Pushkin from the chest of drawers, gave her an extra big squeeze, and then sauntered towards the bathroom to prepare himself for the Homecoming.

16

Duncan yawned.

'Late night?' Margaret was placing her open umbrella on the floor by the counter-top.

''Fraid so. I'm soaked.'

'Where's your brolly?'

'In my briefcase. I thought I'd just dash for it from the car park.'

'There's no rush. Sir and Madam are not in yet. They're on their way, though. Madam rang in on the mobile phone, checking up. Why does it always rain in time for the weekend? I was going to have a picnic with my sister.'

'Are Hazel and Charlotte in?'

'I think they're at the coffee machine.'

Duncan put his things in the office, joined the girls at the coffee machine, and then strolled back with them to Margaret's desk.

'So, Cairns, what kept you up so late last night?' asked Hazel.

'Nothing. I was just pottering around. Lost track of the time.'

'Oh, yeah? He's so secretive!' Hazel winked at Charlotte.

Duncan faked a broad, knowing smile to hide the slight trace of discomfort he felt at that remark and the even greater irritation he felt at the pantomime wink. He disliked being discussed in any way other than professionally. He was relieved at Hazel's follow-up line.

'Just like Nigel and Serena.'

Duncan was not secretive like them at all. They were secretive for professional reasons. He was secretive for personal ones. Hazel's comment had not been a subtle observation on her part. It was just part of her Bash the Boss banter. And any mention of Nigel and Serena always locked the conversation on to them for a few minutes. The coast was clear.

'What *is* their relationship exactly?' asked Charlotte. 'When I had my interview I felt, I don't know, embarrassed almost. Their body language is quite intense. They're like a married couple.'

'They're lovers, stupid. You can spot it a mile off. Everyone does, even all the clients.' That was Hazel's view.

'I've worked for Madam for ten years.' Margaret leant closer to relate her theory. 'You'll soon see. It's all one way: she's never out of his office, but he never goes into hers. She's in love with him.'

'She's in love with him?' Charlotte could barely believe it. 'What on earth does she see in him?'

'He's such a fat old fool, isn't he?' agreed Margaret. 'I can't think what she sees in him. I mean, she's a very intelligent woman. *He* tolerates *her* because she keeps him in his job. That's obvious. But I can't see any attraction in him myself.'

'You couldn't see it with a telescope,' interrupted Hazel.

'I think she's stuck with him and she knows it. MCN'll go for one or the other of them given half a chance, so she stands by him all the time. She only sees what she wants to with him because she has no choice. The consequences for her of losing him are dire.'

'No one else'll shag her,' said Hazel. 'That's her real reason.'

Now Duncan was irresistibly drawn to gossip against his better judgment.

'I don't think they're doing it now. I think they did it once years ago and he wishes they hadn't and she would like to again. And, to be fair, there are even people who believe that there's never been anything between them.'

'Come on, Duncan,' said Margaret. 'When they were at Cannes, I rang his hotel room and *she* answered.'

'They could have been having a meeting,' he suggested.

'At one o'clock in the morning? Hardly. What were they in Cannes for? Nothing. They were just on a jolly. It really annoys me. We've paid for two rooms in nearly every flash hotel in Europe and they've only ever used one. That comes off my Christmas bonus.'

'Can you imagine them at it?' laughed Hazel. 'Bleeugh! I wouldn't go down on him for a million dollars.'

'For God's sake, stop it!' Duncan turned to address Charlotte. 'Just remember that they always support each other. It doesn't matter why. They hunt as a pair.'

'And,' added Hazel, 'they try to isolate *you* from your colleagues. They pick you off.' She fired at Charlotte with her index finger. Twice. 'That's why the rest of us operate a group strategy. Never have a meeting with them on your own. Get me or Duncan or Orlando or one of the others in there with you. Like all dictators, they're cowards. They won't fight you if you've got someone on your side.'

'Duncan was in there with them last night on his own,' Charlotte pointed out.

'I'm on the board and I'm in with the clients. I have enough seniority to survive.'

'Be careful, Duncan.' Margaret moved towards a ringing phone. 'I've been here the longest. No one's safe. I'm like that BBC man at the Falklands War. I counted you all in and I'll count you all back out again.'

She ducked out of the conversation to take the call.

For goodness' sake, thought Charlotte. There's more politics in this little place than in the whole of Saatchi's.

Charlotte followed Hazel into the art files.

'Here,' said the Australian, 'I'll get the stuff we need down from the shelves and you stack it up down there.' She climbed on to the little kick bucket and reached up into the filing system.

'I'd have worn my old clothes if I'd known the place was so dusty.'

'You have old clothes?' asked Hazel. 'I know I've only known you for a day, but I find that hard to believe. This is for your benefit. Duncan is so thorough. He wants you to see all this stuff so you know the history of the accounts as well as we do.'

'Should I bother?'

'Having second thoughts, kiddo?'

'I'm just joking. It's only my second day.' Charlotte was nobody's fool. 'No disrespect, but I'll go by the evidence of my own eyes. I've got the Station TV account. Stella was sweet yesterday. Duncan is great. Orlando is well known in the business and highly thought of. And Serena is an exceptionally able woman with or without her private life. This was a good move.'

'Yeah, you're probably right,' acknowledged Hazel. 'I'm just not getting on that well, which is why I stir it. I'm getting too old just to be an account manager. I'm not much younger than Duncan. Catch this.' She dropped a large stack of polyboards into Charlotte's outstretched arms. Charlotte saw they had press ads mounted on the back of them in a display.

'Can you get promoted here? It's a small company.'

'Oh, yes. Duncan had someone at account director level working for him before, although Nigel fired him. But Nigel will never promote me. I know that.'

Charlotte was keen to talk about something other than Nigel and Serena. Everyone seemed to be obsessed with them.

'How long have you worked here?'

'Seven months. I've only been in London that long.'

'How did you get the job?'

'An English friend in Sydney recommended this person to me who might give me a job. A guy called Alan Josling. So I tried him when I first got here, but his business is all below the line and the company is too small. He used to work at the old C&B with Nigel and Serena and heard that they were hiring. He knew that nobody in their right mind would come to work for what was left of C&B after MCN had done with it, so, even as a foreigner, I had a good chance.'

'I hope you're not suggesting I'm out of my mind to work here?'

'Yeah, well, The Station wasn't such big news last year. Now C&B can get the best.'

She stepped down. The two women carried the boards and

folders through into the main meeting room. Margaret followed them in, pushing a trolley with coffee and tea things.

'I've pinched some biscuits from the kitchen for you. Well, it is Friday. Did you see what Madam was wearing when she finally turned up? I'll give you a clue. Get ready for some Tyrolean yodelling.'

'What?' Charlotte would have to get used to the lack of respect in this place.

'The maroon suede culottes!'

'Not the maroon suede culottes!' Hazel made a puking-face gesture. 'And matching foul jerkin?'

'What else? The weather has turned, you see, so we have abandoned chiffon for suede. Honestly. I didn't know Harvey Nichols sold such ghastly things but obviously they do. It makes her look like that thing in *Jurassic Park*.'

'Margaret!'

The shrillness of the voice froze them in their tracks. Serena popped her head round the door.

'There you all are. I thought I heard you lot gossiping away. I shall have to give you more work to do. What were you talking about?'

'Clothes,' said Charlotte swiftly. She desperately hoped Serena had not been eavesdropping in the corridor.

'Just what I'm working on at the moment. I've got to write a speech for WACL on advertising and the fashion retail trade.'

'Wackle? What's that?' asked Hazel.

'Women's Advertising Club of London. All the top women in the business are members and it's my turn to give a talk. Problem is, I have to cover the downmarket side of things and I don't really know much about how working-class women shop.' She flashed a fake smile. 'I thought you could help me with that, Margaret. You look like a chain-store shopper.'

Jesus, thought Charlotte. What a patronising cow. But Margaret had a riposte to hand.

'Yes, I am actually, Serena. I have to *struggle* on my salary.'

'Rubbish! You're very well paid for what you do, for which, I'm sure, we are all eternally grateful. What were you all doing in here anyway?'

'We're going to be briefing Charlotte on The Station account.'

'What, you, Hazel? Do you think you should be doing it?'

'Duncan's joining in a minute.'

'I suppose you think that'll make a difference. Margaret, go and put some time in my diary for Charlotte, so that I can give her a proper briefing myself. Make sure Nigel's free, too.'

Loyal Margaret rushed off to do Madam's bidding. Charlotte caught her boss before she left too.

'Is that a skirt you're wearing, Serena? Or culottes?'

'Culottes!' Serena extended them outwards like a toddler showing off her party dress. She was proud of her purchasing power.

'They're lovely.' Charlotte pushed her hand through her blonde hair and smiled.

'Thank you!' Serena, chuffed, turned on her heel and was gone.

Hazel looked on incredulously, then realised than Charlotte had been taking the piss.

'Heck! The girl's going to go far.'

'Just watch me,' said Charlotte.

17

Margaret managed to get Nigel and Serena into Christopher's for lunch at 1.30 p.m. With a bit of luck they'd stay there until 3.30 or four o'clock and wouldn't bother to come back for the rest of the afternoon. Serena could go window-shopping in the boutiques in Wellington and Tavistock Streets while he could pop into Penhaligon's and then mosey along to Covent Garden market. Or perhaps they'd nip off for nookie in the Strand Palace Hotel. If Margaret's theory was correct, of course.

'I'd forgotten how boring the menu is in here. I wish Margaret had remembered. If she took more of an interest in her job this sort of thing wouldn't happen. I'm sure I said not to book us in here again.' Serena made a mental note to start next week off with a lecture. 'Are you tired after last night?' she asked.

'No. I'm fine. We've had an easy day, sort of. Nothing to do this afternoon.'

'Nigel, we should be worried. When we ran the old Clancey and Bennett we were run off our feet. Now we have nothing to do. We can't let that go on or we'll both be out. Advertising has changed.'

'I got the message last night.' Nigel stifled a yawn.

'Well, it has. Structurally. Everything now is international. That's how MCN wins all its business. Huge amounts of money walk through that door in Dean Street because of some international alignment somewhere. It hasn't the slightest thing to do with anyone in this country. Our completely talentless board in London then have the cheek to judge our performance against their rate of success and say, 'You're not doing so well, are you?' But they've done no better themselves. They get it all on a plate. It makes my blood boil. Those whiz-kids, so-called, have no right to talk to us in that manner.'

'Thinking of giving up the ghost, old girl?'

Serena's reply was feisty.

'I'll see them all in hell first!' She calmed down. 'We have to be really careful we don't get fired at the end of this year. That's what frightens me. They're all out to get us. No one will lift a finger for us.'

'But what can we do about it? We can't begin to compete on their scale.'

'No. But we need to more than match the main agency on our rate of growth. We need to beat the targets set for us. The financial people always like that. As long as it looks good in percentages on paper they let you be.'

'Well, you'll have to manage that, old girl. I came into the business to sell a few ads to some other chappy over a G&T. Make some pretty pictures. That sort of thing.'

'We all know full well advertising has nothing to do with making ads any more. That's left to the babies to handle.'

'So. What's your plan?'

Serena took a sip of water and held it in her mouth for a moment while she focused into the distance, collecting her thoughts. She swallowed.

'I thought up a plan in the car on the way in this morning,' she said. 'A two-pronged one. First, we need to find a way to either get rid of Duncan or to bring him on-side.'

'On-side? Do we want him on-side?'

'I mean pretend on-side. He's too guarded at the moment. He has a strategy for every meeting, even where he seats us. He cut us right out of that last Carpets meeting because I couldn't make eye contact properly with Stella. And you couldn't see the ads clearly, so you couldn't see what she was talking about.'

'Couldn't I? Can't remember much about it now. I can never see what she's talking about, no matter where I'm sitting. I must say, she's really piling on the weight, old Stella, isn't she? She's the size of a bloody Soviet female tractor driver. As for Duncan, I think you imagine it. Men don't scheme and plan like that. Only women, my dear.'

'Duncan operates like a scheming woman, then. He's trained Orlando only to come to meetings with team support. We never win any of those creative discussions these days.'

'Is Duncan responsible for that?'

'Yes. But perhaps we could charm him, lunch him a bit, give him some Glyndebourne tickets, promise him a better bonus. That sort of thing.'

'Or?'

'Nobble him. He's not *that* good. We need to compromise his professionalism. Make him feel vulnerable and bring him to heel. He's slipped out from under our thumb. We need to get him back under it or get rid of him completely. I'll find a way.'

'Good. I've lost count. You said you had a two-pronged plan. How many prongs did we get in the end?'

'One.'

Nigel's face fell. Oh dear. Only one. Serena carried on regardless.

'Two is: we *must* win some business without Duncan getting involved in it. We need a new account billing at least two million. Business has really picked up in the last six months. We must be able to win something. I think you and I should make an agency video and place it at the Advertising Agency Register. New clients go in there every day to select agencies. At the moment we're mentioned by the register only as part of MCN International. Well, if clients want a small agency they won't look at the MCN reel at all, will they, when it's one of the largest agencies in London?'

'No. I suppose you're right. The last *Campaign* top three hundred list had MCN International almost level pegging with BMP DDB Thingy Thingy, or whatever they call themselves these days.'

'Exactly. We need our own separate identity. We could make a talking-heads film one day next week and put that in immediately. Just you and me speaking to camera. Mention Orlando on it, but we won't even tell him we're doing it. We can craft something better over the next few months, but still with just you and me on it. Then we can prove to MCN it's us who're winning business. Duncan had nothing to do with it.'

Nigel was distracted.

'Oh look, there's that chap.'

'Who?'

'That tall chap. Isn't he famous?'

'I don't know. He looks like a rock star. I can't do young people.'

'Yes, it could be him. I can't remember his name, though.'

'Nigel, are you listening to what I'm saying?'

Serena's mobile phone rang in her purse. She got it out with a flourish. Serena liked having a mobile phone. It made her feel more modern, although she had recently been horrified to discover that her plumber had one too. The same model.

'Hello?'

'Serena. Margaret gave me your number. I needed to catch you now, I'm afraid, as I'm out this afternoon. It's Alan Josling.'

'Alan. Hello.'

'How's that Australian girl I sent you getting on?'

'Oh, we keep her on her toes. We have so much business these days, we're all run off our feet. You know how it is.'

'Listen, I'll come straight to the point. I have a very interesting proposition to put to you. There's three or four million pounds' worth of billings in it for you. Are you free for lunch on Tuesday?'

Serena played it cool and muted the phone for a second.

Nigel was digging into the platter of french fries and not listening.

'Yes. We can manage that.'

'Say one o'clock at Quaglino's, then. I'll look forward to it. You're paying!'

'We'll go Dutch. If we gain anything, we'll refund you!'

Serena switched off the phone.

'I don't know what Margaret thinks she's playing at giving out my private number to any Tom, Dick or Harry like that. She knows we don't like Alan Josling.'

'He's all right. Bit of a crook, I've always thought.'

'I'll have to have a word with her on Monday morning. Still, we might get something out of this if we play our cards right.'

She was dying for Nigel to ask what the call had been about, but he kept his mind solely on clearing up the french fries. She folded the phone away into her purse, but wasn't looking at what she was doing.

'Drat!'

'Something wrong, Serena?'

'A disaster. I caught the salad bowl with my purse and it's knocked dressing all down the front of my jerkin. Charlotte was just saying this morning how lovely my outfit was. I hope it's not ruined.'

'I'm sure it's not. We can pop it into Tuxedo Express for cleaning and spend the afternoon buying you a new one.'

She smiled.

'What a good idea. Something tells me we can afford to.'

The grey Mercedes 300E slowed and turned right into the lane just past the sign 'Wychwood Lea Welcomes Careful Drivers'. Cow parsley fringed the road on both sides in front of dry-stone walls. They passed tumbledown Cotswold stone cottages blanketed in clematis and then turned right again before a Victorian level crossing. On the village green the pink horse chestnut was in full flower. They passed the ancient Swan pub and then drew to a halt outside a three-storey house adjacent to a tiny Norman church. Duncan got out of the passenger side and opened the rear door to produce Pushkin in her wicker basket. She was miaowing at the top of her voice. Michael's duty was to unpack the suitcase and Waitrose carrier bags from the boot.

'Is she all right?'

'She's fine. She just hates going in the car, don't you, baby?'

Inside the house Pushkin growled and sniffed her way round all three floors. The cottage was much smaller than it appeared from the outside, principally because it was only one room deep and had two-foot-thick stone walls. Duncan and Michael had lunch, just some frankfurters, mash and sauerkraut.

'This is my favourite,' said Michael.

'That's because you have Nazi blood in you.'

'I don't!'

'You do. When we were in Berlin you showed me the palace where your great-uncle worked, didn't you?'

'Great-great-uncle. I'm surprised you remember.'

'I remember everything.'

'This is the sort of food we had when I was growing up in South Africa.'

After the food they made coffee in the cafetière and read the Saturday papers. Michael always read the *Independent*. Duncan always read *The Times*. That's what they thought. In fact, as usual they both half read each one and then argued whether either paper was any better than the other. Meanwhile, Pushkin alternated between laps and the small-paned living-room window and then floated upstairs to the study. She lay on her back on the sunny carpet and dreamt of birds and mice and country pursuits.

'Shall we let her out? It's cruel to keep her locked up.'

'No, Michael. She thinks she's still in London. She'll go outside and lose herself and then make her way home in the direction of Maida Vale. They have a compass in their heads that relates to their normal home, not their weekend cottage.'

'You and your theories.'

'It's true. I saw it once on Desmond Morris.'

Later, feeling drowsy-lazy, they went upstairs to the bedroom and lay on the bed in each other's arms, gazing out through the window past the branches of the old yew tree.

'It seems overcast now,' observed Michael.

'It's very changeable. That's because it's the weekend.'

'You were right about this colour. It makes me feel all happy.'

'What? Duck-egg blue? It's sort of a period colour. What are you doing?'

'Unbuttoning your shirt.'

Michael ran his soft hand inside Duncan's half-open shirt and stroked his chest. He pushed downwards over his stomach and slipped his fingertips into the elastic of his Calvin Kleins.

'You've got a hard-on.'

Duncan leaned back into the bed and grinned. 'Undo my belt.'

Michael undid the belt of Duncan's chinos and slipped them down slightly.

'Rub my cock through my underpants, would you?'

'What sort of service d'you think this is?'

'Oh, go on. Make me come. You'll have to kiss me, though, at the same time. I'll take too long otherwise.'

Michael undid the remainder of Duncan's shirt, exposing his torso, then pulled the waistband of his pants down and hooked it under his balls. He pushed his face up to his partner's mouth and posted his tongue between his lips. They began to kiss deep, wet, eating kisses. Michael stopped only to lick the palm of his hand a few times. With his hirsute forearm resting lightly on Duncan's smooth belly, Michael took his lover's erection in his moistened palm and let his fingers do the wanking.

*   *   *

They were awakened by the buzz of the doorbell downstairs. Michael got it. Paul McCarthy, one-time secretary to The Most Difficult Woman In Television, stepped over the threshold and embraced him like a long-lost friend. Well, as far as he could what with carrying enough bags for a trip to the Orient. He was in a state.

'God, it took me absolutely for ever to get here. It's such an ordeal on the M40. I was in such a tizzy I missed the turnoff for Oxford. I had to take the one to Blenheim Palace.'

'That's OK. It's equally valid to come that way.'

'Then I went the wrong way and had to reverse and I scraped some old lady's wall. And she came out and got horribly cross.'

'Did you damage your car?'

'No. But I was nearly in tears. I couldn't understand what she was saying. It didn't really sound like English.'

'They have an accent in these parts. That makes them difficult enough to understand, but they're all interbred anyway. They don't make much sense.'

'Is Duncan here? Oh, there's that cat. Why did you bring it with you? I'm allergic to animal hair.'

Pushkin was only interested in escaping through the open door and into the garden, but Duncan appeared and pushed her back up the stairs. He kissed Paul hello and eyed the bags.

'Hello, Paul. How long are you intending to stay? A month?'

'I need all these bags. I've got this wonderful tapestry to do while I'm here. It's called "Victorian Cabbages". That's what's in that bag and the wool is in that one.'

'Tapestry, eh?' Michael seemed not to approve.

'It's not girlie, Michael. You're a real man if you can do tapestry, you know.'

Duncan mocked him. 'You're a real poof, you mean.'

Paul was getting a bit whiney.

'I can't walk in this mud, Michael.'

'It's not mud. It's earth. They have it in the country, you know.'

'Well, someone's horse has churned it all up. And crapped everywhere.'

'Don't get the horseshit on your boots. We were a bit green when we bought the cottage and had those pale carpets put in. If you tread in anything you'll have to take them off when we get back.'

'OK. OK. I wouldn't have come if I'd realised I was going to be staying with fucking Hitler. Honestly, Michael, you still treat me like I was your secretary.'

'Well, you were once. And I treated you very well.'

'I was only your secretary because I caught fucking Karen Myhill with her knickers down and got fired.'

'I must have been a better boss than her.'

'You were. But you were still dreadful. I was almost as afraid of you. Anyway, it was dead boring in the legal department. Trafalgar only placed me with you to fulfil the last six weeks of my contract and there was no chance of me bumping into her on your floor. I've still got those knickers, you know.'

'What? You mean she gave you a souvenir?'

'They wrapped themselves round my shoe and I trailed them to the Royal Festival Hall before I spotted them.'

'You didn't! How embarrassing.'

'Not really. The whole of the 1970s was a complete embarrassment for me. I put them in a clip-frame and hung them in the toilet.'

'Karen Myhill's knickers?' Michael sniggered gleefully. 'I'd love to see them.'

'They're completely disgusting now. Jamie Hirst got high on coke once. He was larking around with them still in the frame and spilt red wine into the crack at the side. Now it looks like she had a period in them.'

'Yuk.' Michael had a thought. 'Jamie Hirst? Does he do coke, then?'

'I wouldn't know. This was ten years ago, Michael. I fell out with him years ago.'

'Just checking.'

They followed the bridlepath over a low stone bridge which had been there for centuries, and looked down into the bulrushes.

'What river is this?'

'The Evenlode. You are in the lush valley of the Evenlode.'

'You're so lucky to have a house here.'

'I know.'

'You must be earning a fortune.'

'Not really.'

'You and Duncan own three homes between you. I haven't even got one. And look at your cars compared to my old wreck.'

'It's our middle-class gay lifestyle, I suppose. And I inherited quite a lot of money before I left South Africa.'

'Did you? I didn't know that.'

'Yeah. I put part of it towards this house. My grandmother put it in a trust fund for me when I was born. I got it when I was twenty-five.'

'When my grandmother died everything she owned fitted in the drawer of the bedside cabinet by her NHS bed. Is this where the swans are?'

'I don't know. They always have been in previous years. We haven't seen them yet this year. Duncan thinks there's too much swell for them to nest.'

'D'you think we should be heading back now? Duncan said the meal would be ready at seven thirty.'

'I knew I shouldn't have mentioned his name. You just think of your stomach all the time, Paul.'

They turned round and retraced their footsteps.

'It's because I'm not getting enough sex. Food is a great substitute.'

'Not enough sex, eh?'

'I get less and less as I get nearer forty. You know what the scene is like, Michael.'

'I'm forty-two.'

'You're a married man. You've got a little wifey at home in her cottage poaching salmon.'

Michael laughed.

'He'd kill you if he heard you saying that. What happened to your man in Birmingham?'

'Oh, him. He was just someone I met through an ad. I got bored. It was too far to travel every weekend.'

'Was he the piss man?'

'Yes, did I tell you? He wanted me to stand in his playroom in my underpants wearing wellington boots filled with piss. I wouldn't have minded but it wasn't fresh. It was stone cold. He'd fill them up before I got there. The last time, I asked him to warm it up in the microwave. He said no. I think that took the romance out of the relationship.'

Michael laughed again. Now he remembered to show interest in Paul's career.

'How did your programme do on Channel 4?'

'Didn't Duncan tell you? It was the highest-rating arts programme on Channel 4 in April.'

'I wish I'd seen it.'

'I'll lend you a tape. It was called *Man and his Genitals: A Cock and Balls Story*. Of course, they cut half the dicks out of it an hour before transmission.'

'I'm not surprised. Thank God I'm not at Channel 4. Those lawyers must earn their money.'

'Anyway, it's my first go as a director. I nearly had a nervous breakdown. I'm never working with that production company again. I just got dropped in it when the original director walked off.'

'Well, it was probably the best thing for you. Paul, you should have more confidence. You got the programme out, and high ratings.'

'But even you, Michael – and you and Duncan are my best friends – still treat me like a fucking secretary.'

'All of that is in your imagination. You must get over Karen Myhill.'

'No one gets over Karen Myhill.'

'Listen, Paul, before we get too near the cottage I want to tell you something.'

'What? Is it raunchy?'

'It's about Duncan.'

'You've had a threesome! I knew under that tight-arsed exterior he was as big a slut as everyone else!'

'Shut up. We haven't done anything of the sort. Duncan has been approached by Karen Myhill. For a job.'

'Oh my God! Doesn't he know about Mad Max?'

'Don't start all that again.'

'I think I've worked out who his father is.'

'Who?'

'Charles Manson. It could have been him under that basket. He must have been on day release from Alcatraz or wherever he's holed up.'

'Don't be stupid. Listen. Karen and Duncan clicked. She's on the point of offering him a job. She wants somebody to analyse her company and her strategy. He has an impressive knowledge of interactive TV, Channel 4, everything.'

'Yeah, well, people in advertising seem to know everything, don't they? He's a bit cocky sometimes, is Duncan.'

'He's a bright boy, Paul. He's very creative and actually frustrated in advertising. If he could work with Karen it would be a fantastic opportunity for him.'

'If he can work with Karen he'll be the first person to manage it. Did you introduce them?'

'I hardly know Karen Myhill. I haven't seen her for years, not since she left Trafalgar.'

'Lucky you. Does she know he's your lover?'

'I wouldn't have thought so. Anyway, this way Duncan can move straight into television. He has brilliant ideas, you know. It'll not happen any other way.'

'She's the last person he should work for. She's fucking barmy. As for Mad Max, he's demented. Charles Manson might as well be his father. Karen and Max should be in therapy, both of them, not me. Their relationship is sick. They're like lovers, not like mother and son. That's not normal.'

'I suppose walking around in wellington boots full of piss is.'

'Ha ha. Everyone hates them.'

'No they don't. They don't know them. They just know the Basket Case story and that Bob Dresler called her The Most Difficult Woman In Television.'

'He wasn't wrong. She killed him!'

'He had a heart attack.'

'She just happened to be sitting opposite him at the time, I suppose?'

'No one was more distressed than Karen. Anyway, the point is, I don't think Duncan has ever heard the Basket Case story.'

'He must have done! I'm sure we've talked about who Max's father is in front of him. I must have told him my Martin Fox theory. He always was a sly one.'

'You think it's him? Martin Fox was only ever called The Sly

One because his name was Fox. Not because he was devious. You know that.'

'Well, it must be someone with power in tellyland. How else would Karen Myhill be so successful?'

'Because she's genuinely talented.'

'Because she's blackmailing Basket Case. Everyone knows she must be.'

'Everyone is stupid, then. You couldn't blackmail someone over a paternity issue. Not nowadays.'

'Oh yes you could. If multi-million-pound programme budgets were being corruptly handled you definitely could.'

'Codswallop. Why does everyone think it's such a big deal anyway?'

'You're not a programme maker so you don't know. TV is controlled by a tiny handful of commissioning people at Channel 4, the BBC, the ITV network and The Station and the other cable channels. It sounds a lot but there are thousands of producers trying to sell to – what? – less than twenty buyers. It's who you know that counts in tellyland. It's who you've shafted. Or who's the secret father of your barmy love child. You said Duncan knows nothing about Basket Case? I find that rather hard to believe.'

'You and I haven't discussed it for years. I've certainly never mentioned it to him. And he's not in TV, so he hasn't heard it on the grapevine.'

'Well, I haven't mentioned it. I never do nowadays. I've tried to blot it from my memory. That's what I pay my therapist for. I should charge the bill back to Karen Myhill.'

They passed over the level crossing and made their way down the lane.

'Promise me, Paul, that you won't tell him. It's a big opportunity for him if he gets it. If he hears that story and all the rest of it it could put him off completely. You know how correct he is about how things should be done. And pretend I haven't broken the news if and when he tells you he's got the job.'

'I promise. Although I ought to warn him . . .'

'Promise!'

'OK. OK. I'm not your secretary any more!'

'And Paul. Do one thing more for me, would you?'

'What is it now?'

'Take those boots off at the back door. There's horseshit all over them.'

19

Karen Myhill removed her stretched-oval leopardskin-effect replacement spectacles and placed them on her dressing table. Her reflection in the mirror and the room behind her fell away into soft, soapy focus. With the deft, feeling fingers of one who has lived a short-sighted life, she opened the brushed-steel spectacle case that had just been couriered round from the optician's and slipped out and slipped on her trademark bejewelled glasses, repaired. As her reflection returned needle-sharp and crystal-clear in the mirror, so did her confidence return too, with panache and perky optimism. The real Karen Myhill was back in vision and back in business. Spectacles are like stiff, new shoes when they come back from fixing: they need to be worn in and loosened up, to be got comfortable with again. Forefingers fixed at the corner joints, Karen rocked hers from side to side and pushed them further back on her head, and then with one finger pressed the bridge more firmly on to her beaky nose. There. They felt strange somehow, not as familiar as they should be, but nonetheless right, old friends returned. She had worn these glasses, or ones like them, for almost twenty years now. They had got her noticed a bit back then, got her a bit of a reputation, got her talked about. But she had had little need of help in that area for a decade and a half now. For many years it had been Karen herself who was the spectacle, who had attracted the notice, the reputation, the talk – and she knew it. Still, spectacles of note were part and parcel of her personality, her unique monogram, her own personal cliché.

She was pleased to have her good-luck spectacles back just in time. For the conversation she was about to have, she needed all the good luck she could muster, and any lucky charm or talisman she could collect about her was welcome. Quietly, she rose and left her bedroom, descending the staircase to the hallway below. Max was standing there, waiting impatiently.

'Where are we going, Mum?'

'Look. I've got my glasses back. They look fine, don't they?'

'They look exactly the same.'

'That's good, then, isn't it? I hate not having them. You get so used to them.'

'Where are we going? Let's get in the car.'

'Max, don't be so impatient.'

'I'm not impatient.'

'Well, where would you like to go?'

'What do you mean? You know where we're going. I thought you'd thought of somewhere.'

'Why did you think that, darling?'

'Because you said so the other day. You said we needed to go somewhere discreet.'

'Oh, yes, I did, didn't I?'

'You said it was as important a conversation to you as it is to me and that you needed somewhere appropriate to do it. A special place.'

'I know what I said, Max.' There was an edge of irritability to Karen's voice. 'That was before I got all that bad news about our turnover and the money supply. I can't be expected to do everything myself. I've had other things on my mind too, you know. Serious things.'

'This is more serious.'

Karen fiddled with her glasses uncertainly.

'So where are we going, then?' demanded Max.

'Max, don't use that tone. Don't push me.'

'*You're* pushing *me*. You haven't thought of anywhere, have you?'

'Well—'

'Because you're *not* going to tell me!'

Karen felt control of the conversation ebb and slip away from her completely. It was all going to go horribly wrong. 'I am, Max, I am!'

'No you're not! *You're not going to tell me!* I knew you wouldn't. I knew you fucking wouldn't. You're not going to fucking tell me. *You* are the original fucking bitch mother from hell!' He fought back tears.

'That's not true! Oh, Max, please! That's not true! I don't know what to tell you, baby. I don't know what to tell you any more.'

'Yes you do. *Nothing!* That's what you intend to tell me! A big fat nothing! Well, I'll find out myself. I'll check all the records. I'll ask all your colleagues. I'll put an ad in the *Guardian* on the media page. You've humiliated me! I'll humiliate you!'

'Don't threaten me, Max.' Karen reached out with one imploring arm but Max took a step backwards. 'Don't be silly, Max. That's not like you.'

'No, it's not, is it? It's like you, though. See what it's like? This is mental cruelty. Torture. What sort of a fucking mother do you call yourself?' He was very close to crying.

'I try my best. I'm sorry it's not good enough.' Hurt, Karen tried a new route. 'Max, I saw your father's solicitor the other day.'

This blurted-out statement had the required effect. Max was stunned into silence. She waited for him.

'His solicitor. Who's that?'

'Just a solicitor, Max. A very good one. A very annoying one, actually, but I suppose he must be good. He's a very expensive one.'

'What company?'

'Max, you don't know the names of any solicitors' companies so I'm not going to tell you.'

'You're not going to tell me so I can't check up.'

'He wouldn't tell you anything if you did.'

'I didn't know he had a solicitor.'

'Neither did I. It was the first I'd ever heard of him. Look, Max. Come here.' Karen sat down on the third-to-bottom stair and patted the carpet in front of her. Max plonked himself down on the bottom step at her feet. The feverishness went out of their talk. Max sat with his back to his mother and she ran her fingers gently, lovingly, through his hair.

'Max, you must understand that I don't want to say the wrong thing. I know that it cannot look at all right to you or to the outside world that I've not told you or anyone else who your father is, but surely you must realise that I must have very good reasons for that. I'm your mother, Max, and I love you more than you can ever know. You are everything I have. You're my past, you're my present, you're my future.'

'Yuk. You're sounding like a mini-series mom, Mum.'

Karen hugged him affectionately, all-consumingly even, from behind. 'Oh, Max. I love you for being so unsentimental. In my heart I don't really know what the right thing to do is. In my heart, Max, I do know that once I tell you it will be like a Pandora's box, that once the lid is off it won't go back on again. If I could tell you and know that if you didn't like what you heard and it all went wrong and that I could then untell you and you would forget, then that would be all right. But I don't know that and that's what's frightening me.'

'Frightening you? Who is my father? Dracula?'

'No, darling, no one as bad as that. I mean worrying me. No, frightening me.' She corrected herself. Her first choice of word had been more accurate. 'I feel frightened. Everyone thinks I'm this all powerful she-elephant. Well I'm not. I have feelings too. I feel frightened. I'm allowed to be vulnerable too, aren't I?'

'Mum?' Max's voice lifted with a new enquiry.

'What?'

'Is my father alive or dead?'

Karen did not answer.

Max grunted. 'I've always thought he was alive. He might be dead. He might as well be dead.'

'He might as well be, Max. Well might he be.'

'Dead cryptic, Mum! You're doing it deliberately. What was that meant to mean?'

'What would you do if your father were dead?'

'Nothing.' Max shrugged his shoulders. 'I don't know.'

'And if he were alive?'

'I don't know. It's too hard to say without knowing who he is. Dead, alive, alive, dead, living dead. There it is – Dracula, I knew it.'

Karen smiled behind her son.

'Does he know . . . did he know he was my father?'

'Of course. Do you think I wouldn't tell him?'

'You haven't told anyone else!'

'That's true. I told him when I was pregnant.'

'Did he ever come to see me?'

Karen did not want to upset her son further but she answered straight. 'No, he didn't.'

'Why not?'

'I don't know.'

'Don't you?'

'No. Not really.'

'I do.'

'Why? What do you think, Max?'

'I think you wouldn't let him see me.'

'Max, that's . . . not true. Well, not completely. I was very possessive, I suppose.'

'You suppose!'

'You're *my* son, not his.'

'I'm not an object.' Max sighed. 'What did the solicitor want to see you for?'

'Oh, he had some things to tell me.'

'What things? Why did he want to see you now? Had my father asked him to speak to you?'

'Indirectly. Yes, he had. It was arranged some time ago that he would communicate some information to me if and when something happened.'

'What? *What?!*'

'Two things, I suppose. The first thing was a piece of information about your father which I did not know. I had not heard it before.'

'What is it?'

'I can't tell you, Max.'

'Why not?'

'I'm sorry. I'm really sorry, Max. I just can't bring myself to tell you.'

'*Why not?!*'

'Because – because if I tell you it will give you a problem.'

'Mum, I've got a huge problem at the moment, if you hadn't noticed! Just fucking tell me!'

'Max, don't swear. This conversation was going really well a moment ago.'

'It was going well because you thought you were getting away with it. Well, you're not!' He shook his head free from her caressing hands and leant forward.

'Max, it was a piece of personal information. To tell you would create a dilemma for you much worse than just not knowing who your father is. Believe me, I think it's better not to tell you.'

'You think?'

'Max, I'm being honest with you.'

'No you're not. You're totally dishonest.'

'I'm being honest about my intentions, I mean. Give me some more time, Max. Let me think a bit longer about it.'

'Tell me the second thing, then. Let's do a deal. Tell me the second thing. I'll trade you that for the first piece of information.'

'The second thing wasn't nearly so important, Max. Well, it is important, but not quite so. But I'm not allowed to tell you until you're twenty-five.'

'*Twenty-five?!*'

'That's not me, Max, that's not me,' pleaded Karen. 'It's him. Honestly, it's him. It's him who caused all these problems, not me. Please, Max, believe me. Trust me.'

'Oh, for fuck's sake.' Max sprang up and round and kicked the front of the staircase hard. There was a splintering of wood under the carpet which sank inwards, leaving the imprint of his booted toe-cap. 'You really are fucking demented. You're barmy. You're a schizophrenic or something. I've absolutely no idea what you've been drivelling on about. You really are the original bitch mother from hell!' He booted the staircase again. It cracked again. His face was boiling red with rage.

'No, Max, no! Don't say that!'

'Fuck off! I hope you die! Anyone would rather have no parents at all and be brought up in care than have a vindictive bitch of a mother like you!'

He turned to leave and Karen, still seated on her stair, leaned forward and, almost falling over, reached out to grab his arm. Max dismissively brushed her aside and whipped himself away, knocking her spectacles from her face as he did so. He ran down the hallway and threw himself out through the heavy Victorian front door. He banged it hard with a resounding thud behind him.

'Max . . . Max . . .' Karen called softly, but not to her son, to herself. She stood up to follow him but, stepping forward on to the final stair, trod on the left lens of her trademark bejewelled spectacles. There was the galling snap of glass shattering.

'Oh no, I've broken my glasses again.' It was too much. She picked them up and wept over them. 'Oh, Max. Oh, my precious baby.'

20

They were bombing back along the M40 in good time. The Sunday early evening traffic was not as bad as they had feared. For once Pushkin was sleeping in the back.

'Watch your left, Michael.'

'Shut up. D'you want to get out and walk?'

'Well, you're not used to this big car yet. You're driving it like it's a living room up the middle of the road.'

'It's fine. I love it. It comes with the job.'

'You just wanted a Merc to show off in the company car park.'

'Look who's talking.'

'Don't remind me about work. I can't face going back.'

'I can't either. Launching a TV station is so much work. I have to do virtually everything myself at the moment. I can't hire the full complement of legal staff until The Station is on the air.'

'Don't think about it. You're just making it worse.'

'At least you won't have to worry for much longer.'

'If I moved into TV I'd have to worry about money. I'll have to take such a drop.'

'Think of the job satisfaction, Dunky.'

'Man cannot live by job satisfaction alone.'

'You're only a materialist superficially, you know. I've seen that in you. You only use the money to justify staying in advertising. It's not your real motivation. If you move into something more rewarding you'll feel adequately compensated, believe me.'

'Will I?'

'Yes, you will. Dunky, lots of people switch careers in their thirties. It's the decade people sort their lives out in.'

'My life *is* sorted out.'

Michael laughed. 'No it's not. This is the time for you to think about what you really want to do with your life. Owning a BMW isn't everything, you know.'

'I don't even own it. It's a company car.'

'You've proved yourself, Dunky. You got on the board, you got all the trimmings. Now it's time to be yourself, to be more creative. The dosh doesn't matter.'

'I know, I know. I'd love to do something more productive but London is an expensive place. I don't want to go from one extreme to the other. I have to balance my happiness at work with my income.'

'Well, don't put money first.'

'Of course I won't.'

'Did you enjoy the weekend, then, Dunky?'

'Yes. It was fun having Paul there.'

'You didn't mind doing all the cooking?'

'No.'

'Sure?'

'Completely. I like cooking at the cottage. It's therapeutic. That dessert was a little triumph, wasn't it?'

'You're so clever, Dunky. I couldn't do that.'

'It's just a terrine of summer fruits in sparkling rosé wine jelly. It looks so spectacular yet it's very simple to make.'

'Well, I couldn't do it.'

'It's dead easy. You go into Waterstone's, buy *Delia Smith's Summer Collection*, watch the BBC2 series on video, and it does itself after that.'

'It never seems to work for me. My things never look like she says they should.'

'It's interesting you should say that. I think the secret of Delia's success is that she describes exactly what everything should look like as you go along in sort of little word pictures. I always know just what she means. It's amazing no one else can write like that. She assumes no prior knowledge.'

'She must have had me in mind, then.'

'She should retitle her books *Cooking for Men*. I hear her over my shoulder saying, "Don't worry, you're doing quite well, it looks quite good, doesn't it?"'

'God, listen to you. You should marry her.'

'We're both already married to other people, I think you'll find. She'll be a victim of her own success in the end.'

'How's that?'

'Her recipes have gained universal currency. I'm nervous of that *Summer Collection* now. Everyone's got it. Serena, Margaret, Hazel, Orlando. We all got it as soon as it came out. Now, whenever you serve a dinner party, everyone goes "Oh, *Delia Smith's Summer Collection*! I've had this exact same meal twice already this week. Hah, hah, hah."'

'Well, it still doesn't work for me.'

'Yes it does. Your lamb is always cooked just right. You just lack confidence.'

'Just what I was saying to Paul about his making programmes. Why d'you think we all lack confidence?'

'Who's we? *I* don't.'

'You're different. You're in advertising. The industry with a lack-of-confidence bypass.'

'That's not true, actually. Loads of people in advertising are unsure of themselves. It's a front. You have to stick your neck out all the time just to stay still, let alone move forward.'

'I just wonder if we lack confidence because we're gay.'

'Straight people are exactly the same. Michael! Watch that car!'

'Right. That's it. You're walking all the way to Piers's flat!'

Piers MacLelland White was Michael's oldest friend from Oxford. As undergraduates they had been lovers for a short time. That's how Michael remembered it, anyway, as a little romance. Piers always insisted they had slept with each other only three times, and he'd really been concentrating on having as much sex with other men at the same time. Piers was never the relationship type. Hundreds of friends, a thousand acquaintances, but no one special person, no one Significant Other. At forty-four he'd never settled down. He'd never admit it, but Michael was the one important anchor in his life.

Piers had come into money at eighteen and lived in a fantastic flat carved out of the first floor of a white-stucco 1860s house in Cornwall Gardens. In the main room, three seventeen-foot-high windows looked out over the square. Light flooded in from outside. That was because Piers had bought on the expensive side which seemed to get the sun all day, every day, even when there was none.

'I don't look gaunt, do I?'

Duncan had always thought that Piers had a lovely voice. He tended to sit out most of these conversations. Michael and Piers went back way before his time.

'You look slim. Don't worry about it.'

'The tan helps. It makes me look healthy.'

'Where did you go again? Morocco?'

'Marrakesh. For a week. We stayed at the Mamounia. Mother and Father have been there before. It's where Churchill used to go to paint during the war.'

'Really?'

'Father still calls him Mr Churchill. Isn't that funny? Apparently, he held meetings there in his bath. It's been completely done over recently. Sort of Cartier-ised. You know what the Frogs are like. We went into the souks. I bought that carpet there.'

Piers pointed towards a hand-knotted Moroccan rug casually thrown over the back of one of three long pale peach settees in the room. The rug was beige and cream and gold and blue. At first sight the design seemed abstract, but Duncan soon noticed that it was patterned with primitive pyramids and little geometric camels and misshapen dancers in triangular dresses. It was curiously naïve yet terribly sophisticated at the same time, the detail all wrong and asymmetrical, but the whole effect somehow finely balanced and absolutely satisfying. It was frightfully fashionable yet would never date, a classic, like everything else in the room. Duncan thought it was perfect.

Duncan thought all Piers's possessions were perfect. Of all the people he had ever known, and of all the owners of all the homes he had ever glimpsed the interiors of, there was only Piers, he felt, whose taste closely matched his own. Unlike Piers, Duncan, who had inherited nothing nor ever would, did not have a back catalogue of antique heirlooms with which to furnish his own desire for good interior design. And unlike Piers, Duncan was anyway, deep down, a modernist. Nonetheless, he loved the timeless appeal of the choice art and *objets* that Piers had scattered throughout his home. More subliminally, what appealed to the materialist in Duncan was Piers's wealth. He commanded the cash to exercise his taste to the full and exercise it to the full he did. Well, that was not quite true. The Moroccan rug, left floating over the back of the settee, was a typical Piers gesture. It was absolutely right but not absolutely in the right place. Whereas Duncan was a finisher, a detailer, Piers was a great starter who compromised with a general effect and didn't quite care that nothing ever got completely done. Duncan wondered how long the Moroccan rug would lie there, abandoned over the seat-back. It looked good because it was intrinsically good in itself. It would do. But it really should, in Duncan's opinion, be placed somewhere where it could be displayed to the greatest effect. He scanned the room for a suitable space. The walls, huge uninterrupted planes topped by wedding-cake cornices, were peach, the same shade as the three Colefax and Fowler plain fabric-covered settees and all the matching cushions in the room. The rug would work well against any wall, there being space enough, and that space seeming even more spacious than it really was because of the pale peach hue.

That colour, thought Duncan, should be called Piers Peach. It was so him. It was a proper colour, definitely there – not a 'white with the hint of' – and yet, on this scale of interior decoration and with the bleaching light pounding in, it had the safe restraint of a wash, a tone that did not shout loudly, one to be seen and not heard. Duncan thought this shade of peach perfect and had once argued with Piers, who had threatened to change it. He had shown Michael and Duncan a host of subtle swatches of wallpaper, all with subdued tiny prints. There had been so many of them that Duncan had referred to Piers's flat as Swatch City. He was going to make major changes. But he had not. He hadn't made any at all, and Duncan could see the wallpaper swatches now, still stacked at the back of a golden walnut occasional table Piers used for drinks. The swatches were just that, samples of what might be.

They would never turn into rolls of wallpaper. Not now, realised Duncan.

The walnut of the drinks table was repeated in the rest of the wooden furniture, all mid-nineteenth-century large pieces in keeping with the vast scale of the room. A pair of black plaster urns sat on a pair of antique planters on either side of the drinks table. On one of two massive marble mantelpieces, one at either end of the room, sat a pair of green Meissen porcelain jackdaws, which Duncan could not resist thinking of as parrots after an unfortunate observation by Michael at a cocktail party which had brought uncharacteristic hoots of derision from Piers. They were part of his inheritance, of course, and Piers knew the whole history of their provenance, let alone the specific species of bird they represented. In the centre of the mantelpiece was a pure white marble bust of a young boy. Piers could not be so sure about this, it being one of the things he had had to buy for himself. There had been a space for it, he had said. There had been a space over one fireplace for a portrait and over the other for a bust. The space for the portrait was still there, unfilled, nothing suitable apparently having yet come on the market, but when the bust had turned up at Christie's Piers had plumped for it and placed it bang in the centre of the white marble fireplace, out of which it appeared to grow, so appropriately sited was it. It had been a bargain. Not least because it had suffered a terrible accident in the past when it must have fallen flat on its face and its nose and a piece of cheekbone had broken off. Piers and Duncan had amusingly agreed, though, that as a piece of rather fey French eighteenth-century fussiness, the original sculpture was so twee that, had it been unharmed and unmarked, one would have felt seriously obliged to take a whack at it hard in the face with a hammer and crack it open. The damage lent it dignity, Duncan had said, and he had made Piers happy.

To one side of the bust were bundled a few fragments of silk damask for new curtains to match the new wallpaper. It saddened Duncan to think that this was something else that Piers would never do. Duncan would do it. He would finish the room and have everything achieved and accomplished. He couldn't imagine abandoning it. Not if he had been the one who was dying.

'How have your parents taken it?'

Duncan realised he was deep in thought and that Michael was asking Piers an important question.

'Rather splendidly, really. I never told them I was positive but as soon as I got sick I explained it to them. They were marvellous. It must be peculiar to have your child tell you that he'll die before you do.'

Duncan watched as a pang of heartache leapt into Michael's face and then dived for cover. Poor Michael.

'Your parents are elderly, Piers. You'll easily outlive them. You've got years left. And they may find a cure at any time.'

Duncan spoke. 'The *Sunday Times* has been explaining how HIV and AIDS are not necessarily related in the way we've been told.'

Piers was furious. 'I'm really not interested in the rubbish that comic is putting forward. What are they trying to prove? I got HIV. Now I've got AIDS. I know exactly how the virus behaves. I've lived with it scraping around inside my veins for eight years, for God's sake. Why do they have to print all that stuff? It's just anti-Establishment lies.'

'It's written by Nobel scientists, isn't it?' Duncan was defensive. He'd been trying to say something helpful. He looked to Michael to bail him out.

'So, Piers,' asked Michael, 'what are your plans now?'

'I have to go to hospital twice a week. God knows what for. They don't do anything. I've come off AZT. It's too toxic for me. It weakened me so much, I'm almost sure that's why I got ill. I feel so much better now. I'm planning to work a little, just a few projects. And I'll do my BrAIDS work too. We've got the Queen's Theatre to throw a gala night for us soon. You must come. It'll be such fun. You must come too, Duncan.'

Duncan hadn't realised he wasn't included in the first invitation.

'How much money has BrAIDS raised so far?' asked Michael.

'Over a million in eight years. I feel rather proud I've done something with my life in the end. I'm the last left of the four of us who founded it now. You knew Quentin died, didn't you?'

'I'm sorry.'

'I'm not really, to be honest. He was such a pain in the neck. A prissy little queen. He hadn't a clue. I kept saying "Look, it's not about getting Princess Margaret alone over a gin and tonic. It's about raising money for British research into AIDS." But he was always in it for the wrong reasons. Now, you two. I thought it unwise to go out. I get taken short a lot these days. Hence the weight loss. So I've done a little meal for us here.'

'Oh, Piers, you shouldn't have,' said Michael, embarrassed. 'We could have got something in or brought something from the country.'

'I'm not on my deathbed yet, girls!'

Later, Piers turned out a perfectly formed terrine of summer fruits in sparkling rosé wine jelly. Michael gave Duncan a doe-eyed look. With anyone else they would have giggled like naughty schoolboys. But with Piers it was touching. Delia would have been proud.

21

Michael scanned the diners in the dazzling new restaurant The Station had just opened for its employees, seven months late. Like a cross between a cathedral and a conservatory, the staff canteen was actually a massive projecting balcony at the rear of the first floor, cantilevered frighteningly far outward to provide views of the company's Japanese sand garden. They were still taking down the scaffolding on the outside.

This Richard Rogers building, just behind King's Cross, was up for every award going. It was an inspirational crashing together of silver steel and liquid glass, a breathtaking, idiosyncratic gesture that encapsulated everything you'd ever need to know about The Station. The company's American backers had briefed their British architect to house the most creative executives in television in unheard-of, no-expense-spared luxury. More than that, they had asked for the architecture to represent the channel's corporate mission statement, the nub of which was to be interactive with its audience. So Rogers had designed a curved frontage with crystal arms extending outward to pull the public to its heart. And because The Station was to challenge, innovate and alter all perceptions, he had hung the world's largest single suspended sheet of glass at a diagonal off the front of the building as if all six storeys of it were about to crash into the street and shatter into fifty million fragments.

'We're right behind you.'

Michael turned to face Martin Fox, the head of programmes for The Station. He was an old friend. They had worked together in the late seventies at Trafalgar Television, until Martin had left for the Beeb. Michael hadn't seen that much of him over the years. He'd worn well for a straight man. With him was a slight woman in her mid-thirties.

'Hello, Martin,' said Michael.

'Michael, meet Briony Linden. She's just joined the company too.'

So. This was Duncan's client. In the few weeks he had been at The Station, Michael had not seen her around the building. She smiled a warm hello and didn't shake hands.

'I'm Michael Farnham. Recently joined as head of the legal team.' He was conscious of his own formality and her casualness.

'You and Martin know each other from way back, I hear,' said Briony.

'We do. We're old friends.'

'I wish I had an old friend here. I'm completely new to TV. I don't have any contacts. So what's the low-down?'

'What on?' asked Michael.

'On Martin, of course,' joked Briony.

'Oh. They used to call him The Sly One.' Michael laughed.

'For God's sake,' groaned Martin, 'not that old chestnut.'

'They still do,' said Briony.

'God,' said Martin.

'He's pleased, really, of course,' said Briony. 'Even as a newcomer to this business I can see that everyone in telly is just desperate to have a reputation of some kind. Good or bad. As far as I can see, Martin, you're hopelessly un-sly. You don't live up to your name at all!'

'Don't be so sure,' said Martin, making what he thought might look like a foxy wrinkling of his nose.

'He's got a very powerful wife,' continued Michael. 'She's something in the City. And in the Tory Party.'

'Is she?' laughed Briony. 'She sounds ghastly!'

'Hoy. Don't be rude,' gasped Martin. 'She's a fund manager, that's all.'

'A very senior one, or at least she used to be,' said Michael.

'Still is,' said Martin proudly.

'Earned a fortune.'

'Still does. Dwarfs my pay, at any rate.'

'And she ran for Parliament in 1983 and was about the only Tory not to get elected that year.'

'She's still on the party list, actually. Still trying.'

'Oh my God, a power couple,' said Briony. 'She sounds too good to be true, for the Tories at any rate. What's holding her back? Must be her liberal husband in television. What sleazy skeletons do you have in your closet that they're all afraid will come out, eh, Martin?'

Martin laughed. Michael laughed. Briony laughed too. She laughed the least nervously.

'Well, it's nice to know you're very rich and it doesn't matter if The Station fails to get off the ground,' she said. 'Meanwhile, the rest of us are frightened of the consequences.'

'Somehow I don't think we'll fail,' said Martin.

'I'm equally worried about our success, actually. We're about to launch some awful beast and have no idea what sort of a monster it will turn out to be. I can't cope.'

But Michael judged that Briony could cope especially well.

'Can't we smoke even in here, Martin?' she asked. 'Otherwise I'll have to go into the garden.' She turned her bright eyes on to Michael. 'I can't stand this no-smoking policy, can you? If I want to chain-smoke myself to death, surely that's my problem?'

'Actually I've given up.'

'Have you really?' said Martin.

'Don't sound so amazed, Martin.' replied Michael. 'It wasn't that difficult.'

Briony playfully punched Michael's arm. 'I hate you already!' she said.

To Michael, Briony was interesting-looking rather than conventionally beautiful, with nylony hair piled up like spun sugar on top of her head. Her colouring was exceptional, the white-blonde hair almost the same tone as the limpid skin. You virtually couldn't see her eyebrows. On her eyelashes she wore electric-blue mascara. She was further distinguished by long, dangly thin-wire earrings with turquoise bits on them.

'It's amazing, isn't it, the restaurant?' she said. 'I can't believe the expense they've gone to, can you? How much must this lot have cost? They'll be bankrupted before we even launch.'

'It's all capital expenditure,' said Michael.

'Well, I'm supposed to be the head of bloody marketing and I can't see that anyone's ever going to get their money back.' She didn't sound the least concerned. 'I've analysed the research every which way. And I'm the eternal optimist.'

'Well, Briony,' said Martin, 'take a tip from me and don't tell anyone. Now, what's the system in here? It doesn't seem to be self-service. I've got this plastic credit card thing that has to be swiped somewhere.'

Michael couldn't help him.

'The trouble with working in a start-up company is absolutely no one knows how anything works. I've learnt that much over the last two months.'

In the end, it turned out than a helpful woman led you down the great curving slope, round the arched back wall, showed you to your seat and brought a menu. She even brought the swiping machine for Martin's card at the end of the meal. Now they were dawdling over coffee.

'So, Michael, those are all the things we need to get legal clearance on for the launch advertising and PR. No doubt Marketing will send you a memo with the full details. Anything else, Briony?'

'No.'

'You seem to be going full steam ahead, Briony,' said Michael. 'I just seem to be getting bogged down in a mire of logistical problems.'

'Don't you believe it.' Briony smiled. 'I'm struggling to wrap my brain round what interactive television actually means. Not what it is, but what it means.'

'And what do you think it means?'

'God.' Briony concentrated hard. The head of marketing wanted to impress the head of the legal team. 'It's more than having a TV set that allows you to talk back down a telephone line to the programme makers. As a viewer it will be like being your own director or producer. And scheduler, because you can even choose when to order up and receive the movies. Viewing ceases to be passive and becomes not just active but creative. You'll be able to have a full relationship with The Station.'

'I see,' said Michael.

'Does that make sense? I didn't say it very well. Do you get the gist?'

'Yes. It's the best gist I've heard all day.'

Briony laughed. 'Well, if the agency can get all that into the advertising I'll be happy. I just don't want to frighten people off. We're going to hold off explaining the newest technology until phase two.'

'Which technology is that?' asked Michael.

'You know, that we have manufacturers developing wide-screen sets with in-built receivers so you don't need the current box on the wall that you get with conventional cabling. To get the full benefit of the service viewers are going to have to fork out for sets which include built-in mini-cams and microphones so that they can be seen and heard on the participation programmes. Without those features we're no further ahead than an on-line personal computer with a modem.'

'You have a marvellous grasp of everything, if I may say so.'

'It's very easy to make it sound difficult. You try explaining compressed signal broadcasting; that every programme is trans-mitted normally, plus on simultaneous fractional five-, fifteen- and thirty-minute delays to allow viewers to catch up and replay any bits they want; that movies and computer games can be ordered *à la carte* on dedicated strands of your cable link; and that you can use your own split-screen options to see additional bits of news reports in greater depth or get addresses and text information or a sponsor's message alongside the main part of the programme. We're thinking of calling those "side dishes" to the "main menu".'

'That sounds awfully good,' said Martin.

'It sounds awfully complicated,' said Michael.

'The trouble is that it just *is* complicated,' said Briony. 'Three-quarters of households can't even work their video player as it is, you know.'

Michael laughed. 'Yes, I do know, actually. I'm one of them.'

Briony smiled and looked at her watch. 'Are we going to talk *Megabrek*?'

'Have you heard?' Martin was asking Michael.

Michael said he hadn't. He did not know what *Megabrek* was.

Martin lowered his voice considerably. 'I've decided to award the breakfast show to Saturn Productions. Do you know Jamie Hirst?'

'Sort of,' said Michael. 'Well, I know who he is. He was a protégé of Karen Myhill's at Trafalgar, d'you remember?'

'I do, yes. Speaking of whom, when we put out the tender for the breakfast programme, La Myhill proposed the most bizarre show of the lot. I can't think what she thought she was doing.'

'It was hysterically bad!' Briony rolled her eyes heavenward. 'As a newcomer I'm amazed her company's not a standing joke in the business. Apparently, her son thinks up half the ideas and keeps firing the staff. Is that true? Who is this Karen Myhill?'

'Let's just say she's a woman people harbour strong opinions about,' replied Martin. 'She's going to be devastated not to have won it. I can't bear the thought of telling her. Anyway, Jamie and his team at Saturn have come up with a simply brilliant show.'

'It's fantastic, Michael,' said Briony. 'It's called *Megabrek*. It's so cheeky. It's like *The Big Breakfast* on acid.'

Briony was clearly a fan.

'Can you let me see the pilot?' asked Michael. 'What's the budget for the commission?'

'Twenty-two million per annum.'

'Fucking hell.'

'Look around the restaurant, Michael,' said Martin. 'We're

cash-rich. The Yanks have got the right idea. We're going to spend our way into the market and blast a hole in it.'

'Twenty-two million, though. That's more than blasting a hole. That's dropping a fucking nuclear bomb.'

'I'm budgeting seven hundred and fifty thousand pounds on *Megabrek* alone for just the first six weeks of above-the-line advertising,' added Briony. 'Obviously in addition to all the unpaid PR. Listen, guys, the agency people will be here soon. I have to go and prepare. I'm starting the meeting shortly because I need to get away early. One of my daughters is in the school play and you know how headmistresses disapprove of working mothers not showing up on time. She frightens the shit out of me, that woman!'

'You have children?' asked Michael.

'Yes. Two young girls.'

'Who looks after them during the day? D'you have a nanny?'

'No way. No. A husband actually.'

'What, he stays home and looks after the children?'

'And has my bloody dinner on the table when I get back, or else.' Briony laughed. 'No, I'm only joking. But he does look after the kids most of the time. He works from home.'

She checked her watch. 'Shit! I'll see you later, Martin. Very nice to meet you, Michael. Call me.'

Michael rose and acknowledged her goodbye. She dashed off through the crowd like an unrolling ball of string. Michael sat down, at home with his old colleague.

'She runs off like that all the time,' said Martin. 'She's desperate for a cigarette, I expect. Don't balk at the budgets, Michael.'

'It's not *my* money you're spending.'

'Look. You heard Briony. Television is going to change beyond recognition in the next few years. There will be a few smug winners and the rest'll be throwing themselves off the nearest tower block. It's too big a game now to play just for beer money. The BBC is way behind. Look what CNN's done to them on international news. Even ITV is going to struggle. Channel 4 will be niche, if that. We'll be big.'

'I had heard, actually.'

'The other new media are completely caught out by our interactivity. We have the world's most sophisticated technology in our armoury. Sky has such a poor technological base and too downmarket an audience franchise. No one's even heard of half the other cable channels.'

'I know, I know. I don't need a lecture, Martin. Why d'you think I left Trafalgar to come here? For the same reasons as you left the Beeb. I'm already wondering, though.'

'What about?'

'Well, everyone out there is waiting for us to make a spectacular hash of the whole thing. Nearly everyone that's started out like this in telly has gone bust or whatever. Look at BSB. Even Channel 4 took ten years to get a ten per cent share.'

'Pygmies compared to us, Michael. Anyway, look at how Murdoch pulled Sky through. Money. Clout. Certainly not pro-gramming. And we've got over twenty times his budget.'

'Where from? I didn't realise both the Mafia and the Colombian drug barons were behind us.'

'Michael, we just have to make it work.'

'Well, it's much more complicated than anyone has realised. Even just the boring bits I do. This new interactive technology has outpaced a lot of English law.'

'Has it? I suppose it might have.'

'It's all unknown territory. I'm having real difficulty interpreting exactly what we can and can't do on everything.'

Martin fiddled with his coffee spoon. 'Me too. I've realised the independent production sector is completely useless. Saturn Productions were the only company to understand how to use interactivity in their proposal. And even they only just pulled it off in the pilot.'

'Jamie Hirst is very good. You and he and Karen were the ones marked out for success at Trafalgar.'

'He's a lot younger than me. That helps, actually, being young. He's more in touch with the new technology. All the others treated the show like a phone-in. They have ideas, yes, but no strategic vision. None of them had listened. I think one or two grasped it intellectually but they couldn't get it emotionally and it didn't show in their work.'

'It is difficult.'

'Interactivity requires a whole new language of television, Michael. A new programme grammar. Briefing out the breakfast commission was like asking Ancient Egyptians to translate hiero-glyphics into WordPerfect. That's the nature of the revolution. It's that far a leap into the future.'

Michael was getting worn out. 'Briony seems like good news.'

'I think she's terrific. For some reason the board think she's a bit of a risk.'

'Why?'

'She's not from a media background. Her last job was promoting frozen fish fingers or something of that nature. I suppose she is a risk from their point of view. You know the Yanks.'

'Speaking of risk . . . there's something I'd like to clear with you.'

Martin was puzzled.

'We hadn't seen each other properly in years until I came here a few weeks ago. You probably haven't heard I've settled down with a nice young man.'

'What? Michael Farnham's no longer shagging everything in trousers in London? Good for you. I'm pleased.'

'We've been together ten years. It's probably saved both our lives, actually.'

'Ten years? I had no idea gay men could show commitment for that long.'

'Christ, Martin. It's just as well we're old friends. That's an unbelievably contentious statement. I'd go so far as to say it's insulting.'

'Sor-ree! I'm just pulling your leg. Or are we all politically correct these days?'

'Not at all. What I wanted to say is that Duncan, my lover, runs The Station account at the advertising agency. Briony is his client.'

'Jesus. That's one hell of a coincidence. You must know that Karen Myhill was looking for some strategic help on a project of hers and I recommended her to try him. I couldn't think of anyone else.'

'I know.'

'I've never met him myself.'

'I know.'

'Briony speaks highly of him. Does she know about you two?'

'About Duncan and me? God, no.'

'Well. That is a coincidence, isn't it? Is it a problem?'

'I was going to ask *you* that. It *is* just a coincidence, one that came about when I was headhunted to move here. Is it technically a conflict of interest? I'll have to give my approval on legal grounds to all the advertising for the launch and for *Megabrek* or whatever it's called.'

'I see what you're getting at. I don't know. If he were working for GMTV or Channel 4, then that *would* be a conflict of interest. No, I think it's fine. Anyway, Briony controls the advertising in terms of its content. No offence, but you're just detail. I think it's nice that you've got someone.'

'Martin, would you keep it to yourself? Duncan is extremely closety about his sexuality and he's not in a strong position with his bosses at the moment. He seems to think if they found out he was gay and sleeping with someone on the client side, there would be dire consequences.'

'That sounds a bit melodramatic.'

'Well, Duncan seems to think so. It might just be in his imagination but I don't want to find out the hard way.'

'No, of course not. I won't mention a word. It's as good as forgotten.'

'And Briony?'

'She won't hear it from me. I promise.'

22

Thump.

'Two, three, four.'

Thump.

'Two, three, four.'

Thump.

'Two, three, four. Come on. Keep up that energy ... keep going ... two, three, four ... good, everyone, good, you and your thighs'll regret this when you wake up tomorrow morning but you'll love me for it in six months' time – and three, four and ... OK—'

The leggy instructor turned and flicked the off-switch on the ghetto blaster.

'OK, girls. Rest for a second.'

Hazel caught Charlotte's eye. She mouthed an exaggerated contortion of 'Let's go' and Charlotte nodded. They slipped out sideways from the back row of the rainbow of stretch leotards and synthetic leggings. As they swung through the doors an extremely rapid Jungloid track began to batter the air in a frenzy.

'Christ,' said Hazel. 'D'you think it's possible she trained behind the Iron Curtain, that one?'

Charlotte was about to laugh when she spotted the locker-room clock.

'It's five past two, Haze! Fuck!'

'I tried to tell you earlier.'

'Well, try harder next time. There's barely time to shower. What's my hair like?'

'Don't ask! I just hope you've brought conditioner!'

'What? Take two bottles into the shower? Shampoo and egg mayonnaise? Not me. I just wanna rush'n'go.'

'Yeah. And don't care if my hair looks like shit or what! Race ya!'

They scrambled for their bags.

Now they were walking up busy Dean Street as fast as they could, blind to its eclectic mix of small, ancient boutiques, desperately fashionable eateries and large modern offices. They made an unequal pair, one slinky and slim and slightly ahead in a bright red linen suit, the other more square-figured and solid in a long wrap-round skirt, lagging a bit behind.

'He's too young. It's embarrassing.'

Charlotte and Hazel were giggling over the slowness of one of the boys in Production in growing a goatee beard.

'He's only copying the others. Apparently they've nicknamed him Fuzzface.'

'You're way behind, Charlie girl. Now he's called the Pubic Chin.'

They burst into another fit of the giggles.

'Come on, Hazel, we can't be late back. I've only been here a week today.'

'Don't worry about it. Cairns'll just go ahead without us.'

'I don't want to miss the briefing.'

'Well, don't blame me. I told you we'd never get through Dancercise and get back by two o'clock. You're a fit girl, by the way.'

'Yeah, I've always been quite sporty. Mummy's a fab tennis player. She brought us up to be quite athletic.'

'D'you play tennis?'

'I love it. Do you fancy a match, then?'

'Sure, I'll thrash you.'

'Not bloody likely.'

They rushed through MCN reception, saying hi to the black girl whose name Charlotte still didn't know. They jumped into the lift and sprang out again on the third floor. Duncan was there.

'Well, if it isn't Thelma and Louise. Thanks for popping back, you two. I appreciate your squeezing me into your schedule.'

'Keep your hair on, Cairns. We're here and in gear. Yeah!'

'That may pass for wit in downtown Sydney, Hazel, but here it's just trite. Orlando and Steve are waiting.'

'We've got Steve da Silva?'

'If you had stayed in and prepared for this I might have had time to tell you.'

The girls rushed to their offices to drop off their things and pick up the creative briefs, tapes of *Megabrek* and The Station promos. Charlotte got back first.

'Did you come in on your bike today, Charlotte?'

'Yes. Why?'

'That suit. You normally wear leggings.'

'I sometimes change here. It was a great buy last year in the Nicole Farhi sale. She doesn't normally do such bright colours.'

'It *is* a bright red. London bus red, I'd say. Where's Hazel?'

'On her way.' She paused and then picked her moment. 'Duncan?'

'What?'

'Have you heard of the Terrence Higgins Trust?'

A jolt of self-consciousness ran through Duncan. 'Yes. Why?' He over-compensated in case he might sound hostile.

'I'm applying to be a Buddy. You know, to be a friend to a person with AIDS.'

'I know what it is.' Duncan was surprised. He had not taken Charlotte Reith for the Florence Nightingale type. 'Why?'

'Because I'd like to do it, I suppose.'

'Isn't it rather a big thing to take on?'

'I suppose so. I don't know why I want to do it, really. I'm lucky. I've been very privileged and I'm very healthy. I'd just like to do it.'

'So what's this got to do with me?'

'Duncan! Don't you approve? It's not wicked any more, being gay or taking drugs. AIDS is not divine retribution.'

He was smugly comforted to realise that Charlotte had not clocked him.

'Absolutely not. I thought you were going to ask me something about it.'

'I am. Will you be my referee? I've got a form for you. You must have someone from work to say you can handle it. It's not a slight commitment in terms of the hours. I need my boss's approval.'

'Do you think you can handle it?'

'I know I'll be busy here but I do absolutely nothing else with my spare time.'

'I don't believe that for a minute. Actually, I meant can you handle the emotional involvement? Being with a dying person?'

'I don't know. I've never done anything like it before. I've tried to think it through, though.'

'Well, I'll sign your thing for you, or whatever I have to do. I hardly know you.'

'You know me well enough to have employed me.'

'Will they know you've only worked here for a week?'

She didn't get a chance to answer. Hazel ran along the corridor and caught up with them.

'Sorry, guys. Stella's office rang and cornered me about those invoices. Where are we briefing Orlando and Steve?'

'Just as well your board director is here to sort you out, Hazel.

You're meant to have fixed all this up, not me. We're going down to Steve's office. Orlando's gone down already.'

Hazel led the way. 'Let's take the stairs.'

'Hang on a mo. I hadn't intended to have this discussion in the corridor.' Duncan spoke firmly. 'As you both heard from Briony yesterday, she has the authority to let us come up with a new endline for The Station. We're lucky we've got Steve. We need to a have serious rethink with him and Orlando about the creative work to launch The Station overall and *Megabrek* at the same time.'

The girls moved forward.

'Hang on! The distinguishing thing about The Station is that it is interactive. We now need to go on to define more what it actually does and what actually makes it different. The posters which are up at the moment just tell you that it exists and ask you to let it pass you in terms of cable installation, or at least they're meant to. Thankfully, we can ditch that stupid endline. It's virtually incomprehensible.'

Charlotte and Hazel nodded.

'Now. Do we all know what we're doing?'

'Yes, Duncan,' said Charlotte. 'I'm sorry we were late back. It's entirely my fault. I don't even know who Steve da Silva is.'

Charlotte felt completely unprepared. She mustn't let Hazel get her into bad habits.

'He's Mr Yuksville, that's who he is,' groaned Hazel. 'A genuine ball of slime if ever there was one.'

'He's another of Hazel's great friends in the agency, as you can hear. Steve da Silva is MCN's top, top copywriter. His art director has just walked out on him because he's so difficult. Orlando needed someone heavyweight to help him on The Station and none of the C&B teams are free, so we thought we'd take the risk. He and Orlando will make an interesting creative team.'

'Duncan!' It was Margaret. 'Sign this comp slip, would you, please?'

'I haven't time, Margaret.'

'It'll only take a second.' She held out the slip and a pen. He scribbled his signature. Margaret paper-clipped the compliment slip to an agency analysis of BARB data on breakfast TV viewers, and slipped it into a manila envelope. Jamie Hirst, Saturn Productions, it read.

It was Hazel's next line, as they arrived downstairs outside the copywriter's office, which sent a chill of dread and anticipation down Charlotte's spine.

'He's like Conan the Barbarian,' Hazel whispered. 'It's the humungous bulge in his repulsive lycra shorts that I can't stand.'

It was indeed the man from the lift, standing there in a beige cotton suit over a lilac T-shirt, his hair pulled back in a ponytail. He looked past the others and straight into Charlotte's line of vision.

'Well, look who it is,' he said. 'Little Red Riding Hood come to meet the big bad wolf.'

Charlotte wondered how long it would be before he gobbled her all up.

23

Martin Fox, the so-called Sly One, had chosen ZenW3 for two reasons. One was that it was conveniently located for both him and Karen to get home afterwards. She lived just round the corner, in Flask Walk. Two was that it was off the traditional beaten track of telly folk. There was still the danger that in Hampstead you would bump into somebody, but, despite what people said about it being a big anonymous city, that was the risk you took everywhere in London.

He hadn't expected Karen to be on time and she wasn't. Seated upstairs, he ordered a Scotch and looked around the spare, white restaurant. Martin liked this combination of the best of East and West and the contemporary, rarefied look of the place, particularly its light waterfall trickling down the side of the stairs, a series of little glass pools overflowing one into another. He felt safe in this placid atmosphere. The Most Difficult Woman In Television was never at her most difficult in a public place. Karen Myhill, back in bejewelled spectacles, was suddenly upon him, looking more bird-like than ever.

'Sorry I'm late. I dropped in at the house on the way here to pick up my glasses which were getting repaired. And to consult Max, of course.' She sat down.

'How is he?'

'Fine. Difficult.'

'He gets that from his mother.'

'I don't think he gets it from his father.' Karen gave Martin a small smile. 'We had a big bust-up over that subject the other day but he seems to have got over it now. Anyway, I thought I'd better let him know we were going to be talking about the breakfast commission in case there was anything more he thought I could do.'

'For God's sake, Karen, he's still a child. You're treating him like a business partner.'

'And why not? It's a show aimed at young people. Max is a young person. He's my unofficial consultant. I'm too old to get under the skin of that age group now. But Max knows.'

'Well, Karen, I'm sorry to have to tell you that Max didn't know in this case.'

'Aw, Christ!' Karen steeled herself for the very worst news of her twenty-five-year long career.

'I'm afraid we will not be commissioning your company for the breakfast contract.'

'Piss! Fuck! Shit!' Karen's face crumpled in disgust. She was totally disheartened, totally devastated, totally destroyed. She knew what it meant. She was finished. Finished with a capital F. Everything she had left Trafalgar for and gone out on her own for and worked her balls off for was to be wiped off the face of the map with that one sentence. But instead of tears she produced venom. 'You bastard! You've no idea what you're doing, have you? They used to call you The Sly One. The Stupid One would be a better epithet. You and I go back a long way, Martin. You – you of all people – owe me a favour or two. Think of all the times I baled you out at Trafalgar.'

She thumped the table so hard the wooden chopsticks jumped up in their little paper packets. Heads were turning. Martin had known Karen long enough to know that it would not get worse. He gracefully ignored the personal slur.

'I'm sorry, Karen. It's because we do go back a long way I'm letting you hear it from me in person like this. Everyone else got written to.'

'Twenty-two million pounds per annum down the drain. I don't fucking believe it. Martin, do you want to make revolutionary programmes or not? Not, obviously. You're just another nail in the coffin of British television.'

'Come on, Karen. Don't bite the hand that feeds you.'

'Huh! If I relied on your hand feeding me I'd have starved to death years ago. It's all right for you, Martin, you have an extremely rich wife who's got enough money to bail you out of any crisis that ever hits you. Well, I haven't. D'you know, when I left Trafalgar, I had this idea that I'd run my own company, that I'd be in charge and not in hock to all those fat fucking bastards in stained suits who knew fuck-all about communication and entertainment. Well, I freely admit I got it wrong. I swapped them for all the wankers passing themselves off as commissioning editors, so called. And what are they? Useless. Blind. Half of them can't read. The other half wouldn't recognise a good idea if it jumped up and bit them on the backside.'

'Karen, if you're going to be like that then I have to tell you, you weren't even close. We haven't just selected a paper proposal. In the end we secretly made two pilots and live-lined them into our test homes in Milton Keynes. We tested each format on interactivity, we've done projection work on the ratings and we've calculated appreciation indices. A commissioning panel voted on it. Marketing and Research gave their views. The chief executive proposed it to the board. The truth is, Karen, you lost this commission months ago.'

'Research? What does that show? Nothing. Why ask the public? What do they know about television? If they knew as much as me they'd be programme makers, not fucking hairdressers and social workers. So, tell me the worst.'

'What?'

'Who's got it? Whoever has got this will be catapulted to top-dog status overnight.'

'Saturn Productions. Jamie Hirst has got it.'

For the first time Martin suddenly understood accurately the expression 'to burst a blood vessel'. Karen's facial muscles seemed to be undergoing some form of subterranean fermentation.

'Piss! Fuck! Shit! I'll kill the bastard! After everything I did for him, he goes and screws me.'

'Look on the bright side, Karen. That makes you the first woman he's ever done that to!'

'That isn't funny.'

She picked up her chopsticks and tore them from the packet. Martin had not heard before of anyone losing an eye to a chopstick, but Karen Myhill already had an extensive list of firsts to her credit. He was beginning to see why Bob Dresler had given in in the end and chosen to take the easy way out with a face-on fatal heart attack.

A pretty doll-like oriental girl appeared at their side. The atmosphere diffused somewhat.

'You chosen?' she asked sweetly.

'Not yet,' said Martin. 'Could we have five more minutes, please?'

'I'd like a drink, please. A Bloody Mary,' commanded Karen.

'And if you can't manage that, just a glass of blood will suffice,' joked Martin to the confused girl. Karen was on her humour bypass, though, so he switched tack. 'You're all right, Karen. You have some good shows on air. You've got your nomination for best LE series.'

'That means nothing.'

'It means everything.'

'It doesn't mean it's been recommissioned.'

'Hasn't it?'

'I only heard last week. I can't bloody believe it. It's up for an award. But ITV don't care about awards. They care about ratings. I'm not telling anyone yet so don't breathe a word.'

'I can keep a secret.'

'All my series are ending this year, as it happens. I have a strategy, Martin. All these tiny six-part series are no use to me. They're like miserable little cold sores that return once a year. I need a biggy. A backbone for my company. Your breakfast slot was meant to be it.'

'Karen, you'll have to put the breakfast thing behind you. I'm not here to talk to you just about that.'

'Oh, yes?' Karen looked up from stabbing the sugar bowl with her chopstick.

'We can make this a sweet and sour, if you like.' Bad pun, he thought. She's very depressed, so better to tell her outright. 'Karen, I'll give you a straight run at the game-show commission. It's something I should really put out to tender but after the strain of selecting the breakfast show I don't think my team could cope with several hundred more programme proposals. It's nearly as big as the breakfast slot in money terms. It's a late afternoon, early evening slot, half an hour, must be fully interactive. We want our version of *Blockbusters* or *Countdown*.'

'Christ.'

'Come on, Karen, this is a gift. Five days a week, a minimum six months of the year. We'll hold the format and international copyright. We want to bring this one in later to launch our spring quarter next year. You've got until September to make the proposal.'

Karen's sense of relief was overwhelming. This man was giving her company, in its death throes, the kiss of life. 'Why are you doing this, Martin?' She narrowed her eyes and, in a rare move for her, looked into his.

'You know why. We go back years. This is my way of saying thank you for all the times you helped me at Trafalgar.'

The pretty doll-like oriental girl returned with Karen's Bloody Mary.

'Are you going to throw it at me, then?' he asked humorously.

'No, of course not. Why would I do that?'

Martin laughed to himself. In her time Karen Myhill had tipped Bloody Myhills over far greater men then he for far less.

'Did you ever see that guy I recommended to you?'

'The one from the advertising agency? Yes, I did.'

'What's he like? I've never met him, but our head of marketing had just been talking about him when you called me.'

'He's all right. He's fine.'

'Shall I tell you a secret?'

'Is it one I want to hear?'

'That advertising chap is gay.'

'So?'

'So how about this? He's Michael Farnham's lover.'

The blood drained so fast from Karen's face she was compelled to down in one gulped go a full transfusion's worth of Bloody Myhill. It was too small a world and Karen did not like everyone she knew in it to be connected. What might Michael Farnham be telling Duncan Cairns about her behind her back?

After dinner, Karen and Martin parted company outside the restaurant. He pecked her on the cheek. She didn't return the gesture, but hurried across to the other side of the street, running all the way home to the power behind the throne.

Their goodbyes were watched by a pair of surprised eyes through the small eighteenth-century panes of the Café des Arts, the dark-panelled restaurant immediately next door to ZenW3.

'Well, well, well. He is a Sly One.' Jamie Hirst turned towards his young oriental companion and smiled affectionately. He moved the candlestick on the table away from him so that his face fell into shadow, just in case he could be seen from outside.

'I thought you only had eyes for me.'

'I do,' Jamie said. 'But I think I've just witnessed something no one in television has ever seen.'

'What's that?'

'Karen Myhill being kissed by Basket Case.'

'My God! Are you sure?' said the oriental, straining forward to see through the window. 'Who is it, then? Tell me!'

Jamie's mind was ticking over fast.

'You can't see him now. He just got into a cab. But it makes sense. That wasn't an amorous kiss. It was the seal on some deal.' He picked up his fork and pushed it around the perimeter of his plate. 'I wonder if we got the breakfast commission just to put everyone off the scent. And now they're planning something much bigger together. Something much more dangerous.'

His companion now twigged who Jamie was talking about.

'Do you really think so?'

'I do think so. It's taken me years to get this far. We're on the verge of becoming the number-one independent TV production company in Britain, in Europe perhaps, in the world outside the USA, even. There's going to be a number one and that'll be the only number that really counts. That's got to be us.'

'Surely there's room for more than one player?'

'Maybe. But we're not finding out the hard way. What she's doing is not fair. I'm not having her leap-frogging over us and pushing us back down again just because she's got old Foxy by the balls. We want the ladders in this game, she can take the snakes. We mustn't let The Most Difficult Woman In Television get away with it.'

24

At precisely one o'clock, Alan Josling came through the glass doors of Quaglino's. Although he'd been here several times before he still found the layout confusing. He could never remember whether to request his table in the foyer or go on through into the bar. It was important not to do the wrong thing in front of Serena, who would crow about it to all and sundry later. He hesitated until he realised the girl opposite the door was not a meeter-and-greeter, she was just selling things: Q ashtrays, condiment sets and small boxes of roasted coffee beans in plain chocolate. He might buy a little something for Cindy on his way out if he remembered. He went on through into the bar.

One level above the massive restaurant floor, with its glass canopy and enormous vases of luscious flowers, was the slick bar area. Nigel and Serena were already there, seated at the side of the rail, people-spotting. God, thought Alan, I hope he's not been knocking back the gins. Still, it was her he really needed to talk to.

Serena turned and waved in his direction. 'Alan!' She rose in her usual swirl of bright chiffon.

'Hello, old boy. How's business?' Nigel looked ever fatter.

Alan was aware of the strangest sensation. It was the absence of fear. When he had worked at the old Clancey and Bennett they had held his life in their clutches, operating like birds of prey, swooping on the internal competition and eliminating it. Now they were as dangerous as a comedy duo. He hadn't expected it.

'Everything's going very well,' he said, shaking hands. 'It's good to see you.'

'What car are you driving now, old boy? Alan Josling, into fast cars and fast women, is that how it went?'

'I hope not! Actually, I have a lovely little red TVR Griffith. It's rather a neat accessory in the traffic these days.'

'Really? I'm stuck with a Jaguar Sovereign thing. Tricia makes me keep it. I'd like something a bit younger.'

'Nigel has a yacht now.' Serena felt the Jag had not quite levelled the score to one-all against the TVR. The yacht put them in the lead.

'Shall we eat?' Alan led the way down the famous stairs with the Q-railed banisters.

The starters came and went. They broke into another bottle while they waited for the next course.

'So, old boy, what does your company do these days?'

'Well, it's a long story really. In the end I suppose I've found a little niche for myself. You just can't make money above the line these days unless you've reached a certain critical mass. I wanted to keep the company small but highly profitable. So I've slipped, I suppose, out of doing ads and gone into publications – you know, annual reports, leaflets, internal company printing. That sort of thing.'

Serena was fascinated.

'Can you really make more money at that than advertising?'

'Oh, yes, absolutely. You don't have staff who expect sports cars, for a start. Not so many account men. No planners. No in-house production and editing. And although your clients are each spending less, they are somehow more careless with their budgets. It's much easier money.'

'But is it interesting, old boy?'

'Oh, come on, Nigel. We've all been bored with ads for donkey's years. All that "spreads easier" crap. I couldn't face sitting with some spotty guy wittering on about his hydrogenated fat product these days. You must hate it, you two.'

Serena was brisk. 'We'll come to that. You enjoy running a small business?'

'Not that small. There are forty of us now.'

'Really? Nigel and I have only sixteen direct employees.'

'Including ourselves,' Nigel chipped in.

'I mean in C&B, of course. As MCN International board directors we have over three hundred, but we really only attend the big board meetings. We don't run it. Not like the old days.'

'No, we just do our own thing upstairs in C&B.'

'Are you winning business?'

'Some. Serena is terrific, but our creative product always lets us down.'

'You've got Orlando,' said Alan. 'He's not the hippest thing in town these days but he can still craft 'em like no one else.'

'We can't seem to make him understand what we want him to do, can we, Nigel? And one of our staff has ganged up with him against us.'

She took a disappointed sip from her wine glass. Alan almost felt sorry for her.

'You know me, old boy. I'm a big-agency man. I'm a chairman-of-the-board, a how-d'you-do sort of a chap. I work in broad brush-strokes, supervise the big picture. But they've cut C&B down so small, Serena and I have to work like the proverbial darkies we're not allowed to mention nowadays. I'm going to retire in three years. I'll be fifty-five then.'

'No you're not!' said Serena. 'You're not leaving me in the lurch. The thing is, Alan, I suppose Nigel and I have only got ourselves to blame. We sold Clancey and Bennett to MCN, took the money and got trapped. We can't leave on the contracts we've got, otherwise we lose the money.'

'Is it true you got a million each?'

'No it bloody well is not!' The shrillness of Serena's voice swiped clean through the hubbub of the restaurant. Alan was well aware of how rarely she swore.

'And we don't get the final instalment, old boy, until we deliver the goods.'

Nigel gulped down half a glass and gave Serena a weak smile.

Very interesting. Very interesting indeed, thought Alan. He wasn't thinking about their contracts or their ill-deserved money. Instead, a penny had dropped in his head. They were lonely, these two. They were isolated. They had no one else to talk to. They were hurt. Wounded. Their own greed had ruined a once-great British agency. But instead of feather-bedding themselves they had created a bed of nails for each other to lie on. And just as they no longer threatened him, they had forgotten he ever threatened them. They were mistaking him for a friend. The waiter placed their big main-course plates in front of each of them.

'Is this what I ordered?' Nigel was not wild about lean, modern cuisine.

'Yes, Nigel. Just eat it.' Serena gave him the agreed signal to move the conversation on.

'So, old boy, tell us about the millions of billings you mentioned the other day. We're intrigued.'

'Oh, there's plenty of time for that,' said Alan.

He picked up the serrated knife and sliced into his beef. Serena winced as the blood ran out.

The way Nigel was swirling the brandy in the glass was beginning to irritate even Serena. She looked down at her baby Rolex.

'Heavens above, Nigel! It's almost half past four! Honestly, that Margaret girl should have rung my mobile to let us know we were overrunning.'

'She's hardly a girl, Serena. She's a middle-aged woman.'

They were getting picky with each other. Alan felt one of their little tiffs coming on, a sort of married-life bickering they had all used to laugh at, at the old Clancey and Bennett.

'Perhaps your secretary can't ring in down here. We're in a basement, remember. I'd better come to the point, then, and tell you what I had in mind.'

'About time, old chap. D'you need another brandy to help it along?'

'No, but you have one if you like.'

To Serena's extreme annoyance Nigel did just that. Alan began.

'You remember I have a partner?'

'Kevin somebody.'

'Colin Thurrock. Well, his sister was recently appointed European Marketing Director for Japanair.'

'The Virgin competitor?' Serena remembered she had seen the appointment in her press cuttings.

'Yes. They fly a Virgin Atlantic-type service on the London to Tokyo route, but with Japanese technological touches and their level of hospitality. The company is about the size of Branson's and has a progressive, pop-oriented image in Japan. But over here— '

' —they are seen as slitty-eyed, yellow people who'd probably torture you in-flight and make you eat live squid and seaweed! You don't have to say more, old boy, we get the message.'

'Nigel!' Serena did not approve of flippancy. There might be a contract on the way.

'Oh, I like them myself, old girl. I could do with a few people doing all that head-nodding to me. They respect age and status over there. Not like British bloody advertising people, I can tell you.'

Alan wasn't sure whether Nigel was a little worse for drink or really was past it. He hoped he was neither.

'The brand lacks saliency here,' said Serena, willing Alan on to get to the point.

'Spot on, Serena.' Alan continued, 'It's almost unknown and gets confused with JAL and ANA. So they're going to do something about it. My partner Colin has the inside track on his sister, obviously. In a nutshell, she's looking for a dynamic, state-of-the-art agency to handle her business. She's got three to four million pounds above the line. As a private company they want a small agency which is big on personal service but it must be pan-European. That's really why Colin and I can't do it, because we couldn't expand into Paris, or Frankfurt when the airline does. Anyway, she can't give something of this scale to her own brother.'

'We'd be delighted to take it,' said Serena, eyelids aflutter. 'There are no conflicts. What do you want us to do, Alan?'

'Well, Colin's sister knows the temperament of British agencies quite well. Her superiors in Japan will be very hands-on and won't tolerate any aggression or creative battles. She needs an agency that is creatively hot but will toe the line. Japanair's European development and her job will both be axed if they don't do the whole thing correctly. I thought of you. You would do it perfectly. They'd happily go to an agency that handled The Station.'

'Well, old boy, we'll give her a ring first thing in the morning.'

'I don't think that's what Alan has in mind.'

'No. I thought with the sensitivity of the whole thing that I could engineer a sit-down at the weekend with Colin's sister and perhaps slip your names into the conversation. If she picked up on what I had to say about your reputations she might want to arrange a preliminary meeting. You could present your credentials or show her your reel or whatever.'

'Nigel and I are recording a new video about us tomorrow. We could send her that, perhaps.'

'That would be ideal. She lets Colin see a lot of the confidential Japanair thinking. If I can access those documents and pass them on to you in advance, then it would enable you to come up with exactly what Japanair are looking for in the pitch. You'd have a huge advantage over your competitors.'

Serena's mind was accelerating ahead.

'Do you mean Colin and his sister wouldn't know you were acting on our behalf?'

'No, they wouldn't. They wouldn't realise that. I would give the impression I was as impartial about you as about any other agency we might discuss. But I would be rooting for you. I won't mention this lunch – and neither should you.'

'Why's that, old boy?'

'I think that, ethically speaking, she just couldn't risk being seen to dish out four million quid's worth of business to a friend of a friend. She's meant to put all the promotional work out to full competitive tender on a fair basis. If she didn't and got caught that would be corruption and she'd get fired.'

'Bit rich that, coming from the Japs.'

'Nigel, shut up.'

'Colin and his sister would know nothing,' said Alan. 'I'll act as an uncredited consultant to you and with all the confidential documents you'll be way ahead of anyone else. I'll put in a surreptitious good word for you as well, with Colin. He'll give the nod to his sister. I can deliver this to you. I guarantee it.'

'But why, Alan?'

Serena was almost salivating at the prospect of this godsend. Four million pounds plus the sexiest Japanese client to hit Britain. This could snowball. But there had to be a catch.

'I'd expect to be paid for my consultancy.'

'How much?'

'No one must know I'm helping you. It must be in cash and completely under the table.'

'How much?'

'Fifty thousand pounds.'

Nigel and Serena were aghast.

'Bugger me, old boy, that's a bit steep.'

'It's about ten per cent of your first year's income.'

No one said anything for a moment, and then Serena spoke.

'It's nothing to do with the money, Alan – although Nigel is right, it is ridiculous. MCN is a publicly quoted company, here and in the States. We just couldn't write off fifty thousand pounds and not say where it had gone. We don't get expenses to cover industrial espionage, you know. Anyway, who's to say we couldn't win the business by ourselves?'

'Let's just say I doubt you would. I may find my consultancy is taken up by one of your competitors. But it would be a shame if *we* couldn't do business.'

'I'm not saying we can't do business, Alan. We just have to find a way. We don't spend more than ten thousand on any one new business pitch.'

'Well, break the rules. You're the MDs.'

'It's not as simple as that. When we sold Clancey and Bennett we handed over budget control to MCN's finance director. We can't spend anything without his knowing.'

'I'm sorry, then. Looks like we'll have to go Dutch.'

'What?'

'We promised to share the bill for lunch if nothing was doing.'

'Oh no, please, Alan. Let us.'

Serena gave what she hoped was a warm smile and raised her hand for the waiter.

Aha, thought Alan. Serena understood the significance of her gesture as well as she understood the nature of his offer. She might as well have signed on the dotted line.

Both guys were stripped to the waist to reveal hairless bodies which had been expertly developed in the gym. The blond youth squatted down in front of the forest ranger so that his face was level with his crotch. He ran his hand over the bulge of the khaki trousers, unbuttoned them at the waist and slowly unzipped the fly. A long, thick, circumcised cock flopped out and the blond began to suck on it. Meanwhile he got his own equally long but slimmer cock out and began to jerk himself off vigorously. The ranger ran his hands through the blond's hair and pulled his head into his groin so that he was obliged to deep-throat him. After a while the ranger withdrew. His penis was wet with his partner's saliva. As he pulled his trousers off, the boy pulled his own jeans down. Neither was wearing underpants. The blond bent over a convenient fallen tree-trunk and, spreading his legs, pulled his cheeks apart. His backside was shaved smooth like the rest of his body. The ranger masturbated his hard-on constantly so as not to lose it. He looked down at the youth.

'Are you man enough to take it?' he asked.

'If you're man enough to give it,' came the reply.

The ranger then effortlessly slipped his penis in and began to pump the youth's buttocks with long, smooth strokes.

The picture suddenly flickered, blurred and whizzed forward.

'Why did you do that?' asked Duncan.

'This bit's boring,' said Paul, his fingers on the remote control. 'Would you like some more vino? I hate it when they don't wear underpants. It's not sexy. I could make a better porn film myself. Americans have got no imagination. The next scene is more interesting, though. He picks up a hitch-hiker and takes him to a barn and while the hitch-hiker is sleeping he cuts his shorts off with a knife. They're lying on the hay. I came twice over it when I first watched it.'

'I expect you probably did,' said Duncan. Paul put the video player on hold and went into the corridor and down to the kitchen to get the wine. Duncan followed him, glass in hand.

'Where did you get this one, then?' he asked.

'From Malcolm. I love those American boys, don't you? They always have such smooth bodies.'

'They're shaved. All over.'

'Perfect teeth.'

'That's American dentistry for you.'

'Look at mine.' Paul bared his fangs. 'I look like Dracula. They really spoil my looks.'

Duncan did not disagree. Instead he meted out some advice.

'Get them fixed if they bother you. You can get good cosmetic dentistry in London. It's worth it. It'll give you more confidence.'

'I have thought about it. My dentist wants to do it.'

'I'm sure he does. He's one of the best dentists in London who's still got an NHS practice. I even recommended him to my friend Cindy, though she goes to his private place. She says he's great.'

'He is. But he doesn't do cosmetic dentistry at the NHS unit. It has to be done privately at his other practice. And it's too expensive.'

'Save up. Spend less on drugs and invest in your smile.'

'Ha, ha,' said Paul. 'It's the drugs that keep me smiling, darling. I'll think about it.'

Paul crouched down and, forelit by the fridge light, pulled the wine from the door shelf.

'Who's Malcolm?' asked Duncan.

'He's the source of all my blue movies,' said Paul, refilling Duncan's glass. 'Remember you and Michael met him here at dinner once? He has a loft full of porn. He lets me go in and make a selection. It's like a sweetie shop for saddos. We're doing this course on tape at his home every Monday night. It's a self-assertiveness programme.'

'How Californian of you.'

They sat down at the kitchen table.

'Just because *you've* always had an overbearing personality doesn't mean everyone else is in total command of themselves.'

'Is that what you think? That I've got an overbearing personality?'

'Not really, Duncan. You're very sweet most of the time. But you do always seem to get what you set your heart on. Look at your home, your car, your career, your salary. Your lover. And you don't mince your words.'

'Thank you.'

'Don't get smug. Interesting how you're so tight-arsed about your sexuality yet you deal with everything else head-on. You're very focused. You've got all these targets and aims in life and you go for them.'

'I'm just an achiever, that's all.'

'An achiever! Hark!' Paul laughed.

'There's no point in going in for false modesty. If you come from my Scottish background you get up and get out and keep on going.'

'It's funny. I'm totally relaxed with being a gay man compared to you, yet if I had to work with anyone as forceful as you in an office I'd be intimidated.'

'Rubbish.'

'It's true.'

'And I'm not tight-arsed about being gay. I'm just more discreet than you. Not everyone wants to talk about sex all the time and have other people's intimate details shoved down their throat.'

'I know what I'd like shoved down my throat. So where is your husband tonight?'

'He's not my husband.'

'Oh, don't get precious. You're like a married couple, you two.'

'No we're not,' said Duncan defensively, too much so for one who had sought a permanent relationship from the day he had met Michael. 'Gay couples are not like married couples. We don't even live together.'

'God knows why, Duncan. How long have you been together?'

'Ten years.'

'I can't believe I still have to ring you both up separately to invite you out. I thought you were meant to be finding a house together last year.'

'We couldn't move in the current market.'

'Who says?'

'I do. And Michael is under incredible pressure at work at the moment. So am I for that matter. Moving now would make things worse. Anyway, we have the cottage.'

'It's because you're tight-arsed about your sexuality.'

'What?'

'You won't live with Michael because you're ashamed of being gay.'

'Balls.'

'It's true. If you were my lover I'd slap you.'

'You've never had a lover.'

'That's an unbelievably hurtful thing to say.'

'Well, don't lecture me, then. You and I are very different.'

'Do your parents know you're gay?'

'Not in so many words.'

'Well, that proves it. If you can't tell them, who can you tell? I bet everyone in your office knows.'

'I don't know.'

'How old are you? Thirty-one?'

'Thirty-two.'

'And you're not married and can't produce a girlfriend. They must all know. Do you discuss sex in the office?'

'All the time.'

'And what do they ask about you?'

'Eh . . . not a lot.'

'Exactly. Because they all know and they all know you're embarrassed.'

'Oh, piss off.'

'If you and Michael wanted to live together you would. You've organised everything else to be perfect in your life. You like everything just so. The truth is, Duncan, that moving in with him would throw your cover, wouldn't it?'

'We just couldn't at the moment. I have to think about work and my bosses finding out that Michael works at The Station.'

'That's just an excuse and you know it. And if you don't know it then you're even more repressed than I thought.'

'Drop dead.'

'Look at you. Mr All Neat and Tidy. Underneath all that, more than anything, you want to be laid on your back and shagged stupid by a whole raft of American porn stars.'

'Do me a favour. That's your fantasy, not mine.'

'Oh, you're so vanilla.' Paul laughed.

'I beg your pardon.'

'Vanilla sex, darling. All white knickers and boy-next-door kissing. God, Duncan, I'm dreading my phone bill.'

'Why?'

'I got drunk yesterday afternoon with a bottle of wine on my own. You won't approve but I smoked a joint as well and then got out *Boyz* and rang these telephone sex lines. All those 0891 numbers are forty-nine pence per minute during the day. I'm addicted. Yesterday I was on for an hour.'

'That must have cost a fortune.'

'I can't afford it.'

'How does it work?'

'You ring up. It's all done by computer. Guys leave a really detailed message on tape. You listen to it later and leave them a message which only they can hear.'

'You talk dirty to them?'

'Not directly. They leave a pre-recorded message at the end of which you leave your phone number and details of what sort of sex you're looking for. They ring you back later and you arrange to meet up. It's brilliant for me because of my tastes.'

'Have you advertised?'

Paul gave Duncan a delicious smile. Duncan reminded him of one of those prurient tabloid newspapers that profess shock and horror but want to know absolutely all the salacious details.

'Everyone's doing it. It saves all the time and effort and money of going round the bars. It's apparently the most sophisticated way for professional guys to meet up with each other now.'

'How d'you know they're not going to be completely hideous?'

'Most of the guys I've met haven't lied about themselves. What's the point? You meet in a public place and if you don't like each other you leave it there. Otherwise, it's back home for great, uncomplicated sex.'

'What sort of things do you say, then?'

'You wouldn't want to know.'

'I'll be the judge of that. Go on. Tell me.'

Paul laughed. 'Oh, Duncan, you are such a one. The cruise line is best. That's where you talk live to each other, one to one. You can't actually talk directly. You record a description of yourself when you first ring up and then send it on to a bulletin board. You then access the bulletin board and listen to who else is on the line. You can send a message to anyone and wait to get one back.'

'How incredibly complex. You don't need to have a degree in computer science to participate by any chance?'

'It's easy. The message system is designed to protect your identity, I suppose. If you don't like anyone who sends you a message you don't reply. And you can talk to about ten other guys all at the same time. No one knows who's talking to whom. Most of the guys there aren't looking to meet up at all. It's all fantasy. They're just lying at home having a wank. So they describe their body and their cock and what they're doing with it at the moment and tell you what they'd like to do to you.'

'God. It's amazing what technology can do nowadays.'

'All but give you a blow-job.'

'I wonder if The Station could apply the principle to a TV show?'

Paul laughed.

Duncan ignored him. 'I'm surprised it's legal.'

'No doubt your lot will ban it soon.'

'Fuck off. They're not my lot.'

'You voted for them.'

'So? I believe in low taxation and a hands-off government. It's not my fault sexual repression and homophobia come with it. Anyway, the whole point about the Tories is that you can masturbate in your kitchen with a plastic bag over your head or shag some actress wearing a Chelsea football strip and nobody gives a shit until you get caught.' Duncan smiled and cocked an eyebrow. 'Then, as we all know, it's "Move over, matey" time.'

'That's so hypocritical.'

'I know. But it's the British way, really. And it works.'

'Let's go back through.' They headed along the hall towards the TV. 'D'you want some more wine?'

'Is there enough for both of us?'

'Yep.'

'In that case,' said Duncan, 'if you're man enough to give it, I'm man enough to take it!'

'You really are begging for it, aren't you?'

Duncan didn't understand. 'For what?'

'I'm talking ten years in a relationship. You're a horny guy.'
Duncan laughed. 'It's not normal for a gay man to stay faithful
like that. You should do something about it.'

'Yes. Oh yes. Give it to me. Come on, do it to me. Yeah, do it.
Do it. You're great, man.'

But it wasn't Duncan. It was the video player, which had
automatically returned from 'pause' to 'play'.

26

Duncan stayed too late at Paul's and floated through the whole
of the next day. Still, it was Friday and it went by quickly. Now
at six o'clock he was off on a secret mission in the audio-visual
department. Upstairs, Hazel's eyebrows were raised in a question mark.

'Are you sure Nigel and Serena are on their way?' she asked
Margaret.

'I've rung both mobile phones. They're both engaged. That
means that they're in their cars and on their way.'

'They've only just gone down to the car park,' said Charlotte.
'Who are they talking to?'

Margaret gave her a look as if to say 'How green can you get?'

'Each other, of course.'

'Convoy!' Hazel boomed out. 'Did you know, Charlotte, they
even have matching cars? Jaguars. It makes you sick.'

'He got his first—' But Margaret didn't get to finish.

'—and she copied him. Where are they off to this time?'

'The Chelsea Flower Show.'

'Well, I think we've waited long enough,' said Hazel. She

slipped over to her office and came back pressing a whole clutch of bottles of wine to her chest with both arms.

'We can't drink it warm,' complained Charlotte. 'How many people are coming? I didn't realise you had so much stashed away in your office.'

'I take it from client meetings and save it for later. Margaret always over-orders and I retrieve them when Cairns is saying goodbye at the lift.'

'So who's all coming?'

'Just Clancey and Bennett,' said Margaret. 'Orlando and the creative teams, Ben from production, us lot from round here. I haven't told them about the video. They all think it's just Friday evening drinkies.'

Hazel was ferreting away in Serena's office.

'What's she doing in there?' asked Charlotte. 'I thought we were going to view the video in Nigel's office.'

'We are, Charlotte. Hazel's got a duplicate key to Madam's fridge. She takes all Serena's chilled wine and replaces it with the stuff from her own cache. You can get away with it now, since management get the same Pinot Grigio as the *hoi polloi* out here.'

Hazel set up the wine in Nigel's office. Charlotte was dispatched to the kitchen to raid it for glasses and Twiglets. She did better than that, returning with a tray of Perrier, ice, Twiglets, crisps and Bombay mix.

'She'll go far, this girl,' laughed Hazel.

'Stop saying that, Haze. Honestly, you're getting me into really bad habits. This is tantamount to pilfering from the company.'

'No, it's not. It *is* pilfering from the company!'

They laughed.

'Well, everyone does it,' sympathised Margaret.

They didn't normally let anyone into their little group this quickly, but Charlotte seemed to have clubbed extra fast. She and Margaret rang round to the others and soon a group of ten or twelve were assembled in high spirits in Nigel's office.

'Ta ra—!'

It was Duncan. Had they thought about it, his colleagues might have considered his joining in – his instigating even – their conspiratorial behaviour, out of character. Certainly, it was out of character for Duncan to be out of line. But there was a simple explanation: when it came to understanding the difference between right and wrong, Duncan sided with right every time. He treated his team to what he called 'therapy' – occasional office antics behind the backs of Nigel and Serena – and they were all the better for it. So here he was trumpeting the arrival of the videotape. He had spirited it out of the audio-visual department in the basement.

'What's that?' Orlando knew he was up to no good.

'It may have escaped your attention, ladies and gentlemen, but on Wednesday, Godzilla and Dracula filmed a comeback epic curiously entitled *Clancey and Bennett. The Biggest Small Agency in the World.*'

Orlando was simultaneously amazed and furious. 'Those fucking bastards. Is this our new reel, then?'

'Sort of,' said Margaret.

'They've no right to do this without consulting me.'

'I typed the script,' said Margaret. 'I wasn't allowed to tell you. It's just for a few weeks until they can make a better one. It's going into the AAR, or whatever it's called. That place where people who want to be clients go to view agency reels and things. Go on, Duncan, put it on.'

The TV monitor lit up with a frozen picture of Nigel and Serena seated side by side. The assembled throng hooted and laughed and made as many offensive remarks and gestures to each other as they could think of.

'Christ! But she *is* ugly.' Hazel played to the crowd.

'And he's so fat,' said Margaret. 'Look at his neck. It's all bulbous over his collar.'

'Where did she get that dress?' asked Orlando. He put his hand to his forehead in mock horror. 'Look how it strobes on screen. They know nothing, those two. Nothing. I should feel insulted, except that I don't care if their company goes down the pan. No creative judgment.'

Duncan hit the play button and the entertainment began.

'Hello, my name is Nigel Gainsborough.'

Nigel, eyes down, was clearly holding notes below the camera cut-off point and trying to read ahead.

Hazel twisted the knife. 'He doesn't even know his own name!

Cairns, play that bit back. See how he stops and looks down to read out his own name!'

'And this is my, er, partner, er, Serena Sark.'

'Serena Sack, you mean!' Hazel was loving it.

'Serena Suck!' shouted one of the creatives, making exaggerated sucking noises.

'Shhh!' hissed Duncan, his finger to his lips.

'So, what's it all about, really? you're probably asking yourselves. Well, I shouldn't start by apologising, er, but, er, this is just a sort of simple film that Serena and I have put together ourselves. Unfortunaely, our creative director is away, being, er, creative somewhere . . .'

'Oh, piss off, you fat old fool!'

'. . . so, Nigel and I are taking this opportunity to tell you about our small agency with unusual resources.'

'Did she just interrupt him there?'

'It's in the script. I typed it like that.'

What happened next was enough to cause them stomach-ache through laughing. Serena was holding her head at a particularly strained angle, cocked to one side, probably to make her look more relaxed and user-friendly. But suddenly there was a bad edit and the film appeared to leap the Grand Canyon. Serena reappeared with a jump, lit differently and with her head cocked to the other side, like a mirror image. Her delivery speeded up and speeded up some more. A dispatch bike appeared to have been revving up like Concorde in the street outside when the film had been recorded. Serena soldiered on, shrill and shouty, unconcerned.

'That must be the bit they did after lunch,' said Margaret. 'I'd love to send this in to Jeremy Beadle.'

'She's dreadful!' Hazel couldn't take much more, 'That voice!'

'She's so shrill,' said Charlotte. 'It's like she's on fast forward. You can't understand one point she's making. This is supposed to be an advertising agency. I simply can't believe it.'

The creatives had begun to chant 'Shrill! Shrill! Shrill!' in a football-match sort of a way in the background.

'. . . As evidence of both our creativity and our planning skills we won a Gold at Cannes in 1980 and an IPA Effectiveness Award in 1982 . . .'

'1980! 1980! Jesus, some of our clients were still at school then! What are we meant to have won in the 1990s, for God's sake?'

'That's easy,' laughed Margaret. 'Nothing.'

'We won all the top awards in 1851,' mimicked someone else.

'So, there you have it, really. Clancey and Bennett. The biggest small agency in the world. We promise you hands-on management and lots of clout.'

Nigel and Serena were now standing side by side. There was a particularly fetching wide-angled shot of a panel radiator which took up most of the frame. Serena held a big grin and stared out from the screen, bug-eyed. Nigel stood ruddy-faced behind her, frozen, and then just as the picture had been held too long for comfort, stepped to her side, carnally close. She veered over at an angle to accommodate him. They flashed off and were replaced by the C&B logo, bleeding into a too-bright white background.

'He looked like he was touching her up at the end,' was Hazel's final observation. The creatives agreed.

'Hands-on management,' repeated Duncan as he rewound. 'More like "Hands on your money."'

'More like hands on her fanny,' said Orlando. It was a joke but he was bitter.

Charlotte noticed his bitterness. She noticed that this whole exercise was not as light-hearted as it seemed. And she noticed that nobody much cared that Nigel and Serena's selfish power politics had cut out all the requisite talent needed to produce a first-class film. Theirs was not a comedy. It was a tragedy. Or a travesty. Or both.

They had a real Friday-nighter, finishing all the wine and raiding the kitchen of all its Twiglets. Then, at about nine thirty, most of them headed for the pub and half of them were still left at eleven when they shuffled off for a curry, at Hazel's suggestion. Duncan, of course, was long gone by then.

27

Cindy snuggled up to Alan on the floor in front of the settee. They were half watching the news on TV, half chatting at the end of the day, indeed at the end of the week. Alan nuzzled into the back of Cindy's neck from behind her shoulder. She hunched up and giggled.

'Don't!'

'Come on, sweetheart.'

Cindy gently pushed him away.

'Honestly, Alan, all you ever want is sex.'

'Love,' objected Alan.

'Sex,' corrected Cindy. 'What is it about bonking on the carpet that turns you on so much?'

'They say you should make love in unusual places to keep your relationship fresh.'

'They say you should talk to each other first to keep your relationship going. You just like pounding away on the floor for some reason.'

'It makes me feel naughty.'

'Well, let's keep it for bedtime, shall we?'

She winked. Alan's passion was cooled anyway by the appearance on the TV screen of Margaret Beckett, the Labour Party's top woman, composed and calculating in her thoughtful answers to a rather aggressive interview. Alan spoke over her the minute he recognised who she was.

'With those looks she could be Princess Anne's auntie, couldn't she?'

'With those teeth she could be Princess Anne's horse,' came Cindy's riposte. 'Alan?'

'What?'

'I'm thinking of changing the colour of this room. What do you think?'

'It's your flat, really. Do what you like. I always like your taste. You're very clever at that sort of thing.'

'Well, you live here too. It's your home as much as mine.'

'What did you have in mind?'

'I haven't decided. Why don't you help me? We can do it together. You never choose anything. I could barely describe your taste since you never seen to exercise it. We always do what I want.'

'Most women would be thrilled to be in that position. That sort of thing doesn't interest me.'

'Well, it should. I was inspired by that room at Blakes. I thought I could take your clock as a starting point.'

Alan looked up at the antique French clock on the mantelpiece. It was a solid block of matt slate. Its white ceramic face with spidery Roman numerals was edged in gilt. About 1870, Alan had been told by the dealer when he had picked it out as a gift for Cindy a few years earlier. It marked the anniversary of their first meeting, when he had recruited her to work for him several careers ago. 'To record the wonderful hours we spend together, darling,' he had written on a little card. He realised the significance of what Cindy had just said.

'Cindy, you can't paint it *black*.'

'I'm not going to paint it black! A minute ago you weren't interested. Now you want power of veto. I was thinking of British racing green, actually, or one of those dusky colours like plum or something.'

'I like this bluey colour. But it's up to you. Can you afford to do the whole thing? You'd have to change the curtains, and what about the other furnishings? It'll cost a fortune.'

'You're right. I can't afford it at all. I'm just a bit bored. I'd like to buy somewhere new. D'you think anyone will give me a mortgage yet?'

'I think if you're self-employed you have to have three years' figures before they'll give you a loan.'

'I guess so. I shouldn't have left advertising until after we'd moved.'

'I'm sorry, darling. I feel it's my fault. Blame the divorce. I'm earning all this money and I have to pay it to Terri. I wish I'd never bought the house in St Albans. It's her bloody mortgage and I end up paying for the whole thing. There's no way I could help you on that one.'

'Perhaps I could just do something more dramatic with the draperies round the windows.'

'Cindy, they're a fire hazard already. I wish you'd move that wrought-iron stand. One day those church candles'll set the place ablaze.'

'Zeffirelli had them in *Tosca* at Covent Garden. They were good enough for Maria Callas and Tito Gobbi. I got the idea after we saw Pavarotti in the revival.'

'I'm surprised you noticed them on stage with him in the way.'

'Did I see that with you or Duncan?'

'I wouldn't know. I know I've seen Pavarotti in something.' Alan yawned. 'I was talking about Duncan with his bosses the other day.'

'You were? What for?'

'I had lunch with them.'

'You never told me that. What did they say about Duncan?'

'Not a great deal. They spent most of the time talking about their own achievements.'

'Short lunch was it, then?'

'It was strange, Cindy. I'm not afraid of them any more. They can't touch me. In fact, I'm going to make them pathetically grateful to me.'

'How? Why?'

'To help Colin's sister out. She's looking for a new agency for Japanair. Duncan, from what I hear from you, gets on particularly well with female clients.'

'We all know why that is, don't we!'

'Colin's sister would like him. Clancey and Bennett would be ideal to handle the account.'

'Can you arrange it?'

'It's up to Colin's sister whether she goes with it or not.'

'What's in it for you? Why are you helping those two? I can never figure out how your mind works. You used to hate them.'

'I'm just helping Colin's sister out, that's all. Perhaps she can give us some below- or through-the-line work.'

'I hope they're going to pay you.'

Alan responded with a blatant lie. 'Oh, I'll get a lunch out of it, I suppose.'

'A lunch! They ought to give you thousands. How much is it worth?'

'Three to four million.'

'Alan! Sometimes I wonder about your business acumen.'

'Look on it as a favour to Duncan.'

'Duncan? Why are you so keen to suddenly do him a favour? He's *my* friend, not yours!'

'We both worked for the same agency.'

'You left years before he ever went there. Duncan only went to C&B after it was part of MCN. You wouldn't know him if it wasn't for me.'

'Cindy, don't get so agitated. I'm really doing this for Colin and his sister.'

'Now you're doing it for them! What do they ever do for you?' She didn't wait for an answer. 'Nothing. That's what!'

'Well, perhaps I'll get something from Duncan in the long term. You're always telling me how good he is. He'll go somewhere in advertising.'

'Yeah! Through the door marked exit like the rest of us.'

'Well, not for a while.'

Cindy stayed quiet for a moment but felt compelled to tell her lover.

'Actually, Alan, I'm not supposed to say, but very soon.'

Alan moved from her side and looked at her. He didn't like the sound of this.

'What d'you mean? Tell me.'

'I'm not supposed to.'

'I'm your boyfriend, for God's sake. He isn't.'

'Well ... he may be offered a job in television. I think he used his connections with The Station. He's waiting for a detailed offer.'

'God!'

Alan was normally placid. He kept his feelings hidden. Cindy was surprised that the possibility of Duncan's departure was bugging him so much.

'What are you so worried about all of a sudden? Colin's sister can take her business somewhere else, can't she?'

'Too right she can. Cindy? Tell me what you know about Duncan.'

'Duncan? Half his life is a complete mystery. Like yours. Scotsmen don't exactly wear their hearts on their sleeves.'

'I was thinking more about whether he's leaving C&B or not. There's no way the Japanair account can go to Nigel and Serena. They'll never win it. It'll be a disaster.'

'Good. Stitch 'em! That's what I say. Get your revenge. Or are you more worried about missing a free lunch?'

Alan wasn't. He was more concerned about the fifty-thousand-pound backhander he was depending on.

28

'Time to go!' Max leapt off his chair and scrammed out of the kitchen. Karen called after him.

'You've not eaten anything! You can't go to school on an empty stomach!'

'You always say that!' He reappeared and pecked his mother on the cheek.

Sweet, she thought, as they re-enacted their Tuesday morning ritual.

'Have a good day at the office. Don't sit there worrying about not getting the breakfast show money. Get on with the next thing.'

'I would if I knew what the next thing was.'

'How about a game show where kids from broken homes have to pick out the father they've never known from a line-up!'

'Max! That's in unforgivably bad taste.' Karen was not really annoyed, though. If he could joke about it, even bitterly, then he was getting over the disappointment. 'We have to give Martin Fox something that will knock him sideways. Something that uses

The Station's unique attributes. I've no time this week. I have to spend today with the accountant again.'

'School's a doddle. I'll think up something in geography.'

'Well, don't get caught.'

Max zoomed past his mother down the hall and almost out through the wide-open front door.

'Max!'

'What? I'm always late because of you.'

'Max, I'm so lucky I've got you.'

'Too right you are!' He started down the path. He turned back. 'And I'm lucky I've got you!' He whirled round and sped off.

Oh, thought Karen. My precious baby.

Five minutes later, cunningly concealed behind the trunk of a plane tree, Max stood at the corner of Flask Walk munching a Mars Bar. From the corner of his eye he watched his mother's car career down the dense Hampstead street, horn blasting at another driver scraping out from a roadside parking place. Karen Myhill roared off, turning left in a crazy half-circle and narrowly missing a burgundy Volvo estate. At last she was out of sight. Out of sight and out for the day.

Max ran back to the house with a spurt of teenage energy, bent over at a forty-five-degree angle because of the weight of his school rucksack. He let himself in through the heavy, Victorian door, threw his things on to the hall floor and blasted his way into his mother's study. He sat down in front of the Apple Macintosh computer and created a new document on the word processor.

'Dear Mr Abbott, I am sorry to have to let you know that my son Max is ill with a summer cold and will be unable to attend school today. I myself am unable to telephone due to an attack of laryngitis which has left me unable to talk. With best wishes, Karen Myhill.'

Too many 'unables' from the woman who had written three series of *Thameside*. Make one 'cannot'. Max sent the document to print and then erased it from the hard disk. He sorted through the untidy filing tray and pounced on a copy of a letter to Karen's accountant. Great, she had signed it. He took the letter through to the hall and ran it through the fax machine on copy mode. He then returned to the study, buried the original letter back on the desk and found a pair of scissors. He carefully snipped round his mother's signature on the copy he had just made, and rushed upstairs to his bedroom. There, with a squirt of Gloy, he attached the signature to his own lying letter. Brilliant! His headmaster would never spot the deceit once it had been through the fax machine. With the ecstatic glee of a Colditz forger outsmarting the Gestapo, he bombed downstairs and sent the fax through to his school. He then returned to his bedroom and eliminated all traces of the evidence. He launched himself backwards on to his bed and sank into the Ryan Giggs duvet. Fantastic! A day off to do what the fuck he liked. By the time Max was thirty he would either be a millionaire or in prison. Or both.

Max wandered into the kitchen and went round the room kicking the front of the limed-oak cabinets. He pulled open the freezer door and produced a tub of Häagen-Dazs Cookie Dough Dynamo ice-cream out of the frost. He sorted out the largest spoon he could find in the dishwasher and sat down to work his way through the entire half-litre.

Max was bored. School was dull enough but this was even less stimulating. His ennui dragged him through to his mother's study. He picked up the stapler, aimed it high, and fired several salvos into the drapery over the curtain pole. He rummaged on his mother's desk. He found an outline for a celebrity panel game where the likes of Stephen Fry had to write the opening lines of imaginary novels. Christ. Who'd watch that? University dons and who else? Yeah, it was for BBC2. Obviously, his mother intended to go further up her own proverbial backside than even *The Late Review*. He would have to have a word with her.

He took a finger trip through the hanging file system in the drawer under the desk. He peeked at Myhill Productions' salary list. He was never going to work for as little money as some of these guys. Funny how, for all her public statements, Karen paid all her female staff on average twenty-five per cent less than the men. Women, including his mother, could not negotiate. He rammed the file door shut so hard that a tray of paperclips fell on to the floor. Piss. He would have to pick up every single last one of them or she would discover he had been in here.

He crawled under the desk. If only he had a magnet. He inhaled a speck of carpet fluff and coughed. His fingers flicked across the floor picking up the clips. Quite by chance, the side of his hand knocked against a cardboard box, hidden out of sight behind the filing drawer. Hello.

Max wheeled the drawer unit out from under the desk on its castors. He slid the cardboard box across the carpet and into the middle of the room where there was more light. It was heavy. He opened the cardboard flaps on the top. Inside, books and documents were stacked neatly. One black, padded, leather-bound cover was embossed in gold numbers: 1987. How fascinating. A desk diary from half a lifetime ago.

He lifted it from the box, revealing an identical diary beneath embossed with the previous year. He leafed through 1987. It had his birthday in it! But it didn't say what she had bought him. Could he remember? No. Look at all these meetings. Breakfasts. Lunches. Dinners. Hairdresser appointments. Car servicings. Edinburgh TV Festival. Carpet fitters. That was the year they had moved here. Amazing. It was so long ago. Royal Television Society awards. Take Max to the dentist. Yuk. Vote MT. Oh yes, Margaret Thatcher. Karen always told him he was one of Thatcher's children. He had come into the world at the same time as she had come to power. He leaned over the box and dug his hands down to the bottom. He pulled out as many of the diaries as he could manage. Nearly right at the bottom he found the year in which he was born. And there it was in faded ink.

'Maximilian born today. Eight and a half pounds. My new love. The best Valentine's Day ever.' Maximilian. He hated it. Just 'Max' was brilliant. Why did she have to go the whole hog? He touched the writing with his finger. It was special. He wondered if his father, whoever that might be, had been present. Suddenly Max was overcome with investigative fever. He was holding the clue here in his hand. Idiot. He raced through each page examining the meeting entries, the initials, the names, the cancellations and the changes. But there were no give-aways. It could have been 1987 he was looking at for all the difference between this one and the first diary he had searched through. Max was disappointed, annoyed even. He squatted on the floor looking at the summer leaves through the window. Why would his mother not tell him? Why did he have to wait until he was eighteen? What was so terrible about the circumstances of his birth that she could never discuss it?

Max sat bolt upright. He had been looking in the wrong place. There was one diary left at the bottom of the box: 1979. The year of the not-so-immaculate conception.

He gingerly plucked it from the bottom of the container and made his way to the maps at the back. He turned over a few pages, found the first days of January 1980 and counted back by the month into the mists of pre-Max history. One, January. Two, December. Three, November . . . Seven, July. Eight, June. Nine, May. This was it.

The end of May was filled with secretarial interviews. Several dinners with someone called Bob Dresler. God. Perhaps he was his father, whoever he was. Ladies and gentlemen, Max Dresler. Yeah. That sounded cool. What was this? Anti-smoking hypnotherapy. Christ, she couldn't have been that stupid, could she? Ethnic minority scheme people? Who were they? Not his father anyway. And then it all fell into place. This was why he was one of Thatcher's children. Karen had always said he had started at the same time as Mrs Thatcher. Almost literally. There, on 3 May 1979, was the entry, a small and neat reminder. Vote MT. And immediately beneath it, this time huge and carved into the page and almost through it, were two sinister black letters. Max had seen nothing else like this on any of the pages in any of the years in any of the diaries.

MF.

Max could hear his own breathing in the stillness of the room. Who was MF?

Max already knew what these two letters stood for as far as he was concerned. He could not stop himself speaking the words out loud.

'MF. My Father.'

Duncan and Michael had spent the weekend at the cottage but anything exciting was stymied by the rain. Now, a couple of days later and back in London, Duncan was in Charlotte's office with Margaret when his phone rang and, as fate would have it, Serena picked up the call.

'No doubt I'll get a row now for not answering that,' observed Margaret.

'Hello,' said Serena in her archest telephone voice.

'Can I speak to Duncan Cairns, please?'

'Who's calling, please?'

'Jamie Hirst.'

Duncan sped to his phone when called.

'Hello.'

'Is that Duncan Cairns?'

'Speaking.'

'Duncan, this is Jamie Hirst of Saturn Productions. You don't know me. We're going to be making *Megabrek* for The Station.'

'Yes, I know. Congratulations.'

'I just wanted to say that if there is anything you need to help develop the ads for *Megabrek*, feel free to call.'

'I will do. However, I think you'll find everything will have to go through Briony Linden at The Station.'

'Sure. Your agency has a fantastic reputation. We're expecting you to work your magic and come up with a brilliant campaign.'

'We're expecting you to come up with a brilliant programme.'

'We'll have to see about that. Which other shows are you putting support behind?'

Duncan was on his guard. 'We're mainly concentrating on generic advertising for The Station as a brand.'

'I heard a rumour Karen Myhill was getting a big commission from Martin Fox. Are you advertising that?'

'There are so many rumours about The Station, aren't there?' Duncan manufactured a laugh.

Jamie laughed back, equally synthetically. 'Yes. Myhill Productions is one of the real go-ahead companies. I'm sure Martin Fox is very keen on her . . . them.'

God, thought Duncan, if he fishes any further he'll need a rod. 'I'm sure he picks only the best. You must be very proud.'

'I am. Well, if you need anything you know where we are.'

'We do indeed.'

'Oh, Duncan, by the way. Would you thank whoever it was in your company for the BARB analysis on breakfast viewing. We never get the data you agency people seem to.'

'You're welcome.'

'Bye, then.'

'Bye.'

'Duncan!' It was Serena again.

'Yes?'

'I have someone else holding for you. I'm not your secretary, you know.'

Too fucking right you're not, thought Duncan. 'Thank you!'

'Hello?' said Serena. 'I'll put you through. Who shall I say is calling?'

'Michael.'

Serena looked down at the phone as she replaced the receiver. Now whose voice *was* that? she thought. He's always calling Duncan at work. She detected Margaret on the horizon and homed in on her for a roasting reminder on telephone-answering duties.

Duncan was in soft conversation with Michael.

'I just wanted to say "Good luck",' said Michael. 'So, good luck, Dunky. I love you.'

'Thank you.'

Duncan wanted to say 'I love you too', but someone might overhear. 'I love yous' were never for the office. Then, on the pretext of doing some shopping, he slunk out of the agency and took a cab to Arlington Street, Le Caprice and lunch with Karen Myhill.

Unusually, Duncan was nervous. Not about his ability to do well in television. Nor because he didn't think he was capable of persuading Karen Myhill that he would be an asset to her company. He was nervous because he found her a particularly difficult woman to get the measure of. As yet he had no handle on her nor any idea of how to get one. Karen Myhill's was not a personality to be pinned down. Michael's background notes on her had all been career steps and programme notices. They were about her work but not about *her*. Duncan had always got on easily with people in business. He was good at small-talk and keeping the conversation going. He was good at putting people at their ease. He was good at getting difficult points across in a pleasant way and of not compromising his position. He was, in short, pretty successful at handling meetings. But that was with corporate people. Duncan wasn't so hot with eccentrics or oddballs. Neither of those was a fair description of Karen Myhill, of course, but how someone with few social skills and an intrinsic inability to make eye contact could run a talked-about company in any field, let alone television, beat him. During the course of his career Duncan had spotted that, when you got right to the top of a company and met the Mr Big that all the staff talked about all the time and were afraid of or besotted with or mesmerised by, sometimes as an outsider you could glimpse that actually there was not that much there. Perhaps Karen Myhill was one of those small big people who were all power and position but no personality.

They sat in the corner and unlike most diners did not attempt to see who was who. With its pictures by David Bailey and its brittle definition of glamour, Le Caprice could normally reward you with at least a Britt Ekland or an Esther Rantzen. Cindy had even been present on one of the Sundays the Princess of Wales had dropped in. But these two kept themselves to themselves.

Duncan had arrived first. Disciplining himself to concentrate on this crucial conversation, he had set about aligning his cutlery exactly parallel with the edges of the table. He had lifted his dessert fork and spoon from their horizontal positions at the top of this place setting and relaid them, the fork on the inside of the other larger forks, the spoon on the inside of the knives. That, as far as Duncan was concerned, was more technically correct. It was where he liked them, in their proper place. Moreover it created a little territory on the table-top that he could call his own. It meant that, psychologically, he could possess it, cross it and advance over it on to Karen's side should the need arise.

By contrast, when Karen had arrived, she had accidentally swept her side of the table with her chunky shoulder bag. Not the one and only Hermès handbag of the ladies who lunch, the one and only handbag with which to cross the threshold of Le Caprice, the one and only handbag whose twenty-four-carat gold clasp is correctly left open at all times by its designer devotees. No. Rather an unfortunately shapeless black nylon thing with cracked white letters on it. Given out for free at a MIPCOM TV trade fair, it was the one and only thing lying around in the office which was big enough in which to stuff an unsolicited script that had caught Karen's eye a few weeks back and which she had yet to start reading. This bag did not have a twenty-four-carat gold clasp. It did not have a clasp of any sort. It had a zip, a matching black nylon zip, and the black nylon zip was quite definitely *in*correctly left open to reveal the dog-ears of its curling contents. The base of the uncloseable bag had not only scraped all four of Karen's highly polished knives on to the floor where they jangled for the attention of the glitterati, but it had also rucked the starched white linen tablecloth. Even before Karen had descended to floor level to retrieve her missing cutlery, Duncan's grey eyes had already made contact with the waiter's, and by the time she had resurfaced, Karen found the silverware replaced and the items in her hand redundant. A Bloody Mary had also arrived seemingly at Duncan's request. The ruck remained, however, and for the rest of the meeting she had to put up with balancing her glass on the wobble.

'What worries me, Duncan, is why someone who's doing very well and earning big money in advertising wants to come and work for a small, untried TV production company on half his previous earnings.'

'You approached me. It's that simple.'

'Flattery is no reason to take a plunge in income. I won't let you come just because you're chuffed I asked you. My company could collapse in the next few months.'

'Are you offering me a job or not?' Duncan's beaming smile let Karen know he was not becoming impatient or aggressive, only that he was struggling with her style. 'To be frank I'm having difficulty understanding whether or not you are. You seem to be sending out mixed signals.'

'I'm thinking about it. It's a big responsibility for me to encourage you to make a career change and then have to deal with the consequences of your not being happy with it later. D'you understand what I'm saying?'

'Yes, of course I do. But look at your own career. You gave up the highest-profile job of any woman in corporate television. You left a board position at Trafalgar. You left to be an independent, to do your own thing, run your own company and have a go at seeing if you could do it better. It was a risk financially, but worth it. I would be doing something similar, I suppose.'

'I didn't change horses in mid-stream. I'm still in the same profession.'

'That's irrelevant. The real point is that you were seeking satisfaction – in your career, in your creativity. You wanted control over your own destiny. Well, that's what attracts me to working in independent production, too.'

'It is, is it?'

'Ultimately. I will get to answer to myself and my own talent.'

'You'll answer to me.'

'I wasn't being literal. Look, I've done advertising for ten years now. It bores me rigid, to be absolutely truthful. I'm account management. I brief and debrief, and present and sell and take the flak and do the entertaining but I don't get to *create* and to do my own thing. I'm at the beck and call of clients all day long. I enjoy hard work but I want to work on my own projects and be my own master. You are a step towards that.'

'Has anyone told you how difficult I am supposed to be to work with?' Karen decided to give Duncan the chance to mention Michael. She would not bring him up herself.

'Who do we know in common?'

'You tell me.'

'I've heard you're uncompromising. But that's what they say about all creative women.'

'Hmmm.' He had either innocently ducked what she had in mind or deliberately avoided mentioning his significant other.

'Well, I've had to handle difficult clients, you know. Everyone thinks that in advertising your client turns up with five million pounds and says, "Do make a lovely commercial for me, darling."

It just doesn't work like that. It's very difficult and tough and the clients can be hell.'

'Is The Station hell?'

'Absolutely the opposite. A dream company. That's what partly persuaded me I was right to seek this move. I get on with telly people.'

'Do you know many people in television, then? What else have you heard about me? What stories, if any?'

'Stories? Are you that famous?'

'Controversial rather than famous.'

'Are you trying to put me off? You're not succeeding if you are.'

'Well, I don't know, Duncan. My company is small. Even if I halve your salary I can't be sure I can afford you. I'm nervous about giving you a year's contract, but I can't ask you to give up all this' – she gestured round the room – 'just to come and work on spec.'

'What I want to be sure of, Karen, is that you really believe I can do it. I think I have a powerful imagination that can dream up good ideas. But will I be as good as other people in telly?'

'I wouldn't bother about that. Most of them have one average idea per year. It's not about dreaming up amazing ideas anyway. Anyone can do that. It's recognising ideas and turning them into compelling television that is important. Then being able to sell them. What I like about your brain is, yes, the ideas are fine, but your mind is focused. I think you explain clearly and can sell an idea.'

'That's my advertising training, I suppose.'

'Look, Duncan. I'm not sure if we're getting anywhere. I need to resolve this in my mind, talk to a few other people. I can't offer you a job without knowing exactly how I'm going to use you. Will you be an ideas man? A marketing man? A producer?'

'I won't be a marketing man, that's for sure. I'd like to produce. I'd like to run my own production company later. Who do you have to talk to?'

'Oh, no one in particular, not someone in the company.'

Duncan didn't push her. He had already realised that this was the frustrating thing about Karen Myhill. She was slow to make a decision. She would toy with it for ages, the way Pushkin would toy with a bird in the garden, damaging it and defeathering it before going in for the kill. He knew to let her come to her decision in her own way and in her own time. If she was going to hire him, she would. If she wasn't, she wouldn't. That was that. He changed tack.

'I've seen the pilot for the new breakfast show. Not meant to say anything about it, of course.'

'Don't tell me. It's too depressing.'

'Why?'

'I pitched for it and lost. And got humiliated by my former protégé in the process.'

Well, thought Duncan, at least being a protégé of Karen Myhill is no bad thing. Her colleagues and subordinates were sprinkled throughout tellyland, many with the power to pick and choose the plum jobs. He was about to tell her about Jamie Hirst's call.

'Hello, Duncan!'

Duncan nearly leapt out of his seat. The familiarity of the voice and his guilt at discussing a career change set his stomach churning. It was Audrey fucking Goldberg. She was clutching a handbag.

'Audrey! Where did you spring from?'

Meaning, where the hell were you sitting and how much did you eavesdrop on, you nosey old cow?

'I've been right behind you the whole time. I saw you when I came in but you were so engrossed in conversation that you didn't see me.'

Surely an impossibility to have missed the acreage of fluorescent primrose and a thousand golden jangly bits.

'Do I get an introduction?' She swapped her handbag to her left side in case handshakes were forthcoming. They weren't.

'This is an old friend of mine, Karen Myhill. Karen, this is Audrey Goldberg, who is advertising's best-known recruitment consultant.'

'Oh, how sweet, Duncan. You didn't call me a headhunter.'

Karen nodded almost imperceptibly. Audrey gave a completely artificial laugh.

'I've just recruited a lovely young girl for Duncan, haven't I? Ooh, that sounds terrible, but you know what I mean. In fact, I must speak to Nigel about invoicing. The last time, Duncan, your accounts department were slow to pay my fee. I do run a business, you know.'

Duncan couldn't believe they were in Le Caprice talking about the accounts department. Actually, neither could Audrey.

'I must go back to my lunch partner. He's looking for people around your level to move to Hong Kong. Shall I mention you?'

Duncan smiled. He knew she would anyway. And he could put just a little pressure on Karen here. 'If you want to.'

Audrey turned to leave and then changed her mind momentarily.

'Fancy that. Stefanie Powers is over there. Probably having a heart-to-heart!' She gave her artificial laugh again.

Well, at least don't point, thought Duncan.

Audrey returned her Hermès handbag to her right side. Its twenty-four-carat gold clasp was tightly shut. She was gone.

Karen was examining the bill. 'Has your friend had a facelift, by any chance?'

'She's not my friend. And chance had nothing to do with it. She's had them *both* done, apparently.'

30

'Ladies and gentlemen, the head of our legal team, Michael Farnham.'

Martin Fox left the stage and handed over to Michael, who strode to the lectern and addressed the audience. As he was speaking, he became conscious that this was unrehearsed and that it was always a good idea to have had a technical run-through first. Of course, all the programme people had had theirs, but there hadn't been time, apparently, for the boring bits such as his to be included.

He found the room daunting. This was the circular lecture theatre in the basement of The Station's extraordinary building. It was illuminated from overhead by natural light flooding through an enormous skylight. This lay beneath a glass and steel footbridge over which visitors walked from the street into the main reception area on the ground floor. Michael felt he had two audiences: the one hundred or so faces in the foreground and the stream of curious folk above him trying to peer down to see what lay below.

'You know, when I came into television – and don't let that legal bit fool you, I *am* in television – I rather imagined I would be at the beck and call of chief executives determined to stop errant producers midway to bringing down the government with an outrageous libel or two. I anticipated that, on more routine days, I would have the Mary Whitehouse brigade to deal with, because foul language and dangly bits had made themselves apparent before the nine o'clock watershed.

'So here I am today, head of the legal team at The Station, the most talked-about television channel in the history of British television, and about to launch the UK version of what our friends across the Atlantic endearingly call the Superhighway. By an Act of Parliament, no less, The Station is uniquely positioned as the sole company to hold both a franchise for the production and broadcast of programmes and the delivery of them into the home through digitally compressed signals sent via multi-strand two-way fibre-optic cables.

'At this breakthrough in our broadcasting culture and on the brink of this momentous and already legendary commercial investment, to whose attention do you think I have completely devoted the last twenty-seven working days and a lengthy stream of Rumpolean correspondence? No less, I repeat, no less a figure than Mrs Doreen Whipsnade of 37B, Glebe Crescent, Milton Keynes.'

The audience gave a polite laugh. They'd had an hour already of light witticisms and showreel clips and trailers. They were nearly all from the advertising industry having their egos, their palms and their wallets massaged as part of the trade communications and marketing strategy.

'Mrs Whipsnade is not happy about our contractors' excavation of Glebe Crescent to bring the Superhighway past the roots of her flowering weeping cherry.'

Those in the audience still listening laughed a little more. The others flicked through their programmes or eyed the clock.

'I can tell you, ladies and gentlemen, that cherry and I have much in common. We're both imports to this country from warmer climes, we've both had our lives uprooted by The Station and we both spend all day weeping for Mrs Whipsnade.' This time nobody laughed, not even Martin Fox, and Michael realised he was trying too hard. 'You will have noticed that for the last six months we've been running the line "Do Let It Pass You By" on all our advertising. I think Mrs Whipsnade hasn't quite understood our intended double meaning.'

Michael gritted his teeth in a smile and paused. There was so much to do in getting The Station off the ground. He had not calculated on the time that would have to be dedicated to PR events such as these. You spent half your day just meeting people. It meant that the time in which to get the real work done was even more precious. He wondered whether in the long run he could take the strain. As he took a sip of water before getting down to the nitty-gritty, he ran his eyes across the audience. He had been looking forward to seeing Nigel Gainsborough and Serena Sark for the first time after having heard at length from Duncan for the last two years about this gargoyle couple who obsessed their employees so much. But there appeared to be no one in the audience who fitted the caricature he had in his mind's eye. Maybe Duncan's secretary was right. Perhaps they did skip half the events in their diary and nip off instead to a cheap hotel for an afternoon shag. Well, no matter. He wasn't going to meet them up close, was he? He returned to his notes and began his summary of the complex legislation under which The Station would operate.

Nigel strained. He couldn't see this chap very well at all. He was feeling more than a touch tired, having made the mistake at lunch in Charlotte Street of having a risotto as a starter followed by pasta as a main course. Rice and pasta combined was a bit of a killer. He would love to undo the waistband of his trousers under his jacket. If this went on much longer, he would. Nigel and Serena had turfed up late. Advertising people at their level always did. So they hadn't got seats together but were separated in the back row. Something had caught Serena's attention, Nigel could tell that from the way she was screwing up her face. She must have spotted a new business opportunity.

Serena was deep in thought. She found all this fascinating, of course, but there was something about television which was lost on her. She never watched it. Well, not never, but almost never. Her experience of advertising was gained from showreels and bought-in tapes in the office, not from home viewing. Sometimes she might catch *The Money Programme* or *Question Time* and she would certainly watch *Channel 4 News* and *Newsnight* if she were ever about at those times. But the truth was that she *was* never about. The rest of British viewing appeared nowadays to be forcibly concentrated on either smut masquerading as the double entendre or Cilla Black – a woman, in Serena's opinion, of intrinsic vulgarity. No. Serena's decided preference was for Radio 4. *The Times* could do the rest.

Why wasn't she concentrating? She glanced at her agenda to remind her where they were. This was going to go on too long. There were three other speakers still to come. This was Michael Farnham, the head of the legal team. Honestly. Why had they put him up? Advertising people just wanted to know how it worked, how much it cost and could they sell it to their clients? Not the ins and outs of Acts of Parliament. Still, he was quite good-looking. About her own age, she flattered herself. Had she met him here before? Something about him was familiar. She liked his voice – quite plummy and English-sounding, no trace of the ghastly South African mentioned in his succinct c.v. – and clearly a good brain. She approved. Still, enough was enough.

She tried to catch Nigel's eye but to no avail. In the end she had to get up and push past the whole row to get out. She tapped Nigel on the shoulder and after a kerfuffle as he slipped out of his seat, they exited through the double doors at the back. Briony Linden was there, exhaling fumes from a stolen cigarette, not her usual Camel Light.

'Hello, you two.' She laughed. 'Christ. I feel as if I've been caught round the back of the bike sheds by the headmaster and mistress!' Whoops. That came out like not the sort of mistress she had had in mind. 'Don't tell anyone, will you?'

'Aren't you allowed to smoke, Briony?' asked Serena.

'Absolutely not. This really *is* an American company. Californian political correctness is the order of the day here.' She secreted the butt in her hand.

'Oh dear. I'm sorry we have to slip away.'

'That's OK. I'll send you the typescripts.'

'Oh, will you? That would be immensely useful. I think all today has confirmed, really, is that what we need to be doing is an awareness job, not an educating one. Do you agree?'

'Well—'

'I'm never wrong about these things, Briony, as you know. All the research and analysis shows that there is a crucial target group of social leaders, I suppose you call them. Upmarket, younger people. Once they hear about something new in the technological or media or leisure area they investigate it for themselves. They are sophisticated enough to make their own judgments. It's a case of "You can lead a horse to water but you cannot make it drink". The rest of society will follow on from them later when they've seen The Station in other people's homes and heard from word of mouth about how successful it is.'

Briony nodded. Serena sailed on.

'Our campaign should be about image, status, emotional pull. We shouldn't let it get bogged down in technological high jinks and schedules and times and dreary details.'

Briony continued nodding. Serena had an uncanny ability to sum up months of work in a few simple sentences. But she did go on a bit.

'I do hope Duncan's not leading you down the detail route. He's obsessive about small things for some reason. One needs to keep an eye on the long term, on the big picture. Nigel, what *are* you doing?'

Nigel, face scrunched up, was bent sideways, clutching at the jacket of his suit, round about where his waistline once was, and appeared to be writhing from side to side in discomfort.

'Are you ill?'

Briony suppressed hysterics as Nigel, for some reason, grappled with his trousers inside his jacket. He was obviously in some sort of contorted difficulty.

'Terribly sorry, old girl,' he said sheepishly. 'It was that damned risotto.'

He pulled his trousers up under his jacket and tried to fasten them. Serena gave him a withering look and turned to Briony, rolling her eyes heavenward. Better to ignore his idiosyncrasies.

'I liked the last speaker. I thought I knew him. Have I met him here?'

'I don't know. I wouldn't have thought so. He's quite new.'

'He's rather dishy, don't you think? He must be making some woman very happy.'

Briony laughed knowingly. 'Well, some*one* very happy.' She laughed a bit more. It was an excuse to get out the laughter she was suppressing at the antics of that complete twit, Nigel Gainsborough.

Serena stood riveted to the spot as Nigel and Briony turned towards the outer doors. A giant penny dropped inside her brain, crashing down like the demolition of an unfashionable tower block. Her mechanical mind ticked over as accurately as always. It was the voice she had recognised, not the face. It was the voice that called Duncan regularly. Michael Farnham, the head of the legal team, was probably calling Duncan Cairns every day. Unmarried Michael Farnham. No wife and children on his c.v. Unmarried Duncan Cairns. No mention of any personal life at all in his conversation. And Briony Linden knew. No wonder Duncan and she seemed to get on so well. No wonder he spent half his days over here. No wonder he knew the ins and outs of The Station so well.

After the penny had dropped, and as the dust settled, everything else fell into place. Serena Sark had discovered Duncan Cairns's Achilles' heel.

31

Paul McCarthy was on his way to buy a panama hat. He was waiting for the tube. Where the fuck was it? This had to be the last tube station in London not to have an overhead display telling you when the train was due. God, London was dirty. For all the money they spent stone-cleaning and relighting, you'd think they could pay someone to sweep the tube platforms, wouldn't you? They had used the IRA as an excuse to rip out all the litter bins, supposedly in case bombs were planted in them. They'd never bothered to put them back. The result? The place was a tip. A skinhead with a swastika tattooed on the back of his head was smoking about ten feet away from him. There were signs everywhere telling you not to smoke. Look at all those people who died in the King's Cross fire. Still, Paul was not going to go over and get his face permanently scarred by 'doing his duty', as his grandmother would have called it. Was the skinhead with that denimed girl, or not? Paul couldn't tell. The seventies were clearly back: the skinhead was wearing those incredibly tight tartan bondage trousers with the inter-leg straps that Vivienne Westwood had made trendy two decades ago. They were dead tight and ripped across his thighs. If Paul cocked his head back a little he could see the boy's backside. He was wearing his tartan trousers right up the crack of his arse. Very sexy. Bet he was a dirty bugger in bed.

An incomprehensible message was broadcast overhead. The announcer's accent was Indian or Pakistani. Why couldn't they have someone who spoke decent English? Even then, you couldn't have heard anything – they could be frying chips inside the speakers. Ho hum. Paul was looking forward to next weekend. He would have his new panama hat to wear. He adored the Cotswolds in June and the English country house – not that the cottage was in that league, but they might go and visit one this time. Michael and Duncan had kept the place sparse. No, spartan was a better word for it. But then, they were only there at the weekends and they spent most of their time entertaining. They had been good to him over the years, really. Well, Michael had. Duncan never parted with a penny unless it was spent on himself. He complained he never had money. No, Duncan, just a huge flat with a garden in Maida Vale and a BMW and three Stateside or equivalent holidays every year. He ought to try living on social security and the occasional morsel of piecemeal work in half-baked TV production companies. Then come home to a poky damp flat in North London where you could hear the squatters upstairs shitting in their toilet because the landlord hadn't bothered to obey the law on soundproofing.

A welcome cool blast down the tunnel signalled the arrival of the train. My God. Wonders would never cease. It was a new one. One of those ones with bright red and blue paintwork and picture windows. Its destination was Heathrow. It would travel right through the heart of the West End and way out to the other side of London.

The doors opened and Paul got on. He sat down opposite a middle-aged lady, the sort his grandmother would have called a Shirley Williams. No make-up, not even lipstick. Her shoes said librarian, the neck-bow prison visitor. The denimed girl, who was not with the skinhead after all, placed a nylon sports bag by the doors and sat down beside Paul, her hair falling over her face.

'Don't you think it would be better to keep your bag with you?'

The lady had committed the cardinal sin of the London Underground. She had spoken to another passenger.

'I can see it from here.'

'I wasn't thinking so much of you, dear. I was thinking how other passengers might react if they saw an unattended bag.' She gave the girl the smile of a nun.

'It's not unattended.'

'I don't think you're helping terrorism, do you? Once we all become used to seeing unattended bags, then it's so much easier for them.'

'I can't put it here, can I? Someone will trip over it.'

The lady leant forward. Paul fixed on an advert for Premence. Something to do with women's periods. How revolting. The print was too small, he thought.

'Are you a Londoner, dear?'

'I don't think that's any of your business.'

The tube train rattled along.

'I'm sorry. I can't hear you.'

'I can't fucking believe this. Look! I'm getting up and standing by my bag. OK?'

She got up and did just that. The lady sat back and smiled like Mother Superior. Paul self-consciously concentrated on his hat.

The train came to a halt at King's Cross and sat there for what seemed like years. Mother Superior and the denimed girl had got off and gone their separate ways. Paul only had two more stops to Holborn and then he would change on to the Central Line and take it to Oxford Circus. Come on. Hurry up. This is boring. He watched the throng on the platform. As this was a major interchange with British Rail, the place seemed to be full of confused non-Londoners battling their way underground under stress and under strain. The skinhead with the peach of a backside walked past, his Doc Martens like concrete boots pulling his dead feet back to the ground. He obviously couldn't find the right exit. Paul examined a large poster for Hennes and Mauritz. A Kate Moss-type model crouched with her knees where her breasts might have been, wearing a see-through white blouse with dagger collar and wide-flared white pants. Yes. The seventies were indeed back. Paul had hated the Seventies, at least his time at Trafalgar Television. Thank God that was well in the past. When he came to think about it, this was King's Cross and half of that lot were now working somewhere overhead at The Station. Not right at the moment, this being Saturday, but on weekdays. Who was there exactly? Michael. Who else?

Martin Fox. The Sly One. Jesus. That was him walking along the platform. Perhaps he was working over the weekend. Well, he probably was with the biggest revolution in TV since colour television to launch in a few months' time. Well preserved for a straight man of his age. He was going to get on this train. Paul hoped he didn't see him. He didn't appear to. Fancy him using public transport. The train finally lurched alive, stopped dead with a shotgun bang and then shuffled forward.

Would Martin recognise him nowadays? Of course not. Martin had been somebody at Trafalgar. Everyone knew *him*. Everyone knew The Sly One. But Paul was just a faggy secretary with five minutes of fame to his credit as Karen Myhill's doormat. The doormat who ratted on her getting laid in the security film library. And who was doing the laying that day? Martin Fox? Could be. Paul was never that sure. When he had come into work the following morning, not knowing whether or not he still had a career in TV, he had ignited the inter-company secretarial bush telegraph with the hottest story to hit TV for years. Margaret Thatcher's general election victory paled into insignificance in the Trafalgar Television offices. People had been staggered that Karen Myhill had had sex at all, let alone on the office floor and with a man wearing a wastepaper basket on his head. The story soon developed a life of its own. Everyone was *desperate* to know who the guy was. For a start because it was Karen Myhill, The Most Difficult Woman In Television. Anything she did was worth talking about. And it was a great office mystery. Everyone had been bonking everyone else anyway, but no one had thought anyone was bonking La Myhill. And because people had been rushing off early to vote that evening lots of people could not account for their whereabouts.

But there was more to it than that. The election of Margaret Thatcher coincided with the first of the big revolutions in British television. No longer would it run like the old Hollywood studio system with the BBC versus ITV. The government had quickly made sure that the BBC and ITV's duopoly was broken. Now there was going to be Channel 4. Sky. Cable TV. The Station. Independent production was born alongside Max Myhill. And with it the commissioning system, the tender, the deal and the TV entrepreneur. Most of the old dodderers had no idea how to get ahead. It was a new generation who took over. It was a bit like when sound came to Hollywood – who had survived the transition to talkies and who had not. Karen Myhill had survived. She had flourished. She had made money. She had won awards. She had gone from strength to strength. And when asked or when interviewed or when written to, she always replied that Max was her secret weapon, her consultant who earned his weight in gold, her passport to the future. No wonder tongues wagged. Basket Case must be a top TV string-puller. Only he seemed to be Karen Myhill's puppet.

Paul had narrowed the mystery down in his mind to three candidates. Bob Dresler. His heart attack later could be explained by Karen's blackmailing and his arguing over Max, couldn't it? She was supposed to have been cataclysmically hysterical when she had rushed out of his office screaming he was dead. She had killed her own son's father. Or had she?

The best candidate was Martin Fox. He was now the head of programmes at The Station. It was funny where people ended up. He had been great buddies with Karen Myhill back then. They were in cahoots with each other. It would be out of character for Martin to cheat on his wife, but on the other hand, as Paul knew only too well, most men will fuck anything given half a chance. And look how Karen had repaid him. She had not exactly destroyed his career as she had done just about everyone else's. Part of Martin's success story was that he could work with The Most Difficult Woman In Television. She appeared to rate him, to like him. What was the kiss of death for the others had turned out to be his elixir of life. They probably were fucking each other, then. It probably was Martin Fox's arse he had seen. It probably was Martin Fox who was Max's father. And he had a rich wife, didn't he, a powerful wife, a wife with political ambitions? Karen Myhill could easily have wrapped around her little finger the husband of such a woman whose Something in the City career and parliamentary profile would hardly be helped by her husband fathering what the tabloids used to call a love child. Or, these days, a little bastard. That must be it. That *must* be it.

Probably. But not certainly. His third suspicion caused a Mona Lisa smile to settle on his lips. Most men *will* fuck anything, particularly in London in the seventies. Particularly highly pro-miscuous men leading a certain lifestyle. That was his boss's lifestyle back then. Not his boss Karen Myhill. No. His second boss, Michael Farnham. Oh, Paul. Would you ever have the guts to ask him? 'Michael, are you Max's father?' No, you wouldn't.

The train pulled into Holborn and Paul got off to change trains and to go and buy his panama hat.

Nigel stood in the doorway of his office. He took a short step forward, then one back again, then turned to go back into his office, then turned once more and stepped back out again. He was dithering.

Oh, make up your mind, thought Margaret.

Margaret was grumpy. 'She didn't say what it was about. Are you going to take it out here or in there in your office?'

'I'd better take it in my office, I suppose.'

'OK. I'll transfer it now.'

As he disappeared behind his door, Margaret tapped the recall button on her phone.

'Hello, Audrey? I'm just transferring you now.'

She tapped in Nigel's number and the phone rang in his office. He popped out a moment later. He sounded accusatory.

'She wasn't there when I picked it up.'

'She must have been!' Margaret was cross.

'Well, you couldn't have done it properly. You've lost the call.'

'It wasn't my fault,' she snapped back.

Serena rocketed out of her office. Madam had been listening behind her Venetian blind.

'Margaret, I really don't think it's your place to answer Nigel back. Obviously if Audrey Goldberg wasn't on the line when Nigel picked it up, then you must have lost the call.'

Your place. What century was she living in? Who did she think Margaret was? The parlour maid? She sent a watery smile in their direction. Old hag. Stupid old duffer.

Margaret worked off her annoyance by dropping back into her seat and pulling on her audio earphones and hitting the word processor keys as hard and as fast as she could.

Duncan silently pressed the door of his office shut with his foot. When he had heard Audrey Goldberg was on the phone for Nigel, he had acted smartly. What she was up to he didn't know, but he wasn't going to risk the lunch at Le Caprice repeating on him. As soon as Margaret had transferred the call to Nigel he had pressed 'call intercept' and diverted Audrey to his own line. A neat trick. Nigel and Serena could barely work this new-fangled phone system and didn't understand such features.

Audrey was fine and quite happy to speak to Duncan. She should have been paid within fourteen days of a new candidate starting and she had got nothing out of the MCN accounts department for Charlotte Reith. She ran a small business, cash flow, etc., etc. After he had reassured her and passed a few pleasantries, he was confident she had not understood the significance of his lunch at Le Caprice. Audrey was incapable of not pummelling him for information if she thought something was going on. So that was one less thing to worry about.

Serena strode into Nigel's office, where he was sitting at the round table. She pulled the door shut and slipped to the internal window and closed the blinds.

'What do you think we should do?'

'About what?'

'Duncan.'

Nigel didn't have an answer. 'I'm still coming to terms with him being a poofter. Fancy that. I've even been out for a drink with him.'

'It's obvious. I don't know why I didn't think about it before. He's over thirty. He keeps his private life very private indeed. I've just never thought about it before, that's all.'

'I wonder whether he takes it or gives it?'

'Nigel! That really is unacceptable! We don't need to know any more than we do. Really, Nigel, you mustn't bring your public-schoolboy attitudes into the office.'

'It's public-schoolboy attitudes that built this country, you know.'

'Rubbish. We haven't had a public-school prime minister for generations. This one didn't even go to university.'

'That proves my point. Ever since Supermac said we'd never had it so good, we've never had it at all.' Nigel sat back in his swivel chair and swung from side to side, rather pleased with his witticism. That was quite good for him. 'Anyway, old girl, what are you suddenly defending the great unwashed for? You subscribe to the Snob Club, not me. I'm hardly prejudiced. You know we're friends with that lesbian woman sort of across the street from us.'

'Where? In Chelsea?'

'Yes. Tricia and I speak to her. Well, we did once when Flounder went missing. At least, I think Tricia did. Or perhaps she didn't. Perhaps she just dropped the note thing through her door. Anyway, we toot or wave to the old dyke and her lezzy friend in their sort of garden thing when we drive past. You know who I mean.'

'I've absolutely no idea who you mean.'

'I mean that writer woman. She wrote that thing.'

'What thing?'

'That thing. I can't remember the title. It got very good reviews apparently. Didn't sell. Well, no wonder, really. Who wants to read about all that muff-rubbing in the sack.'

'Nigel! You're being deliberately offensive!' Serena sounded irritated. 'Well, it's not working.'

'Oh yes it is. You're all cross now. You're becoming shrill.'

He laughed and pointed at her. He had scored a point.

'Don't say that word. Look, concentrate on the matter in hand.'

'What plan are you scheming up this time? Just fire him, for God's sake. There're plenty more fish in the sea.'

'We can't fire him. Not on the grounds of sexual orientation. That's not allowed nowadays.'

'More's the pity.'

'The crucial point is not his homosexuality or gayness or however one is meant to term it. Nobody cares much about that any more. I mean, it used to be the love that dare not speak its name. Nowadays it hardly ever shuts the blazes up. The point is the fact that he's hidden from us a relationship with a client. One that could compromise our business. It's a conflict of interest.'

'Is it? I wouldn't know about that sort of thing. It seems to me the other chap is only in the legal department. I mean, he's not in marketing or anything to do with us. Does that count, then?'

'Of course. We'll make it count. He's a senior manager on the client side in a position of influence. But, Nigel, the thing is . . .'

She stopped and drummed her Tiffany pen on the table-top and then put it to her pursed lips.

'What?' Nigel yawned. Surely it must be lunchtime?

'The way to get Duncan—' She lowered her voice to a whisper. 'The way to get Duncan is to play the public persona against the private one.'

Nigel's face expanded into a flummoxed look. Serena went on.

'Duncan doesn't want anyone to know he's gay. He's obviously ashamed of it. That's our weapon. Not that he *is* gay but that he is ashamed to *be* gay. Frankly, we don't care if he's gay or not, as long as he gets the job done. After all, we're relaxed about that sort of thing. We're frightfully progressive. But he cares very much about us knowing.'

She put her pen down flat on the table, finished.

'Listen, old girl. Are you absolutely sure you haven't got this wrong? I mean that chap's voice—'

'I'm one hundred per cent sure.'

'Well, we need to be one hundred and ten per cent sure. Otherwise we'll end up with egg all over our bloody proverbial.'

'I know I'm right.'

'That makes a change!'

'Nigel . . . I shouldn't admit to it, but I had a rather brilliant idea, even if I say so myself.' Serena plucked her earring from her left lobe and massaged that part of her ear between two fingers. 'I've got proof.'

'Proof?'

'A friend of mine happened to ring me up and ask me about my pension arrangements. Well, of course, I was able to say that MCN had one of the best company schemes in London. And that set my mind thinking.'

Whatever effect it had had on Serena's, it had none on Nigel's. His stomach rumbled. Serena continued.

'It occurred to me that every member of the scheme has a form in the personnel department on which they have to state who will get their company pension or insurance money in case of death.' She smirked. 'I just wondered who was on Duncan's form.'

'Good God, old girl. All that stuff is strictly P & C. Even you can't go nosing around in the private files. It's not above board.'

'I am the board, I think you'll find. And so are you, for that matter.'

'Well, I hope no one's been leafing through my file, I can tell you. Rattling the skeletons.'

'Of course not. But I am able to pull strings. I just switched on my normal charming personable smile for that rather brainless girl they've got in there in Personnel and she let me check Duncan's files for pay rises. Pay rises are due soon, so it made sense.'

'Damned clever, Mrs Peel.'

Serena, pleased as punch at the reference, ceased preening herself and returned her earring to its lobe.

'So, what's the score, old girl?'

'At the foot of Duncan's form it states that, in the event of his death, MCN's insurers will pay out a lump sum of three hundred and fifty thousand pounds . . . to one Michael Farnham.'

'Three hundred and fifty grand? That's not bad, I suppose.'

'Uh! The point is who's to get it, not how much it is. That proves their relationship.'

'I thought you could only leave it to your trouble and strife.'

'Don't use that expression in my presence, please.' Nigel swallowed his snigger. 'Interestingly – well, I found it so – where it asked you to declare your relationship to the person you had named on the form, Duncan had written in "not a relation". Why couldn't he just write "friend"? Or "boyfriend" even!'

'Yuk! That would spread like wildfire round the building.'

'I suppose you're right. Anyway, that proves it. Awfully clever of me, don't you think?'

'Oh, yes, of course. But . . . thinking about it, there's not much we can do about it this side of Christmas. We need to keep Duncan on right through the launch of The Station. We can't rock the boat then.'

'That's precisely when we'll get him. Immediately before the launch of The Station. When he least expects it. The client won't be able to do anything about it. If they fired us then, it would throw the whole launch completely. It's not as if they could switch agencies at that late date. And by the time it's all up and running we'll be back in firm hands-on control.' She gave a little cackle, not quite in the Wicked Witch of the West league, but pretty convincing nonetheless. 'He's only got himself to blame.'

33

Cindy opened the door to a big bloke with strawberry-blond hair and a shirt and tie under a sports jacket. He was about her age. When he saw how she looked he gave her an especially wide smile. She was expecting a structural engineer, not a salesman.

'Why do want your property valued, Miss Barratt? Are you thinking of selling it?'

'I might do.' She ran over to the Sony system and turned down Marilyn Horne and 'Mon Coeur S'ouvre à Ta Voix'. 'I'm more interested in doing it up. Perhaps extending it at the back. I need an idea of what I can afford to spend on it.'

'Conservatory?'

'No, a second bedroom.'

'I see. Hmmm.' He was moving round the internal walls quickly and superficially. 'Not exactly a great conversion.'

He gestured with a damp-meter.

'I know. It could be laid out better. I'm forced to use the other room as a dining room. It could have been a bedroom if the kitchen wasn't on the far side of it.'

'Actually, I meant the standard of the building work. The finish of the newer walls and woodwork is sloppy, if you don't mind me saying so. The corridor wall is cavity with plasterboard. Not great for security.'

'I know. You could cut your way in here with a penknife! I didn't pay much for it. None of these old houses is properly converted. This is one of those cardboard cut-out 1980s ones. Would you like some coffee?'

'Fantastic. White with two sugars, please, Miss Barratt.'

As she turned her back on him he looked her up and down appreciatively.

She was wearing thin gingham check Capri pants. He noticed her white panties underneath. Just as he had clocked the faint imprint of her nipples through her white Gap T-shirt when she had opened the door. He followed her into the dining room and put his clipboard down on the table. He loosened his tie and unbuttoned the top of his shirt to reveal a tuft of gingery chest hair.

'You've done a great deal with it, though. All the candlesticks and hangings. Old pine.'

'It's all repro,' she shouted through from the tiny kitchen. 'You get a lot of it in Camden on Sundays.'

'I like your black clock. On the mantelpiece.'

'It makes a feature. Now *that*'s real.'

He heard her accent more clearly now she had raised her voice.

'Have you been in this country long?'

'About twelve years.'

'Did you come as a child?' Even he couldn't keep the smile off his face delivering that one.

'Did I hell!'

She rustled up the coffee in big, bright Italian pottery cups with hand-painted piggies on them. She held them up at tit level.

'Nice cups.' He said it straight. See if she picked up on the double entendre. She didn't.

'I got them in Divertimenti. It's a kitchen shop in Fulham Road.'

They went through the kitchen and out on to the patio, the patio that never saw the sun of summer and was instead hung with shadow on walls already gloomy with the matt-grey bricks of North London. Cindy floodlit it with the halogen security lamp that had been a bargain at one of the big DIY sheds on the North Circular Road. The engineer examined the ground and the outside walls. They discussed how she might build out and whether the plumbing could be rerouted.

'You've still to see the cellar and the bedroom.'

Hello. Cellar first. Finish up in bedroom.

He knocked into the Apple Mac on the desk.

'You work from home, then?'

'Yes. I'm a marketing consultant.'

'Busy? Or are you in a recession too?'

'There hasn't been a recession for at least two years, you know. That's one thing I tell my clients. Stop feeling sorry for yourselves. Get out there!'

'It's very damp in here. But you know that.'

'I do.'

He pressed his damp-meter against the wall. It emitted a high whine, the highest yet. They went back up the half-landing to the bedroom, on the darker side of the house. During the day any direct sunlight was netted by romantically draped broderie anglaise.

He laughed.

'I like your toys.'

'It's a bit girlie, isn't it? I even have names for them all.'

He laughed again. 'You don't. A big girl like you?'

'I do. The round bear with the shaggy beard is Lucy.'

'Lucy?'

'Yeah. As in Fat Lucy. You know, Pavarotti.'

He didn't know, but nodded anyway.

'The big black cat is Jessye Normous. And the little pink bunny is Rosé Carreras . . .'

Cindy giggled. She wouldn't go through the more obscure ones, so she avoided those and got back to business.

'This is the best room, with the fireplace and cornices and everything. It's all original in here.'

'I can see that. Very solid.' He tapped the walls and plonked his damp-meter on to the chimney breast.

'Except for the ceiling. You can hear the couple upstairs through it.'

He paused and looked her head on.

'Their television?'

'Their lovemaking.'

She blushed and felt conspicuously self-aware. How long had he been looking at her like that? Dirty beast.

Cindy was never instantly aware of the effect she had on the men around her. In fact, it was amazing, really, that she had ever seen a penis in its natural limp state. It was just as well she could not see this man's, throbbing hungrily away inside the pouch of his tanga briefs. She pushed past him and returned to the living room warmed by the red evening sun. He stopped off to pick up his things from the dining room and joined her.

'It'll take me a couple of days to put my report together, Miss

Barratt. Would you like me to come back and go through it with you? I could do that.'

'Just pop it in the post. That'll be fine.'

'It's no trouble.'

'Do I pay you now?' She was trying to sound more abrupt. 'You take Amex, don't you?'

'Yes. Er, do you fancy a drink? I saw a pub down the road. We could go there.'

'What? Now? No way.'

'Some other time, then?'

'I don't think so.'

'Do you mind me asking?'

She handed him her Amex card. 'I probably should, I suppose.'

'Do you have a boyfriend?'

Not a great detective, she thought at first. He had not spotted Alan's things in the bathroom. 'Although it's none of your business, I do have a boyfriend, as a matter of fact. He'll be home from work any moment.'

'Oh.'

He filled out the triplicate form in embarrassed silence. It took him for ever and he made more than the usual number of mistakes. What seemed like ages later for both of them, he said goodbye and hurried down the path and out of her life.

Cindy sighed and pushed the door of her flat shut with her back. She moved across to the CD player and relocated Marilyn Horne's mesmerising performance as Dalila.

Men, Cindy thought to herself. You just can't trust them, can you?

34

Towards the end of the day Duncan took a call from Briony Linden, his client at The Station.

'Can we meet, Duncan? Something's come up.'

'Sure. I'm free. Shall I come to your office?'

'No. I thought I could meet you at the agency or, if you want, we could go for a drink round the corner somewhere. You're spoiled for choice in Soho. I can't say the same about King's Cross!'

'Well, come to the agency, then. What time will you get here?'

'Say six forty-five, seven o'clock?'

'I'll see you then.'

By the time reception rang up, Duncan had arranged a room, a bottle of Pinot Grigio, some water and some coffee. Briony opted for the wine, produced her Camel Light cigarettes and lit up with relish.

'Is everyone else still working?'

'Orlando's still in his office round the corner, I think. Most of the others have gone to a softball match in Regent's Park. It's the one time people leave a bit earlier.'

'I hope I didn't stop you from going?'

'No way. I was glad to have the excuse. I'm not very sporty. What did you want to talk about?'

He opened his black leather folder and took the top off his Cartier pen. He loved his Cartier Pasha pen, named after the Pasha of Marrakesh for whom such a pen was originally designed. Duncan's, however, was not topped with a cabochon sapphire. Nonetheless, he had still forked out the best part of five hundred pounds for it. It was chunky and tactile and good for playing with in meetings like this where the client wanted to chat that *strictly entre nous*-type stuff. Briony wasn't speaking, though. She was smoking slowly and trying to think of things to say. She needed to get going. She made a stab at it.

'We must, *must*, move the campaign on quickly, Duncan. As I was coming through reception and looked at that poster I realised that although it's a breakthrough in metallic printing or whatever, it doesn't actually tell you what you really need to know about The Station.'

'I know. It doesn't now. It did at the time we ran it, though. It's that awful line at the end. It's a real company line that means nothing to the public.'

'Well, we've dropped that now.'

'I know. Good. So . . . well . . . I'm not really sure how you want to progress.'

Duncan turned his Pasha pen over in his palms. He was conscious of its layers of hand-applied black lacquer and the great weight of its fluted, solid gold cap. Briony upended her plastic lighter on the table-top and watched it fall over on to its side. She pushed it along with one outstretched digit, her head down and her focus following her finger.

'Oh, the campaign is not what I came over to talk to you about. It's something personal.'

Duncan's antennae tingled Red Alert. He stopped playing with his pen.

'Oh, really? Personal about you or personal about me?'

Briony looked up and tried to smile as warmly as possible. 'Personal about you, I'm afraid,' she said. She paused and puffed away.

Duncan instinctively knew what was about to come. It was an extraordinary moment for him; one he had always known he would some day have to face and one that he had recently realised more and more was coming closer and closer. And although he had not literally anticipated this moment, he had always wondered how he would react when he was outed. Outed? Exposed was more old-fashioned and melodramatic perhaps, but right now it felt like a better word for it. Exposed *was* a better word for it, decided Duncan, who had been a well-brought-up and well-behaved child and whose adult incarnation could only regard honesty as a necessary personal virtue. How honest had he been with everybody? How honest had he been with *any*body, including himself? Not honest at all. Now, to serve him right, he would be exposed. Exposed as lying by omission. Duncan had never lied, of course, Duncan had never told people he was straight. But he had never told them he was gay either. He had just never told them anything at all and had made absolutely sure they did not ask him. He had cleverly constructed and repeatedly rehearsed whole formulae of words and expressions that avoided the question or avoided the answer or simply changed the subject. From his teens onwards he had become first skilled and then masterful at this game. It was a golden art in which he was a self-taught alchemist, singularly articulate but doubly economic with the truth. Interestingly, the techniques he had picked up along the way had turned out to be just as invaluable in the world of advertising, where lying by omission or changing the subject seamlessly or operating unobserved were crucial political skills that had well served each successive step in his career. But did that at all justify his acquisition of such traits? Duncan knew in his heart that, for the sort of man he was or rather the one he tried to be, it did not.

And now here he was with Briony, a client no less, one worth millions of pounds to his company and tens of thousands of pounds to his own personal income, and he was to be outed, exposed, declared, labelled, branded, whatever. Curiously, amazingly even, now the great moment had at last arrived it did not seem so bad. Would it be worse if it were his parents he faced? Of course it would be. His oldest friends? Absolutely. His educational peers? Yes. His employers? Well, yes again, of course, it would be very much worse, and perhaps it was just as well it was not any of those as all of them were more important and more complicated and more repercussive in the tangle of his mind than Briony Linden. However much he liked her and respected her and needed to get on with her in meetings, in the end she was just a client colleague and she did not count very much in the total scheme of things. The long-imagined devil was not going to rise up from beneath the ground and drag him into the furnace of hell. Duncan did not feel terror, or fear, or guilt, or sin. Instead, he was unexpectedly overcome with relief, a new sensation for Duncan Cairns.

Briony spoke. 'I heard an incredible piece of gossip about you today.'

After everything he had just thought, Duncan's heart still skipped a beat. 'Did you?' His tone was dead flat.

'About you and Michael Farnham.'

'Well. Now you know.' Poor Duncan wanted to give a speech or say something of unsurpassed profundity. But he couldn't. He felt drained. He could only be unremarkable.

Briony was sensitive enough to storm on enthusiastically. 'I don't know him very well, of course, but I like him enormously. He's already one of my favourite people in the whole of The Station. Everyone in The Station rates him phenomenally highly. You're very lucky to have him.'

'Thank you.' She was laying it on a bit thick, wasn't she?

'How long have you two been together?'

You two. Duncan hated that. 'Ten years.'

'Gosh, that's a long time.' She paused. She puffed a bit more. She was giving Duncan the chance to say something. He realised this was probably just as difficult for her as it was for him.

'It must have been difficult for you. Coming over here like this to tell me. I'm . . . I'm embarrassed, I suppose.'

'Duncan. Don't be. I think it's terrific. I do. Really.' She blew a steam-engine's worth of smoke directly into the air above her, extinguished one Camel Light in the ashtray and immediately lit another. 'You organised the room, didn't you?'

'Yes. It was late when you rang. Margaret wasn't around.'

'I always know when you've done it, because I get an ashtray. A rare occurrence for me these days. Mr Attention to Detail.'

'That's just a courtesy. It's not meant to encourage you to smoke.'

Briony laughed.

'Who told you about me and Michael?'

'My secretary.'

'How did she find out?'

'Someone else told her.'

'Anyone I know? Or is it just all over London of its own accord?'

'Come on, Duncan. Don't worry about it. If you wish to keep it a secret, I'll honour that wish. I'm on your side. She heard it from Martin Fox's secretary. I don't know who told her.'

Duncan's blood boiled. Or rather it simmered. He controlled his temper, but he was furious. He was not furious with the secretary. He was not even furious with Martin Fox. He was furious with

Michael fucking Farnham. The blame for anything that went wrong now could be placed firmly at his door – and would be. Why had he fallen in love with this lawyer who believed in principle, moral courage and pernickety fucking detail? Duncan knew those were admirable things and that he loved Michael, not just for sex or security or anything selfish like that, but for those other qualities that made him so special. But it was precisely those qualities that had led to Michael betraying him. Michael had put legal niceties before love. He had put principle before passion. He had put duty before Duncan. Duncan didn't need somebody *that* special, thank you very much. He realised now – and was dreading it already – that he would have to have very serious words with Michael about the consequences of all this. Telling Martin Fox had been an incredibly stupid mistake, just as Duncan had told Michael it would be. They say straight men do not gossip, but they do. Everybody gossips when the story is a bestseller.

'Well. You've caught me out. I don't know what to say. I'm very closety about the whole thing. I hope you feel I haven't deceived you.'

'I'm not your mother, Duncan. One guesses that a good-looking man over thirty with no sign of a girlfriend is probably gay.'

There. She'd finally said it. Gay. 'So, is that what everyone thinks, then?'

'I have no idea. Come on, Duncan. The girls and I are hardly going to talk about that sort of stuff behind your back.'

'Oh yeah?' Duncan laughed.

'Orlando asked me once if I thought you were. I said I didn't know. He'll never ask you outright. He's a very private man himself. Well, he seems to be to me, anyway.'

'I'm not ashamed, Briony. I was a late developer, I suppose. Late into it and late to come to terms with it. I know what the business is like and so do you. You don't give unnecessary ammunition to those around you. Some people, mentioning no Clancey and Bennett directors in particular, can be very personally spiteful. Their backs are up against the wall, what with all the politics of a big company like MCN International. They've fired a whole tranche of people before me for less. I'm not making an excuse for not being honest with people. That isn't the whole story but it is part of it.'

Briony smiled. 'You don't need to be so defensive. That's actually what I came over to tell you. Something amazing happened today. It's funny how, when news hits you, it doesn't trickle out, but floods out. I think Serena knows about you and Michael.'

Her last sentence was a mortal body-blow to Duncan and he had not seen it coming. Briony Linden obviously did not have the real measure of Serena Sark otherwise she wouldn't have trotted out her little report quite so matter-of-factly. Duncan was staggered. He felt sick.

'Oh, God. How?'

'She saw him at the conference today and I think something rang a bell.'

'She sometimes speaks to him on the phone here . . . perhaps that was it.'

'I'm afraid I didn't get the lowdown on you until just before I rang you. As luck would have it, earlier in the day, I made an oblique reference to Michael in front of Nigel and Serena. I'm awfully sorry. I don't know that she knows, of course, but I think she might be on to your tracks.'

'God.'

'If she did guess, she was very relaxed about it. I'm sure she's not prejudiced. What could she do even if she was?'

'Cause me a fuck of a lot of trouble, Briony. When they get down to it, Godzilla and Dracula are malicious. They're paid-up members of the Nazi Party. Advertising's very own Adolf and Eva alive and well and out of the bunker. Anyway, it isn't who or what sex I'm sleeping with, it's where he works. As far as they're concerned, I'm having an undeclared sexual liaison with a client.'

'I'm the client, Duncan.' Briony's deep, dependable tone made it clear who she thought would be calling the shots if there was to be any fuss. Duncan hoped she was right.

Briony finished her cigarette and made a move to leave. Once she was inside the lift and had said goodbye, she thought better of it and returned. She gave Duncan a peck on the cheek – she had not done that before – and headed off down the stairs.

Duncan returned to his office and sat down at his desk, fatigued.

He thought no thoughts, but a loch-sized tear filled one eye and flowed outward down one cheek. The phone rang. It was Michael, concerned about the time.

'Are you still there, Dunky?'

'Yes. I'm still here,' said Duncan quietly.

'Shall we meet up?'

'Yes, let's. We need to talk.'

35

'Let's not go home yet,' said Duncan.

'Are you speaking to me?' Michael was not looking at him. Instead his eyes were glued to the horizon of the restaurant floor, willing a waiter to come up from downstairs.

'Don't push it, Michael. Let's go for a drive.'

'Where?' asked Michael. 'I have to be up early tomorrow. I'm not coming over to sleep with you tonight, by the way. I need to stay at my place.'

'Did you think you were invited?'

'Duncan, if you so obviously can't stand the sight of me, why d'you want to go for a drive?'

'We need to talk this thing over.'

'We've talked it over. I already know what you think. I don't need another fucking lecture. You just want to have an argument, Duncan. I'm not in the mood. I've had a long day.'

'And I haven't, I suppose?'

'Oh, don't get into one of your defensive Scottish gloom-and-doom moods, Duncan. You should see your face. You've gone all jowly. For a good-looking boy, sometimes you can make yourself look incredibly unattractive. Let's get the bill.'

When it arrived Duncan searched his pockets. It was unlike him to have left his wallet at home, but then he had assumed that Michael would pay. Now, after an increasingly acrid conversation, he was not so sure that he would. The waiter politely explained that the restaurant did not take Amex.

'Typical.'

Michael paid by scribbled cheque. They sat in silence. The waiter brought the cheque back. Michael's cheque card would only cover fifty pounds and the bill was for fifty-one pounds something.

'Jesus,' spat Michael unpleasantly. 'That's Britain for you.'

'Why do you all come to live here if none of you like it?' retorted Duncan.

'I didn't say that.'

Duncan barely absorbed what happened next. Michael appeared to be going out of his way to cause a scene. He had a stand-up row with the waiter over the non-acceptance of his cheque. His well-argued solicitor's points were beyond the waiter's endurance. He called the manager. So then Michael had a stand-up row with the manager of the restaurant. He made an exhibition of himself. Everyone was looking at him. Everyone was looking at Duncan. After some careful parrying by the manager, when service was deducted it was realised than the bill was under forty-nine pounds. The total could be met. The solution had been found.

'Come on, Michael, let's just go . . .'

Outside, Michael seethed on. He couldn't help himself. Unfortunately, Duncan couldn't help himself either.

'I have a two-hundred-and-fifty-pound cheque card.'

'You fucking would, wouldn't you? Well, fuck off!'

'Well, what use is a fifty-pound cheque card? No one has one nowadays. What could you buy with it?'

'You had no fucking wallet, that's what you had, Duncan.'

Duncan felt himself falling into an even fouler mood, and that foulness fermented in his mind. They crossed over Kensington Park Road and got into the Mercedes. They headed back not to Maida Vale or St John's Wood but down towards Notting Hill Gate. Michael drove along Bayswater Road, past the Russian Embassy and the touristy hotels, across the top of Hyde Park. The broad-leaf trees were illuminated and glowed yellow-green with baby leaves. They sped down Park Lane and past the Dorchester.

'I love that tree outside the Dorchester, all lit up with light-bulbs,' said Michael. 'Are you feeling better now, Duncan? Or are we still feeling down?'

'Of course I'm feeling fucking down. What d'you expect?'

'Jesus. Don't bite my fucking arm off. Is it all my fault?'

'Yes.'

'I can understand how you feel.'

'No you can't.'

'Yes, I can, actually. But I still think I did the right thing.'

'God! If you could just hear yourself. There is no such thing as the right fucking thing. Or, if there is, that wasn't it.'

Michael sensed that Duncan was set on having a big scene. He'd already had his with the restaurant staff. He had no energy for another. He thought that circling Hyde Park corner and taking in the graceful architecture might help defuse the situation. The gas-burning lamps on the portico of the Lanesborough Hotel were blowing in the breeze.

'They don't really work, those things,' muttered Duncan. 'Not with the wind.'

'Shall we go into Knightsbridge?'

'Let's not.'

'Where, then? Home?'

'I couldn't face it. I won't sleep.'

'Pushkin will cuddle you.'

'Don't try and fob me off with the fucking cat, Michael.'

'You're the one who calls her your baby.'

Duncan tutted sullenly. 'Don't take the piss. Haven't you done enough damage for one day?'

'Let's go down the Mall, then.'

They sat at the lights facing the recently restored monumental stone gate into Hyde Park, a sort of triumphal-arch arrangement by Decimus Burton.

'London is a very beautiful city,' said Michael.

'It's laid out all wrong.'

'Nothing pleases you ever. How?'

'You can't see any of the buildings properly. Not like in Paris. Or in Edinburgh.'

'Edinburgh!'

'Edinburgh is a beautiful city. It's all laid out in rows and circuses and it's neat and symmetrical. I happen to like that.'

'You like everything neat and tidy, don't you?'

'Yes I do, actually. So do you, judging by your recent behaviour. I'd like to pick up all the buildings in London and lay them out neatly in a grid pattern and put all the nice ones next to each other for tourists to look at. Bring order out of chaos.'

'And then go home and iron your underpants.'

'Fuck off. I don't iron my underpants.'

'You ironed your swimming trunks when we went to California last year.'

'I never fucking did. Piss off.'

'It's a sign of being sexually repressed.'

'Are you itching for a fight?'

'I thought you were.'

'I'm not sexually repressed, Michael. What I am is discreet and in a very vulnerable situation at the moment and what you have done is to completely shatter the whole scenario.'

'Don't be such a little drama queen, Duncan.'

Duncan, who anyway detested being referred to as a queen, smarted at the tone of dismissal in Michael's voice. 'Don't use language like that about me.'

'You *are* repressed!'

'You just can't see what you've gone and started, can you, Michael? You always have to put me down and treat me like some little runaround because I'm ten years younger than you. Well, I've grown up since you first met me, only you don't seem to have noticed. I'm equal to you. We're supposed to be partners. You're supposed to talk things through with me and agree things, not stitch me up and finish my career behind my back because it seems a sensible move in your own dreary career.'

'Balls! You're just worried that everyone will find out you're gay. Well, have I got news for you. They all know already, Duncan.' Michael meanly spelled it out. 'They All Know!'

Duncan bit his lip and fought back the tears of defeat from running into those of seething resentment. Right now he needed Michael more than ever, but he also wanted to hurt him more than ever, too. He tried to concentrate on their surroundings.

Constitution Hill seemed rural and plain compared to the other more formal streets, flanked as it was by the sandy bridleway on the left and the unadorned brick walls of Buckingham Palace garden on the right. The Mercedes shot out past the forecourt of the palace and spun round one side of the Victoria Memorial. Michael had one hand on the wheel and let the power steering take them round.

'Buck House looks so white, like a big cake.' His chattering cheeriness was hugely irritating to Duncan, and he knew it. 'Why doesn't the old Queenie-pops have it all lit up?'

'It's not a music hall.'

The full length of the Mall was dressed with Union Jacks and green and yellow and black flags repeating all the way to Admiralty Arch.

'Whose flag is that?' asked Michael.

'How d'you expect me to know?'

'Normally, you know everything.'

'Fuck off.'

'It looks African. Must be a Commonwealth person visiting. I think it's Zimbabwe. I'll look in the *Independent* tomorrow and see if Mugabe is here.' They proceeded past Marlborough and Clarence Houses and towards the massed white stucco of the Nash terraces. 'Still angry with me?'

'I'm extremely angry with you. I'm also deeply wounded.'

'Don't exaggerate. That's one of your friend Cindy's soap scripts talking.'

'Leave her out of it. I just can't believe you told him about me.'

'I had to.'

'You did not *have* to. You *chose* to. Because you've got the fucking pernickety mind of an up-his-arse lawyer.'

'You'll get over it.'

For the first time ever Duncan felt like thumping Michael. Hard.

'Duncan, I'm not lying to cover up your insecurities.'

'No one asked you to lie. I asked you not to volunteer the information. That's an important difference that even you should be able to grasp. What was Martin Fox ever going to ask you? Nothing. But, oh no, you had to go ahead and spontaneously spill your beans in front of him because you're more interested in covering your own fucking arse than helping me. Can't you see what you've done, Michael? Obviously not. You've been completely insensitive to my needs and totally obsessed with your own. I'll just get fired and humiliated and lose my home because I can't pay the mortgage. But you'll have your fucking principles intact.'

'I've thought about it. It can't have come from Martin Fox.'

Duncan's chest tightened with gasping, disbelieving, maddened astonishment. 'Well, who told his secretary, then? He did. Of course he did. He's gossiped it all over the building. You don't know, Michael, do you? If you're an out homosexual, people are always so right-on in front of you. Well I'm not out and I know what people say behind your back. And it's not pleasant.'

'Don't snap. I'm bored of you wallowing in your own self-pity. Face it. You brought this on yourself, Duncan, not me. You can really ruin an evening sometimes.'

'Sorry I ruined your evening. You've just ruined my life.'

'Is that what you think?'

'Yes.'

'Really?'

'Yes!'

'Do you hate me?'

'Yes! Yes, I do, now you come to mention it.'

'Shall we split up?'

'Yes!'

'What? Really?'

'Yeah. Why not? We're completely unsuited.'

'Is that what you think?'

'Yes!'

'Well, thanks for wasting the last ten years of my life, then. I could have been with someone decent who loved me.'

That was more than Duncan could take. 'Stop the car.'

'Come on, Duncan, don't be childish.'

'Stop the car!'

'Nope.'

'Just stop the fucking car. If you don't stop I'll jump out while it's moving.'

'Go ahead! Make my day! Throw yourself into the middle of Trafalgar Square, you silly arsehole. See if I care.'

Michael's forced, patronising, laughing response cut Duncan to the quick.

'You cunts!'

It was not Duncan that was now the object of Michael's wrath, but a pair of anoracked tourists stepping on to the pedestrian crossing in front of one the great bronze lions at the foot of Nelson's statue. Michael braked sharpishly and both he and Duncan were shot forward and then slumped back in their seats. Incensed, Duncan quickly flicked open the lock of the passenger door and sprang out of his seat-belt. He was on the pavement in a second and slammed the car door brutally hard behind him. Mad, he marched off along the pavement in the direction of Haymarket and Piccadilly Underground station. Michael kerb-crawled for a second behind him, the electric window on the passenger side rolled down.

'Get back in the car, for God's sake.'

Duncan pretended not to hear.

'You're making an exhibition of yourself.'

Duncan ignored him.

'Well, don't bother calling me, then, you stupid little bastard.'

The window shot back up and the Mercedes sped off. Duncan did not slacken his pace. Instead he strode on more purposefully than before. He glanced over his shoulder to see if there was any sign of a cab. He realised it would have been quicker to have headed for Charing Cross which was nearer than Piccadilly Circus, but this was all a gesture of pain and anger and hurt, not a test of the quickest way home. He was struck by a sudden thought.

'Fuck.'

He had come out without his wallet. Michael had been paying for dinner. Duncan had no money for either a cab or a tube. He would have to walk all the way home. He had never walked far across central London like this before. He had never forgotten his wallet like this before. He had never forgotten himself like this before. He pulled his navy blue four-button jacket around him and wrapped it nearer his body. Duncan shivered with the stinging slap of the cold night air on his drawn face. But that was nothing compared to the chill he felt inside, the inner coldness of the consequences of what he had just done: of being alone and unloved for the first time in ten years.

36

Max Myhill sat thinking in his black bedroom in his mother's house in Hampstead. His milky face was luminescent, lit from below by the the green type on the monitor of his computer. Consequently, his features took on the mystic glow of an underlit monument at night. His mother's bird-like face was suddenly there at the door, all beak and wide-oval bejewelled spectacles. Sensing her presence, Max cleared the screen and turned slowly and silently, pre-empting her.

'Kar?'

She was taken aback.

'Don't call me that, Max.'

'Kar.'

'Don't call me that, Max! I don't like it. Call me Mummy or Mum, please.'

Max replied with cool disdain.

'Kar, young men do not refer to their mothers as "mummy".'

'Well, mum, then. Or even mother.'

'I've decided to call you Kar.'

'You've decided? Christ, Max, don't be so pompous. I've never been called Kar in my life. It makes me sound like a – well, a car. I don't want you calling me Karen either. I don't want you calling me by my name.'

'Why not?'

'Because I don't, that's why. God, you're being irritating.'

'On the contrary, Kar. You are being irritating. You are being irrational. We can debate whether I call you Kar or Karen. I accept that. But the "mum" bit isn't on.'

'Don't try it on with me like this, Max. What's got into you? Mummy is under a lot of pressure. And you're not helping.'

'I thought I'd given you a great deal of help actually. Kar.'

'Oh, you have, darling, you have. Just don't call me that.'

'Why?'

'Because sons don't call their mothers by their first names, do they?'

'Some do.'

'Well, it's not the done thing. It's not conventional.'

'Not conventional?' Max might have laughed if he ever laughed. But he didn't, so he didn't. 'Convention isn't exactly alive and well and living in our house. Is it?'

'Oh, Max, please don't be cruel. Don't make me feel guilty.'

'It's not conventional to be brought up in a single-parent household—'

'Yes it is! It's completely normal. You've been listening to those Christians in the government again, haven't you?'

'No need. I'm quite capable of thinking up my own original thoughts. Anyway, you voted for them. And you interrupted me.'

'I know what you're going to say. You were brought up by a woman who will not tell you who your father is.'

'Good. That shows that you have at least understood my predicament.'

'Max, I've told you time and time again, I will tell you about your father and my relationship with him when the timing is appropriate. I'm sorry I suggested it was recently, but the turn of events meant that it wasn't. I've said I'm sorry.'

'I'm old enough to know now, Kar.'

'No you're not. And calling me by that name when I've repeatedly asked you not to is a sign of your emotional immaturity.'

'Hardly.'

'Max, when you're older you'll understand that intelligence and intellectual ability are not the same thing as being able to deal with life and relationships and trauma and love and sex and things like that. You're very clever but you're still a child.'

'That's something I'm working on every day. I think you won't tell me so that you have power over me. It's a well-practised management technique, albeit a lousy one. The retention of power by the withholding of information.'

'Jesus Christ! God only knows how I gave birth to a child who talks like a fucking management training manual!'

'God knows, but Max doesn't. You hold the solution.'

'Max, you're being exasperating. You're a reptile.'

'You should be pleased I'm like this. Other single mothers' sons at my age indulge in truancy or drug abuse or transvestism.' His face took on a threatening expression. 'Or worse . . .'

'I'd happily exchange all three any day of the week! They're normal! You, on the other hand, have the personal traits of a computer.'

'Lucky I do, then. Kar, it really is time you updated my technology. I'm long overdue a powerbook.'

'What? One of those portable things? A waste of money, Max. They cost twice the price and do half as much. You don't need one anyway. You never go anywhere. Where would you take it?'

'I go to school. Only, I might add, to comply with the law.'

'Well, you're not taking one of those things to school. It'll get stolen in two seconds flat. Brain of Britain you may be, but streetwise my son is not.'

Max slumped into silence for a while, then realised his mother was going to continue hovering.

'What is it?'

'Well . . .' Karen was quite excited, and now she let it show. 'That advertising person we've been talking about.'

'Duncan Cairns. Stop calling him "that advertising person".'

'Max, don't be so sullen about everything. I've almost made the offer to him. We've discussed terms.'

'I thought the company was about to go bankrupt. I thought we were on the edge of the abyss. How are you going to afford him?'

'Well, there's The Station game-show commission.'

'If we get it.'

'It's chicken and egg, Max. If I don't bring in the right person now we won't get the commission. But I can't afford to bring in the person without the funds from winning the commission.'

'That's a Catch 22, not a chicken and egg.'

'Whatever it is, Max, I just need to think it through a bit more. He'd have to take a huge cut in salary. And leave his career. I have to be sure I'll be committed to him. I can't go round ruining people's lives.' If the television community had heard that one!

'What's he going to do?'

'Programme development. Come up with ideas.'

'You and I do that. We don't need him.'

'No. He's good at the sorts of ideas you and I don't have. He's got a very focused mind. He talks about strategic thinking and management of creative resources.'

'Blinding you with science, by the sounds of it. Don't hire him.'

'Do you think I'm making a mistake?'

'Yes. We don't have the funds. He has no experience. What good idea has he told you so far?'

'Well . . . not one specific idea I'd go with, really.'

'Talked himself out of a job already, then. Myhill Productions is just too small and too rickety financially to take on freeloading executive staff. Even if you halve his pay he'll still be a drain on resources. Then I'll never get my powerbook. Stick to freelancers and short-term contracts.'

'So you think I should say no?'

'I didn't realise I was being that mysterious, Kar.'

Karen wanted Max's approval. She could not contemplate hiring Duncan against Max's wishes. And saying no and calling her that name all in one sentence was too much. She blew her top.

'Don't call me that, Max!'

'OK. Let's make a deal on it. We'll have an equal two-way relationship. I'll call you "mum" if you reciprocate and call me "son".'

Karen was so angry she stormed out of the room and slammed the bedroom door so hard that Max's picture of Richard Branson slipped from the shelf and smashed on the floor.

Max returned to his computer. He reopened his document, a masterpiece. Employing as an inspiring guide a commercial research questionnaire on the usage of and attitudes towards frozen foods, something that had recently been randomly shoved through the letter-box and addressed to his mother, Max had produced a simply stunning example of a seemingly generic research survey of the nation's demographics and attitudes to modern lifestyles. Only, while it looked as if twenty thousand people across the country would be receiving one, Max's questionnaire was intended to be sent to just two candidates. Two candidates – the only ones in his mother's Psion organiser with the initials MF.

Max pulled open the topmost drawer of his desk and drew it forward on its silent runners. He produced his mother's mobile telephone, surreptitiously slipped out of the glove compartment of her car. At this time of evening all local calls were free and would not register later on her itemised printout. He first pressed 141 so that his call could not be traced back to source and then called The Station's number.

'Night security.'

'Good evening. Could I just quickly check a couple of job titles on your phone list, please.'

'Oh. I don't know if I can help you there. What was it you was wantin'?'

'The correct job title for Martin Fox. It's on your phone list.'

'Right you are. 'Ere it is. Fox, Martin P., Controller of Programmes.'

'What's his room number?'

'Free four two.'

'And Michael Farnham?'

'Farnham, Michael. No initial. Head of the Legal Team. Two two six. Is that what you was wantin' to know?'

'Yes indeed. Thank you very much. That's very kind of you.'

'You're welcome, madam.'

Madam! Max was momentarily maddened, and then almost immediately delighted that his youthful pitch had helped further to cover his tracks.

Had he thought of everything? Could he fall at the final hurdle? One late ruse entered his mind. He pressed last-number recall on the telephone.

'Night security.'

'Hello, it's me again.'

''Allo, madam.'

'I forgot one name. Could you tell me who the marketing director is, please. I know it's a woman.'

'Hang on. I'll have to go through the list.' Max listened attentively to the rustle of papers as a ragged fingernail was run up and down the long list of names.

'I can give you a Head of Marketing. I don't know whether it's a woman or not. I can't tell from the name.'

'That'll do nicely.'

'Linden. I can't say the first name. I'll spell it for you. It's B.R.I.O.N.Y. Initial also B. Free free nine.'

'Thank you. Goodbye.'

'Bye now, darlin'.'

This time Max really resented the mistaking of his gender and the over-familiarity, but at least he had achieved exactly what he had set out to.

Briony Linden. Head of marketing. As a smoke-screen she would receive the same generic questionnaire into attitudes to modern lifestyles. Marriage. Divorce. Affairs. Single-parent families. Half-brothers and half-sisters. Children born out of wedlock. That sort of thing. Your attitude to these subjects. Your experience of (in strictest confidence). Please tick relevant box. Please specify. Write details in space provided.

They would answer fairly and fully in the safe knowledge that their strictly private and strictly confidential and strictly unidentifiable responses would be known only to the company that had issued the questionnaires. Max smiled smugly to himself. His opening of an anonymous post office box number at Trafalgar Square post office, where the returns would be received, was, he thought, a stroke of genius bordering on the criminal. Watch your mail, Martin P. Fox. Watch your in-tray, Michael Farnham. Watch your answers, both. One of these two guys would indirectly admit to being his father and unknowingly write back to his own son to tell him.

'We should go somewhere and drown our sorrows, you and I,' said Cindy.

'Let's not bother,' said Duncan. 'There's nowhere round here, anyway.'

'That's for sure. Isn't this ghastly? I wish we had some choccies.'

Duncan was driving Cindy on a rare foray into the shabbier parts of the East End. Her lack of interest in map-reading and his dejected driving had combined to put eternal minutes on their journey. Traffic lights, painfully planted on every corner, greeted them by turning red and glaring at them for daring to drive down deserted roads, making them wait for no apparent rhyme or reason. Nothing crossed their path.

On a whim of Cindy's, to cheer them both up, they were heading for the London Architectural Salvage Company, a treasure-chest of outsized Gothic goodies ripped from the vandalised walls and ceilings and floors of London's past and, according to Cindy, laid out for sale like the props from *Citizen Kane*. These two had every intention of looking, touching, fantasising but, between them seasoned Sunday shoppers, none of buying.

The Sabbath streets were deserted. In fact, much of that part of London looked like a wasted no-man's land. It was difficult to believe that anyone still lived here or even came here any more. Even some of the decrepit wholesale shops selling saris were boarded up. On the side of one high, white-painted corner building, the names Sami and Salim were spelled out vertically in huge bright blue plastic letters running down several floors. An eyesore anywhere else, here the building had all the relative beauty of the Taj Mahal, surrounded as it was by scrap and squalor. This place had been first besieged and then deserted by generation after generation of immigrant ghetto groups who each in turn had worked their way out of some hell or other and into the social assimilation the British prefer. The Huguenots had come and left first, then the Eastern European Jews. Now even most of the Asians from the sub-continent were long gone too. There didn't seem to be any new takers for the East End. It looked to Duncan as if that was it. It was time for the East End to shut up shop.

There were more windowless walls here than it was possible to imagine. They just went on and on, never running out of brick, never running out of grime. You couldn't see the end of the road, just the thin, uneven lines of brick on either side, wavering ever onward. Duncan decided he was developing an aversion to brick. As a Scot he had never liked the nineteenth-century brick buildings of London. That century in Scotland was a period of stone. Brick spelled out manufactured poverty to one raised on the quarried grandeur of his native Edinburgh. Also bored with the view, or rather the complete absence of one, Cindy spoke.

'We're nearly there. I remember this bit.'

Duncan did not reply.

'Oh, cheer up, Dunky. This is meant to be fun. Turn left here.'

Duncan flicked on the indicator. A green light winked at him from the dashboard. The indicator stick clicked back upwards again. Still he said nothing.

'Duncan, it really doesn't sound as final as you seem to think. It's just a short-term rift.'

'Two days.'

'Huh!'

'Don't be so unsympathetic.'

'I'm not being unsympathetic. God, if you only had the relationship I have! I hardly see Alan from one end of the week to the other. I go days without a telephone call.'

'That's precisely it. I don't have the relationship you have. I don't go days without a telephone call.'

'Here it is. Pull in here.'

Duncan parked the car in the empty one-way street. Old industrial buildings lined the right-hand side of the road just like all the others in this part of the city, but on the left, behind a high mesh fence, loomed a vast, ugly, Victorian Gothic church. It could never have welcomed worshippers. It was simply too frightening. But its forecourt was filled to the brim with an antique jumble of florid metal furniture and fantasy fountains and free-standing columns. Even from the car Duncan could see that every pedestal had a pillar on it and that every pillar sprouted a gargoyle or a tortured shape in rusted wrought iron.

'Norma Desmond lives here,' quipped Cindy. She fumbled with the door lever. 'Hey, you've locked me in. Do you wear iron knickers or what?' She tried to be more understanding of Duncan's condition. 'Good idea, though. I wouldn't drive round here on my own.'

Duncan released the central locking and they got out of the car. He hit the infrared beam on his key fob and the central locking clunked shut again. They stepped on to the pavement and Cindy stood back, sucking up the spectacle. She tried to pull Duncan by his sleeve but something else had grabbed his attention. There was a crumpled Pepsi Max can lying beside a full bin at the side of the street. To Cindy's astonishment, Duncan broke away from her grip and stepped over and impulsively booted it into the gutter and along the edge of the road. It clang-clanged as it went.

'I wish other people weren't so untidy,' he moaned. 'Where are the street cleaners? They should be doing their job.'

'They don't have street cleaners out here, I shouldn't think.' Cindy smiled. 'That was a very un-Duncanish thing to do. Look. You've scuffed your shoe.'

'I don't care.'

They walked into the laden forecourt. The sun appeared not to shine past the street entrance and the busy space in front of the church was dancing with shadows. It was as if they had wandered into an Aladdin's cave of architectural styles, as if the Royal Opera House had piled up its theatrical gimmicks one upon another. Only this was all real and everything seemed to be oversized, an oversized reminder of an oversized century built around an oversized empire. The lot was here: Gothic, Neo-Classical, Indian, Egyptian, French Empire, general European, made-up foreign, non-identifiable. Real wood, real stone, real marble, real iron, real remnants of real history and real people. To the left, dwarfing Duncan and Cindy, a Gothic metalwork church screen, like an overworked garden gate in three panels each some forty feet high and twenty feet wide, provided a backdrop to the stone ornaments.

'That was here when I came the first time,' said Cindy. 'No one's bought it, not surprisingly. It's from that Catholic church that burned down in Eaton Square a few years back. Do you remember? The one where debutantes were always getting married?'

Duncan nodded.

Cindy squeezed past a wide stone fountain, hung with scallop shells in three tiers like a dumb waiter, and ran past a couple of worn obelisks, a pair of scaled-down versions of Cleopatra's Needle.

'Look,' she called. She wrapped her arms around an extremely tall fluted column supporting a Corinthian capital, one of six spaced out in front of the church screen. 'Aren't they fab?'

'For God's sake, don't pull it over,' snapped Duncan. He looked at a price label on a set of four cast-iron balls mounted on lions' paws. 'Jesus. These are nine hundred and fifty pounds. Excluding VAT.'

'Not each?'

'No. But still . . .'

'I didn't say it was cheap.'

'Nobody lives in a house big enough for any of this stuff.' Not even Piers, he thought. Piers would love to ramble round here. He would tell him about it.

Cindy had never seen Duncan so down-in-the-mouth. She had always enjoyed their explorations and adventures together. Duncan was nearly always game to tag along with her. Usually his company provided her with a rare combination of intelligence, knowledge, humour and the preparedness to indulge with her in deliberately appalling lapses of taste. Not this time. Worse, Cindy knew she had neither the necessary sentiments nor the vocabulary at hand to comfort and console her friend. She drifted away. She ventured up the steps of the church and into the interior. Duncan followed her. The Aladdin's cave continued, now with rows of marble fireplaces big enough to entertain in, now with lines of etched mirrors that had once reflected back scenes of coming-out balls, now with stacks of cherry panelling that had once clad the smoke-filled rooms of gentlemen's clubs. When Duncan at last caught up with her, Cindy was dreaming.

'It's sad, isn't it?' she mused. 'It's all so dusty and cobwebby. This place is like a cemetery for unloved buildings.'

'No,' said Duncan. 'It's an abattoir. This is the corpse of

Old London, its ribs, its heart. Everything is chopped up into saleable lots, dissected into take-away chunks. Look. There are twelve matching chandeliers over there from some old hotel in St Marylebone. But they're being sold off separately. They'll never be a set again.'

'It's a shame, isn't it? All this stuff is so magical. How could they rip it all out? In Australia this would never happen.'

'In Australia this would never happen because you would never have had it in the first place.'

'This is true.'

They wandered on, past painted Arabian Nights double doors thirty feet high where Cindy loitered and languished and reclined vertically in the bulb-shaped frame.

'Scheherazade or what? Go on. Tell me a thousand and one tales, big boy.'

'I'll tell you just one. It'll depress you.'

Cindy tutted and dragged Duncan on upstairs to a false floor suspended under the wide pointed arches of the church. Here were cinema fittings and polished furniture and lamps from the blown-up Baltic Exchange topped only by vitreous enamel basins and carved marble baths from decayed Art Deco hotels in the provinces of France. Duncan was strangely quiet when he next spoke.

'I'm feeling very un-Duncanish at the moment.'

Cindy released her grip. Obviously he had been dwelling on her earlier remark.

'Don't take it out on me, Duncan. I'm trying to be understanding.'

'Try a bit harder, then.'

'Piss off! Honestly. I've spent the whole afternoon listening to your "Woe is me" speech. I'm trying to be sympathetic but it's very difficult. You're still a lot better off than I am. The depths of your love-life are just about the same level as my peaks.'

'That's not true.'

'They are. I'm alone most of the time. Without you I'd barely have any friends. I've invested so many years in Alan but I don't know what I've got in return. I don't seem to be any further on with him than when I started.'

'Perhaps there's not any more to him.'

'God. You know how to cheer a girl up, don't you! I'm more worried there's not any more to me. When I came to Europe I had high hopes and generally I've achieved everything I dreamt of and yet there doesn't seem to be that much there. My life doesn't seem very interesting to me and yet it should. Lots of women would like to live my life. Why don't I? And I don't blame Alan. I blame myself. I think I'm suffering from arrested development or something. I feel lonely a lot of the time. Me and Princess Di.'

'We seem to be talking about you now.'

'Oh, sorry. I forgot you as a topic was monopolising the conversation.'

'You're always talking about yourself.'

'I'm a very "me" sort of person. Come on, Duncan, what's the big problem?'

Duncan sighed. His shoulders rose and then fell back lower than before. 'One of the problems is the pressure we're all under. Launching The Station is a much bigger thing than we all thought we were getting into. It's changed the nature of my relationship with Michael. He's so irascible these days.'

'How old is he?'

'There're ten years between us.'

'Mid-life crisis.'

'It's just work. He wasn't like this when he worked at Trafalgar TV. They were laughing there.'

'Trafalgar's old news now. You and Michael are working on one of the biggest events in media in this country.'

'And don't we know it. When we went out for dinner Michael was really bad-tempered.'

'You didn't push him to it?'

'It was some format of a new show they're doing. He felt he couldn't clear it because it's too like something else. He had a row with the head of programmes. So he was not in the mood to talk out what we should do about me.'

'You should have left it to later, Dunky.'

'How could I? I need to sort it out *now*. I *had* to talk to Michael about it in the restaurant. It was safe territory.'

'Yeah, but you should go easy if the other person is tense and irritable.'

Duncan sighed again. He was exasperated and did not know what to do.

'Hey, Dunky, cheer up,' said Cindy. 'All you've had is a bust-up with Michael. Has the ceiling caved in? Has the earth opened up and swallowed you? What's the big deal?'

'The big deal is . . . that every piece of my life was exactly where I wanted it. My relationship was long-term and loving. My personal life was discreet and locked away. My career was progressing along conventional high-flying lines. I knew what I was doing. I knew where I was going. Now, all of a sudden, everything's fallen apart.'

'Oh, it hasn't! Don't exaggerate. You're just depressed. Get something for it from your doctor. Prozac.'

'I don't have a doctor. I'm never ill. My life just seems unsure. I hate that. I may never see Michael again.'

Cindy scoffed.

'I may be outed at work and lose my job or suffer some other humiliation.'

'That's all in your own head. You're good at your job. You're holding business there. They won't take you on. They wouldn't dare.'

'They would. And I realise I've been side-tracked by Karen Myhill. She's let me take my eye off the ball and yet she's come up with nothing. I'm relying on her to make a decision and she's never even come back to me. She's let me down and I'm falling between two stools.'

'Give her an ultimatum.'

'I'm in no position to do that. She'll just say no.'

'She may not say anything if you don't.'

'I'm well aware of that. That's part of the pressure on me, Cindy.'

Cindy had turned her back on him and now she turned round again with a glittering prize pulled off a shelf.

'Look at these taps. Is that brass or gold? The water must come out of the dolphin's mouth, I suppose. Did you see *Now Voyager* the other night?'

'What?'

'It's an old Bette Davis movie. They keep running it on TNT.'

'I know what it is, Cindy. I'm just affronted that when my life is lying like a shattered mirror in a thousand fragments you're wittering on about what crap you've seen on TV. Sometimes you can be so fucking insensitive.'

Cindy smarted. 'I was going to tell you the message of the film, given half a chance. I'm not insensitive. I'm just not like you. And that shattered-mirror crap is hardly original. That was Maggie Thatcher's metaphor when she was playing for sympathy after she was ousted.'

'Ousted. Outed. What's the difference? Well, I knew someone had said it.'

'Duncan, what you have to realise is that your life is charmed, not jinxed. You've always handled everything really well and done really well out of it.'

'That only gives you further to fall.'

'Drivel. Look at yourself. You plan and order and organise and predict and calculate. It makes other people sick how you've got your life all down to a T. The rest of us just wake up in the morning and wonder if we'll get through the day, what next is going to hit us and whether we'll cope with it. Stop trying to control everything. You can't. Stop trying to be in charge. Join the rest of us. Join the copers.'

Duncan felt chastened by Cindy's outburst.

'Am I overreacting?'

Cindy manoeuvred. 'I hope not. I hope I'm wrong. Why don't you give Michael a call? That's what's really worrying you. One of you has to come down off his high horse first.'

'Why should it be me?'

'Why shouldn't it? Look, I know I'm no role model but when Alan and I bust up we bust up big. It's always me who has to get on the phone and do the crybaby bit to get him to come back. I have to crawl but I'm not proud.'

'You're a woman.'

Cindy was put out by Duncan's unintended sexism. 'At least I am a woman. You're just a big girl.'

Duncan tutted. His mind was clearer but he was just as miserable as when they had started.

'Tell you what, though, when you do all that weepy bit down the phone you can expect great choccies. Book a table somewhere expensive as well. Pretend you didn't realise. He won't complain. How can he?'

Duncan laughed. Cindy descended so easily into self-parody. 'I'm sorry I shouted at you.'

'Oh, don't worry about that. That's what friends are for. For falling out with.'

'That's what lovers are for.' Duncan looked down at his scuffed shoe. He did care.

'Compromise and be happy. That's what Bette did in the movie. That's what you should do, Dunky.'

At the door Duncan spotted a small classical terracotta pitcher. He checked the price tag. It was only thirty-five pounds. Michael would like that, he thought. He stopped and touched it with just one finger. It was dusty. Absent-mindedly he wiped the dust onto the corner of his jacket. He tried a smile for Cindy but his face was too heavy to manage one. He put Michael to one side and took Cindy up on her point as they left and returned to the car.

'Do you compromise?'

'All the time.'

'And are you happy?'

'I thought you were the topic for this afternoon, not me.'

'Just answer the question.'

'What was it again?'

'Don't pretend. You know. Are you happy?'

'Oh, don't make me answer that. Er . . . I don't know.'

'That means no.'

'No. It means, Duncan, that I don't go around thinking about it. I don't think about anything. That's my secret.'

'I can't stop thinking,' said Duncan. 'That's my problem.'

Duncan entered his flat. Even with Pushkin miaowing away behind the door the place seemed empty. It shouldn't. After all, Michael didn't live here. He never had. Perhaps that was part of their problem. He walked up the hall and into his cream-carpeted bedroom, Pushkin wrapped around his leg, bushy tail aquiver.

He removed his light summer jacket and threw it on to the bed. He should have put it in the wardrobe in its correct place but for once he felt like being a slob. Pushkin climbed into it and rolled herself up into a ball. He couldn't be bothered chastising her. Instead he accused her of being a hedgehog. He bent over to tickle her tummy. She had already managed to saturate the interior of the jacket with her moult.

'How am I going to get that off, baby?'

Pushkin purred.

The telephone on the bedside table rang.

Duncan stood and fixed it with his nuclear stare. Was it him? It had four rings to go before it would switch over to the answering machine. Letting the answering machine take the call was a cop-out. Three rings left. Anyway, if it was Michael, he wouldn't leave a message on the machine. Two rings. That would be too humbling. One ring. Duncan grabbed the receiver.

'Hello?' It blurted out of his mouth all breathy and high-pitched.

'Hello, darling. What's up with you?' It was Paul McCarthy. 'You sound as if you're in the throes of orgasm. In which case you shouldn't be picking up the telephone.'

'I'm not.' Duncan was annoyed. He did not like to be taken to task by Paul McCarthy. He sat down on the bed. 'What do you want?'

'Charming! I don't want anything. I'm just being sociable. Still, if that's the way you're going to treat me—'

'I was in the middle of something.'

'Having a wank?'

'No, I wasn't actually. You disturbed me.'

'Don't be so dismissive.'

'Paul—'

'I'll go if I'm not needed.'

'No. Stay. I need to talk to someone.'

'Oooh! Why?' Duncan had no trouble imagining Paul settling in for a chinwag. He might as well tell him. 'Michael and I have had a row.'

'You're always rowing, you two.'

'No we're not. Anyway, this was bigger than usual.'

'And?'

'And we've not been in contact for two days.'

'Two days?' mocked Paul. 'Is that all? That's a tragedy and a half, isn't it?'

'Be serious. I feel down.'

'That makes a change for you.'

'I want sympathy. I feel all alone in the world.'

'Where's Pussy?' Paul laughed.

'Pushkin is here. But she's not a substitute for a lover.'

'No. She's a substitute for a child. Well . . . I don't know . . .'

'What d'you think I should do?'

'Go out and have lots and lots of sex. That'll cheer you up. Use the opportunity. I know I would.'

'The opportunity?'

'You'll get back together with Michael. I have no doubt of that. I give you one more day. Then you won't be able to have sex again with someone else without being unfaithful. And since you're the only faithful gay couple in town, I know how much that means to you. So get out there now! It isn't infidelity when you've split up.'

Duncan laughed. 'You're ridiculous, you are.'

'I'm not. Sex is very therapeutic. I've just been on the phone all afternoon on my sex line.'

'Oh God. How did you get on?'

'Fabulously. Not that you'd approve. I have a hot date with these two guys this evening.'

'Two?'

'Why don't you join us? Make it even numbers.'

Duncan couldn't think of anything he'd rather not do than have sex with Paul McCarthy. The idea of doing it virtually in public was an even worse prospect.

'You don't seem very interested in me and Michael.'

'I'm not. You haven't split up, just had a tiff. If you were my lover I'd slap you. I've told you that before.'

'Why?'

'Because you're so prissy, that's why.'

'Look who's talking.' Duncan didn't want an argument. 'So you're running up your phone bill?'

'It's worth it. You should try it.'

'I wouldn't know where to start.'

'Have you got a pencil handy?'

'What for?'

'I'll give you the number. It's an 0891 one.'

'Don't bother.'

'I can hear the tone in your voice. You're desperate. Sex is a great reliever of tension.'

'I don't need the phone to relieve tension.'

'Hmm. The primitive type, relying on wanking?'

'That's my business.'

'Were you wanking when I rang up?'

'No, I bloody well wasn't. You're incorrigible, you know.'

'I know! Isn't it fantastic? Anyway, I've got the number now.'

Paul read the digits down the telephone. And, picking up a sharp company pencil on the bedside table and using the memo pad placed there, Duncan found himself writing them down.

38

'D'you want to stop now, Haze?'

Charlotte bent over to pick up the spare tennis ball rolling along the base of the net.

'Do you?' Hazel called back.

'The light's fading.' She used the back of the hand holding the ball to wipe the beads of sweat from her forehead and push back her damp blonde hair.

'Come on, Charlie, it's not bloody Wimbledon! It's not as if we're playing a game or anything. I thought you were meant to be "simply fab" at tennis?'

'Piss off! That was my mother I was talking about.'

'Oh-oh. She's in a temper!' teased Hazel. 'I know why. You took one look at me in these shorts and thought, "Christ, her backside is as big as Ayers Rock," didn't you? Didn't expect me to race round the court like Steffi.'

Charlotte stepped forward to make some caustic response but her sly expression was wiped clean away by a bullet tennis ball that almost struck her in the face. Instead it just skimmed the surface of her hair. She stood frozen in shock for a moment, then burst into nervous laughter.

'You all right, Charlie?' Hazel ran forward, thought better of leaping the net, and zig-zagged her way to her friend.

'I'm fine. I'm fine.' She started to giggle.

'What fucker did that, then?'

Hazel's stance suggested she could take on all comers. She and Charlotte were on the last of the line of clay courts at Paddington Recreation Ground in Maida Vale. They scanned the groups of adjacent players, but there was no sign that any of the thirty or so people further up the row was going to come and claim their ball. Charlotte pushed her hair back again.

'You need an Alice band, sweetie. Suit you.'

'A bit of a whopping cliché for a girl like me. Let's play the best of three games, then go back to my flat.'

'Brilliant. I spotted a Thresher's on the corner by the tube station down the road. We can drop in there on the way and stock up on some booze.'

They started on their three games. Charlotte couldn't really concentrate, though, and became progressively more hopeless. She was swiping at the ball and serving pathetically like she was sifting flour.

'What is it about you British girls? You're looking more and more like Sue Barker! She couldn't get it over the net either.'

'Piss off! Just because you're butch enough to cut it with Martina.'

Hazel stopped short and drew up at the net, laughing with mock shock.

'I can't believe you just said that. I am *not* a lesbian.'

The two middle-aged men playing beside them gave them a sideways look and muttered in low voices.

Hazel walked round on to Charlotte's side of the court and whispered it a second time.

'I am not a lesbian.'

'Oh, who's touchy now? I know you're not. I wouldn't be inviting you back to my flat for a shower on a Friday night if you were.'

'Well, actually, now you come to mention it . . .'

They were snorting with laughter when a second ball struck Charlotte on the side of the head.

'Ow!'

'That looked like that hurt. Who's the fucker that's doing it?'

The two middle-aged men looked across and shrugged their shoulders. Hazel's eyes flicked across all the other courts. Then another ball, now softly lobbed, landed between them and bounced away. Charlotte turned round and gulped.

Striding across the other half of their court was Steve da Silva, swinging a metal racket and fielding a lupine grin. His glistening black hair was blowing out behind him. He was dressed in a black and lilac lycra body suit with cycling short legs. The definition of his dark-skinned, muscled body was only slightly softened by the evening light. In the crotch department, weightily swinging as it was from side to side, nothing was left to the imagination.

'Isn't that disgusting?' hissed Hazel. 'I think I'm going to throw up.'

'Y-e-e-s,' said Charlotte dreamily. 'He's like André Agassi.'

'Well, that's not my idea of a recommendation. At least Agassi wears shorts over his pants. *That* is revolting.'

'What's he's doing here? This isn't his neck of the woods.'

'No. He's bound to belong to some smart club somewhere. He wouldn't play here. Knowing him, he probably followed us here from the agency. I wouldn't put it past him, that one.'

'Why would he do that?'

Hazel rolled her eyes skywards and tutted at Charlotte's naïvety.

Steve walked right up to them on the other side of the net and leaned over it. The top of the net formed a ledge on which he just happened to place his massive genitals, presented, seemingly, for inspection. Out of the corner of her eye, Charlotte reviewed the troops.

'Hi, girls. Enjoying the game?'

'Not the one you're playing, matey,' said Hazel. 'You could really have hurt Charlotte, you great kid.'

'Rubbish. It was just a bit of fun.'

'What are you doing here, anyway? Did you follow us?'

'Oh,' said Steve, 'I'm just out for a bit of sport.' That was about as much attention as Hazel was going to get. 'How much longer are you staying on court, Charlotte?'

'Oh, we were just finishing.'

'And?'

'Charlotte's invited me home with her for a drink.'

'Then what have you got planned?'

Hazel seethed. 'What did you have in mind, da Silva?'

His answer was clearly directed at Charlotte only.

'I thought you might want to go clubbing or something.'

Charlotte, true to habit, pushed her fingers through her hair. Her lips seemed dry so she ran her tongue across them. 'I'm not really a club person. Why don't you come back with us?'

Hazel looked at her, gobsmacked. She tried to break in on Charlotte's mind with her fierce expression, but remained unobserved.

'Are you showering here?' Steve asked.

'No. I only live in St John's Wood. We shower at my flat. I've got my bike here.'

'Sounds just like what I need.'

He yawned and stretched his big arms out wide. As his chest expanded, a large near-black nipple floated out from under his lycra outfit and then slipped back in.

'How are you travelling?' asked Charlotte.

'I came like this. I cabbed it here. I keep my things in the office.'

'Haze, d'you mind walking down to Thresher's and picking up the booze?'

Hazel was outraged. She didn't have to say anything.

'Well, you know much more about wine than me. Then tube it round to my flat.'

'Maida Vale's the wrong line, Charlie.'

'I'm sure you can get a taxi there easily. I'll take Steve on the back of my Ducati. It's so close, he won't need a helmet.'

Hazel let out a frustrated 'Christ!' and stomped off to the pavilion to collect her things. With Steve feigning help, Charlotte collected the loose tennis balls together and started off in the direction of the pavilion herself.

'Where's your bike, Charlie?' Steve asked.

'Just out there on Randolph Avenue.'

'I'll find it.'

'You won't mind riding postilion, will you?'

'Are you one of those fast-lady types?'
'You bet.'
'Then I'll just have to sit close and grab on tight, won't I?'

39

'Duncan, there's a phone call for you.'

'You take it, Margaret. We're just leaving.'

'He said he needed to catch you before your meeting.'

'Who is it?' Duncan was half hoping it would be Michael and half hoping it would not be. There still had been neither sight nor sound of him.

'He wouldn't say. Come on, Duncan, take the call. I'm bored sitting here holding.'

'Don't get grumpy with me, Margaret. I'm not the one who annoys you around here.' He couldn't decide what to do. He braced himself for the worst. 'Put it through.'

To Duncan's surprise it was not Michael. It was Piers MacLelland White. He had never called Duncan at work before. He explained that he was at The Station and would be presenting a debrief of a consumer research project he had carried out for the research department. He had just heard that Briony Linden from the marketing department was going to be there and was bringing the agency with her. Piers would, of course, be discreet. Perhaps they could meet up with Michael afterwards for a drink. Duncan winced. Michael had obviously not spoken to Piers in the last few days. He opted for stalling and, playing unsure of his diary, agreed to catch up after the debrief. He replaced the receiver and chased Hazel and Charlotte down the corridor.

The debrief was moderately interesting but Briony had already commissioned similar research through the agency earlier in the year. Duncan liked the way she sat there, confident and slightly spiky owing to lack of nicotine. Not once did Briony let on to the head of research that she already had her own lowdown on the take-up projections for The Station's breakfast service. Duncan, thoughts of his personal battles segmented away, was amused by this in-house rivalry. It was funny how all companies had their politics. It was also reassuring that she trusted him and the girls so implicitly that she did not bother to say 'Don't mention it' to him or the team. But then again he trusted her enough with his own personal 'Don't mention it' which was private just between the two of them.

Piers looked well. He was still tanned, and, with silver temples, he also looked wealthy and debonair. His weight loss was likely to be read as athleticism. Duncan had not seen him at work before. Apparently, Piers used to do quite a lot of TV research when he was younger, but he had worked less and less in general and almost not at all in the media field as he had got older. Piers didn't need the money. He did it for fun. No, not for fun. For something interesting to do which he could pick up and drop as he chose. Freelance market research projects fitted the bill. The truth was that he was not a natural researcher, coming from a class that took little interest in mainstream society. A light TV viewer, he struggled with programme references. Consumer goods' brand-names he knew mainly from AGB or Nielsen charts rather than from personal purchase. But he was an Oxford graduate who could turn his mind to any exercise and produce competent, if less than thrilling, results.

The research department people shuffled out with their copies of the document. Piers packed up his charts and switched off the overhead projector. Hazel yawned and looked at Charlotte. They needed to make a quick exit to hit the tennis courts again on time. First, though, they had some agency trivia on which to catch up with Briony. As the three women chatted through the routine pleasantries Piers gently gestured to Duncan that he would go down to reception and ring Michael from there. Duncan made eye contact and smiled, but he was really looking into the future and wondering if Michael would be part of it. He wanted to see Piers but he didn't feel this was quite the right time.

Perhaps Michael would wriggle out of it when Piers called him. He couldn't face seeing Michael for the first time since the split with Piers – Michael's oldest and closest ally – there at his side. That way Duncan would be rendered awkward and young and outnumbered. On the other hand he did not want to leave Piers and Michael to go off on their own and discuss him behind his back. Somewhere inside he was pleased that Piers had come along to resolve the situation unintentionally.

Piers said an utterly charming goodbye to Briony. Hazel and Charlotte made their excuses and fled, leaving Duncan alone with his client. He wished they wouldn't run everywhere together. It lacked the dignity appropriate to their career status.

'How goes it?' Briony asked.

'Fine.' That was a social lie. That was allowed.

'No problems?'

'None yet.'

'I'm sure you won't have any. Relax. You'll be fine. D'you fancy a drink?'

'Actually, I'm supposed to be meeting up with . . . a friend.'

'I think I know the friend you mean!'

'Actually, you don't. Not this time.'

'Oh, sorry. OK. Some other time. Sit back down for a moment. I've discovered some more information.'

Duncan sat down on the other side of the meeting-room table from Briony. It was a wide, thick, frosted-glass affair. It would make a stunning centrepiece to a modern dining room, thought Duncan, if you had the money. Briony looked tired.

'How are you?' asked Duncan. 'If you don't mind me saying so you look worn out.'

'I'm just a bit overworked, I suppose. I could do without the research department doubling my workload by repeating everything I've already done with you.'

'It wasn't uninteresting.'

'That just about sums it up. Anyway, no worries. I could have bigger problems. And I will have, believe you me. Anyway, what I was going to say was, I discovered the source of the old bush telegraph.'

'Really? Who is it?' Duncan pretended he did not already know. He could tell her, however, that it was Martin Fox.

'Michael used to work at Trafalgar, right?'

'Yes.'

'And you used to phone him every day?'

'I suppose so.'

'And he had a secretary?'

'Yes. Several. One that was there for five or six years.'

'And you used to talk to her and got to know her. Well, she now works at Saturn Productions.'

'So?'

'For Jamie Hirst. And you replied to a request of his for some research data on The Station. The secretary saw your name on the compliment slip and rang a friend here to tell her the good news. As it were.'

'Aw! *Fuck!*'

Briony was alarmed. Something had gone wrong. She had never expected that placid Duncan could be this displeased. 'What's the matter?'

'Fuck, fuck, fuck. I have a lot of apologising to do, that's what's the matter. I thought Michael had told someone he shouldn't have. I mean, I know who he told. I thought they had told someone else. But I don't think they have. Fuck!'

'No. I'm afraid it's just a small world.'

'Micro-fucking-scopic,' said Duncan. 'Am I going to have to eat huge helpings of humble pie!'

'What?' Briony did not understand.

'Oh, nothing,' smiled Duncan. And his smile became a beam and he swung his legs beneath the table, happy that at least one problem was sorting itself out.

Michael spoke. 'I've asked Piers to come down on Saturday when Paul comes.'

'Oh, that's a good idea,' said Duncan. He felt empty. He wondered if he was still part of the plans for the weekend. 'I hope the weather holds.' In front of Piers their conversation was polite and strained, almost enough for him to notice.

The three men were walking to a wine bar in that part of London referred to by commercial estate agents as Fitzrovia. It was characterless, but discreet. Duncan felt uncomfortable that he had been dragged unwittingly by Piers into exactly the situation he was trying to avoid. At the wine bar they ordered spritzers and after Duncan excused his lateness, Piers excused himself and slipped to the toilet.

For the first time in a quarter of an hour Duncan was able to catch Michael's eye. He looked at his lover numbly and reassessed him. His was the face of a stranger, or perhaps of someone seen in photographs but not in the flesh. Duncan was aware of the distance between them that they had to make up. It was distinct, it was measurable. He tried hard to think of something to say but he did not get the first word in.

'He has to go to the toilet a lot these days – Piers, I mean.'

'I know. It's sad.'

'Do you think he's guessed?'

'Guessed what?'

'That we've split up.'

Those were depressing words. Duncan knew he would have to make the first move. 'No, of course not.'

'He's known me for the best part of twenty years.'

'Why would he have invited us out together if he thought we'd split up?'

'To get us back together again. His dying wish. That's why he's left us alone. To kiss and make up.'

'I think he just needed to go, didn't he? Anyway. We haven't split up.'

'Haven't we? You leapt out of my car at speed. You said we were unsuited.'

'The car wasn't moving, actually. I'm not a lunatic. You said you'd wasted ten years of your life on me. And you swore. You've never done that before. You said much worse things to me than I said to you.'

'I did not!'

'Yes you did. You hurt my feelings.'

'You hurt mine. You're the sort that doesn't even notice other people have feelings.'

'That simply isn't true. I'm sorry if I hurt your feelings. I didn't mean to. But you *meant* to hurt my feelings. Although I take that as a sign of true love.'

'Eh?'

'People only try to hurt the feelings of those they really care about. It's one of love's paradoxes.'

'God, she's off. You're sounding like Jeanne Moreau or some such person. That's the sort of trash that Cindy comes up with.'

'It's not trash. It's true. You're only vindictive with those you're in love with. It's only with them that you can be. You don't care enough about people you hate or you're finished with to try to hurt them.'

'You've been through the mill of love enough times to know, I suppose?'

'Michael, don't be so dismissive of me.'

'I'm not being dismissive.'

'Yes you are.'

'I'm not.'

'Don't argue. Look. I know the real source of the story. It wasn't Martin Fox. So I'm apologising.'

'My God. I can't believe I'm hearing this.'

'Don't make it more difficult than it is, Michael. Despite the fact that I still think you were wrong to tell Martin Fox about us, I admit he doesn't seem to have told anyone and that I was premature in blaming you for compromising my position.'

'Martin Fox can keep a secret.'

'Maybe. But aren't you going to congratulate me on my climbdown? I think it's very big of me, myself.'

'It is very big of you. But that's why I like you. For your self-deprecating modesty.' Michael sniggered.

'Just "like"?'

'What?'

'Not "love"?'

'Do you love me?'

'Yes. Yes, I do.'

'Enough to tell all the world?'

'Enough to tell you. That would have been hard enough on its own yesterday.'

'You're a funny boy. Do you really think we're unsuited?'

Duncan sighed. 'I think gay relationships are destined to be mismatched in some way or other. Men and women can give and take more easily between them because they're different.

Two men are too much the same. What d'you call the positive and negative points on a battery?'

'I don't understand. D'you mean the electrodes?'

'Yes. It's like if you put two positive electrodes together you get sparks.'

'Sparks can be fun.'

'I know they can be but eventually you damage the battery and it won't work any more. Let's not let that happen to us.'

'Oh, Dunky. That's a clever thing to say. Did you just think it up or have you been practising?'

Duncan tutted. He sipped from his spritzer.

'You're so sweet sometimes.' Michael took his hand across the table. Duncan swiftly snatched it away.

'People will see.'

'Oh! Oh! Panic. Panic.' Michael laughed. His eyes twinkled. 'You'll never change, will you, Dunky?'

'I am trying. Just try and help me, not hinder me. Please?' He looked up. 'Here comes Piers. I'll tell you the whole story later.'

'I can't believe you've apologised.' Michael took the public opportunity to chide Duncan playfully and turned to Piers to do it. 'He's getting better as he gets older.'

'Yes, he is, isn't he? I remember a headstrong young Scot who used to upset my dinner parties.'

'I did not! You just used to have a bunch of vapid queens round, that's all. People should be told to their face they're being stuck-up and pretentious and queenie.'

'Those were the days,' sighed Piers. 'Half of that crowd are dead now. The other half are HIV-positive like me. A generation wiped out.'

Piers exaggerated but then he was entitled to. If he wished to cry into his drink, so be it. He had been happy executing his little project. It was over now. How many more would there be? Michael and Duncan shared a long, private look. They had had their ups and downs and now they'd even had a trial separation for all of three days. Yet they were happy and in love. Lucky them.

The phone rang. Nigel answered it. It was Margaret.

'She's here.'

'She's here,' repeated Nigel.

'About time,' said Serena. 'She's a junior. She's no right to keep us waiting. I wish we knew more about her. I really think Alan Josling could have come up with a better background briefing. Bearing in mind he's ripping us off for fifty thousand pounds for it. It beats me how these third-rate people survive in the business nowadays.'

'Oh, he has quite a good approach to things, I think. He has that sort of Jewish manner about him.'

'Jewish manner? He's not a Jew.'

'Isn't he? Looks like one to me.'

'Well, he's not. And you shouldn't be so prejudiced.'

'I'm not. I meant it as a compliment, really.'

'What you meant, or should have meant, is that we shouldn't trust him. Not one inch. The thing about Alan Josling is that he is a man of mystery. I've never worked out what makes him tick.'

Serena stacked her papers on the table-top and stood up. She smoothed down the fuchsia silk dress with Margaret Thatcher neck-bow which she had selected specially for the presentation. Actually it was by far her oldest dress, twelve years, but it had become her lucky outfit during a run of new-business wins the decade before. Serena felt its classic line hadn't really dated. She turned towards Nigel and crossed the room. She used her free hand to wiggle his tie-knot into place.

'There,' she said. 'Perfect.'

'Good luck, old girl.'

'We don't need it. Not today. We have inside information. D'you know, it's a shame there isn't a British mafia. I think we'd be rather good at it, all this skulduggery. Our trouble is, we've been far too nice to people for years.'

Adopting a two-faced mask of authority and charm, they

marched round to the lift. The doors opened. The prospective client was amongst them. She addressed the reception party.

'Hello. I'm Louise Thurrock, European Marketing Director of Japanair.'

'Serena Sark, Director of MCN International. I run Clancey and Bennett, with my partner, Nigel Gainsborough.'

'Hello, hello. Welcome, Lorraine.'

'It's Louise,' the young woman corrected him.

'So it is. Well done.' Nigel gave her a plump and jolly handshake. He always preferred it if the client was a man. Men were not exactly thick on the ground these days. Still, for four million quid he'd put up with another of the monstrous regiment. Whatever her name was.

'And this is Tako,' said Louise, looking back into the lift. 'Come on, Tako. Don't be shy.' A timid Japanese, a boy in a suit, followed her out from the shadowed interior of the lift. 'Tako is a trainee in our Tokyo office. His English is not up to much. In fact, he can't understand anything at all. He's on secondment to me for a fortnight so I thought you wouldn't mind if I brought him along.'

'Not at all,' said Serena, though her expression suggested otherwise. She faced the young Japanese and turned up the volume. 'Hello, Tako from Tokyo.'

'Hurro,' said Tako meekly. He nodded.

'Hurro,' chortled Nigel back, greatly amused at his own sense of bonhomie. He bowed deeply and brought his face up only after the blood had rushed to his head and left him looking like a crimson candidate for a heart attack. Louise Thurrock, somewhat surprised, raised her eyebrows at his seeming insensitivity.

'Shall we go through, Serena?' burbled Nigel, unaware.

'Yes. Come this way, Louise.'

They walked through into the meeting room where Duncan and Orlando were waiting for them.

'Look at those two bootlickers. Hello. Hello. Welcome. Welcome. I'm Serena and I'm Nigel. I'm too thin and I'm too fat. I'm Dumb and I'm Dumber.' Hazel, spying from Margaret's counter, was her usual caustic self. 'It makes you sick, doesn't it?'

'She spoke to that young Japanese man like she was making a

platform announcement at King's Cross station. They must have heard that in reception. And did you see the expression on her face when Madam waltzed forward in her fancy frock?' Margaret swayed her arms and hips a little to imitate her boss. 'You'd think with all her money she could afford something new. She's been wearing that old rag for donkey's years.'

'I can believe it. It's very old-fashioned,' said Charlotte, only too happy to join in for a good bitch. 'Why does she insist on wearing either chiffon or silk? I mean, it's not exactly 1990s, is it? And that bow! Presentation in advertising is everything. That makes her look such a has-been.'

'Well, she is,' said Margaret.

'And he's a never-was,' added Hazel for good measure. 'Are they actually pitching today?'

'God, no,' said Margaret. 'Wait till that happens. We'll all be up all night for weeks beforehand. This is just a presentation of credentials, although Nigel's got some ads or something up his sleeve supposedly. There was a real palaver over whether Duncan was to be in the meeting. Orlando insisted in the end.'

'Why?' asked Charlotte.

'Because Duncan worked on some American airline in his last agency. Orlando felt it was stupid not to make use of his experience. And Madam is so keen to get this she saw sense. In the end.'

'That wasn't what I meant. Why was there a palaver?'

'Well, they don't want him in there doing it all for them, taking it away from them, do they? Because Sir and Madam have their backs to the wall. And Duncan is the young Greek or whatever you call them.'

'Young Turk, I think you mean.'

Nigel had one last roughly mocked-up press ad to present.

'Now what's this one again?' He propped it up on its stand on the table and looked over the top of it.

'I wouldn't know. It's upside down,' observed Louise Thurrock dryly. She was being a lot more blunt than Serena felt someone of her age ought to be.

'Is it?' asked Nigel. 'So it is.' He turned it over. 'Well, we showed this one too to our businessmen in our little piece of creative research and—'

'What's it meant to be?' asked Louise.

Serena stepped in. 'It actually encapsulates in one ad what I believe the essence of your strategy should be. Simple strategies are strong strategies. It's pointing out the end benefit of your schedules from Europe when compared with your rivals. Because Japanair flights fly out of the West in the late afternoon, you deliver the businessman fresh in Tokyo at the optimum time – you know, at the start of the next day – so he doesn't lose any valuable time by arriving out of working hours.'

'I see.'

'Yes,' Nigel went on. 'The real thing would be photographs, of course, but just for the research we've drawn a face on the left which is all tired and baggy-eyed and sleepy – that's your rivals arriving through the night – and on the right-hand side drawn a face which is bright-eyed and bushy-tailed. That's the man who flew with Japanair.'

'And did they like it in your research?'

'Yes. Well, sort of. Well, not altogether.'

'Are we talking thumbs-up or thumbs-down?' There was irritation in Louise Thurrock's voice.

'They didn't get it, I'm afraid, because of the way we've drawn it up,' said Nigel apologetically. 'Better blame Orlando for that one. He only thought of it at the last minute. Because it's only a sketch, they assumed the wide-awake face was a European with normal sort of eyes and the sleepy face was a . . . you know' – he nodded towards Tako – 'a Jap, with slitty eyes.' He raised his two forefingers to the corners of his own eyes and pulled them upwards for the full effect. He gave a buck-toothed grin and held it.

Duncan cringed and then tried desperately to avoid eye contact with Orlando, whose heaving shoulders suggested he was having internal hysterics.

Although Tako appeared to have followed none of the meeting at all, Louise Thurrock, hugely aware of her colleague's presence, was horrified. So horrified in fact that she could think of absolutely no appropriate comment whatsoever.

'There are some things you still have to convince me on. Japanair is a young, go-ahead company. It's like a Japanese Virgin.'

'I wouldn't know. I've never met a Japanese virgin,' sniggered Nigel.

Serena ignored him. 'Absolutely. We think so too.' She leant forward and pressed the remote control to silence the fan of the slide projector she had used earlier. She pressed another button to bring up the parabolic spotlights over the meeting-room table.

'How can I say this?' said Louise. 'In your presentation there was a lot of good stuff, obviously, but some of the C&B successes were . . . rather old.'

Serena was surprised, almost intrigued by the remark.

'Do you really think so?'

'Don't you think you're relying on some rather old case histories? One of the awards you mentioned you'd got – well, I was still at school then.'

'I think that's more a reflection of your lack of experience in the business than any fault on our part.' Serena was determined to keep a lid on this girl. 'If you've been paying attention, what we've been trying to demonstrate is that we have a long and distinguished track record. Some of the other agencies you might be seeing are a bit green around the gills. You know if you look at the really classic accounts they stay with their agencies for generations because of trust and the relationship and everything. It takes years to build a brand.'

'I know that, although I hope you don't intend to take years to build mine. But there didn't seem to be much recent success. You know, since Clancey and Bennett came into the network.'

'We're getting new slides made,' said Nigel weakly. 'All that stuff will be in our new presentation.'

'Anyway, what I'm sure an experienced marketeer looks for in his or her agency is a genuine feel for their market. Hopefully Nigel's review of our research ads will have convinced you we can do that. Duncan!' Serena made it clear who was in charge. 'Pour Louise some more coffee.'

Orlando tried hard not to laugh as Duncan gave the client a knowing look.

'I've already declined, thank you,' said Louise.

She smiled at Duncan. This had not gone at all as she had anticipated. Duncan Cairns, when he was able to interject, had a reasonable handle on things, having run an airline account before. He appeared to be an able and co-operative Scot. Also, he was fun. Orlando, the creative director, didn't say much. Nice clothes, though, almost like silk pyjamas. He had a robust showreel and seemed easy-going. These two were what Alan and her brother had led her to expect. Fair's fair. But the other pair? Tweedledum and Tweedledee were bizarre enough to be fascinating. Louise had seen their video. It was like the 'before' half of one of those John Cleese tapes you used to get which showed you how *not* to run a business. She was beginning to lose faith in Alan's advice to ignore it as a hurried one-off. In real life, Serena was sharpish and just a bit shrill. When she wasn't scoring points, she reminded Louise of the Queen delivering a 1950s Christmas Day message to the people of the British Commonwealth. And as for him? Advertising's answer to Inspector Clouseau. Unfortunately he seemed to be in charge. To be scrupulously fair, Serena had given an immaculate and insightful review of the market, although her presentation was far too long. But she had nearly allowed her partner to sabotage it with irrelevant interruptions and proto-racist remarks. Hmmm.

Serena unscrewed the top of a bottle of Highland spring water as if she were wringing a chicken's neck. Her face cracked into killer wrinkles until the hiss of the carbon dioxide signalled victory. She poured herself a full glass and didn't offer the bottle around. That's a bit rich, thought Duncan. The whole time she didn't remove her headlight stare from her new client-to-be. Hopefully.

'How long have you been at Japanair, Louise?'

Serena already knew the answer. She was just feigning interest.

'Three months. I need to get my skates on and appoint an agency within the next twelve weeks. The internal politics is difficult, though, as you'll understand. Everything goes to Tokyo, where Tako works, for approval. Do you have an office there?'

Serena was quick on her feet. Unfortunately, for once so was Nigel.

'Yes.'

'No.'

They tried again.

'No.'

'Yes.'

Louise laughed incredulously. 'Make up your minds, for God's sake.'

Serena gave Nigel a sharp kick beneath the table.

'What we mean is that Clancey and Bennett is unique, as we've said. But as part of the MCN network, you'll find a sister office in most countries in the world. That's what we mean by "resources".'

'Clout,' added Nigel.

'So is there a small, separate bit like C&B in the other agencies in the network? Personal service is a very important part of my brief.'

'D'you know, old girl, I'm not absolutely sure how the whole thing works.'

Louise caught her breath. What had he just said? 'You're not sure? How do the other international accounts work?'

'The local foreigners run them.'

'Foreigners?' Foreigners! The man was talking as if we still had India. How on earth would he handle the Japanese?

'Isn't there international co-ordination? Isn't that what you do?'

'Well, sort of. It's a complicated business, this sort of thing. We travel round, enjoy a good chinwag and an overnight stay – we've been to Vienna, Milan, New York, even Tasmania in the last eighteen months. Lots of places. And it sort of sorts itself out.' Nigel pressed his portly frame into the table-top and leaned over to give Louise a good tip. 'Personally, I try to avoid doing business with companies in countries who've got green in their flag. Don't trust 'em.'

That thought almost stalled Louise Thurrock. But not quite. 'Who would be responsible for the international side of my business?'

Duncan jumped in. 'I think, with your area of responsibility, Louise, we're only talking about Europe, aren't we? And by Europe we principally mean business travellers from Heathrow, Charles de Gaulle and Frankfurt airports. So, in Paris we have a small agency within the main agency which we work with now on our Bencelor business. MCN in Frankfurt is regional, therefore quite small already. Rest assured, Louise, I could act as international account director to lead your business from this office and, with you in charge in London, I'd closely co-ordinate the whole operation. It's no big deal, really. Now—' Duncan stood up and reached across to the drinks trolley, 'what would you say to a glass of wine?'

'I'd say "Hello, glass of wine"!' Louise laughed and explained. 'One of Eric Morecambe's. My father's always doing that one.'

Duncan and Orlando laughed with her. Tako, munching a custard cream, laughed too, although clearly uncertain as to why.

Nigel and Serena smiled wanly. They had failed to pass the baton between each other. And having dropped it, the little bugger had scooped it up. He had just worked his way on to this Japanese airline account. If they got it, that is. Still, Serena was wearing her false smile. There was time for another oriental pleasure before the airline business was landed. Death by a thousand cuts.

41

Karen put Duncan's contract into the feeder of the fax machine and held up his business card in front of her glasses. She tapped out Clancey and Bennett's number on the keypad. He had said it was all right to fax it to the office, hadn't he? The machine beeped and whirred a bit. Then she heard the ringing tone and the ear-piercing noise. It was on its way.

'Kar!' Max came flying down the stairs.

No. It was not on its way. Karen couldn't press 'stop', whip the contract out and stuff it into the pocket of her coat on the peg fast enough. Dammit. She should have done this from the office, not from her own machine in the hall. None of the contract had gone through.

'What are you doing?'

'Nothing, Max. What brings you out of your room for once?'

'Were you using the fax machine? You were, weren't you?'

'Somebody started to fax us, but it didn't come through.' She tore off the end of the paper roll and crumpled it in her hand, pretending it was an error of some sort. 'Perhaps it will come through in a moment.'

'I didn't hear it ring, Kar.'

'Max, don't call me that dreadful name. I've told you before. Mummy's going out for a walk.' She slipped her coat off the peg and on to her wine-bottle shoulders.

'What? Now?'

'Yes, Max. Now. That's what normal people do, from time to time. They go outside, they don't stay indoors all the time. I'm going for a walk on the Heath.'

'Don't pick up any strange men, then.'

'I think you'll find the ones on Hampstead Heath are more interested in each other, actually. You can take a pizza out the freezer and shove it in the microwave if you're hungry. Or one of those Marks and Spencer fajitas things.'

'I'll just have a drink of something.'

'I got that Sainsbury's cola for you to try. Apparently it's better.'

'You just mean it's cheaper. You know I'm a Tango man.' He thumped his way into the kitchen.

'Lift your feet!'

He thumped them harder.

'And lock the door behind me.'

She undid the bolts and chain on the door and scurried out on to Flask Walk. That was Max all over. When it came to pizza and Tango, he was a kid. When it came to Karen's making oblique references to homosexuality or drug abuse, he was an informed and sophisticated adolescent. When it came to television and her production company, he was the senior partner. Which is why she was scurrying out of her own home like a sneak caught in the act. What to do? What to do?

She squeezed her way along the pavement, that narrow strip between the cars parked like sardines in the road and the protective garden walls of the rich and famous who constitute the chattering classes of Hampstead. She continued into Well

Walk. This so-called village on the hill somehow got darker at this time of year. In winter the tree-lined narrow streets were bright and airy, but as spring progressed into summer the dense foliage of the giant plane trees obstructed the sky to those at ground level. She hurried past the houses which got bigger and bigger as the eighteenth-century English domestic style gave way to nineteenth-century turreted fantasies. Boy George was supposed to live in that one, but Karen had never seen him.

She waited for a couple of cars to flash past her on East Heath Road and crossed over on to the grass. A sudden bout of panic overtook her. She clutched at her pocket. Duncan's contract was still there.

Karen realised she had slowly metamorphosed into a real Londoner. Nowadays, she imagined the breeze was purer on Hampstead Heath and that the landscape was interchangeable with the countryside. It was, though, wasn't it? Oh, what to do? What to do?

You see, the problem came in two parts. First there were the work issues.

What would Duncan really add to her company? Her first instinct had been to hire him. He was extremely bright, perceptive, thoughtful and original. The Station's head of marketing thought so too, according to Martin Fox. But she was not a programme maker. And, Karen admitted, she herself was no great judge of people. Only *The Word* had ever put worse presenters on television than she had. Also, with the hiring came the expenditure. Her initial plan to hire somebody had been more than embryonic before she had learnt of her future fiscal disaster. Myhill Productions had been heading for closure. Now it had a tiny glimmer of a chance of keeping its head above water. Would Duncan help it to swim or would his coming on board sink it? The company could not afford Duncan but nor could it not not afford him either. She couldn't entice him to halve his salary without the promise of some genuine involvement in the business. She would be obliged to put him at the heart of her company.

Second, there was the battle on the home front. There was Max. He had not met Duncan, but perhaps Max was right. Or perhaps he was jealous. Max was good with figures, though. The company was still small. It could not afford an executive team, really. On the other hand, she couldn't go on relying on Max. When he was eleven years old he had helped her win those crucial commissions. But they were aimed at eleven-year-olds. He was completely wrong about the breakfast thing. He had lost her a twenty-two-million-pound commission on a hunch about underground trolls and computer games. With hindsight, she realised she had made herself a laughing-stock at The Station. Thank God it was Martin who was head of programmes there. Not someone like Bob Dresler. Don't think of Bob Dresler, Karen. Please.

She stood at the crest of the hill and looked towards the City as thousands had done before her. A middle-aged woman in a woolly cape passed by in the opposite direction, walking a golden retriever. Off she goes home, to her family probably, thought Karen. Her husband. Karen would never have a husband. Not now. Could she ever have? She was lonely, really. Max was everything in her life at the moment. There were her parents. A few friends – well, sort of – picked up on her career. No one close, though. No firm arms to pull her nearer in bed. No warm breath on the back of her neck as she slept at nights. And Max was changing. He'd get progressively more difficult for a while and then up and leave for university or backpacking round the world or some such thing. The golden retriever barked in the distance. The thought crossed her mind that perhaps the woman had a dog because she was a lonely old spinster.

She walked on and once again clutched at the contract in her pocket. What to do? What to do? By the time she came to the big tree where she always turned round, she had made up her mind. She aimed her face into the breeze and headed back.

42

Paul got defensive. He felt like the junior partner in all this. He did usually just with Michael, but with Piers MacLelland White there as well, it was worse. He couldn't quite read all the nuances.

'I don't want to cause an argument.'

'We're not having an argument,' retorted Duncan.

'No, Duncan?' said Michael firmly. 'You're causing one. It's up to our guests to do what they want to do.'

Piers had opted out of this. Sometimes Duncan could be sheer bloody-minded. And stubborn. Duncan went on.

'Exactly. And what they want to do is visit a country house or a garden or something. Not spend the weekend inside the cottage eating and drinking just because you do.'

'Well, I don't care what we do,' said Paul.

Duncan pounced on his lameness. 'No wonder you never get your own way, Paul. You always avoid confrontation. You should stand up for yourself.'

'I do! I'm trying to be polite. Just listen to yourself, Duncan. You're being dictatorial.'

Piers's measured tones settled it. 'Let's take your car, Michael, and go to that place Duncan suggested.'

'Woldcote.'

'All right, Duncan, Woldcote. If the big house isn't open we'll just tour the garden. And if there's no tearoom or whatever we'll go into Stow-on-the-Wold or somewhere else on the way.'

'That settles it,' said Michael. 'Come on, then. Paul, get a move on. You know what you're like.'

'Don't be so rude. I'm supposed to be your guest.'

'Supposed to be,' joked Duncan, 'but we enjoy punishing people.'

'I've noticed,' said Paul, actually a little upset. 'I've also noticed it always seems to be only me.' He sneezed. 'And you know I'm allergic to that cat!'

Half an hour later, Paul joined them by the Merc. He had

changed into linen jacket and trousers and his new panama hat.

'Oh my God, it's Cecil Beaton,' sniggered Michael.

Paul was hurt by the comment on his specially selected head-gear, and even more hurt that the others made no comment at all, not even an insulting one. He decided not to push for compliments.

'I couldn't find my moisturiser. I've borrowed yours, if you don't mind.'

Michael rolled his eyes, then turned into the Spanish Inquisition.

'What's in that bag? You don't need to bring anything. It's a lovely day.'

'It's my tapestry.'

'Jesus Christ! You're not bringing that fucking tapestry out with us in public.'

'I'll just do it in the car. I can leave it in the boot.'

Piers looked out of the open rear window.

'Come on, girls. A stitch in time saves nine.'

The house was closed, but the gardens were open and almost empty. Woldcote's green copper onion dome and great curving Eastern-style orangery looked out over a stunning English landscape garden. In the distance, full, leafy oaks stood out against pretty wild-flower meadows where slow-walking ewes stumbled over their suckling lambs.

Piers headed off on his own, alone with his thoughts, across the formal lawn, down the Cotswold stone steps and through the rose garden to take in the view. He wanted to absorb the stillness and the space and the peace and take some of it home with him later.

Oh, England, England. I don't want to leave you, he thought. Not just yet. The countryside *does* roll, he noticed. And it *is* green and pleasant. And the air . . . He filled his lungs and walked on. He would stroll among the sheep. Ever since that day when he had come to terms with the knowledge that he was going to die, he had begun to appreciate the company of animals. Dumb animals had meant nothing to him previously. In fact he couldn't abide them. Why anyone wanted to own a pet had always escaped him.

Now that same dumbness was a source of great comfort. He wasn't exactly sure why. It was probably that age-old simple observation that with animals there was no judging to be done. Each of you just accepted that the other was there. You just were. You hadn't let down your side. Your homosexuality didn't disappoint. The AIDS virus was not silently screaming between you, ripping your relationship apart.

Michael and Duncan, still with making-up to do, had sloped off on their own on the pretext of examining the design of the house. They left Paul prissily adjusting his panama hat of which he was constantly conscious. Annoyed to have been dumped on his own, he meandered into the Victorian kitchen garden. The brick walls were, what, twenty feet high? Fan-trained fruit trees from a hundred years ago still lined the south side, standing crucified on their rusting wires. Plum, pear, peach, quince, greengage. There was an interesting attempt to lay out a floral cabbage and lettuce patch as a centrepiece in front of them, but it was too minute in scale to be of any significance. They should get in Rosemary Verey, the famous country gardener, to do it properly. He thought of her Laburnum Walk. It would be coming into flower about now. They should go and see it tomorrow if Piers wasn't too tired and Duncan was prepared to do what somebody else suggested for a change. He walked over to the old glasshouses. They looked Edwardian and were in an appalling state, completely fallen in at one end. He peered in through one of the panes of the door. Perhaps no one had been in here for most of the twentieth century. But they had. And their eyeballs were suddenly exactly opposite his.

Paul leapt back in complete fright and let out a campy shriek.

'Oh, my goodness. You terrified the living daylights out of me.'

A young, dark-haired plantsman, a seedling tray in his hand, opened the dirty glass door and came out grinning broadly. He had big square teeth like Scrabble pieces.

'Did I frighten you, sir?'

He had an accent broader than his chest. He was in rolled-up shirt-sleeves and wore an earth-stained green apron. His jeans were tucked into green wellingtons. Don't think wellingtons, thought Paul. Instead, he recalled Maurice and his Scudder. He was instantly in love with this gorgeous young man.

*   *   *

After a really touristy strawberry and clotted-cream tea in an over-curtained, frilly, fussy place in Stow-on-the-Wold, they floated home in the big, comfortable Mercedes, the late afternoon sun highlighting the brilliant yellow squares of rape on the swelling land behind the hedges. Piers was out for the count.

'So, go on, then. Did he give you a blow-job in the rhododendrons?' Michael was being mischievous.

'It wasn't like that,' answered Paul, pretend cross. His eyes were closed in half-slits as he concentrated on aiming his needle into his tapestry. 'We just exchanged phone numbers. It was platonic, although subliminally he must have known I'm gay.'

The others did not wish to rush in and agree that he was a classic screaming queen and the poor boy would have to have been a blind, retarded yokel not to have noticed.

'Why else would he have given you his number?' asked Duncan.

'Well, I said I was looking for a plant and could he get one for me and call me when it comes in.'

'I wish I'd seen him,' said Duncan. 'Was he very good-looking?'

'I rather thought so. He didn't have great teeth, but then I'm very conscious of teeth at the moment. Oh, Duncan . . . ' Paul was suddenly gushing. 'Did I tell you I'm taking the plunge? I'm getting my teeth fixed at last.'

'You are?' Paul was surprised that Duncan left it there. But Duncan, for all his sophistication, was at thirty-two still intrigued by some of the ways of the world and how other men picked each other up. He returned to Paul's encounter. 'What sort of plant did you say? An indoor one?'

'I said I needed it for my garden.'

'You don't have a garden.'

Paul laughed. He was enjoying being the centre of attention for a change. He drew his wool through the tapestry with a long, slow single pull.

'Let's not get stuck on the details.'

43

They had been *in camera* all day behind closed blinds. Lunch was finger food from the kitchen on a tray. Earlier she had popped out into her own office and unlocked the contracts file, had a good rake round and then gone back into Nigel's room. No calls were to be put through.

'What's up, kiddo?' Hazel had asked Margaret.

'They're up to no good in there. Planning something.'

'It's me, isn't it? I'm up for the chop.'

'I can't say I've heard them sharpening the blade.'

'No? She'd do it with her bare hands, that one. Aw, fuck. I shouldn't have answered Fatboy back in that Bencelor meeting.'

One look from Margaret told her that this was not as much of a joke as Hazel had hoped it might be. Down in the dumps, at lunchtime she dragged Orlando and the creatives off to Pizza Express for some comfort food and a few beers.

Margaret checked with Duncan. Duncan would have told her if Hazel was for it but he had no idea what was going on. Meanwhile Charlotte had her head down in the accounts department, sorting out the billing for the next month and dutifully trying to clear up historic debts that Hazel had continually ignored.

'What's going on, Margaret?' Charlotte was back. 'I've been sitting half the day outside the financial director's office, you know, by his secretary? Serena's never been off the phone. She's been kicking up a fuss about something.'

'Oh?' Margaret was all ears. 'What did you hear?'

'Not much. One exclamation of "Fifty grand, you must be joking!"'

'Blimey. Well, they're not discussing my pay rise then, are they? Don't worry, you'll be all right. You're too new.'

Charlotte didn't buy that for a second.

Serena plucked out the last stalk of celery left in the glass and bit into it with a sharp crunch. They had a solution. In one fell swoop they could find the fifty thousand pounds for Alan Josling; pick up Japanair and its profitability to secure their future; sideline Duncan and, later, remove him. They would retake control of their little empire. Serena ticked off her shopping list, memorised it and then started to run it through Nigel's desktop shredder.

'I don't know how you can go near that thing, old girl. First and last time I used it, I caught my tie in it. Damn near strangled myself.'

Serena was animated. Her shrill voice had a sing-song tone to it. 'This is fun. I like shredding things. It's a bit like making coleslaw. Only this will leave a more bitter taste in a few people's mouths. Hah!' Finished, she opened the door on to her kingdom and brought her servant up sharpishly. 'Margaret? Ask Duncan to come into Nigel's office.'

Gosh. Madam was being especially officious this afternoon. Her voice was at least a semitone up on usual. That meant she was expecting trouble.

'What for?' asked Margaret, insincerely sweet. 'A meeting?'

'Yes, Margaret, a meeting.'

'What shall I say it's about?'

'Don't say what's it about. It's just a catch-up.'

Oh. Margaret decided to pry. 'On The Station? D'you want him to bring his files and things?'

'No. That won't be necessary.'

Margaret hovered, mind-searching Serena's brain.

'Margaret, go and do it now. I haven't got all day. Honestly, it would be quicker telling him myself.'

Why don't you, then, you old hag? Do your own dirty work. Margaret padded round like the Pink Panther into Duncan's office.

'Lady Macbeth wants to see you,' she said. She carefully closed the door behind her and lowered her voice. 'They're on the warpath.'

Duncan looked concerned. 'What about?' he asked.

'I don't know. Take them on, Duncan. Oh, go on. Only you can. Briony Linden and Stella Boddington will always back you against them. You know that. And Orlando.'

'God, Margaret, what's got into you? This is my career I'm having here. It's not *Win, Lose or Draw* we're playing.'

'Duncan, I've worked with her for ten years. I know how nasty she can be. You've no idea. They're afraid of you deep down inside. Which means they'll play dirtier than ever.'

Duncan knew what *that* meant.

Nigel and Serena sat directly opposite him. She did the talking and was brisk about it.

'Duncan, you know we went to that conference at The Station?'

Here it came. 'Yes.'

'There are a number of things that we learnt there, Duncan, that we really ought to have heard from you first, you know. It really isn't your place to sit on information and not pass it up the line. We could have been embarrassed by our apparent lack of knowledge of some of the details.'

'That surprises me. Could you give me an example? Then I'll know what to circulate in the future. I try not to bog you down with trivia when you're both so busy on other things.'

'I can't think of an example right now, Duncan. You're very lucky you work for Nigel and he's so diplomatic at these events. I don't know where I'd have been without him.'

Nigel sat there looking more puffed up than usual. He fiddled with his tie, butter-fingered Oliver Hardy to her vinegary Stan Laurel. Madam continued.

'We heard the head of the legal team speak.'

He was obviously meant to react at this stage, but Duncan had been practising for this moment ever since the dry run with Briony. 'Was that interesting?'

'Very interesting, Duncan. I recognised his voice. He's phoned you a few times here, hasn't he?'

'Yes, he has.'

'In what capacity?'

'How do you mean?'

'Is he talking to you about business or, how shall I put it, personal things?'

'Serena, if you mean is he a friend of mine, and do we have personal conversations, then yes we do.'

'And how close is your relationship?'

'Frankly that's one of your business. No more close than yours is with Nigel.'

Serena's face creased into corrugated rage. She couldn't lose her cool, though. She wanted Duncan to know that they knew and he had to fall into line. Well, now he knew that they knew. He was holed below the waterline. She changed tack. Full steam ahead.

'Duncan, what we really wanted to do was to let you know about our plans for the company. We're telling you as a courtesy now. Orlando and the others will hear it at the appropriate time from us, not from you. Understood? Money is very tight.'

'Not if we win Japanair.'

'That will be an expensive piece of business to pick up. There are hidden costs involved which we are unable to discuss with you. But we will not be able to afford to employ Hazel beyond the end of this year.'

Duncan swallowed. 'I find that hard to believe. She doesn't earn *that* much.'

'Duncan, don't interrupt. If we say we can't afford her, we can't. The reason is we're not happy with Orlando working on his own without a writer. Working with writers from MCN, like that grotesque young man Steve da Silva, for example, is jeopardising C&B's position. He was very rude to me once about an item of clothing I was wearing, but that's not the point.'

'He thinks you don't like him because he's black.'

'I beg your pardon?'

'*I* don't think that. *He* thinks it. He thinks you're a racist.'

Serena scowled. 'There's no point in my arguing that one because I couldn't win it. I think you'll find, Duncan, that it is better not to let the fashion of political correctness stand in the way of one's critical faculties. My opinions about that young man downstairs have nothing to do with his being coloured and everything to do with our creative integrity. The creative work *must* come out of here, meaning C&B. If it gets out we can't do our own ads we'll have failed as an agency. So what we're going to do is hire a writer for Orlando. Our choice, not his. He'll report to Nigel and me, not Orlando.'

'Serena, you can't do that. Orlando is the creative director. That's unheard-of.'

'No it's not. *We* hand-picked our creative teams at the old

Clancey and Bennett. Orlando has to stop working for you and your little club and start working for the agency. Understood?'

He let it ride. He had never before seen Serena this brittle.

'The new writer will be expensive. Hence we'll have to drop Hazel. She earns the most after you. You encouraged us to pay her too much when we recruited her. I don't underestimate her intelligence, but she barely puts the hours in. She's developed an uncooperative attitude. You really should have handled her better, Duncan. You've not kept her motivated. In fact, if we could afford it, we'd send you on a basic management training course. Heavens knows, you need it.'

Duncan gave her a filthy look. Of all the nerve. But he could see her counting the points out on her bony fingers. He might as well let her get through her shopping list.

'We will replace Hazel with a trainee who'll report to Charlotte. If we win Japanair – and you must help us to win it, Duncan – then you won't need to work on it. There will be a lot of foreign travel that Nigel and I will clearly have to handle ourselves. And Charlotte and the trainee will report directly to Nigel. That way, we can make sure that Charlotte will be developed in the right way.'

She sat back. She had delivered her speech in an uncompassionate way. But the flickering pulse in her eyes told Duncan she was triumphant.

'Pay rise, old girl,' muttered Nigel.

'Oh, yes. As part of the financial stringency, there won't be a pay rise for you at the end of the summer. We can talk about that later.'

Duncan sat motionless. He let Nigel play with his tie a bit more. Obviously, they wanted a grovelling, pleading response.

'Could I have some of that mineral water, please?' he asked.

Serena passed the bottle across the table and Duncan ceremoniously unscrewed the cap and let the contents glug out into his glass. He took a sip and looked up.

'You've clearly put a lot of thought into what you've just said, so I hope it won't upset your plans too much . . .' He pulled a sheet of yellow fax paper from his inside jacket pocket. 'I'm handing in my resignation.'

'What?' It was Nigel who blurted it out. But they were both taken aback.

Duncan sipped some more water and, giving the impression of a lack of interest, ran his eyes over his contract. 'I'm resigning.'

'What about your mortgage?' asked Serena. 'Your commitments? You can't afford to leave.'

'Actually, Serena, I think you'll find my private finances, like my private life, are none of your business. I *do* have a new job to go to, as it happens. A new career, actually. I'm moving into television production.'

'What? Making ads? You've no experience. Who'd employ you?'

'Not ads. Proper programmes. Grown-up television. I might be making programmes for The Station. That would be funny, wouldn't it? You coming along to see if you could advertise them.'

In Serena's mind's eye her plans unravelled and fell apart. This was a disaster. They were left too exposed too quickly. 'You'll have to work six months' notice as a board director.'

'I don't think so. Nigel ought to have renewed my contract when I went on the board but I never signed anything. I'm still on the original six weeks.'

This was an emergency. Serena just wanted Duncan out of the room as fast as humanly possible while she reviewed her tactics with Nigel.

'Duncan, give us time to think about what you've just said. It was very inconsiderate of you just to spring it on us like that. I demand that you keep this strictly confidential. Understood?'

'I'll do my best. Unfortunately, though, they sent the contract through by fax. I hope no one else saw it. You know, you two, how tongues like to wag, don't you?'

Serena raged silently. She could get up and give it in the neck right now to Nigel for duffing up on the contract. To her irritation, Duncan made no move to go. Instead he poured himself some more water.

'I never thought I'd make a move like this,' he said. He recalled an appropriate line from his childhood in Scotland and deployed it to full effect. 'Funny, isn't it, Serena, how the best-laid schemes o' mice an' men gang aft a-gley?'

44

'Do you think they're ever coming out of there?' asked Charlotte.

'Doesn't seem like it,' said Margaret, checking over her shoulder to see if the blinds were still shut. 'No. I'd say not.'

'I wanted to get away early.' There was a slight agitation in Charlotte's voice. 'Well, not early exactly. I mean on time. The time that most normal folks leave an office.'

'Most normal folks don't earn what you earn, Charlotte, that's why you have to work harder. What are you up to tonight, then? Something nice?'

'Nothing much. I'm meeting someone, that's all.'

'Anyone I know?'

She got no response.

'A man or a woman?'

'Margaret, don't be nosey.'

Margaret clucked. 'I'm not being nosey,' she answered back. 'I'm just being friendly.' A big knowing smirk grew on her face.

'It's not who you think it is.' Charlotte's voice rose in self-defence as well as in volume.

'Oh?' Margaret pretended ignorance. 'Who's that, then?'

'You know full well who I mean. I heard you and Hazel gossiping about it earlier on. Where is Hazel this afternoon, anyway?'

'She and Orlando went out for lunch and then they went to a casting session. Male models. Swimsuit parade, I think Hazel said. They won't be back.'

Margaret disappeared under her counter-top and surfaced again with her shoulder bag and a Marks & Spencer food carrier bag. She collected her things and she and Charlotte made their way to the ladies'. In front of the big mirror there, Margaret vigorously brushed her dyed chestnut hair and applied a dash of scarlet lipstick, while Charlotte slipped out of her red linen suit and into leggings and yet more lycra.

'So are you and Steve da Silva an item, then?'

Charlotte ignored her.

'Is love–love the score on the tennis court?'

'Oh, for God's sake!' Charlotte blushed. 'Nothing happened!'

'That's not what Hazel said.'

'I heard her stirring it. If Briony Linden hadn't rung I'd have come out and brained her. I did not snog him, if you must know. He and Hazel left my flat together at about one in the morning. He gave me a peck on the cheek, that's all.'

'Look in the mirror,' said Margaret. 'You've gone all red. He's a bit of a ladies' man, you know, that Steve da Silva.'

'Margaret, he's really not my type. I don't even know why we're having this conversation. Honestly. We spent most of the time talking about *them*' – she waved her hand in the direction of Nigel and Serena's offices – 'and *Megabrek*.'

'What's that?'

'The Station's breakfast show.'

'Oh yes.' She remembered it now from typing the brief. 'Who's going to watch that? It sounds worse than that Chris Evans used to be. Everyone says 'Isn't he good?' I suppose he is if you're aged five. Personally, I can't stand him. All that ginger hair at breakfast. It turns my stomach. I like Chris Tarrant on Capital.'

'Just as well you're not in the research groups, then. Fuck. I forgot to tell Briony about the recruitment details. Never mind, I'll do it tomorrow. She can't do anything with it tonight.'

Charlotte stuffed her red linen suit into her bag and swept out of the ladies' with Margaret following closely. She popped into her office and picked up her crash helmet.

'I'll wave to you from the bus-stop,' said Margaret, grinning. 'Give my love to Steve!'

'Piss off.' Charlotte ran towards the stairwell. 'By the way, you've got lipstick on your teeth!'

Charlotte pulled her bike into the side of the road. This was it. She looked among the residents' parking places until she found a gap big enough to squeeze the Ducati into. Residents' parking restrictions lasted until 6.30 p.m., but time was almost up. She'd risk it.

It was a much grander address than she had expected. She began to suspect that, because of her public-school accent, the

Terrence Higgins Trust had assigned her to someone quite wealthy
and high up the social scale. She suddenly wished she knew more
about him. A briefing down the phone seemed a bit lightweight
considering she was dealing with a terminally ill human being.
On the other hand, she rationalised, she was not a nurse or a
replacement for any official help. She was just an extra friend to
someone not in a relationship.

She had spoken to him on the phone, but only very briefly.
He had just said 'Come round', and hadn't wanted to chat there
and then. He was in his early forties. Perhaps he would think she
was too young. Perhaps he would think she was too young to
understand him, too young to deal with his lifestyle, too young
to deal with his death. Or perhaps that was what Charlotte really
felt about herself. She realised she was just a touch nervous. She
tried hard to clear her mind.

She climbed the steps of the white stucco house. His flat was
on the first floor. She thought about the training scheme. Some
of the training had been quite draining emotionally. The big deal
was that you couldn't drop out once you had been assigned
as a Buddy. That could harm the health and welfare of the
person to whom you were meant to be a support. A lot of the
others training with her had been gay and HIV-positive. Sweet,
really, that those afflicted should rally round each other. It was
heartening to see how gay people stuck together in a crisis.
She imagined the advertising community struck down by some
deadly disease. It would just be a case of 'When you're dead,
can I get your company Porsche, or has some other bastard got
it already?'

She found the name on the button. At least he was a professional. That other girl had got a terrible case. A teenage coke
addict who'd been a rent-boy since he was thirteen. How would
Charlotte have coped if they'd given her that one? She didn't
know, only that she would have tried. At least with this man,
they could talk about handling their clients and dealing with
people. That would help to break the ice. Charlotte wondered
whether he was still working.

She pressed the button on the video entryphone and waited.
A light came on inside and she spoke into the grille.

'Hello. It's Charlotte from the, er, from the Trust.' Better not advertise the name halfway down the street. Everyone knew what it was nowadays.

'Hello,' the voice came back. What a beautiful speaker, she thought. 'Come on up to the first floor.'

When she came round the corner at the top of the staircase he was framed in the doorway. Handsome, immaculately dressed in classic, casual clothes from, she guessed, the likes of Simpson's of Piccadilly, and, healthwise, in the pink. You never would have known he was carrying the killer virus.

'Hello. Come on in. I've just come back from Christie's. Bought a new painting. You can help me find somewhere to hang it.'

'Hello. I'm Charlotte.' She offered him her hand, her hand of friendship. He took it and shook it warmly. Their lingering ever so slightly on the greeting was significant. It was their bond.

'What sort of painting is it?' Charlotte had at last thought of something to say after what seemed an age.

'A portrait. I've been looking for one for yonks. It's to fill a space over a fireplace. What d'you fancy? Red or white wine?'

'Oh! I'm easy. White, please, if you would like that too. Not too much for me. I'm on my bike.'

'I know. I watched you from the window. I was interested in what you would be like.'

So it was as big a moment for him as it was for her. 'Heck. Would you have let me in if you hadn't liked the look of me?'

'Oh yes. Probably.'

'Would you have preferred a man?'

'I don't know.'

'I've never done anything like this before,' she confessed.

'Don't worry. This is my first terminal illness. It's a new experience for me too.'

She tried to reflect his sympathetic smile. 'I intend to do my best. I work in this incredibly demanding job but apart from that I have no commitments. I must give you all my contact numbers while I remember. And I've got my notebook so I can write down anything you want me to do. I'm really very organised—'

'Hey. I invited you round for a drink. Not to plan my funeral. Not yet, anyway. Let's just relax, shall we?'

'Sorry. Am I being too keen?'

'Just a smidgen. I don't intend to shuffle off my mortal coil that easily. You haven't even crossed the threshold yet and entered my world. So, white wine, was it, or shall we head straight for the gin bottle?'

'Even better.' She giggled and went in. He closed the door behind her.

Hell, thought Charlotte. I'll like him too much. I know I will.

45

Paul lay back in the leather chair with his mouth wide open. It felt rather sexual. Did everyone think that about going to the dentist, or was it just him? He'd ask Duncan, his sexual litmus test.

'You certainly have the fangs of a vampire. I never noticed that when I first met you.' The dentist pulled back from his mouth. 'Rinse, please.'

There were two glasses of sparkling pink fluid on the side by that small thing that always looked like a miniature toilet bowl. Paul took a swig from one of the glasses. He was so taken aback that instead of spitting out he swallowed.

'What's that?' he gasped.

'Which one? Oh, that's Mateus Rosé.' The dentist laughed. 'You've never been to my private practice before, have you? I don't serve *that* on the National Health Service in the North London unit. Don't worry, the other glass contains regular mouthwash for the less adventurous.'

Paul gave the dentist an incredulous look and restarted their conversation.

'Isn't that what a dentist always notices about anyone first? Their teeth?'

'No. I'm a dentist second and a homosexual first. I noticed your arse, followed by the size of your basket. I'm a basket case!'

'You said it. Where *did* you first meet me, or should I say, pick me up. You've got a good memory. Was it at the Embassy?'

'Yes. One Sunday evening in 1979. I'd just come to London after the Shah went into exile. You were working for Karen Myhill then.'

'Don't remind me.'

'She was one of my patients in those days. We didn't know we had her in common then, did we?'

'If we had, I wouldn't have had sex with you.'

'Strange how I remember you, but not the sex. One had so much of it then.'

'So much, but never enough. Why is sex like that?'

'Because it's a drug. And we're all addicts.' The dentist walked over to the workbench on the side. 'Did you find your way here all right?'

'Yes. I never realised there was such a difference between your two practices. And I'd have preferred not to have a nine o'clock appointment.'

'It was the only time I could fit you in at short notice. Anyway, it'll do you good to get up early for once. I'm sorry you had to come all the way to Kensington, but I don't do the private treatment out of the North London practice. That's where I rush through all you poor National Health people. They get nothing cosmetic. Just the basics.'

'It's so unfair. Why should poor people be denied the best treatment?'

'What do they need it for?'

'Sometimes, Rik, you make me so angry I could hit you. You're so right-wing. You despise ordinary people.'

'I don't. I was just brought up in a different culture from you. In Iran, there are different rules. The lowest don't expect a free handout from the state.'

'Listen to you, Rik. Just because your family are rich Indians.'

'We're not Indians. We're Persians of Asian descent.'

'Whatever. I can barely afford to pay for this, you know. I should get a reduction.'

'What for?'

'Sleeping with you.'

'That was fifteen years ago. I wouldn't sleep with you now.

You're far too old. I can have some nice young boy. With his own teeth!'

'They only sleep with you for your money.'

'Balls. Lots of humpy young men like Asian looks like mine. All that dark skin and body hair.' He laughed. 'Now look. This is what I think we can do. I'll crown or cap the four front upper teeth. The middle two we'll lengthen slightly. The incisors we'll leave so that they form a neat row of six. No one will see any of the others, so save your money.'

'It won't hurt, will it?'

'It'll hurt like hell, Paul.' Rik gave a shrieking laugh. 'Now, where are my rusting pliers?'

'Stop it. You're mad, d'you know that?'

'Yes!' He grabbed Paul's cheek and squeezed it playfully. 'Now.' He pushed himself on to a high stool. 'When d'you want to start? D'you want to think about it?'

'No. I trust you, God knows why. As soon as possible. Whenever.'

'OK. Three o'clock the day after tomorrow. I know that's free because someone else just cancelled. Fix it with the receptionist as you leave.'

'I'll see you then.' Paul got out of the chair. 'You could have great sex on this dentist's chair, you know.'

'I do know!' Rik gave his shrieking laugh again. 'I've tried it! Lots of times!'

46

'Charlotte, Charlotte, Charlotte!'

'My God, Hazel. What's up? Give me time to get into my office and put my things down, will you?'

Charlotte had lain awake most of the night thinking about her Terrence Higgins man and how she would feel if a death sentence hung over her own head. She didn't feel like facing her list of twenty things to do today.

Hazel clipped her heels as she pursued her into her box-like office. She pushed the door shut.

'My God, Hazel. What's happened?' Charlotte slumped down into her swivel seat.

'You don't know, do you?'

'Know what?'

'Weren't you here yesterday afternoon?'

'Yes.' Charlotte pulled out her little make-up bag and produced a hairbrush. She attacked her hair vigorously. 'But I left on time for once. I thought they were never going to come out of that meeting.'

'Cairns has resigned!'

Charlotte stopped brushing and sat there for a moment, paralysed with the shock of the news.

'Duncan's resigned? Has he been fired?'

'No.' Hazel could not get the grin off her face. 'He's ditching his career and is going to work in television.'

'Television? On the marketing side?'

'No. As a producer or something. Godzilla and Dracula are stumped. He's stitched them. Isn't that brilliant?'

'Who's he going to work for?'

'Some production company. The name meant nothing to me. Brilliant, though, isn't it?'

'God, Hazel. You're so short-sighted. It's us who've been stitched. We'll never get through all this work. How on earth are we going to cope with *Megabrek* and The Station?' In her mind's eye the hours of tortuous late-night meetings were already clocking up and the volumes of anticipated paperwork weighed heavily upon her. Her thoughts shot back to her secret meeting with her Buddy the day before. She had just taken on a huge commitment of both her time and her emotions. How was she ever going to cope? She was not proud of the feeling, but she found herself deeply resenting what Duncan Cairns had gone and done behind her back. 'Where is Duncan, anyway? The traitor. What sort of notice is he on?'

'Six weeks.'

'Is that all?' Charlotte was sickened. Lowering her gaze, she absentmindedly noticed a tiny black thread that had been somehow pulled loose from the neckline of her blouse. She eyed her desk for something to cut it with but found nothing and thought better of tugging at it and seeing what happened. Enough had unravelled already and the morning had yet to begin.

'Margaret says Fatboy forgot to revise his contract when he went on the board. Otherwise he would have had to stay for six months. I can't wait to see Briony Linden's face. Or Stella Boddington's for that matter. The whole place'll fall apart now.'

'Hazel, I can't believe what I'm hearing. You seem delighted by the whole thing. It's a disaster. It's a goddamn fucking disaster. I should get on the phone to Audrey Goldberg straight away and get my next move sorted out. God.' She propelled her seat back from under her desk and half rose. 'Is Duncan in? I must talk to him.'

'They're in a board meeting. It's meant to be confidential, by the way. Don't tell anyone I told you.'

'Who did you hear it from? Margaret?'

'No. Ben in production. Which means the whole world knows anyway.'

'They'll buy him back. They'll have to. Not even they can let twelve million pounds' worth of business just evaporate.'

'Oh yes they can, kiddo. Apparently they're in a real quandary about the whole thing. They can hardly go crawling to him, can they? Anyway, how can they buy him back? He's not leaving for money or position or better accounts or anything they can do a deal with him on. He's left them with no negotiating stance. What a stitch-up! Good old Cairns!'

'Oh, Haze. This is dreadful.' The arm holding the hairbrush hung limp by Charlotte's side. She felt tired and run-down and depressed all at once.

'There's going to be no work done here today,' said Hazel. 'Let's go out for a slap-up lunch with Cairns, shall we? Get the whole thing from the horse's mouth.'

'I can't, Hazel. I've got loads and loads to do. So have you. Someone needs to call Stella Boddington and find out where she is on launch dates.'

'She's off ill again.'

'Again? She's always ill.'

'Yeah. I spoke to her accounts department. She's not in. So nothing to do there, Charlie.'

'We're meant to be seeing Steve at ten to go through what he and Orlando have done on *Megabrek*.'

'When in crisis, her thoughts turned to lover-boy.'

'Piss off, Haze!'

'Watch where you're pointing that brush, sweetie! That's a dangerous weapon in the hands of a wronged woman.'

'I know you've been spreading it about me.'

Hazel began to make her exit. 'Don't worry, kiddo,' she said. 'I've got a much better story for the old bush telegraph now.'

'Well, that's one less account man to deal with.'

Steve da Silva sat at his desk in his office downstairs in MCN. Today his hair was tied back and he wore a Hugo Boss mushroom suit and a Paul Smith shirt with small checks.

'It's meant to be confidential, Steve,' said Charlotte. 'Don't tell anyone I told you.'

Steve laughed at her concern that she might be caught telling tales out of school.

'Come on, Steve,' she said. 'You may think it's funny, but it's not. Clancey and Bennett really relies on him to hold on to its two biggest accounts. You know he gave you a really good brief on this *Megabrek* thing. If it wasn't for Duncan, Nigel and Serena would never have let you near it.'

'OK, OK. I know Orlando rates him. They'll get somebody else. You'll see.'

'I came here to work with *him*, not with somebody else,' said Charlotte. 'Anyway, when Duncan came here, nobody out there really knew about Nigel and Serena. Well, they do now. They'll only bring in some clone of Nigel. God. I can't bear to think about it.'

'You came here, Charlie. You're good. Duncan came here too. So will someone else, you'll see. *You* didn't know about them.'

'That's because I met Duncan first. I ignored them. I didn't pick up on them at all. God, why am I so impulsive? I wish I was more mature sometimes.'

'Why don't you come here and sit on my lap, babe, and I'll cheer you up.' He patted his crotch.

'Piss off. What are you? A walking sex machine?'

'Yes, if you must know.' He grinned. 'You'll love it. Just wait and see.'

Charlotte flushed. 'You're disgusting.'

'I was talking about the *Megabrek* work. Let's go through it now.'

'I should wait for Hazel.'

'She'll be late for her own funeral, that girl. Anyway, it's you I want to show it to. You can take her through it later.'

'Are you sure Orlando won't mind not presenting it to us himself?'

'He'll be OK. You're such a worried little flower, aren't you?'

'I'm sorry. I'm not feeling myself today.'

'How about me feeling you instead, Charlie?'

'Don't be disgusting!'

He laughed. 'I know you public-school girls. You love it when a big black man talks real dirty to you.'

'That's tantamount to sexual harassment.'

'So's that outfit you're wearing. I can see your nipples through that top. It might as well be sprayed on. And you're not wearing knickers.'

'How dare you!'

'I can tell. No VPL.'

'If you must know, when I wear leggings I wear a G-string. Anyway, you're one to talk. You virtually go around with your knob hanging out.'

'When I see you it's not hanging down, Charlie. It's standing up big.'

He had pushed her too far.

'Fuck off, you!' she said.

She stormed out of his office and banged straight into Hazel.

'Where are you off to, kiddo? Has he shown you the work?'

'No. I came to get you. Hazel, you'll have to stop being so late for everything. I didn't want to be left alone in there with that monster.'

'He showed it to you, did he?' She laughed, but saw the strain on Charlotte's face. 'I'm here now. Let's go through the work together, then nip round the corner for a coffee. No one will notice we're gone for twenty minutes. You look like you need it. The campaign'll be fine, don't worry. Steve's work is always brilliant. Even I admit that. Orlando'll tweak anything we can't get through Godzilla and Dracula. And Cairns still has plenty of time to sell it to Briony. She'll love it.'

'Are you sure? I feel sick.'

'Do you? Do you want to take something? I trained as a nurse in Australia, you know.'

'A nurse? You didn't. You're having me on.'

'I did,' said Hazel. 'Really I did. Any time you're not up to it come and see me.'

'I don't believe you.'

'It's true. I know all about emergency first aid. I'm like one of those St Bernards that turns up just in the nick of time with a barrel of brandy.'

'Except in your case the flask would be empty. You'd have drunk it yourself! Come on, let's go in and sort out those ads.'

'What do you think?' Now Charlotte was in Duncan's office, looking over his shoulder at the roughs of the revised posters for The Station and *Megabrek*.

'I think you must be getting on very well with Steve da Silva.' Duncan laughed.

'Don't you start, Duncan,' she sighed in exasperation. 'What with Hazel and Margaret and Orlando, not to mention half of the media, production and TV departments . . . I can't stand it any longer! There is nothing going on between us. Absolutely nothing! No one is the slightest bit interested in your leaving. All they want to know is whether Steve and I are screwing each other.' She pushed her hair back from her face and made a brave attempt at concentrating on the matter in hand. 'Are you happy with the tweaks? I really need to know now, so I can get Orlando or someone in the studio to draw them up properly for this afternoon.'

'Yes. I'm very happy indeed. This poster campaign is fantastic. It's spot on. *Megabrek* should get off to a great start.'

'Well, it's getting off to a really horrendous start as far as I'm concerned.'

Duncan looked her in the eye but said nothing.

'Serena was saying that your enthusiasm is rapidly on the wane because you're leaving.'

'And you believe her?' He mimicked the voiceover of an American automobile commercial. 'Would *you* eat half an apple from that old witch?'

'No,' said Charlotte. 'But if it was me leaving, I couldn't care less about staying committed. I left Saatchi's the day I resigned. Why should anyone bother to work their notice?'

'In my case, because I need the money I can earn here over the next few weeks. I'm taking such a drop when I leave. And because I don't want to leave my clients in the lurch, do I? Particularly when I might be trying to sell the same company programmes in the near future.'

'You must be mad.'

'I thought "traitor" was your description for me.'

Charlotte was shot through with embarrassment. 'Who told you that?'

'A little bird.'

'It wasn't a kookaburra, by any chance? I love Hazel, but one day I'll damn well kill her. You might as well run a forty-eight-sheet poster campaign across the nation as speak to her in complete confidence.'

Duncan laughed.

'Anyway, you are a traitor, Duncan Cairns. I feel gutted. I hate that expression. I don't know why I used it but it's the truth. I haven't felt this miserable in ages. I went and saw my Terrence Higgins man last night for the first time, too.'

'Have you started already? That was quick. How did it go?'

Tears welled in Charlotte's eyes. 'Oh, Duncan, it's going to be so difficult. He was so lovely and charming and kind to me and I'm going to be completely bloody useless.'

'You'll be fantastic.'

'I've no idea what I've got myself into. Now I haven't even got you here on my side.'

Duncan leaned past her and pushed the door of his office quietly shut. He turned his seat face on to the door so that Charlotte could look at him and at the same time avoid her tear-stained face being seen from the outside. She sniffed. 'Honestly. I hate you. You've really let me down.'

'Don't say that. You're making me feel guilty. You'll be fine, you'll see.'

Though internally quite affected by his account manager's plight, Duncan remained calm and soothing. Charlotte's tears were flowing freely now.

'God, this is so pathetic. I hate women who cry in the office,' she wept. 'It lets the side down.' More than that, it let *her* down in front of Duncan, who was a stickler for correct behaviour. More tears poured out. 'I really only came here because of you, you know.'

'Rubbish. Of course you didn't.'

Charlotte suddenly found herself edging back ever so slightly as Duncan leaned towards her. With his upper body looming close in front of her own heaving bosom, for a ghastly moment she thought that for some reason he was about to kiss her. She became momentarily awkward and flushed with the prospect of something that to her could only be outrageously incestuous. For a sliver of a second she was confused. But she almost instantaneously realised she was reading him wrongly. She spotted that Duncan's right hand contained a small pair of black-handled steel scissors drawn from his black plastic desk-tidy. Lowering them to an inch in front of her nose, he deftly snipped away the dangling thread she had spotted earlier on her neckline.

'There! That was irritating me,' he announced. He dropped the offending thread into his black wastepaper basket. Charlotte was staggered by this oddity of Duncan's attention to detail, and then felt reassured and relaxed by such a tiny but tangible sign that her boss cared about her. Which was precisely the effect that Duncan had aspired to create.

'You'll be fine,' he said. 'If you can get Steve to produce copylines like these and mix and match them to Orlando's visuals, then you don't need me. Whatever your relationship with him is, you've obviously got the best out of Steve professionally. I couldn't have got these results myself.'

'You're just saying that.'

'Charlotte, if you knew me better, you'd know I never just say anything.'

'Do you really mean that?' She sniffed again, loudly this time.

'That was most unladylike!' chided Duncan.

Charlotte managed a little laugh.

'I do mean it,' said Duncan. 'Now, cheer up and go and get these drawn up in the studio or wherever.'

'Do we have a budget for that?'

'No. No budget—'

He was drowned out by a shriek of hysterical laughter from Margaret's corner. Duncan and Charlotte left their little quiet moment behind them and popped out to see what was up.

'Look!'

Margaret was holding up a large black and white studio portrait photograph of Serena in which she was smiling her widest smile.

'What's that for?' asked Charlotte, composure recovered. This was something they could all have a laugh at. 'She looks as if someone's rammed a coat hanger in her gob sideways.'

'Wish I'd had the pleasure,' said Duncan.

'She looks like the Queen, don't you think?' said Margaret. 'It's her publicity photograph for this year's MCN brochure. She always has it done this size so that they'll print it big. They never do, of course. They want to encourage clients to come here, not frighten the living daylights out of them. It's always right at the back, the size of a postage stamp.'

'Has Nigel got one, too?' asked Charlotte.

'Oh, no,' said Margaret. 'He just uses the same old thing from years ago, before he ballooned up. He's got dark hair in it, all bushy like a Brillo pad. And a big kipper tie. If he keeps it for a couple more years it'll probably come right back into fashion. I'd better go and take a photocopy of this and then put it back in the envelope before she catches me. She's popping in any moment now to pick up their Glyndebourne tickets. Sir forgot to take them with him, needless to say.' She scurried off in the direction of the photocopier.

'What do you need a photocopy of Serena smiling for?' asked Charlotte.

Duncan and Margaret laughed together.

'It's become a bit of a tradition in the creative department,' Margaret called back. 'They like to have it for their dartboard.'

*   *   *

Briony exhaled her usual jet of Camel smoke. She smiled generously.

'Brilliant. Really brilliant. Did Orlando do this?'

'Yes,' answered Duncan.

'All by himself? He wouldn't write lines like these, would he?'

'No. One of the copywriters did those.'

'What? In Clancey and Bennett?'

'Er, possibly.'

Briony cottoned on immediately. 'Who did them, then? A freelancer?'

'No. We never use freelancers.'

'Who, then? You didn't write them, did you, Duncan? Or you, Charlotte?'

'Stop asking questions, Briony.' Duncan was hedging.

'I'm entitled to ask questions. I don't care where the work came from. It's brilliant. I'm just surprised you got it done so quickly.'

'Well, if you must know,' said Duncan, 'we used a copywriter in the main agency. His partner left so he was at a loose end.'

'Really? What's the problem in owning up to that?' asked Briony.

'Serena's worried that MCN will get the credit publicly, not C&B,' replied Duncan.

'Well, I don't mind,' said Briony.

'No, but we do. So, what d'you want to do now?'

'I need to get them through Martin Fox and then the board. And pass them on to Saturn Productions as a courtesy. It'll take me a couple of days. Oh yes.' She winked at Duncan. 'I'd better check them with our legal department.'

'Is that likely to be a problem?' asked Charlotte.

Briony roared with laughter.

'What's so funny?' asked Charlotte innocently.

'I'm sure there'll be no problem.' Briony laughed and puffed a bit more. 'Where's Hazel this afternoon?'

'She's at a stills shoot for one of our other clients, Bencelor,' answered Duncan. 'Charlotte's really done most of the work on this lot.'

'Have you?' said Briony, pleased. 'Good. Very good. You and

Duncan seem to make a good team. You must be looking forward to your partnership together, eh, Charlotte?'

'Oh, yes. Working with Duncan is one of the main reasons I came to Clancey and Bennett,' said Charlotte, not without irony. 'I *am* looking forward to it! How about you, Duncan?' She turned to face Duncan and looked at him with playful expectation.

If Duncan had been sitting any closer he would have kicked her beneath the table. They were under strict instructions not to tell any of the clients he was leaving. He suddenly realised he was keeping a different secret from each woman.

'Briony?'

'Yes, Duncan?'

'I think we need to get moving on the production side. Even an extra two days would be a big help. We're really way behind on these posters. And we also need to brief the team to spin them off into national press and radio ads as well.'

'You're right. Go ahead. Assume they'll get approved just as they are. No revisions.'

Duncan turned to Charlotte. 'Make sure you get that for the contact report. Looks like you and Steve da Silva are going to be working a lot of late nights for the next few months. I hope that won't be too much of a strain for you?' Now it was Duncan's turn to turn full face and look with playful expectation at Charlotte.

This time the boot was on the other foot, and if Charlotte had been sitting any closer *she* would have kicked *him* beneath the table. She would miss him when he was gone.

Paul settled back into the dentist's chair and looked up into Rik's face.

'Are you nervous?' asked the dentist.

'Are you joking?' said Paul in a tremolo voice. 'I'm shitting myself. I simply can't stand pain.'

'Well, Paul, you won't feel a thing when I'm filing down your teeth,' said Rik. 'But that's after the injections. There are four of those which *will* hurt, like hell, I'm afraid. You know I wouldn't cause pain unnecessarily, but in this case, there is nothing I can do about it. Now is the time to withdraw if you don't want to go ahead.'

'Don't encourage me or I'll be out of here like a shot,' said Paul. 'The thought of spending twelve hundred quid just on my smile is enough to unnerve me. I must be mad. I can't remotely afford this. This is next year's payment to the Inland Revenue.'

'Think how cute you'll look when I've finished with you.' Rik was talking while sorting through some cards. 'Now, what I'm going to do is file down all four front teeth and then take casts of them. From the casts we'll make the crowns. That'll take about two weeks. After I've made the casts, I'll give you temporary caps. They may make you look a bit goofy, but you'll only have to wear them for a fortnight.'

'Jesus.'

'Now, because it's your front teeth, I have to give you four main injections in the roof of your mouth.' Rik had replaced the cards in his hands with his syringe kit. He began to assemble his weapons. 'Then there'll be four teensy-weensy injections in the gum around each tooth.'

'Jesus. How many?'

'Twenty injections in total. That's more pricks than even you've had in your mouth at one time. Ha ha!'

'Fuck off.'

'OK,' said Rik. 'Rinse out. Uh-uh. Not the rosé. Use the real stuff this time, please.'

As Rik placed the water spray in the corner of his mouth, Paul screwed his eyes tight shut. He could still envisage what was happening, though. In his fantasy, Rik was dressed in a sequined sari, wielding a huge, shining spear, roasting it over a blue flame until it was white-hot and then brandishing it in the air before he impaled his sacrificial victim. Paul flinched. He felt the sharp point of the needle find the seam where the back of his front tooth joined his gum. The needle slipped surreptitiously up into the space behind the joint and proceeded to travel into the roof of his mouth. Flesh and bone pressed and resisted and fought back, but to no avail. The needle forced its inexorable way onwards. It was the most excruciatingly painful sensation he had ever experienced. Although his eyes were shut firm, tears welled up inside his eyelids and waterfalled out. His brain could no longer understand where the syringe was headed. Jesus fucking Christ, it must be inside his *nose*. His sinuses screeched with pain, ripped apart by a slow-motion dumdum bullet. That fucking syringe must be nearly the length of a knitting needle and now, rupturing his nasal passages, it was headed deeper and *deeper* inside his skull. Paul was now cruelly aware of all of the bone in the interior of his head jarring and shuddering as it went into shock. Burning nerve-ends he didn't know he had introduced themselves, crying out in torment. Surely his cranium would be punctured from within. This massive steel rod would erupt volcano-like, as a Hunnish spike through the top of his head. Imagining fountains of blood, Paul simply could not bear the sensation of searing pain any longer and let out a single-toned, feminine scream straight out of the Hammer House of Horror.

'Sh, sh, sh. There we are. All finished.' Rik skilfully withdrew his rapier blade in one lightning stroke and stood back, proud of his sensitive touch. 'Only three more of these biggies to go,' he chirped. 'Then we'll canter through the last sixteen.'

Paul's head rolled senseless to the side, his eyes and tongue lolling insanely like a cow with bovine spongiform encephalopathy. He had fainted.

'If you wriggle around any more I'll have to strap you to the chair.'

Rik pulled some tissues from the box on the side and wiped away the tears on Paul's face. He gave him a second bunch to hold for himself. 'You may want to use these when you start drooling.'

'I hate you, you bastard. If I ever get off this chair alive I'm going to kill you. I swear it.' He sniffed in a horrendous amount of mucus. 'Oh, my God. I think I'm going to throw up.'

'No beauty without cruelty, sweetie. Just think of the sex you'll be able to get when you're cruising around with four fab new teeth.'

'I want that in writing.'

'Now, we'll just have to wait for five or ten minutes for the injections to take their full effect.'

'I can't feel anything beyond my nose already. It's like you've sawed through the back half of my head and removed it.'

'I think you're confusing me with Dennis Nilsen. Talk to me. Take your mind off the pain.'

'I can't.'

'Go on. Let's see. Tell me who the latest love of your life is.'

'Oh, he's gorgeous. His name is Jolyon.'

'Jolyon? He sounds very upmarket. Do I know him?'

'No, no. He lives in the Cotswolds. He's a gardener in a stately home. He's a plantsman.'

'Really? That sounds novel. Where did you meet him?'

'In his greenhouse.'

'What? He poked you over the petunias, did he?'

'No, it's not like that, *actually*. He's very sweet. We haven't done anything yet. I've been talking to him on the phone but so far I've only met him that once.'

'*Brief Encounter*. Yes,' said Rik. 'I can see you as the Celia Johnson type.'

'Piss off,' said Paul. 'It's very romantic. He's rather charming and polite. He's a real country boy. He's looking for a certain plant for me, and when he's got it, he's going to come down one weekend and stay with me. I'll show him the sights.'

'Yes. I bet you will. What tricks are you up to in the meantime?'

'Nothing. I'm saving myself for Jolyon. This is the one.'

'Well, you can impress him with your new teeth.'

Paul thought of Jolyon's creamy teeth and that old line

about eighteenth-century gravestones. There was no way Jolyon noticed teeth. 'Oh, God. My entire head feels numb. I feel I'm slavering from my mouth.'

'You are. But that's not the injections. That's jolly old rumpy-pumpy Jolyon doing that!'

Paul had cheered up a bit by now. Rik picked up his filing implement and switched it on. It let out a high-pitched, menacing whine that spelt danger and instilled sudden new fear into its victim.

'Oh my God, it sounds like an electric chainsaw,' said Paul, panicking. 'I'm not so sure about this now.'

'I can't understand what you're saying any more,' said Rik. 'You've lost the feeling in your lips and you're slobbering. Here goes.' He raised his arm and launched his attack.

Paul looked up into Rik's leering face. It could have been Jack Nicholson in *The Shining*. Petrified, he scrunched his eyes up as tight as possible and dug his nails into the padded arms on either side of the chair. Right now his knuckles were whiter than his teeth were ever going to be.

48

In the throng of the Queen's Theatre foyer, it was Duncan's eagle eyes which spotted Piers first. He looked distracted.

'We'll just say hello and go to our seats,' said Michael.

'Suits me,' said Duncan. 'It's so crowded with luvvies, I can't believe it.'

'How's my bow-tie?' asked Michael.

'Still straight, which is more than can be said for half the men here tonight.'

'How's my hair?'

'Still receding slowly,' said Duncan. 'Oh, look. He's seen us. Doesn't he look excited?'

'Well, imagine if *you* pulled this off.'

'Hello, hello,' gushed Piers. He *was* distracted, mainly because he was people-spotting and collecting invitations not otherwise easily obtainable. 'Have you seen who's here?'

'The Princess of Wales?' suggested Duncan.

This irritated Piers.

'She probably would have been here had she not gone into bloody retirement. It's so unfair. We at last get someone decent in the Royal Family who'll support our lot and then it all falls apart and she becomes a Trappist nun overnight. I'm afraid we don't have a royal patron yet for BrAIDS. But we're working on it.'

'Get Princess Margaret,' said Michael.

'She doesn't do AIDS officially. It's not one of her things,' said Piers. 'They don't do just anything, you know.'

'Some of them don't do just anything at all,' said Duncan.

'How much is this gala concert raising?' asked Michael.

'About sixty-five thousand.'

'Is that good or bad?' Duncan wanted to know.

'I think it's good. Don't you? If everyone was a mean Scot like you, Duncan, we'd have made bugger-all.'

'But he's so handsome!' Michael tweeked Duncan's cheek.

'Stop it!' said Duncan. 'People will see.'

'Let them. I don't care.'

'Well, I do.'

'Stop it, you two,' admonished Piers. 'You're always quarrelling. Now off you go to the bar while I play the hostess with the mostest.'

Michael and Duncan pushed on towards the grand circle while Piers swept off into the bustle.

'Quite the grand duchess in her element,' observed Michael, with a flourish of his wrist.

'Don't do that,' said Duncan. 'I hate it when you get all queenie.'

'Well, it is the Queen's Theatre.'

'I know. Couldn't they have chosen somewhere less of a joke?'

'You're worried that Nigel and Serena will turn up, aren't you?'

'Not at all. They're at Glyndebourne.'

'Really? What's on tonight?'

'I'm sure they've no idea. He still won't know, even when it's over.'

'He can't be that bad.'

'He is. So is she. I can hear her tomorrow. "I preferred the old Glyndebourne. It had more class. They let common types in these days."'

They passed on fighting their way to the bar when they saw how busy it was and eventually found their way to their seats, with Michael chatting up the prettiest of the programme boys on their way into their row. Duncan looked down into the stalls to spot the glitterati. He loved it. What he did not spot, however, was the top of the head of his best friend, Cindy Barratt, sitting patiently in her black lace gown and checking her watch.

Cindy was wondering, as usual, where Alan had got to. Half the fun of something like this was chatting together about how absolutely gorgeous or completely dreadful so-and-so looked close up in real life. As the house lights dimmed and the enthusiastic applause rippled from the front of the stalls up to the very back row of the gods, Alan joined her – just in time. The orchestra struck up and the audience settled in for an evening of thrown-together standards from under-rehearsed old favourites. Nothing taxing. It was all in a good cause.

'Piers! Halfway through already! It's going well.'

'Hello, Rik.' Piers squeezed the arm of a floating young companion and gave him the subtle signal to move on. He was quaffing champagne and becoming a little merry. Piers was an old friend of the dentist from the A-list gay circuit and tended to bump into him at just this sort of event. 'I haven't seen you for ages. Thank you for coming.'

'It's a great success,' said Rik. 'Congratulations.'

'Well, I'm only responsible for the sponsorship and some of the organisation. The performances and the speeches are up to the dear old luvvies. Poor old Whatserface. She can barely stand, let alone sing. They pull her along on wheels till she's right in the wings, then just give her a bloody good shove. Still, it's the thought that counts.'

'Who cares?' said Rik. 'You just want the money, don't you?'

'A little bit of prestige as well, if you don't mind. We really want this lot to come back next time. Have you something to drink?'

'I won't bother, thanks,' said Rik. 'I can't bear the thought of fighting through all these dreadful people just to get to a glass of warm champagne.'

'Oh, no, it's no problem. I have a bottle behind the bar. Follow me.'

Rik shadowed Piers as he helloed and air-kissed his way to a crammed and darkened corner at the end of the bar. He made a small overture to the bartender, who produced a champagne flute which was quickly filled and passed to the dentist.

'Now, Piers,' said Rik. 'Let me ask you a question.'

'Oh, no. What?'

'Who was that handsome young man you were squeezing the arm of when I caught you?'

'Oh!' Piers laughed. 'I couldn't remember his name for the life of me. Someone I picked up once at a dinner party in Earls Court.'

'He looks divine,' said the dentist. 'Very *moi*. Introduce me.'

'I can't. I can't remember his name!'

'I'll just have to use my own talents, then.'

'I'm sure you're not out of practice.'

'I'm sure you're not, either.'

'Oh, well. Hmm! I can't say anything about that. Not since I got involved in BrAIDS.' Piers was gushing just a little. In fact, he had not drunk that much but, mixed with his daily cocktail of life-prolonging drugs, the champagne was affecting his speech.

'Hah! I know what that means,' said Rik. 'That means you're still tricking!'

'It's not a crime, you know,' said Piers defensively. 'As long as it's safe.'

'So, who's the latest? Or are you just stringing them along as usual?'

'Oh, no one in particular. Well . . . no . . . hmm!'

'Go on, Piers. We're old friends. You can tell me.'

'Well, I was up in the Cotswolds not so long ago. At a stately home. You know the sort of place.'

'National Trust.'

'That type, but it wasn't one of theirs. Anyway, I picked up this young guy there.'

'A tourist?'

'Oh, my dear. He wasn't a tourist at all. He was working there in the garden. A sort of plantsman. A very horny twenty-seven-year-old. He's been down to London a couple of times since.'

This struck a chord of recognition in Rik's mind but he couldn't think why.

'So. What's he into? Go on, tell me!' He gave Piers a nudge. The five-minute bell rang and an announcement was made asking the audience to return to their seats. Nobody paid the blindest bit of attention.

'The usual stuff. He's really wild in the sack. No holds barred. Loves it in the derrière. I'm only too happy to oblige, of course.'

'You old bugger! As long as it's safe.'

'That's not a problem. He's positive too. At least, I assume he is. He insists I don't spoil it by wearing protection. Calls himself an old-fashioned boy!'

'Well, he must be,' said Rik, one eyebrow raised.

'What? Old-fashioned?'

'No. I meant positive. I mean, he wouldn't let you fuck him, would he?'

Piers was slipping into giggliness and Rik was feeling uncomfortable all of a sudden. It began to dawn on him that Piers was over-excited and a bit tipsy. It was out of character for him to talk sex in mixed company, even if no one else was eavesdropping. Rik racked his brains to recall who else had recently told him about a plantsman, but he couldn't place the story. He must have got his wires crossed. He just hoped that Piers was not avoiding telling people he was not just HIV-positive but actually in the first stage of full-blown AIDS. He couldn't get away with that, could he? Although, come to think of it, if you hadn't known him before, you'd never know now. No one in their right mind would let themselves get fucked without a condom these days, would they? Although there were rumours all round the scene about the queens who lived dangerously for added kicks. This was not the time or place to dwell on it, though.

The final bell rang and the audience trickled back to their padded seats for more 'I am what I am', 'Life is a cabaret, old chum', and 'I'm still here', uproariously sung on this occasion to a brand-new, specially written lyric:

'I'm still queer. And I'm damned well here.'

49

The agency was quiet, almost tranquil. He heard her soft footsteps approach.

'Hi. How are you getting on?'

Charlotte wandered into Steve da Silva's office on the pretext of bringing him up to date on her latest meeting with Briony Linden and chasing him up on the press and radio elements of the *Megabrek* campaign. He looked up from his word processor.

'Still here?' Steve sounded surprised. 'Are you working late, too?'

'Absolutely. I've got loads to do,' she replied. 'I thought I'd report back on the client's comments. Everyone's very pleased with your work.'

'Thank you.'

'Thank *you*.'

'Still mad at Duncan?' asked Steve.

'You bet. Actually, that's partly why I'm still here. I keep thinking about what's going to happen instead of concentrating on my work. And partly why I came down to see you. I need cheering up. Shall we go for a drink?'

His wolfish grin appeared. 'Are you the only one left upstairs?'

'Yes, and don't I know it. Nigel and Serena are at Glyndebourne, so they left early afternoon. Everyone else cleared off on time.'

'If there's no one else up there, why don't we raid the drinks cabinet rather than go out?'

'OK,' said Charlotte, 'if you want to.'

Steve got up and switched off the computer. 'I'll print that lot off tomorrow for you.'

'There's no rush really. I need to debrief you on the meeting first anyway. I really only came down for a chat.' She smiled at him and he smiled back. She held his gaze. Steve opened the door of the cupboard that he used as a wardrobe.

'Gosh, haven't you got a lot of suits?' said Charlotte. 'How much did that lot set you back?'

'No idea. I earn so much money these days. It trickles through my fingers like water.' He absent-mindedly wiggled the fingers of one hand as he spoke. He pulled out a pink linen jacket and pulled it on over his T-shirt. Linen trousers and loafers completed his lightweight look.

'For one ghastly moment there,' said Charlotte, 'I thought you were going to strip off and change into one of your active lycra numbers.'

He grinned. 'We'll do that one later!'

'You're terrible.' She giggled. Steve pocketed his money and keys from his desktop and they strolled out of his office.

'You ought to get a padlock for your wardrobe door, you know,' said Charlotte. 'We're not insured for personal possessions in the office.'

'You can tell you're on the management side, can't you?' said Steve. 'It would never occur to me to know about things like that.'

'Probably not. But then, you're talented in other ways.'

'Would you like a demonstration?'

'Stop it!' said Charlotte, but her mock annoyance suggested 'Yes, please' to Steve.

'You're quite the little cat burglar, aren't you?' observed Steve, languishing in the swivel seat. He had kicked off his loafers. He wasn't wearing any socks. Charlotte did indeed look feline in her skimpy black sleeveless blouse and black lycra leggings. She ran her fingers through her hair.

'I ought to feel awful,' she said. 'I picked it up from Hazel, all this sneaking around in the boss's office and stealing the wine. It's nice, though, isn't it?'

They were in Serena's office, having rifled the fridge under her desk. Charlotte got up to go back to her own office but a new note in Steve's voice stopped her.

'Jesus. Look at this.'

'What? Don't, Steve. You mustn't go through Serena's things. We're in enough trouble as it is if we get caught.'

'Miss Goody Two Shoes! You just helped yourself to two bottles of Pinot Grigio. Anyway, look!'

He held up the publicity print of Serena over his shoulder, while he searched the desk for other titbits.

'I saw it earlier,' said Charlotte. 'Isn't she ghastly? She looks like a grinning gypsy.'

She walked over to get a closer look. Steve swung round and they were less than half an inch from each other. He leant down and kissed her gently on her winey lips. His own were like wet pillows.

'Don't,' she said, not very convincingly.

He leaned forward again and this time slipped his tongue into her mouth and began to explore. Without Charlotte realising, he expertly rid himself of his wine glass and removed hers. He put one large hand on the small of her back and, with the other, pushed his fingers through her hair. He grabbed it at its end and pulled it sharply down to bring her face flat up so that he could devour it greedily. Charlotte went through the pretence of pushing him away but he pressed her to him and pulled her into his chest. Then he sprung a surprise on her. He lifted her up and spun her round on to the desktop. With his wide thighs he pushed her knees apart and stepped forward into her open legs. He withdrew from her mouth and tongued his way down her languid neck. With one flick he undid his ponytail and shook his hair out behind him in a cascade. Charlotte's fingers ran their way into it and were lost for a second before she continued to stroke his back and arms.

He placed both hands on her shoulders and pinned her blouse there, while with his teeth he undid the top few buttons. Then he produced her breasts, one in each hand. They were not large but firm, perky and pointing upwards. He licked and kissed and nibbled each nipple while Charlotte kicked each shoe off her feet behind him.

Steve stepped back and grinned at her. She pulled her blouse, still partly buttoned, down round her waist and slipped her arms out of the armholes. Steve stretched one powerful arm upwards and with the other unpeeled his T-shirt straight off and over his head. He shook his hair back into place. Then his hands went straight to the waistline of her leggings.

'Lift up your bum,' he ordered.

Charlotte bumped up off the table for a second and, as a magician might pull a tablecloth off a full table without displacement, Steve whipped off her leggings and G-string in one go. They fell to the floor behind him.

Again, he used his huge body to stand between her legs and push her thighs apart. He put two fingers to his mouth and moistened them, then ran them between her legs and stroked her mound. She sighed as he fondled her and then began to work his finger magic on her clitoris. Meanwhile their tongues were intertwined, tying and untying lubricant knots with each other. Charlotte was completely lost in time. Serena Sark could have walked in and she would neither have noticed nor cared.

Now Steve stepped back, undid his belt and ran it out through the loops of his trousers. He unbuttoned his flies and his loose linen trousers fell to the floor. He was wearing pale yellow silk boxer shorts which could not conceal the beefiness of his massive semi-erection, its sheer weight causing it to hang extended yet limp. If Steve had not taken Charlotte's breath away with the oral plunder of her face, he did so now. He slipped his shorts down, kicked them off, and took his big, black circumcised dick in his hand. Charlotte had seen nothing like it outside of a delicatessen. Its extreme darkness contrasted with the lighter skin of his torso; its thickness filled the palm of his right hand. He pulled on it mechanically to work up its hardness. Pre-cum oozed from the glistening glans.

He used his other hand to find the small of her back again and pull her slight body to the edge of the desk. Then he took the giant head of his knob and rubbed it up and down and round and over the entrance to her pussy. Meanwhile her hands caressed his face, his hair, his neck, his arms, his back, his fleshy backside. He continued to kiss and suck on her nipples and anywhere else his tongue could reach. They were both in abandon now and both thoroughly wet as he began to push his way into her. Charlotte was amazed not to tense up. Instead she dropped her head back and her hair hung down loose. She let go of Steve and placed her hands on the surface of the desk. He took her hips in his hands and began to slide in and out of her, first slowly, then faster. Charlotte had never been fucked like this before. It was pure animal porn-film sex and it was driving her wild with unreleased, pent-up sexual tension.

'Don't come inside me,' she gasped as Steve continued his rhythmic fucking.

He grinned. 'Don't worry. Be happy,' he grunt-sang. He pulled out of her. She thought for a moment it was over but instead he rolled her over on the desktop on to her knees and mounted her again from behind. In deeper now, he tweaked and tugged on her tits which were hanging down and swinging backwards and forwards in time with his furious pummelling. He gradually increased his speed. Charlotte and he were breathing simultaneously in rhythm.

'I'm going to come now,' he announced.

She looked over her shoulder. He pulled his penis out of her and held it pointing it downwards and to the side. A jet of thick white spunk shot straight out, followed by two smaller arcs. He stood, knees bent slightly, milking himself dry. He wiped his forehead and grinned at her.

'Enjoy that, Charlie?'

'You're impossible!' she laughed. 'I can't believe we just did that.'

But Steve was not finished. 'OK, babe. Now it's your turn,' he said. 'Sit back on the edge of the desk as you were before.'

She dutifully did as she was told. To her surprise, Steve dropped and squatted in front of her, then nuzzled his face into her blonde vulva and began to eat away. As his tongue licked and flicked upon her, Charlotte ascended into seventh heaven. It was multiple-orgasm time. She stretched each arm out to the side and pressed her hands hard on to the flatness of the desktop, unaware that the thumb of her right hand had found the publicity photo of Serena Sark and the space between her eyes. As Serena's smile remained ever-wide and ever-constant, Charlotte pressed more firmly down into her boss's face, now furrowing her forehead, now caressing her beneath her chin, now puckering her extended smile. As she arched her back in climax, blissfully unaware than her superior had somehow joined her in a threesome, she unwittingly pummelled Serena's cheeks with her clenching and unclenching fist, as if to check her for her bare-faced intrusion on a stolen sexual moment. At last, Charlotte squealed and squirmed with pleasure and fell back, surprised, sated, spent. Steve da Silva had more than lived up to his reputation as one of London's biggest creatives.

Old Zena shuffled through the stale offices at five thirty in the morning, spray polish, duster and bin liners in her hands, decaying carpet slippers falling apart on each foot. She finished tidying up Mr Gainsborough's office and went into Mrs Sark's. She collected up the dirty wine glasses and tipped the contents of the wastepaper basket into her black bin liner. As she gave the desk a rudimentary wipe over, her eye spotted something hanging drip-like on one of the metal drawer handles. At first it looked like that foamy stuff found on the stems of plants, where some insect has laid its young in a sort of spawn. Then she understood what the congealed blob was. She gave a hoarse laugh and with a squirt of her aerosol rubbed it away. Mr Sheen really does wipe everything clean. She gave the surface of the desk a good going-over and lastly picked up the grinning picture of Mrs Sark. She used her duster to remove the thumbprint smack in the middle of her face.

'You and that Mr Gainsborough! Still at it, you naughty girl.'

She laughed again hoarsely. Her laugh degenerated into a smoker's cough and she shuffled on her weary way.

It was nearly a fortnight since Duncan had resigned. Hazel's head came into view round the edge of Charlotte's door.

'Are you staying late again tonight, Charlotte?'

'Yes. There's so much to do. I've been put on new business. You know, that Japanese airline thing.'

'Have you?'

Not a good sign. Nigel and Serena had bypassed Hazel completely on that one.

'I'm just doing some background reading. Serena was meant to be briefing me this evening on it, but she'd forgotten about Henley.'

'So you're not working on *Megabrek*?'

'No.'

'It's just that I have an appointment with somebody and I really need to get away,' said Hazel. 'But I don't like leaving you here on your own slaving away every evening.'

'Oh, don't worry about me,' said Charlotte. 'Off you go. I'll be fine.'

'Yeah, but you don't think I'm pulling my weight at the moment, do you?'

'I don't think that at all, Hazel. I'm a bit of a workaholic. Always have been.'

'Always have been! Listen to you. You're just a baby compared to an old-timer like me!'

'Just go!' Charlotte shooed Hazel away with her hand.

Hazel went off to the lift but, checking over her shoulder in case Charlotte was spying on her, bypassed it and took the stairs down to Steve da Silva's office. She crept along the corridor. Yup. She could hear him tapping away at his keyboard. This was the fifth time those two had been hanging around after everyone else had fucked off. Interesting. They were definitely an item. God. How could a gorgeous girl like that fall for a slimeball like him? It was enough to make you barf.

*   *   *

Hazel gave a small wave of her hand.

'Hi. It's me. I'm Hazel'

Alan Josling came over to the table. She was seated outside Le Pont de la Tour, a classy, expensive Thames-side restaurant, located in the old brick Butler's Wharf and packed with immaculately groomed diners on this balmy summer evening. The colossus of Tower Bridge, for one hundred years the gateway to London, loomed over them in all its theatricality, unreal and two-dimensional, like a giant version of the picture postcards Hazel knew from childhood. This was London at its best, she thought: a location that was completely unique, with a fabulous sense of its own presence.

Alan had met her only once, the previous year, so he shook her hand rather than kissing her.

'You didn't remember what I looked like, did you?' chided Hazel.

'It's always difficult to spot people in restaurants,' said Alan. 'You look different. Have you changed your hair or something?'

'Yup. One difference between London and Sydney is that you can get a really chic short haircut here. I've also put on a ton of weight. The diet here is so high in fat. Here, have some of this.'

Alan realised she was halfway through a bottle of Semillon Chardonnay.

'Not so much,' he said. 'I'm driving.'

'Don't you just love Tower Bridge?' said Hazel. 'It's fabulous.'

'I suppose it is,' said Alan matter-of-factly. 'I never really pay much attention to that sort of thing. *Britannia* is moored just down the river. It was on the news.'

'The royal yacht?' Hazel cast her eyes across the water down to the post-modern mirror of Canary Wharf on the skyline.

'You can't see it from here. They're bringing it up for celebrations on the river. The Prince of Wales is coming.'

'Charlie boy, eh?'

'Oh. You're one of those republicans.'

'Not me. I love the royals. I don't want Australia to have a boring old president. I'm an Anglophile. At least I was before I got here.'

'What's made you change your mind?' He didn't wait for an answer. 'There are supposed to be fireworks tonight.'

'Fantastic! What time?'

'I don't know. Later on. Have you looked at the menu?'

'No,' said Hazel. 'I always start on the wine list and work my way back from there.'

They ordered and dined slowly and comfortably. Alan realised he could not match Hazel's drinking capacity, but even at half her rate he was soon pleasantly relaxed. He picked up the bill and they strolled out on to the riverside walk, prettily illuminated with pearly strings of white light-bulbs. A crowd was beginning to assemble to watch the fireworks. Tower Bridge was itself lit up against the darkening sky, even more of a set-piece from the musical theatre than before. They walked in front of Butler's Wharf and the Design Museum, past the diners and the ornamental anchors, trying to identify the historic ships moored on this section of the Thames. Hazel leaned over the riverside wall and looked at the twinkling reflections in the water.

'I had a reason why I wanted to see you, Alan,' she said.

'I supposed you must have,' said Alan, 'what with not having been in contact since you got your job.'

'Well, you were very helpful to me when I first arrived. I knew nobody at all. But the truth is, it hasn't really worked out.'

'Nigel and Serena up to their old tricks?'

'You bet. They are dreadful!' She dwelt so much on the last word she almost spelt it out. 'They'll never promote me. And Duncan Cairns – you know him, don't you? – is leaving.'

Alan was not pleased about that. 'Is that for sure?' he asked.

'Yeah. Why shouldn't it be?' replied Hazel. 'Anyway, I'm thinking of chucking it in and going back to Sydney. I wanted to get to be an account director in London and go back to Australia. London's regarded as the world centre of advertising so, from a top job here, I could have walked into anything I chose. But to go back as a thirty-year-old account manager . . .'

'I'd hang around if I were you.'

'At C&B or in London generally? I don't think with the market the way it is anyone else will consider employing me, because I'm a foreigner. The law says they have to take people from the European Union first. The old empire doesn't count for much these days.'

'Have you spoken to a headhunter?' suggested Alan. 'Audrey Goldberg, for instance.'

'She's awful. Showed no interest. Too difficult to place.'

'Well, C&B could win new business,' hinted Alan. 'Things are picking up.'

'Nigel Gainsborough is not picking up. He's getting worse. They'll never win anything.' She laughed. 'I'm doomed.'

They turned and walked in the direction of the bridge again. Alan put his arm round Hazel to guide her round a clutch of tourists using a camcorder. He kept it there. Hazel felt uncomfortable but said nothing.

'I don't know what advice to give you, Hazel. I'm sure a nice girl like you will have no problem.'

They walked on under the arch of the bridge spanning the riverside walk. In the darkness there, in front of the souvenir shop, Alan stumbled. As he recovered he had to pull himself closer to Hazel and his hand slipped from the small of her back on to her bum. She stopped immediately.

'What are you doing?'

'Nothing,' he said apologetically. 'Do you want to stay for the fireworks? I thought we could go back to your flat and continue over a drink or something. It's not too late.'

'Yes it is too late,' she snapped back at him. 'I hope you don't think buying me dinner gives you the right to come on like that?'

'Like what?' said Alan, apparently confused. 'I think you've misunderstood.'

'I have not misunderstood, buster,' said Hazel, her voice rising. 'You're not interested in me or my problems, are you? You're just out to get your leg over!'

'Come on, Hazel. You're overreacting. Let me give you a lift home.' He tried to smile consolingly, but her ire was up.

'I'll take a taxi, thank you.'

She abandoned him and fled up the steps to the bridge above and into the floodlit night. As she sped through the crowd gathered on the world-famous landmark, a thunderous bang walloped in the air over the Thames and she was fleetingly silhouetted against the first fireworks in the sky, a burst of neon chrysanthemums radiating outwards in rainbow colours.

But Hazel kept her head down. British men, she thought. You just couldn't trust them, could you?

51

'You have called Duncan Cairns. I'm sorry I'm unable to come to the phone at the moment. Please leave a message after the tone and I'll call you back.'

Michael waited and spoke after the tone.

'Hi, Dunky, it's me. It's lunchtime. I'm just leaving the office for St Mary's hospital in Paddington. Piers collapsed this morning. He got very weak suddenly. Oh, Duncan, it's so sad. I'll be there for a while if you're looking for me. I don't know how long. I should be all right for this evening. I'll call you when I'm leaving. Be a good boy. Bye.'

'Doing anything for lunch?' It was Martin Fox.

'I wish I wasn't. I have a friend who is seriously ill in hospital. He's dying. I'm going to see him now.' Michael picked up his car keys and checked in his jacket pocket for his wallet. His hands flapped round his desk, desperate for last-minute organisational things to do to occupy his mind.

'Is it AIDS?'

'Yes,' said Michael, resigned to it.

'I'm sorry,' said Martin.

'I've cleared the advertising for *Megabrek*.'

'We don't need to talk about that now.'

'I thought you ought to know. I had no problems with it.'

'Well, there's a surprise. I'm sure you saw it before any of the rest of us.'

'No, I didn't, as it happens,' said Michael. 'Actually, Duncan is leaving the agency. Don't tell Briony, though. It's confidential and the agency haven't told their clients yet. Believe it or not, he's going to work for Karen Myhill.'

'Who is?'

'Duncan.'

'Good God, haven't you warned him? Has he met his new boss?'

'Of course he's met her.'

'No, I meant Mad Max. He who hires and fires more people in this business than I do. I saw him the other week. Took him to the cinema.'

'Did you?' Michael was intrigued. He ought to dash but this was too good an opportunity to make bigger than usual small-talk. 'Why did you do that?'

'Well, I visit him occasionally. Karen needs a break sometimes. The boy has no father figure.'

'Not one that we know of.'

'She'll never, ever live it down, will she?' said Martin.

'I don't know. I half suspect she enjoys the notoriety. I haven't been to the movies for ages. I really ought to make the effort. What did you go and see?' asked Michael.

'God! Max's choice. It was called *Stalingrad*. In German, with subtitles. It's the grimmest, most thought-provoking film about the Teutonic spirit I've seen.'

'I've never seen any, so I wouldn't know. Max always was a precocious bugger.'

'Absolutely,' agreed Martin. 'We once tried to adopt him. Thank God Karen wouldn't agree.'

Michael was well taken aback. He'd not heard this before.

'Did you? Why?'

'Well, those rumours,' said Martin. 'It wasn't clear Karen would want to keep him. She was at the peak of her career then.'

'And you approached her about it?'

'Yes. We worked out what we had to do technically, if it was allowed and so on, and then went round to see her.'

'How did she react?' Michael was curious to know as much as possible.

'Bizarrely – meaning her normal reaction,' laughed Martin. 'I think she was touched and insulted at the same time. I suppose we were well-meaning but tactless.'

'My God.'

'I know what you're thinking,' said Martin. 'My wife still thinks it sometimes.'

'What?'

'Oh, don't pretend. You're thinking that I'm Basket Case.'

'Are you?'

'Hey.' Martin gave him a mock warning look. 'You'd better get a move on.'

Michael walked along the glaring corridor. There was a policeman at the door of Piers's room. He opened it for Michael without looking him in the eye. Michael went over to the bed and sat down on the standard-issue visitor's chair. Piers was sound asleep. Michael didn't know if he was drugged or if this was his natural state. He had been placed on a drip with a plastic tube inserted into his arm and another inserted in one nostril. His right arm lay outside the sheets. Michael took his hand in his.

'Oh, Piers. I hope it doesn't end now. Not like this.'

Michael felt tearful for a moment and then sighed and sat back in his chair. He sat there completely still for an hour and remembered his oldest friend.

There was a knock on the door. The policeman popped his head into the room. 'Would you like a cup of tea, sir? I'm going to see if I can get one for myself.'

'That's very kind of you. Are you sure you should be leaving your post?' he said sarcastically. 'He might get up and run away.'

'It's procedure, sir. I know he can't do anything. It's also for his own protection. How d'you take it?'

'Er, white without sugar.'

'Be back as soon as I can.'

Michael sat for five minutes. When the door opened this time, however, it was not the policeman but a white-coated doctor. He was a young Asian with heavy five o'clock shadow. Michael stood up and moved away from Piers.

'Mr Farnham?' The doctor was softly spoken. 'I'm Dr Barani. You're his solicitor?'

'No, I'm not actually. I *am* a solicitor by training, but I'm here first and foremost as a friend. I'm the head of the legal team at The Station.'

The doctor smiled politely. 'So, what's the problem with the police?'

'Oh, it's absolutely ridiculous. It's so ludicrous it's farcical. This man is lying here dying of AIDS and the police want to arrest him for something that's got nothing to do with him. They have no evidence and no case, basically. It's outrageous. I can't believe this country, sometimes.'

'What's he supposed to have done?'

'Nothing,' said Michael petulantly. 'That's the whole point. Apparently they've busted a paedophile ring based around a group of under-age rent-boys. One of the rent-boys is helping the police with their enquiries, i.e. telling them anything they want to hear in order to get himself off. This boy was caught with an electronic personal organiser thing which contained Piers's name and address and phone number.'

'I see.'

'Well, it's hardly grounds for treating someone like this.' He pointed towards the policeman's post on the other side of the door. 'They're complete bastards, the police. Look at that one out there. He's just a thug in a uniform.'

The door swung open and the policeman tiptoed in gently and passed Michael a polystyrene cup of tea, smiled sweetly, winked and then crept out. Michael noticed the doctor's wry smile.

'Am I getting hysterical?' asked Michael sheepishly.

'No. You're fine,' said Dr Barani. 'You've had a bad shock. Excuse me for asking, but is Mr MacLelland White your partner?'

'No, he's not. Once upon a time he was.' He looked across the room at Piers. 'He's my oldest friend.'

Michael lost his composure and sobbed. He put the cup down on the table at the end of the bed and took a moment to pull himself together. Dr Barani looked on sympathetically but made no move to comfort him.

'I'm sorry,' apologised Michael.

'It's OK,' said the doctor.

'I bet half of the so-called boys are over eighteen.'

'I thought they changed the age of consent.'

'It wasn't the law at the time.'

'The police wouldn't prosecute on charges involving men aged over eighteen. Not now, would they?'

'Yes, they bloody well would. They're obsessed with homophobia.'

'I'm sure some of them are. Racism, too,' said the doctor. 'Basically, they're good, though, I think. I support the police. They're just not strong on getting it right on liberal issues.'

Michael looked at Piers lying by their side.

'He's been in here before,' he said. 'He made a fantastic recovery.'

'I know,' said the doctor. 'Quite remarkable.'

'Will he get better this time, do you think?'

'He's very weak. It's difficult to say.'

'Is that it, then? The end to his life. In this room.'

'We'll wait and see. Some hang on for ages, others fade away very fast. It's difficult to know which is better.'

'I suppose I should ask you some things while you're here.'

'Yes?'

'Is he sedated or sleeping naturally?'

'He's sedated. He's had problems with his digestive system. His immune system has virtually disappeared now. You know about T-cells? Well, his count is almost non-existent, which means that, really, the slightest little thing now could end his life. The consumption of solid food was causing him to have convulsions. So he's being drip-fed through that tube.'

'Will he come round?'

'Oh, yes. He's got at least a little time. He should be awake tomorrow in the late morning or afternoon.'

'The police will want to question him. They want to eliminate him from their line of enquiry or charge him while they still can.'

'Well, Mr Farnham, why don't you go home for tonight and come back tomorrow. If he comes round, I'll call you first. I won't let the police get at him without you being here.'

'Thank you.'

'Shall I show you the quick way out?'

'No thanks. I'd like to stay a little longer with Piers, if I may.'

Dr Barani left and Michael resumed his place by his friend's side, their hands clasped for a short while once more.

52

'I can't wait for you to remove these things.' Paul was back in the dentist's chair. He was referring to the temporary caps fitted on his four top front teeth. 'They make me look like Muffin the Mule.'

'Are you ready, then?' asked Rik.

'Let me just have another sip of this Mateus Rosé,' said Paul, being kittenish. 'It's rather a fun way to spend an afternoon, getting merry in the dentist's chair.'

'Well, don't get drunk,' said the dentist. 'You know how girlie you get. I can't stand you when you get like that.'

'Oh, piss off and just do your job. That's what I'm paying for you, isn't it?'

'Hark at the proper little madam.'

It took half an hour for Rik to pull off the temporary caps and fit and fix the four new porcelain teeth over the filed-down stumps he had created two weeks earlier.

'Let's test the bite once more.'

Paul bit into an imprint detector sheet that Rik had placed over his lower teeth. There were no marks this time, meaning the porcelain crowns were now positioned correctly. Paul ran his tongue over his new upper teeth. How much more even and smooth they felt. Rik held a mirror over Paul's face and mimicked Loyd Grossman on *Through the Keyhole*.

'Who lives with a mouth like this?'

'Wow. Brilliant.' Paul beamed, and not just to check his new smile. He was genuinely happy. 'You've done a terrific job,' he told Rik.

'Thank you. Say "S".'

'Why?'

'Don't be awkward, just say "S". We need to check your enunciation. Sometimes people end up speaking a little differently.'

'S. S. S-S-S-S-S. How's that?'

'Thimply fantathtic.' Rik roared with laughter at the look of annoyance on Paul's face.

'Honestly,' said Paul. 'I don't know why I bother to come here. You treat me like dirt. I'm paying you through the nose for this.'

Rik played mockfully hurt. 'Don't you love me any more, darling?'

'No. I never did. I was just after sex. Now I love Jolyon. D'you remember I told you about him a fortnight ago? He's a plantsman at a stately home in the Cotswolds.'

'Yes.' Rik sprang up and went over to the counter at the side of the room. 'Yes, I do. I do now. I didn't before. But I do now.' This was going to be awkward.

'He's lovely, although you could fix his teeth for him,' Paul prattled on. 'He's got even less money than me, though.'

'Paul?' Rik's mood had changed. He sounded pensive. 'How did you meet this guy?'

'Jolyon?'

'Yes.'

'We visited the stately home where he works. It was a lovely day and I wandered off on my own. I was exploring the walled kitchen garden. I bet you don't know what the difference between a quince and a pear is?'

'Who were you with?'

'You know them all, actually. Michael Farnham, his lover Duncan and Piers Thingy White. We spent the weekend at Michael and Duncan's cottage. You know Duncan, don't you?'

'Yes, a bit. I know Michael and Piers from when I was first in London. This all makes sense.'

'What does?'

'I'll tell you in a minute. Answer me honestly, will you?'

'God, what are you on about? You're coming over all religious.'

'I just want to know the truth. Have you been having sex with Jolyon?'

'I told you last time I was here. I've only met him once. I've not seen him since that first day. But he's coming down to London this weekend, or the next one. He's getting a plant for me for my garden.'

'I didn't know you had a garden.'

'I don't. That's going to be a huge, huge embarrassment, but there you are.' Paul laughed. 'I'll just have to make up for it with my huge, huge dick!'

'And you didn't have sex with him the first day?'

'No. It wasn't like that. It was all dreamy and romantic. John Thomas and Lady Chatterley. That sort of thing. Now stop sounding like Hercule Poirot and tell me what you're going to tell me.'

Paul lay back and held the mirror closely over his face. He stretched and puckered his mouth this way and that to see what effect this had on his gleaming new teeth.

'Well, I met Piers the other night at a function.'

'Where?'

'It doesn't matter. These days I rarely see him. He'd had a little too much to drink.'

'That doesn't sound like him.'

'No. He was all talkative. He told me he'd picked up a plantsman in the Cotswolds and had been having sex with him.'

Paul's last excruciating expression for the mirror sat frozen on his face. He was stunned. He lay immobile on the dentist's chair like an abandoned waxwork from Madame Tussaud's. 'You're joking?' he said after a while. 'Please say you're joking.'

'That's what he told me.'

'It can't be the same one. Piers wouldn't do that. It's indecent.'

'Oh, come on, Paul,' said Rik. 'It must be. The reason I'm telling you is that Piers has obviously got the big A.'

'Not obvious enough as far as Jolyon's concerned. I can't believe he would do that. He seems so sweet. I'll just have to woo him with my charms when I get my hands on him.'

'I haven't finished, Paul. Piers has been having unprotected anal intercourse with him.'

'That's impossible,' snorted Paul.

'Well, not according to Piers,' Rik replied. 'Your plantsman friend must be HIV-positive or a complete fucking lunatic. If I were you I'd drop him like a hot potato, if that's not an unsuitable term for a vegetable grower.'

Rik had built a beautiful new smile for Paul over two weeks and had taken barely more than thirty seconds to wipe it from his face. Tears welled up in Paul's eyes yet again in the dentist's chair. He was completely crushed.

'Oh, Rik. It's not fair. I'll never find a lover,' he wailed. 'I'm destined to be all on my own for ever and ever.'

Charlotte positively bounced out into the muggy lunchtime warmth. She turned left into Dean Street and, in obvious good mood, strode her way up towards Oxford Street. She negotiated the pedestrians thronging on the pavement there, and, running out in front of a snake of taxis belching out black fumes, crossed over to the north side of London's great high street. It was tacky – well, some of it was. If you ever went into one of the souvenir shops, and no real Londoner ever did, you might find some amusing piece of plastic in the shape of a London double-decker bus or a City of Westminster street sign that you could at least give to someone at an office party. The souvenir shops were legit. What *was* tacky was the new breed of store like the one she was peering in now, where an empty shop, which had been ground into defeat by a lethal combination of recession and business rates, had had its premises taken over for a sort of fly-by-night auction of audio and TV technology well past its sell-by date.

I'm sure half that stuff is stolen, thought Charlotte.

An announcer with a cockney accent was squawking through a microphone at the back of the store, telling a curious crowd of old and poor Londoners peppered with stray Germans and Swedes that there were no set prices and that every item was a bargain. They were about to close the doors to avoid the store becoming overcrowded. What a load of crap, thought Charlotte. It's against the law to lock people in a store, anyway. The real purpose was to give the salesmen a captive audience whom they could con. Margaret had told her that what they did was to have three or four women make purchases to give the audience 'permission to spend'. The women would then leave, stand round the corner, and return ten minutes later, hopefully having started a trend. Where were the police? Margaret had said that commercial squatting wasn't yet against the law, and that's how they got away with it. Charlotte stopped caring and moved on.

She turned up Rathbone Place and then walked into Charlotte Street. She looked up at the sign. She knew it was extremely childish, but she liked seeing her name up there. When she was a little girl, her father had walked her up here from Oxford Street and said, 'Look, Charlotte. This is your street. It will always be here and it will always be named after you.'

'Is it mine, Daddy?' she had asked.

'Yes, it is,' he had said. 'It's yours.'

Which is more than could be said for her father. Once Mummy and her father had divorced, her relationship with him had grown strained. It was like he was accusing her of siding with her mother. She hadn't sided with either of them, but Mummy had played it all up a bit too much. These days she did get on better with her father, well enough for him to have bought her a Ducati. It was a friendly but not close, not special, thing. Not for someone who had once been Daddy's golden girl and still wanted to be.

Strange how as a grown-up she had got her first proper job in Charlotte Street, at Saatchi and Saatchi. It seemed ages since she had left. She hadn't seen any of her old colleagues since starting at Clancey and Bennett. She didn't particularly want to now, come to think of it. They were probably watching her through the windows of Café Italien or Chez Gerard. So, to avoid being spotted, she turned right into Windmill Street and then walked up Tottenham Court Road to Heals department store.

Charlotte had decided to buy a token gift for Steve. He had wined and dined her quite a bit. He said he was putting it all on expenses, but that wasn't the point. She wasn't remotely sure where this relationship was going and she didn't love him or anything like that, but it was great fun and it was making her happy. She was able to consume vast quantities of work at the moment because Steve was invigorating her with vast quantities of sex. And lots of varieties of it, too, not just the conventional, fast-food sort of bonking that her public-schooly boyfriends had used her for. For the most part, though, Steve was like all the others. He just wanted to hump as often as possible. So far, he hadn't shown much interest in talking to her or finding out what she thought about any particular thing. But, to be fair, he was interested in giving her pleasure, making sure she enjoyed it. She decided not to think about who in the past he may have experimented on to learn his choice techniques. She just hoped it wasn't someone she knew. It gave him a great kick, he had said, to make a woman squirm with pleasure and come back for more. It clearly also gave him a kick that she was white and a toff, a lot more socially advanced than him. This was the *frisson* that lent their liaison a sexual charge and the rush of adrenalin that comes with tasting forbidden fruit. What would Mummy say if she saw Steve? Charlotte would have to explain his ethnic heritage – half from the West Indies, half from Goa – and that he wasn't fully black, but half-black and half-Eurasian, a quarter Indian and a quarter Portuguese, to be precise.

She went into Heals and moved through the ground floor, past the contemporary dining tables on wrought-iron bases and past the acres of striped, comfortable settees, any one of which would have filled her whole flat. She arrived at the bit where they sell kitchen appliances and dinner services alongside chocolates and boxed teas. Everything was rather expensive-looking, but Charlotte felt that if she bought just one thing and took it out of its setting, it might not look like much when she got it home.

She went through into the next area. Here was fabulous glassware and wickerwork and picture frames. And mirrors. One range was jewel-like, each mirror the size of a large platter. One of those would be ideal for a narcissist like Steve. They were hand-made in beaten and polished stainless steel. Each was unique. She picked out one with jagged points leaping out at the edge to form a flaming sun. She turned it round. It was eighty-five pounds. That was a bit expensive. On the other hand, she didn't have much of her lunchtime left. Steve *would* definitely like it. It would go in his minimalist flat in Notting Hill. He could even hang it in his bathroom. Every morning he could get up and examine his beautiful face and preen himself. He was in love with his own self-image. But when he drooled at himself in this it would be Charlotte who was reflected back at him. She took the mirror gingerly in her hands and approached the sales desk. She could put it on her charge card. Steve *was* worth eighty-five pounds, wasn't he? She looked down into the sunny silver-looking glass and saw her own golden, happy reflection, convincing her he was.

When Charlotte had first told Steve she was going to hold a dinner party she had become quickly aggrieved at the balefulness of his hangdog expression.

'I do have other friends, you know.'

'Spend your time with me, babe.'

'You are invited.'

'They're all wankers, your friends. The double-barrelled set. Sloane Rangers.'

'That's completely untrue.' Her voice broke with mock annoyance. 'I can't think of more than one person I know who's got a double-barrelled name. Apart from you.'

'Huh?'

'"Da" and "Silva". That's as good as double-barrelled.'

'I'm from an ethnic minority, for Chrissake.'

'Just the one? I thought it was two, West Indian and Goan. A double-barrelled name and a double-barrelled heritage.'

'I've a good mind to take you across my knee and spank you.'

He had then chased her around the flat screaming until she allowed him to catch her and they fell on to the settee and he squeezed her and she kissed him passionately while his mercurial hands rippled up the inside of her clothing.

'Stop it! It's broad daylight.'

Steve howled with laughter. 'What's that got to do with anything?'

'It's not the right time of day to get undressed. You're always rummaging through my clothing. Half the time I have to run to the phone with my knickers round my ankles.'

'It's called lurve, ba-a-a-a-be.' He said it like a rock DJ.

'It's called sex. You don't love me. You just love having sex with me.'

'Whatever.'

Later on they had got round to discussing the guest list.

'Don't have all those people from work.'

'Why not? We like Duncan. Haze is my best friend. You work with Orlando. Anyway, that way you'll know some people.'

'I see them all day in the office. I don't need to see them at night.'

'You see me all day in the office and you seem to need to see *me* all night, every night.'

'You're different. You have an edible pussy.'

'Don't be disgusting.'

'No one can hear.'

'I can!'

'You love it when I talk dirty.'

'Stop saying that. It's not true. Who are we going to invite?'

'Not the whole of Clancey and Bennett, that's for definite. We'll only end up talking about your bosses or The Station and bore the rest of your friends who'll bore us all back. Let's not bother with the entertaining, babe.'

'You're worried they'll see you rolling joints at the table and tell everyone else in the office.'

'Everyone does that. That's no big deal.'

'I don't think any of them do. Duncan is rather prim and proper.'

'He's repressed. He thinks no one knows he's a queen.'

'Steve, don't be nasty. We don't know that and if he is we wouldn't mind. I couldn't tell you anything about Orlando or Margaret's private lives either. Or Hazel's for that matter.'

'She's not getting it, that's for sure. That's what makes her so damned spiky all the time.'

'She's not spiky. She's just an Australian. They're all like that, aren't they? Anyway, she's really unhappy at work. She's not getting anywhere. Neither am I, for that matter.'

'You got me, babe.'

'I got you, babe,' sang Charlotte. 'Not exactly the Sonny and Cher of St John's Wood, are we? Listen, this dinner party is important to me. It's the first one I've had in my flat and I want to make everything nice.'

'So you keep saying.'

'Just because you never entertain.'

'I do. I put on a performance for you every night, honeychild. And you love it.'

Charlotte chorused the last line with him. 'Stop saying that. You just speak in clichés all the time. Has anyone ever told you? I suppose that's what makes you a great copywriter.'

'I have an office full of gold awards. You only get those for originality. I am an original.'

'You'll be a starving genius if we don't hurry up and agree about this dinner.'

'Drop the office people.'

'Well . . . all except Haze. She's my friend. And she's good at talking. She can get the conversation going.'

'I can get the conversation going.'

'You'll be helping me in the kitchen.'

'What?' Steve's lupine grin resumed its hangdog expression once more.

Steve had rolled another joint and offered it around the table but the others once again declined. Charlotte dwelt on Steve's softened looks in the candlelight. She was pleased with how everything had gone.

'Now we've all had a rest, would anyone like some more dessert?' she asked.

'No, thank you. I'm full,' said one of her guests. 'That was a perfect dinner, Charlotte.'

'Delicious,' said another.

'Don't tell me now! You're supposed to write a notelet next week and go into orgasms of compliments. I want it in writing!' Charlotte removed some of the plates and went through into the kitchen. 'Heavens,' she called over her shoulder. 'It's ten past twelve. I had no idea.'

'D'you want us to go home now?'

'Of course not. I'm just going to make coffees for everyone.'

'Do you have herbal tea?' asked one of the young women.

'I've got camomile, I think. Will that do?'

'Perfect,' came the reply.

Steve stayed silent. The others chatted on until Charlotte came back in with a tray of miniature coffee cups in cobalt blue and gold, decorated with little stars and moons.

'What pretty little cups,' said one of her girlfriends. 'Everything is so well chosen.' Charlotte popped back out into the kitchen.

'Apart from the boyfriend.'

Charlotte's friends were stupefied by what Hazel had just said under her breath.

'Don't worry. He's off in another world,' she said, smiling, pleased to have got away with it. 'It beats me how people like him can be on a health kick and then take drugs, even soft ones.'

Charlotte returned with the tea and coffee.

'Charlotte, is it true you're working for the Terrence Higgins Trust?' an old schoolfriend asked her.

'Yes.' She looked at her guests. 'Don't worry, people. You can't catch AIDS off the cutlery. Not even if I haven't washed it.'

'I know that,' said her old chum. 'I just thought it was a brave thing of you to have done. I wouldn't do it in a million years. We're all proud of you.'

'I'm not very proud of myself.'

'Why?'

'Because . . . I don't think I'm any good at it, really.'

'I'm sure you are,' said the schoolfriend reassuringly. 'Think how you handle your clients.'

'It's hardly the same thing. You can't organise somebody's decline and death like a business meeting. It doesn't work like that. I find it really difficult.'

'Who is he?' enquired one of Charlotte's other girlfriends.

'A man. He's lovely. Really special.'

'Gay?' asked the girlfriend.

'Yes. He's rich. Sophisticated. Funny. Gentle. Charming. Well educated. Professional career of note in his field. Sometimes I think how fantastic he would be as someone's husband or father. If he was he wouldn't be left on his own. What the hell I'm meant to be doing with him, I don't know. He's so intelligent and perceptive compared to me. I suppose because he's older. He gives me help and advice with my career and . . . anything really. I have nothing to offer back. I'm just there for him.'

'I'm sure he enjoys your company,' said the girlfriend. 'You probably take his mind off it. If I had a terminal illness I wouldn't want someone standing over me counting out the seconds.'

'I didn't think of that.'

'Why did you do it in the first place?' asked one of the young men.

'Because . . . I don't know. Now I do it for him. But originally I think I did it for myself.'

'For yourself?' There was surprise in Hazel's voice.

'Yes. I've had everything in life compared to most people.'

'You wanted to give something back to the community,' proffered the old schoolfriend comfortingly.

'God, no. I can't stand the community. I can't articulate it. I wanted to be more important and needed, and not just a terribly girlie account manager quaffing champagne and running around going, "The client this, the client that." Everything in our business is style over substance. It's so shallow. Everyone thinks it's glamorous. Well, it is. But it amounts to nothing other than a huge spending of money on chunky morsels of gristle-free liver or freedom during your frigging period.'

'It's terribly important to the economy.' Charlotte's old school-friend was definitely strong on reassurance this evening.

'I know that. But it's not terribly important to me. He is, though. He is now. I'm glad I stuck the training. If he goes, when he goes, I'll remember all the brilliant things he's said to me and carry a little bit of him with me for the rest of my life.'

'Are we upsetting you?' asked Charlotte's girlfriend.

'No. It's good to talk about it. *He*' – she nodded at Steve – 'has no interest in the subject whatsoever. I can see you're all staring at this coffee.' She began to pour.

'You're very lucky to have got this flat,' said one of her friends.

'I know.'

'You're good at this game, girl, aren't you?' said Hazel.

'What game?'

'Entertaining.'

'Thank you. Speaking of games, shall we play something? Go on.'

'Oh yes,' said the old schoolfriend. 'It'll be such fun.'

'Brilliant. I love charades. We used to play it at school. You were brilliant!' She egged on her old chum. 'Come on. Steve, you'll play, won't you? Steve!'

'Hi, babe.' Steve was woozy, dreamy-eyed. 'Anything the lady desires.'

'Would everyone mind helping me fold the table away? It'll give us so much more room.'

An hour later they were happily spread out on the floor and in cahoots of laughter. Steve had come down a little after a factory-line of tiny coffees from Charlotte. She had given up trying to make the others keep the noise down. The people in the flat below would have complained by now if they were ever going to. They had moved on from charades to another game that no one knew the name of, or the rules of, so they were making it up as they went along. In turn, they had to think of a famous person and then answer questions on him or her and the others had to guess who it was. They'd already done Hugh Grant, Princess Di and Naomi Campbell.

'Does anyone want more coffee?'

'More vino, if you don't mind.'

'Hazel, you're drunk enough already. You're slurring your words.'

'Please. I'm not driving or anything.'

'You can stay here tonight,' offered Charlotte. Steve made a face at her. She stuck her tongue out at him. 'If you don't mind sleeping on the settee.'

'What, with you two bonking in the next room? Count me out. Just point me in the direction of the fridge.'

'I'll get it for you.' Charlotte stiffened at Hazel's comment. She went out and came back with another bottle of wine and filled Hazel's glass. As she leant over she whispered in Hazel's ear. 'Less of the bonking references, sweetie, or I'll ram this bottle down your great Australian gob, OK?' She checked the candles. 'OK. Who's next? Have you thought of someone yet?'

Her girlfriend said, 'yes.'

'Male or female?' asked Charlotte.

'Female.'

'If this person were a colour, what would they be?'

'Pink.'

Hazel next. 'If this person were an animal, what would they be?'

'Er . . . a little white fluffy lap-dog.'

'Oh, I know!' shouted Charlotte. 'What's her name? That old hag. Barbara Cartland!'

'Yup. It was too easy, that one. Sorry, everyone,' apologised the girlfriend. 'Whose turn is it now?'

'Mine,' said Charlotte. 'Let me think. Oh, I know.'

'Male or female?' asked one of the young men.

'Male.'

'If this person were a colour, what would they be?' asked the school chum.

'Grey.'

'John Major!' Everyone except Steve shouted it out at the same time. They chuckled.

'Uh! That was even easier than the last one,' laughed Charlotte. 'I feel sorry for him.'

'It's all his own doing.'

'I couldn't think of anyone else. I don't know any famous people. Steve, you go next.'

'I can't be bothered.'

'Steve,' warned Charlotte. 'Yes you can. You're supposed to be creative, for God's sake. Do someone good. Who we've all heard of. Not anyone obscure.'

'OK.' He was lying on his back on the floor. Charlotte sat squatting behind him. She removed the band on his ponytail and loosened his hair. He moved his head back into her lap. 'OK. Ask me a question.'

'You have to say whether it's male or female first.'

'Female.'

'If this person were a colour, what would they be?'

Steve stared across at the girl who had asked him, so penetratingly hard that she dropped her gaze. Time passed. Charlotte rhythmically slid her fingers through Steve's long black hair. He spoke mellifluously.

'If this person were a colour she would be the blaze of primal fire, a colour you could never determine, never catch and hold in your hand, never explain and never understand, simply be beholden by.'

For a moment no one seemed to know what to say.

'My God! You can tell he's a copywriter. If this person were an animal, what would they be?'

'If this person were an animal she could only be a cat, a lithe feline, languidly stretched out overhead on her branch, her blonde coat of silken fur glowing gold in the sunlight, a creature whose every movement is the definition of grace, one to be tamed only by Cartier and turned into a dazzling bejewelled ornament for a duchess who stole a king's heart.'

His audience was bemused.

'I can't think. If this person were a song, which one would they be?'

'This person is more than a song. She's a symphony of strings, a mother's tender lullaby, a rousing march to battle, a celestial choir of angels, a hymn to glory, an overture to romance. A prelude to love.'

'What a load of crap,' scoffed Hazel. 'She sounds like one mixed-up bitch, whoever she is.'

Steve raised his head from Charlotte's lap. 'One of these days, honey, someone's going to take that wine bottle you seem to date all the time and shove it down your constantly open mouth.'

Hazel laughed. 'Your girlfriend's already beaten you to that one. Another unoriginal line from the great writer himself.'

Over Steve's head Charlotte shot Hazel a warning look.

'What is it with you?' replied Steve. 'Salman Rushdie was a copywriter, you might like to know. He wrote "Naughty but nice" before he wrote *The Satanic Verses*. And which one, do you think, has entered the national vocabulary? I'm proud of what I do.'

Hazel caught Charlotte's eye and retreated. 'I'm only pulling your leg, buster. Go on. Tell us who the jungle pussycat is who's all aflame, before we call a taxi. We're all dying to know.'

'Work it out. Good night, everyone.' Steve rose, shrugged off Charlotte's catching arm, and walked into the bedroom. Charlotte was grateful he did not bang the door. Everyone stood up and prepared to say their thank yous and leave. Charlotte busied herself. Their movement diffused any tension.

'He's very tired, everyone,' said Charlotte. 'People don't realise how much pressure we're put under in advertising. Agencies are set up like war zones. It wears you down. I'll call cabs for you all.'

'I'll do it on my mobile,' said her old school chum. 'I have the number in the memory.'

'Who do you think it was then, Charlie girl?' asked Hazel, bringing some glasses into the kitchen.

'I've no idea. We might have found out if you weren't so obviously the descendant of convicts. You're so bloody brutal sometimes.'

Hazel laughed. 'Come on. You know me. I love you, Charlie. I'm dead jealous of you. You're beautiful. Your home is beautiful. Your clothes are beautiful. Your accent is beautiful. You have a good job. You earn good money. Shame about Conan the Barbarian in the next room, but not even you can have everything.'

Charlotte laughed. 'I've bought him a rather *avant-garde* mirror.'

'That figures. The only person he thinks is more gorgeous than you is himself.'

'I haven't given it to him yet. I'm waiting for the right moment.'

'There'll never be a right moment. And what have you got for me?'

'Nothing you can buy. Just my friendship.'

Hazel, sozzled though she was, was touched. 'Oh, Charlotte.' They hugged each other hard.

'I'm so glad I've got you at work, Haze. I couldn't bear it without you. You can stay overnight if you want.'

'No. I'll go.'

At the front door Charlotte again hugged Hazel, the last to leave.

'Sleep well,' winked Hazel.

'He doesn't love me, you know.'

'Don't be so sure.'

'He doesn't. I'm enough of a girl-about-town to know.'

'Charlie, don't you see why I asked you in the kitchen who the answer to Steve's game was?' Charlotte looked blankly back at her. 'He didn't take his eyes off you the whole time he was raving about his mystery lady. And only you couldn't get it. Sweet, really.'

As Charlotte pressed her back into the front door of her flat to push it shut she fell gently against it and allowed her body to be flushed by a deliciously warm internal caress. It was something she was feeling for the very first time.

The bedroom was flooded with the yellow light of the summer morning sun. The presence of this golden sunlight was quite tangible, filling the air like thin golden honey or runny lemon curd. If she could have tasted it, it would have been just as sweet and just as warm and just as deliciously pleasurable. In that half-state that lies between dreams and reality, Charlotte became blissfully aware that she was wrapped not just in the strong arms of her sleeping lover but within his whole slumbering body. The white luminous skin of her curled-up figure was a letter of secret thoughts folded into his manila envelope. His river of jet-black hair tumbled in sprays into her own pool of blonde. The one white linen sheet that was cover enough on close London nights had fallen away, in hours just past, to the end of the futon on which they slept. This morning Charlotte felt no chill, no need to reach down and pull it up over her bare flesh. Instead she slipped back further into Steve's protective mass. Her left hand stroked his right forearm which protected her breasts. His walnut-coloured skin was smooth to her touch, satiny and hairless, emanating heat enough to warm them both.

She sensed his awakening as his heart beat to a quickened rhythm and his breathing was flecked with soft moans. She turned a corkscrew spiral within his grip, weaving their hair together to bring her face in front of his. She looked up into his closed eyes and allowed an age to pass until his long dark lashes lifted and she was looking into his peat-black eyes. She spoke so softly that only the coming together of her lips and tongue carried her greeting.

'Good morning.'

His frame now drifted away from her and he rolled over on to his back and stretched himself out, leonine in the lemon light, his arms rising up the wall behind the futon, his toes tight in the knot of the linen sheet at their feet. Suddenly, with a throaty roar, he scooped her up into his arms and launched them both off the limboland of the mattress and into the middle of the morning. Ultrasonic laughter squealed out of Charlotte, ambushed and surprised, as Steve, standing nude and spread-legged in the centre of the room, spun her round like a drumstick in his grip, so that her knees were uppermost, bent over each of his broad shoulders, and her head hung down, her fine blonde hair both a curtain for his black manhood and a tingle on his inner thighs. Disoriented by being dangled upside down and with her waist locked against his chest by his forearms, Charlotte squealed again as Steve charged out of the room towards the shower.

There, to the sound of Charlotte's gulped giggles and his own strained snorting, he fumbled with the tap until he finally forced it open with one elbow, not before Charlotte had slipped down a half foot against his skin.

'Don't drop me! Don't drop me!' she pleaded, and looked up, up beyond her breasts, up over her own supple frame dew-dropped with water, up into his fabulous face. His hair was long and wet and sleek and glossy and pouring like molten molasses, totally revealing of his perfectly formed skull. As the warm water sprinkled from the shower-rose and lubricated their bodies, Charlotte craned her neck upwards to drink in his forehead, his eyebrows, his eyes, his nose, his lips. And his tongue. Her resistance collapsed and she hung her head down loose as Steve eased her thighs back over his moistened muscled chest and on to his shoulders and ate his way into heaven.

'*Croque monsieur.*'

'BLT baguette.'

'And – are you having your usual, Steve? – and an ordinary cappuccino and a decaff cappuccino.'

They were sitting terrace-style in Clifton Road outside Raoul's, a small but smart contemporary café nestling amongst the chic little shops at the Little Venice end of Maida Vale. It was chock-a-block for breakfast. It always was. But they had waited patiently to sit outside and soak up more of the Sunday sunshine. Charlotte had decided to come over here after Steve had returned from his run and she still could not stomach the washing up from the mother of all dinner parties the night before. Still, she was satisfied. Steve and Hazel's little bout of fencing aside, it had been a

success and she would plan another soon. They had donned
T-shirts and shorts and meandered hand in hand along the great
boulevard of Hamilton Terrace and over Maida Vale proper and
along the side of the tree-lined eighteenth-century canal where
all the prettily painted houseboats are, before turning in front of
the creamy white stucco of the grand double-fronted houses of
Little Venice. It was the long way round but, as Charlotte sang, it
was 'Oh, what a beautiful morning. Oh, what a wonderful day.'

She licked the powdered chocolate off the top of her cappuccino.
'I feel light-headed today. After all that booze last night my head
just feels completely empty.'

'That wasn't last night, babe. That was me this morning, fucking
your brains out.'

'Don't be so vulgar. You really know how to spoil everything,
don't you?'

'Here it comes. The lecture after the walkout the night before.'

'I wasn't referring to that. You were right to turn in then. Hazel
doesn't know what she's saying when she's been drinking.'

'She doesn't know what she's saying when she's sober.'

'Which isn't often,' said Charlotte, cheekily behind her friend's
back. 'She comes from the other side of the world. They call a
spade a shovel over there.'

'She calls a spade a whole fucking mechanical digger.'

'Tell me about it. We've been brought up, or at least I was, to
always find other people's dinner party conversation fascinating
and to generally agree with them. You're not meant to declare
World War Three over the mackerel pâté and Parmesan garlic
Melba toast.'

'What shall we do today, then, Charlie?'

'Sit here and watch the world go by.'

'I can't sit still for that long. I get too twitchy.'

'Go back to bed and snuggle up together.'

'I have too much energy for that. Unless you want another
seeing-to.'

'Christ, Steve! For someone who came out with virtually
spontaneous literature last night, you can turn a really common
phrase just as well as any lager lout.'

'I am a man of the people,' he joked. 'Only I'm more man than
most people.'

'Yes, well I can vouch for that. D'you know at one stage I thought I was going to crack my head open on the shower tray.'

'Never. Uncle Steve will never drop you, babe, and that's a promise.'

Charlotte felt charmed. She was under Steve's spell and she loved it. 'We could go the National Gallery. I've not been there for years.'

'The National Gallery? What on earth d'you want to go there for?'

'Isn't that what young lovers do? Mooch around embracing in front of the Titians and Tintorettos, all romantic and gooey?'

'It's what old ladies do, isn't it? They go round on their own all horny and look at the cocks on the statues.'

Charlotte giggled. 'Balls!'

'Yeah, they look at those too.'

'I'm not even sure if they've got any statues in the National Gallery. They do in the V&A. We could go there.'

'When I was a kid, we went somewhere on a culture trip once. You know, with the school.'

'We used to do that too.'

'I don't know where it was, it didn't interest me. I was going through puberty at the time – that's part of the story. We went round and saw all that Greek stuff with guys with their cocks torn off and whatever, and it was dead funny. We got told off for sniggering, but you know what kids are like. Then in this other room there were all these statues of young Greek gods with their willies still intact and they were tiny, like little worms or something. And I was petrified.'

'Petrified? Why?'

'Because even then I had a huge knob only I didn't know it and, you know, guys always worry about the size of their dicks and I was worried mine might be small. And then when I saw all these miniature numbers I thought they must be the normal size and that I was some kind of freak. I didn't know that they sculpted them dead tiny, much smaller than average. So I had the reverse problem of most guys. I mean, it's nice to be bigger but not abnormal. I didn't know how lucky I was.'

'I would still say bigger was an understatement. Does that mean you don't want to go to the V&A either?'

'It means that in this country with their prudent sex education they manage to fuck you up whoever you are. It's ludicrous.'

'I wouldn't worry about it. They'll change it. It's only old people that are holding things back. Once they all die off things'll change.'

'Die off? They get replaced all the time if you haven't noticed.'

'I disagree. I think there's a huge difference in society between the attitudes of those over fifty and those under forty.'

'Oh yeah?'

'Absolutely. We do more attitude surveys in advertising than anyone else—'

'Bloody research! You account people and your research reports have ruined more good ads than I've had hot babes.'

'Surely not that many? You have a way of making a girl feel particularly special, Steve. Look – Britain is a continental country for the younger ones. We eat fantastic food, take drugs, cross borders with no cares, shop all over the world, sleep with whoever we fancy of whatever sex whenever we feel like it, abort our children or get a nanny, don't worry about debt or the mortgage and just have a bloody good time. The trouble with the older generation is they go around worrying about things over which they have no control that just don't matter.'

'Such as?'

'Such as that the local vicar might be gay. Who cares if he is? Virtually no one goes to church any more in this country, anyway. Including all the people who think he should resign or preferably be the subject of a public hanging. But everyone gets all hoity-toity about it. I mean, I wouldn't recognise the Archbishop of Canterbury if he was standing stark naked in front of me!'

'Allow me to introduce myself.'

'Don't be silly. You know what I mean.'

'I hope you're right. But people change as they get older. They must do. Wait and see. You'll end up a proper little Maggie Thatcher.'

'No way. Although I wouldn't mind running the country. I'd introduce bike lanes for a start and bring in the electric chair for drivers who can't use their mirrors.'

'So you'd call yourself a liberal, then? Are you finished?'

'Almost. I'm a girlie. I can't wolf everything down like you. Inside your mouth there must be a sign saying Hoover.'

'Listen to Miss Dainty Little Bite-Size Chunks. These people here must have no idea how much cock you can get in your mouth.'

'*Steve!*'

'Stop acting all finishing school. You love it when I talk dirty.'

'I do wish you'd stop saying that.'

'Let's get the bill and go for a stroll in the sun.'

They chatted to the waiter who stopped for a break outdoors and then they walked back round to the canal. Steve's bare arm slipped round Charlotte's waist and he held her close to him. Two swans sat still on the surface of the water. Ducks quacked and dipped their heads underneath in search of brunch. Steve and Charlotte read the names painted on the sides of the barges and houseboats and picked out the ones they would own and those they would not. *Poacher. Theophilus. Sir Walter. Firefly.* A pleasure barge with a mid-Victorian black and gold castellated funnel and a long awning topped with stacks of orange tyres slid past. They read the name *Gardenia* on its stern and watched the young man standing aloft at the stern manoeuvre it into the old tunnel under the point where the Edgware Road becomes Maida Vale. Above it sat spectators eating out at Café Laville, a former florist's glasshouse perched directly over the canal. The *Gardenia* disappeared into the darkness of the tunnel.

'Where does that go?' asked Steve.

'Underground for quite a bit. Then it comes up in Regent's Park and you can get off at the zoo. Or go on to Camden Lock.'

'Let's do that, then. Go to Camden Lock and go to the markets and bric-a-brac places.'

'What a brilliant idea. We have to walk a bit further down to get on.'

They strolled on past the floating art gallery and stood on the little Venetian-style bridge over the water.

'That's Browning's Island,' said Charlotte, pointing to an isle bearing a copse of weeping willows. 'It's a bird sanctuary.'

'I can only see swans and geese and ducks.'

'Well, they need a home too, you know. Robert Browning's house was like those white ones in Blomfield Road. It was over there on the other side of the lagoon, but Mummy said they pulled it down in the sixties and built those matchboxes.'

'They look OK to me.'

'I know. But it's hardly the same as having Robert Browning's house, is it? Mummy told me he came back here after Elizabeth Barrett Browning died in Venice and bought the house by the canal to remind him of her and their time there. So sad and romantic. The weeping willows just set the whole place off, don't they?'

She swung round to face Steve, placing both her hands in the small of his back. He brought his own face down within an inch of hers and, with a palm placed on each of her buttocks, pulled her even closer. He nuzzled his nose in her ear and whispered.

'"How do I love thee? Let me count the ways. I love thee to the depth and breadth and height my soul can reach, when feeling out of sight for the ends of Being and ideal Grace."'

Charlotte was unexpectedly moved.

'You amaze me,' she purred.

'Don't be so surprised. I do have a degree in English literature, you know. I am a copywriter.'

'A bloody copywriter.'

As she ended the last syllable their lips made contact. She was consumed by his kiss.

56

Duncan and Michael were lying on Duncan's Victorian bed, reading. They had been contemplating whether to go out for dinner or not. They'd got nowhere as they were both in a do-nothing sort of a mood. Pushkin had slipped her way in between them and was purring away like a simmering pot of fur.

'Are you sad it's your last day soon?' asked Michael.

Duncan flicked through the second section of *The Times*, looking for a review or something to inform himself with.

'Yes and no,' he said.

'It's exciting, though,' said Michael. He yawned. 'As of a week on Monday, you'll be in television.'

'I know. Don't remind me. No previous experience, no one reporting to me, no company car, no mega-salary.'

'You'll love it. You'll be creative. People will get to see how talented you are.'

'Or not, as the case may be. If it all goes wrong I'm blaming you.'

'Why me? What have I done?'

'Encouraged me, that's what. I'm beginning to think I'm off my head. I've got to hand in my car this week. That's a killer. I won't be able to afford another.'

'Yes you will. You've got all that money in the building society.'

'That's to pay my tax next year. My accountant says I have to put it away.'

'God, Duncan. Nobody *does* that,' said Michael. 'You're over-organised. You'll have new money next year. Go out and buy yourself a car, some old banger.'

'I don't want some old banger. Somebody might see me in it. Anyway, I've only got to go as far as Paddington each day. I can walk it in twenty minutes. You can give me a lift everywhere else.'

'I'm not a taxi service.'

'Speaking of cars, look at this.' Duncan had spotted something in his paper.

'What?'

Duncan held up a double-page spread of an advertisement for the new MG. 'If I was staying in advertising I would get one of those next year.'

'Well, maybe you'll make a lot of money in TV.'

'That hardly seems likely. You know, I think I'm growing away from advertising already. This copy reads like so much twaddle it's an embarrassment.'

'I've been telling you for years that that's what everybody else thinks of advertising. You've just never listened.'

'When I first went into advertising cars were sold on eighties sex and glamour and performance. Nowadays it's all boring nineties safety and security.'

'Is it?'

'Yes, it is. Mind you, this copy could sum up you and me.'

'What?'

'Our relationship. It puts it in a nutshell.'

'What does?'

'This car ad. Listen to this: "Isn't it reassuring to know that there are crumple zones, side impact bars and high-tensile steel built into its sleek form."'

'What on earth are you talking about?'

'Well, when we met and I was young it was all constant sex and glamour.'

'I don't remember that.'

'Well, I do. Just. Then it became all safe and secure.'

'But you like that, don't you, Dunky?'

'I do. And we need it too. After all, we had our big crash.'

'Eh?'

'The night you abandoned me in Trafalgar Square.'

'You walked out on me.'

'Whatever. But all the years we've had knowing each other . . . neither of us could throw those away. They protected us. Like the crumple thing in this ad.' He sniggered.

'Sometimes you spout rubbish, you know that, Dunky?' Michael leaned over and kissed the back of his neck. 'That's why I love you.'

Pushkin was getting squashed and made a complaining noise to register her presence. She rearranged her front paws under her chin and embedded herself further into the duvet. Michael found the top of her head and tickled her behind the ear.

'What did you think when I left you that night?' asked Duncan.

Michael thought hard. 'Can't remember. Nothing.'

'Interesting. I thought nothing as well. I mean, I deliberately didn't think about it. It didn't bear thinking about.'

'Don't dwell on it, Dunky.'

'Did you think it was the end?'

'No. I just thought it was you being stupid.'

'But you didn't contact me.'

'I was waiting for you to ring me.'

'But I was waiting for you.'

'I didn't know whether I should make the first move. It's much harder for me, you know, because I'm so much older. I didn't want to be rejected twice. That would have been twice as painful.'

'Well, imagine if we had both waited. We'd never have seen each other again.'

'I doubt that's what would have happened. Dunky?'

'What?'

'Will you still love me when you're rich and famous?'

'Don't start that again.'

Michael wailed in pretend hurt. 'That means you won't.'

'I will.'

'You won't. I'll be all old and wrinkly then.'

'You are already. And so will I be. At the rate I'm going I'll be eighty-five by the time *I* hit the big time.'

'That'll make me ninety-five,' said Michael. 'D'you think we'll still be together?'

'Yes.'

'We won't have other big fall-outs?'

'Probably. But I'll never be able to get rid of you, more's the pity.'

'You'll become rich and leave me for some younger man. Someone who's not going bald and growing hair out of his ears. Someone who's got a big willie.'

'You're unlikely to be beaten in that department, so I wouldn't worry there.'

'Do you feel lucky to have me? I feel lucky to have you. When I saw Piers today I thought how lonely he must be sometimes. Friends are not the same as lovers. He'll die alone with no one special at his side. Poor Piers. I feel so sorry for him. No one deserves what's happened to him.'

'Don't depress yourself, Michael. He's got his parents. And friends. He's got you. You've virtually given up your job to research his case. That's real friendship. Mind you, you'll be the one that ends up devastated when you find out he's guilty.'

'Duncan, he's not guilty. You're the first to point the finger the moment you don't approve. You're such a little fascist.'

'I like that. One minute you're promising me undying love, the next I'm some fucking Nazi. Michael, I don't approve of underage sex.'

'Only because you never got any as a teenager.'

'Just because you trashed your way through every boy in your school when you were fourteen doesn't make paying kids for sex legal or moral.'

'You really are a middle-aged woman trapped in a young man's body. D'you know that?'

'There *are* absolutes.'

'Like remaining innocent before being proven guilty,' said the solicitor. 'I'd hate to have you on my jury.'

'Well, how did Piers's name end up in a rent-boy's electronic address book? Answer that one.'

'I'm working on it. I'm—'

'Michael, shut up and stop wittering on,' said Duncan. 'I'm trying to read the newspaper. Read your book.'

Michael squeezed his lover hard from behind and nuzzled his face in his ear. Pushkin complained again.

'Stop it, Michael. Your squashing the cat.'

'You've always got some excuse, haven't you?' laughed Michael. He returned to *England under the Tudors* by G.R. Elton.

Duncan sighed, exasperated. 'I'm bored, Michael. Let's go out.'

'Where?'

'Somewhere cheap.'

'Well, you think about it while I go and clean my teeth.'

Michael got up and went through to the bathroom. Pushkin rolled over on her back and put her little paws in the air and wiggled them around.

'D'you want me to tickle your tummy, baby?' asked Duncan.

He and his next-best friend played their favourite game for a moment or two. The phone by the bed rang. Duncan picked it up.

'Hello, Duncan?'

'Yes?'

'It's Karen Myhill.'

He immediately wondered if she was about to withdraw her offer. She had no other reason to call him. Fuck.

'Hello, Karen.'

'Duncan, I know you haven't quite left your old job yet, but I thought you might like to put your thinking-cap on over the next ten days.'

He relaxed instantly. 'What did you have in mind?'

'It's the game show for The Station. If we get this contract the company will be bankrolled for the foreseeable future. It's terribly, terribly important that we win it. I can't tell you how terribly important it is.'

'Obviously terribly important.'

'Yes. Martin Fox wants a daily interactive game show for younger adults.'

'What sort of age exactly?'

'Just not old ones. I've been racking my brains and I'm not sure what direction to go in. Perhaps that's because I haven't got a really good idea myself, or perhaps it's just the pressure of absolutely having to win the damn thing. Anyway, we're having a development meeting on the Monday you start and I remembered, Duncan, that you were going to be in it. And who knows most about The Station, Duncan? You do! So why don't you think of something to present on your first day.'

Christ. How could she land that on him? 'OK. I'll have a go,' he said. 'It's not much warning.' In advertising you usually got at least four weeks to have an idea. Longer for a good one.

'I have my best ideas in five minutes.'

Bully for you, thought Duncan. Michael came back in and started fondling his hair. Duncan gently pushed him away.

'Is there any direction you would like me to go in?' he asked Karen.

'Whatever you think, Duncan. The important thing about any game show, even if it's not interactive, is that the audience can play along at home. Think about that carefully.'

'OK.'

'See you a week on Monday. Bye.'

She had hung up before he had time to respond further.

'Who was that?' asked Michael.

'Karen Myhill.'

'Really?'

'Not exactly the world's most specific brief. If anyone briefed like that in advertising they'd get fired.'

'Well, it's TV. It's probably different from advertising. She *is* good, you know.'

'I know. I've to think up a new programme.'

'Ooh, Dunky. That's exciting.'

The phone rang a second time. Duncan picked it up.

'Sorry, it's me again,' said Karen. 'Do you know where we are and everything?'

'Yes. Don't worry. I won't get lost.'

'And we start at ten a.m.'

'Yes, you've told me that already.'

'Fine. Love to Michael.' She banged the phone down again.

'She said "Love to Michael".'

'Did she? Well, don't read anything into it.'

'What's that supposed to mean?'

Michael had momentarily forgotten his pact with Paul not to allude in any way in front of Duncan to Basket Case. 'Nothing,' he said.

'She's not meant to know. Honestly.'

'Well, she was to find out sooner or later.'

'I wonder who told her?'

'Not me. I haven't spoken to her in yonks.'

'I'll never get used to starting so late.'

'What?'

'At ten a.m. I hope I come up with something.'

'You will, Dunky. You'll be brilliant.' Michael gave him a hug. 'Now come on. You'll think better on a full stomach.'

Pushkin rolled over on her back again and gave them the come-on. They both fell for it. Dinner could wait just a few minutes more.

57

'I hope we're not the first here,' said Margaret. 'I hate being the first.'

'Is this it?' asked Duncan. 'Do you recognise it?'

'It looks like it.' Margaret peered through her large plastic-framed sunglasses. 'He said to turn left at the out-of-town Sainsbury's.'

'Why are we doing this?' called Hazel. She had been sleeping in the back of Duncan's BMW until just a few moments before, despite his having the roof down. She shouted in Margaret's ear. 'I'm only here, Margaret, because you press-ganged me.'

'Oh, no,' said the secretary, 'they're quite good fun at parties.'

'Well, let's face it,' said Duncan, 'they've had a lot of practice.'

'Well, I *can't* face it,' said Hazel. 'A day on a boat with Mummy and Daddy? Let's mutiny and throw them overboard.'

'Oh, yes,' laughed Margaret. 'Let's make them walk the plank. Feed them to the sharks.'

'The sharks wouldn't eat them,' said Hazel, sullenly. 'That would constitute cannibalism.'

Duncan shifted down to second gear and continued along the private road into the car park of Southampton Marina. It was still not yet ten. They parked and, while Duncan sat and waited for the roof to glide back into place, the women attempted to exit from the car.

'How d'you open this door?' asked Margaret, pulling at the handle. 'This thing is stuck.'

'You're locked in,' said Duncan, and he flicked the central locking switch. The system burred and clicked deep within the heavy frame of the BMW.

'God, Cairns,' said Hazel. 'You're really tight-arsed, aren't you, locking us all in?'

'He's got very good attention to detail,' mocked Margaret, and the women sniggered while Duncan took it all in good grace, as a man who had handed in his resignation might do. They trooped round to the boot of the car and unpacked the vast quantities of food they had bought at Marks & Spencer.

'Oh,' said Margaret. 'I mustn't leave my camera in the car. I thought I could take some nice souvenir snaps.'

'My God,' said Hazel, taking in the size of the marina and the number of yachts. 'There's thousands of them.'

'His is down there, somewhere.' Margaret pointed somewhat ineffectively with a hand laden with two carrier bags. 'Can anyone see Orlando's car?'

'He'll never be here yet,' said Duncan. 'He's always late.'

'Why has Charlotte gone with him, then?' asked Margaret. 'Wouldn't it have been easier for you to have given her a lift?'

'Because Orlando wanted the pleasure of her company,' replied Duncan. 'Obviously he doesn't know about Steve da Silva.'

'Ooh,' said Hazel. 'Is he coming?'

'Are you kidding, Hazel?' said Margaret. 'Madam wouldn't have him to her summer party if it was the last thing she didn't do. As far as she's concerned he's an uncouth foreign type.'

'Yeah, well, she's not wrong there,' said Hazel.

They set off down the boardwalk in the direction suggested by Margaret. In fact, they walked the long way round, but, in the end, they spotted a becapped Captain Gainsborough, in long navy shorts and deck shoes, standing legs apart on the deck of his small schooner. He was doing something mysterious with a length of rope.

'Hello, hello, land-lubbers!' he chortled, waving a cheery arm.

'He's been at the rum,' whispered Margaret through clenched teeth. 'Next thing he'll be flying the Jolly Roger.'

Hazel laughed.

'He could replace the skull and crossbones with a nice picture of Serena grinning with her arms folded!'

Margaret sniggered.

'Permission to come aboard, Captain,' Duncan called out.

'Right, that's it, Cairns,' muttered Hazel. 'I'm off home.'

They climbed aboard the rocking yacht and staggered from one side to the other until they got used to the rolling motion. They were laughing and commenting on each other's white legs, exposed in shorts, when Serena's head popped up from the cabin below.

'Hello, people.'

They were taken aback. Margaret made an aside to Hazel.

'What's she doing here so early? Bet she spent the night down here with him.'

'There's lots and lots of booze down below if anyone wants to start,' said Serena. She was going to try hard to mix with her crew, one of the key objectives of the day's outing sailing in the Solent. But they failed to notice her novel use of the word 'booze'. 'We've got champagne and Pimms and agency wine. There are soft drinks too.'

'Is there coffee?' asked Duncan. 'I'm tired after the drive and pushing a trolley round Marks at eight thirty this morning.'

'Show some gumption, man,' laughed Serena.

The confrontation with Duncan had ended in stalemate. Nigel and Serena felt they had come out at least equal and had decided to let Duncan live in peace until he departed. Serena's strategy was aways to reserve her strength for battles she could win, and there were more of those to come.

'Coffee's just a bit difficult,' she said in answer to his request. 'You can walk back to the cafeteria if you like.'

'No. I can't be bothered,' said Duncan.

'What did you get at Marks & Spencer?' asked Serena. 'Lots of nice things, I hope.'

'You bet,' said Hazel, who had helped to stack the trolley with over two hundred pounds' worth of top-notch pre-prepared grub. 'Dressed lobster, for a start.'

'Blimey!' That was another rare use by Serena of a word socially beneath her. She really was one of the boys today. She thought.

The newcomers picked up all the bags and went below and started to lay out a fantastic feast on the cabin table. Nigel joined them. His hands wandered over the ready-to-eats on the table. Margaret playfully slapped the back of his hand, just a bit too hard, she hoped.

'Hands off my cheese straws,' she admonished her boss. She was taking the plastic off a punnet of citrus fruit.

'What are those baby orange things?' asked Nigel. 'Are they tangerines? They're too small.'

'No,' said Margaret disparagingly. 'They're kumquats.'

'Oh, is that what kumquats are? They look a bit fussy for my liking.'

'You don't peel them, Nigel,' said Margaret. 'You eat the whole thing.' She popped one in her mouth. Nigel tried to pick one out himself, but Margaret slapped his hand again. 'They're for later!'

She spoke with her mouth full but he understood and backed off. Nanny knew best.

After an hour the stragglers had turned up. Orlando, Charlotte and two of the creatives were the only other attendees, everyone else having pulled out as the date approached. Nigel and Serena had taken the yacht out of the harbour and into the Solent, referred to by Orlando as 'the motorway'. Apart from what Nigel endearingly called 'rather a close thing', when they were almost sandwiched between a skyscraper of a cruise liner and the Isle of Wight ferry, the sailing passed without incident. The sun was round and bright yellow when it came out from behind the clouds and there was a reasonable wind, allowing them to move out at moderate speed.

'He can't even sail his own yacht,' Hazel pointed out to Duncan. 'She's doing it nearly all for him.'

It was true. Serena quickly instructed Charlotte and Hazel in the art of raising and lowering the sails. Duncan took over shakily at the tiller and chatted nineteen to the dozen to Orlando. Margaret stood queasily at the top of the cabin stairs, Cerberus guarding her Hades feast from the locusts of the creative department. Her Kodak Instamatic hung round her neck and from time to time she would point and fire it at one of the crew, looking smiling and windswept. After a while, Nigel and Serena went below to study *Reed's Almanac*. They closed the door behind them. Five minutes later they opened it to hand out a cache of booze and then shut it again. Wicked tongues wagged at their lack of discretion.

Charlotte took the opportunity to be alone and stumbled off to sit astride the prow of the yacht, her blonde hair blown straight back, her face catching the spray. It was invigorating, although the cold blast penetrated her clothing. She pulled her turquoise nylon waterproof tight round her neck. She stared at the ocean-going traffic ahead as they cut through the foam. She cleared her thoughts and believed that she was thinking of nothing, but gradually she became aware of all the questions turning over in her mind. What was she doing here? Why had she given up her Saturday, her Steve, herself, for this? What had ever appealed to her about Clancey and Bennett? Why had she come to this little place with this bizarre gaggle of people? She realised she had momentarily lost sight of her career path. First, she had come to work with one specific person in mind, only to find he was leaving within a few weeks of her arrival. She liked Duncan. She was drawn to him. She respected and admired him. His daring move into television was courageous. She listened to him. She laughed with him. She enjoyed his company, which was enriching. But she was not as close to him as she would like to be. She felt she did not really know him yet. She would learn nothing from him now. And that was a loss. Had he let her down by leaving? Or had she let herself down by jumping at the first decent interview with the first decent person to come along?

Second, she had befriended a girl who played at her job, who didn't care what happened next and who drank heavily. Worse still, Charlotte copied her bad habits. She had joined in a conspiracy against her bosses and was obsessive about them. But Charlotte liked Hazel. She had time for her. She admired her. Her coming halfway across the globe was courageous. She gossiped with her. She was led astray by her. She laughed with her. She enjoyed her company, which was riotous. But she was as close to her as she could get. She felt she did not really know her yet. What trouble were they going to end up in together? That was the worry. Would Hazel let her down by leaving for home when the shit hit the fan? Had Charlotte let herself down by allying herself with her to run rings of deception around her employers?

Last and no longer least, there was Steve, the man by whom she had been skilfully seduced and with whom she now spent half her waking hours in bed as well as all her sleeping ones. She liked Steve too. She – almost – worshipped him. She admired him. His choice of a lone career path as a highly successful black man in a white world was courageous. She confided in him. She was driven wild by him. She laughed with him. She enjoyed his company, which was exhilarating. But she was not as close to him as she ought to be. She felt she did not really know him yet. What lessons had she to learn in love? In life? That was all a mystery. Might he let her down by leaving her? Or had she let herself down by jumping into bed at the first sexual invitation to be offered in the agency? It was all too much. It was all over the top. She would have to do something about it. But when? There was The Station to launch. She needed that on her c.v. And the Carpets Company was OK business too. Then there was being a Buddy, which would take up more and more of her time. But once the autumn was over . . .

Without warning, the yacht suddenly lurched violently and unpredictably to one side. Charlotte's heart leapt within her chest as she nearly flew sideways off the prow into the water. Behind her, the land-legged crew were flung ascatter in panic. There was a moment's genuine fear followed by mirth and wry comment.

'Whoops! Sorry!' said Duncan. 'I'm not as sure a hand on the tiller as I had hoped.'

'Cairns, you're a bastard,' laughed Hazel, recovering her composure. But her face then bled pale in an instant at the sound of a woman's scream.

'What was *that*?' called Charlotte, as she clambered back along the edge of the yacht.

The shocked group of colleagues stood transfixed as the door of the cabin swung back. Serena, as if struck down with consumption, crawled in an undignified and wretched way on all fours up the cabin steps. Her hard helmet of black hair had disintegrated to hang in spidery strands over her ashen face, seemingly racked with agony.

'Help me! Help me! Help me!' she implored in ungainly sobbing gulps.

Each of her amateur crew stood rooted to the deck for the first and only time that morning. Each was frozen in horror at this unprecedented view of the devil woman whose spell was cast over their working lives. Each was unable to move, unable to react, unable to relieve her tragedy.

'Help me! Please help me! Someone!' she wailed into the wind. 'It's Nigel. He's dead!'

Charlotte looked at Duncan. Hazel looked at Duncan. Margaret and Orlando and the creatives looked at Duncan. Duncan returned their look, the same one. It was the look of guilt.

58

'Your mum's dead famous in telly, isn't she?'

'She's not famous. She's well known and respected in her field.'

'Same difference.'

'No it's not, actually. My mother is not a star, she's an executive. The public haven't heard of her.'

'We have.'

'That's because you're our neighbours.'

'Does she take you with her on to the sets and things?'

'Of course. Sometimes. I give her quite a lot of advice, particularly on the younger shows.'

'I bet you don't really.'

'I bet you I do. I'm a salaried consultant.'

'La de da. Have you met anyone famous? Have you met Prince?'

Max corrected her. 'The artist formerly known as Prince.'

'No one calls him that. Have you met him? No, obviously.'

'Actually I have. Well . . . seen him, anyway. He's very slight.'

'Slight?'

'Small.'

'Amazing. Did you get his autograph?'

'No.'

'Why not?'

'Because you only do that if you're a sad fuck, that's why. Anyway, he doesn't even write his name in English.'

'Dad says your mum's been nominated for an award and they're going to show it on telly.'

'You'll only see her if she wins.'

'Won't they show a clip of her or something even if she loses?'

'I assume they'll show a clip of the programme, but she didn't appear in it. She won't have lost if she doesn't win. She'll receive a certificate as a runner-up. She'll still be one of the top four executive producers in the country.'

'You're a right know-all, aren't you, Max?'

'I'm extremely well informed for my age and experience, if that's what you mean.'

'Can you talk as well about sex? I bet you can't. I bet you're a virgin.'

'I can talk well on most subjects. Would you like to have a sexual conversation? I only dropped round to hand back your father's powerbook.' Max stared his neighbour's fifteen-year-old daughter in the eye. 'Why don't you initiate it?'

She felt uncomfortable. There was always something sinister about Max Myhill and the way he looked at you. 'You think you're dead clever, don't you?'

'I know I am. But I don't let it go to my head.'

'What do you let it do, then?'

'I could use it to twist you round my little finger.'

'Fuck off,' scoffed the girl.

'I use my intellect to help my mother run her company. I'm going to bypass university and go straight into television when I leave school.'

'Would you like to snog me?'

'If you want me to. I don't really fancy you, though.'

'Big brain, small willy.' She was cross that Max did not rise to the bait. 'I don't fancy you either.'

'Then why did you ask, small-tits?'

'Fuck off. It's what adolescents do. They get all horny. You wouldn't know about that.'

'I tend not to think of myself as an adolescent.'

'That's because your mum's not married.'

Max was puzzled. 'My mum's not married?'

'That's why you act all adult in a kid's body.'

'I am past puberty, you know.'

'Prove it.'

'I'm more interested in you proving the point you were making. Albeit not very successfully.'

'My dad says it all the time. In single-parent households with a single kid the kid ends up playing the role of the woman's partner, not her son. It's not a natural relationship.'

'What else does he say about me and my mother?'

'He didn't say it about you. He made a general point.'

'I suspect he was quite specific.'

'Where is your father, anyway?'

'I don't . . . He lives in London.'

'Does he visit you?'

'We have an arrangement. Look, I only dropped by to hand in the powerbook. I must go home now.'

'OK. Suit yourself. You don't have a father, do you?'

'I do.'

'No you don't. Everyone round here knows that.'

'I do so. Everyone has a father. It's a biological fact.'

'It's a biological fact you don't know who yours is.'

'I do.'

'Who, then?'

'I can't tell you. He's famous.'

'Famous?'

'My father is famous. That's why I can't tell you who he is. My mother is well known and respected in her field and my father is famous.'

'Who is he? Go on. Tell me.'

'I can't.'

'Oh, go on. Tell me. I promise I won't tell anyone. I don't even know anyone who knows you, Max. Go on.'

'I . . . I can't.'

'You're making it up.'

'I'm not.'

'Prove it.'

'I don't need to prove it to the likes of you. I can give you a clue, though.'

'OK.'

'His initials are MF.'

'MF? Give us another clue. What does he do?'

'No more clues. Except that one day I'm going to adopt his surname and everyone will know who my father is. Then I'll be the artist formerly known as Max Myhill.' He sniggered.

'You're weird. I can't tell whether you're serious or not.'

'Dead serious. And you can tell your father not to talk about me and my mother behind our backs. Otherwise we'll put you on telly.'

'Can you get us on TV? Fantastic!'

'Not in the show I have in mind.'

'Look, sonny, we said we'd call you if and when you received something. You're a real pest, you are, but as it happens an envelope did come in this morning.' The post office clerk feigned a smile.

'Give it to me.'

'Try saying please.'

'Just give it to me. You're holding up other people.'

'Don't be so sodding ungrateful.' He handed over the sole item contained in the shiny grey nylon sack that was Max's anonymous post office box number at Trafalgar Square post office. 'Look. We had that whole sack all ready to bulge with your mail and that's all you've got. Arf, arf.'

'I'm expecting more. Keep it open.'

Sweating, Max made his way uneasily to the other side of the modern utilitarian floor of London's busiest sorting office and stood at the chest-high counter that ran round the full-length windows fronting on to the street. The slim white envelope reflected back a single band of sun that beamed in from over the buildings on the other side of the street. It bore the first-class company frank of The Station.

'The Sta-a-a-a-tion. The Sta-a-a-a-tion. The Sta-hey-hey-hey-hey-hey-hey-shun. Do let it pass you by.' Inside his head Max heard The Station's advertising jingle from the car radio twist and turn in dissonance and discord. But this, the contents of this envelope, he could not let pass him by. He tugged at the corner. A tiny piece came off and fell on the floor. He pushed a finger inside but, instead of slitting open, the envelope crumpled and seemed to get all mangled up. That beam of sun was like a laser gunning for his head. Max felt he was boiling alive in the microwave of the window. He stepped back from the counter and rested in the shade against a concrete pillar supporting both the ceiling and a slate of benefit forms. He murdered the envelope with his bare hands as it gave birth to his first returned trick questionnaire, crumpled by his poor delivery of it as it emerged from its cover. To Max's fright and fascination the questionnaire was not all the envelope contained. There was a letter too. Not just the answers to his questions but a letter too.

His disappointment was immediate and absolute. Every question had been replied to, each box ticked, all the spaces stuffed full of comment. But it was not from MF, neither Martin Fox nor Michael Farnham. It was from Briony Linden. He read her letter. It was crushed. Max was crushed too. Max was having a very bad Saturday.

'From the office of Briony Linden, Head of Marketing, The Station. To whom it may concern. Dear Sir or Madam. As the Head of Marketing for the most exciting new development in interactive multi-media in Europe, I am constantly on the lookout for new market research techniques and new market research companies with whom I can work in partnership. I am interested in developing new consumer models and a new method of tracking the increasingly fragmented marketplace of televisual communications. I was quite dazzled by the unprecedented insight and sophisticated approach of your social issues questionnaire (enclosed), and would like to meet you to discuss how we could perhaps develop a similarly insightful tracking study covering a communications-oriented target market.

'For some reason I have been unable to trace your company's telephone number through directory enquiries and I would be most grateful if you could call me by return to discuss arranging a meeting. With best wishes. Yours sincerely.'

Max was saddened and pleased. His ruse had worked perfectly, so perfectly she wanted his pretend company to run the sodding research for The Station. She thought he was dazzling and sophisticated. Max sighed. He didn't want to be this clever. He just wanted to find his father.

'Max! Max!'

Karen Myhill lolloped the length of her back lawn, to the little wrought-iron love-bench under the spreading horse-chestnut. Max sat there.

'Max! I've been looking everywhere for you. What are you doing down here? You never come into the garden. Max? Max, answer me. You look like a lost soul sitting here all in the shade.'

'I am a lost soul.'

'Max, have you been crying?'

'No.'

'It's all right for boys of your age to cry, you know.'

'I haven't been crying.'

'Mummy cries a lot. Everyone drives me to tears, that's why.' She was speaking more to herself than to her son.

'I haven't been crying.'

'What makes you a lost soul today, then?'

'It didn't just start today. I've always been like this.'

'No you haven't, Max.'

'Everyone makes fun of me because I don't know who my father is.'

Karen sighed. 'Max, that simply isn't true. Did you take the powerbook back?'

He nodded.

'It's that Collins girl again, isn't it? She's growing up into a proper little cow, that one. I could wring her fucking neck! I'll call her father—'

'You'll do no such thing! You've humiliated me enough already with your stupid game without her telling everyone else I'm a mummy's boy. It's my life you're playing with, Kar. They all talk about us behind our backs.'

'I don't give a flying fuck what they talk about, Max. It's none of their damned business. You have much to be proud of. Most people would be glad to have just one parent like me, rather than two nonentities like hers.'

'Her father's the chairman of a City company.'

'He virtually inherited that job. And how much time does he spend with his daughter?'

'This is typical of you, Kar.'

'What is?'

'It's maddening because you don't even realise you're doing it.'

'Max, stop being cryptic. Doing what?'

'Moving the debate from why you won't tell me who my father is to assessing the brilliance of your own qualities as a mother. Since you're employing a diversionary tactic and fishing for compliments at the same time—'

'I'm doing neither!'

'Yes you are! So let's get all that out of the way first. Yes, you are a good mother. That is not in dispute. Although you are neither a role model nor a template for the exemplary mother—'

'Gee, thanks.'

'—you are nonetheless a first-class example of an idiosyncratic, creative, working, middle-class single parent.'

'Ever thought about running the Civil Service, Max? You have a way with demographic description that's uncanny in a teenager.'

'Funny. Somebody else just made a similar comment. Don't sulk.'

'I'm not the one that's sulking! You are!'

'You're becoming upset because I spotted your diversionary tactic and am clearly going to work this conversation back to where I want it. I am in control.'

'Max, don't be such a weasel. As it happens I am always in control of this particular conversation.'

'You are?'

'Absolutely. Because I know the answer to your question and you don't. And knowledge is power.'

'Absolute knowledge corrupts absolutely.'

'Huh. I'm not telling you! So there!'

'Don't be childish.'

'Me? I'm not being childish! I'm the adult! You're the child!'

'I sometimes wonder. Who's playing games here?'

'You are, Max—'

'No, you are, Mother! You are! You can't seem ever to understand that I might need to know who my father is. That that might be important to me. That you might be fucking up my life because you haven't told me. Doesn't it ever strike you as even just the slightest bit odd that a mother would not tell her son who his father is? And that the son might lie awake at night tortured by wondering whether his father's a murderer or a prominent politician or the next-door neighbour or that his mother doesn't even know who his father is? You are selfish, Kar. You are a cold, calculating, selfish bitch. I only have one parent and that just about sums her up. Jesus!'

He stood up. Both he and his mother would not make eye contact now as they were both crying.

'Mummy has very good reasons for not discussing the father

thing, Max. I'm sorry if it hurts you. It hurts me too. If you had any sense in that adorable stubborn skull of yours you'd realise that it was for your own protection that I do not tell you.'

'Those reasons are your own selfish reasons, Kar. They have nothing to do with protecting me. You're protecting yourself.'

'No, no, that's not true, Max. They have everything to do with protecting *you*. I've told you I will tell you when the time is right. Max. Max?'

Max did not look round.

'Max, the time will be right. Very soon. Something is going to happen very soon and then the time will be right.'

'Oh yeah? What will happen?'

'I can't tell you.'

'What's about to happen, Kar? Tell me.'

'I can't.'

'Oh, for fuck's sake.'

'Language, Max.'

'Fuck off.'

Max stomped off towards the house.

'Max! Max! Please come back. I'm only thinking of you, darling. You must know that. I'd never do anything to hurt you, you know that. Oh, Max, let's do something together,' she called. 'There's still time to go out today. We could go and see something in London or go to Thorpe Park or go and see a film or whatever you want . . .'

Max did not look back and disappeared into the house. Karen's voice trailed away and she waited wretchedly until she heard the bang of the bedroom door reverberate all the way down to the bottom of the garden.

Oh, my precious baby, she thought, and burst into tears.

'This is like something out of a James Bond film.'

'No it's not.'

'It is. And I mean "film" and not "book". The books make more sense.'

'I just wanted to be careful.'

God knows why, thought Michael Farnham. He had agreed to meet Jamie Hirst, the creator of Saturn Productions' *Megabrek*, in the recently revamped London Planetarium, the huge green semi-sphere that has always looked as if it has just crash-landed from outer space beside Madame Tussaud's. Under a state-of-the-art computer-generated night sky winking against the black-domed ceiling, the two men from television lay side by side, legs in the air, seemingly dropped like upturned beetles on their backs, planted in huge dark bucket seats set at a forty-five-degree angle to the floor. Each man gazed directly ahead into the twinkling techno-heavens that, despite the wizardry, seemed feeble and fuzzy compared to the real thing. Michael wondered if his eyesight was failing or if the computer-generated images were a bit out of focus. He remembered a once-in-a-lifetime visit to Europe as a child and the uplifting pinpoint sharpness of the old display of flashing light-bulbs. The moons of Jupiter were orbiting overhead and spun past to the accompaniment of the actorly voice of Sir Ian McKellen.

'This is the first thing I've heard him do in years that isn't a plea for gay rights,' said Michael.

'Really? Haven't you seen his *Coriolanus*?'

Michael laughed. 'There's definitely a rude reply to that one. This is ridiculous. You could quite easily have come to my office during the week.'

'We shouldn't be seen together.'

'We shouldn't be seen together behaving oddly and furtively like this. There's no problem with you coming into my office and talking to me there. We could be discussing the ground-rules for *Megabrek* or something. This way if we're spotted people will jump to conclusions. They'll think the gay mafia is up to no good again.'

'I disagree. This is preferable. Anyway, we're old friends. We're allowed to meet up for a chat.'

'Who the hell comes to the Planetarium for a chat?'

'The man from Saturn.'

Michael smiled. 'I've barely seen you since you left Trafalgar. I hear on the grapevine you have a new boyfriend.'

'I do. He's Chinese.'

'I love Chinese boys. They're so smooth.'

'And you're still with your Duncan.'

'Yup. After ten years, believe it or not. He's off sailing this afternoon. It's brilliant weather outside. I don't know why we're stuck here in the pitch dark.'

'Because I need you to shed light on something. I need your advice. I have reason to believe that Martin Fox has given Karen Myhill a straight run at The Station game-show commission.'

'Yes?'

'Well, has he?'

'Jamie, I can't discuss Martin Fox's commissions, real or imagined, with independent producers. You know that.'

'Why not?'

'Because you're competing in the marketplace. I can't leak confidential inside information.'

'Your Duncan is going to work for Karen Myhill now, isn't he?'

'Yes, he is, as a matter of fact.'

'Well, he must know what she's up to.'

'He might not do. He's not started yet.'

'But if he did he could tell you and then you could tell me. That wouldn't be a breach of anything you'd learnt internally at The Station.'

'What are you on about, Jamie?'

'Martin Fox is not allowed to dish out a huge multi-million-pound commission to his girlfriend Karen Myhill without putting it out to competitive tender. Saturn Productions, and everybody else in the TV business for that matter, has the statutory right to be asked to pitch on a fair basis for any large commission. What Martin Fox is doing is illegal.'

'Where on earth did you get that idea?'

'I saw Fox and Myhill hobnobbing it together in Hampstead one evening. I've put two and two together since. Everyone knows the light entertainment brief should have been issued ages ago. But no one's had sight of it. Except La Myhill. She's screwed it out of him, the cow.'

'Stuff and nonsense.'

'I've also found out she's about to go bust. That series she's been nominated for an award for hasn't been recommissioned by ITV. She's desperate and Martin Fox is bankrolling her and Max's future for them.'

'You've no idea what you're talking about.'

'I think I do. Call it industrial espionage, if you like. Or pillow-talk. One of my employees is going out with one of Karen's. It all comes back to me.'

'Huh, rumours! I meant, where did you get the idea what Martin is doing is illegal?'

'It is. It's anti-competitive. There are industry rules.'

'Balls. We're not the BBC. He can commission who he likes, when he likes, how he likes. We're a private company.'

'He's obliged to put it out to tender. I've checked. There would be questions in Parliament if he did not. It's worth nearly twenty million quid. What would the Americans say if they knew he was giving that much business to his old girlfriend just to settle an old score? What would the Monopolies Commission say? What would the European Union Media Affairs Committee say?'

'Bugger all, I should imagine. It's not illegal nor is it business malpractice in any shape or form.'

'Well, you would say that, wouldn't you? So you admit it's true.'

'I . . . Jamie, what is this all about? You've just won the breakfast show contract. There's no way in a million years The Station will give you its next-biggest commission as well. Saturn couldn't handle it. It's not remotely in our interest to give one production company two daily shows for the next five years. You know that. You shouldn't be expecting to get a bite at that particular cherry. Why are you getting so hot under the collar about this?'

'I'm getting hot under the collar, Michael Farnham, because

independent TV production is tough enough as it is without corruption and blackmail and bedhopping being responsible for how most of the fucking business is awarded. Karen Myhill has to compete on fair terms with everybody else. These are make-or-break days. There are nine hundred little production companies at the moment. By the year 2000 there'll only be fifty of us left and it'll be only the fittest that survive. Everyone knows Martin Fox is Basket Case and she's using Mad Max as a hold over him. His wife is a prominent Tory councillor. She's tipped as a future member of a Tory cabinet if she gets into Parliament. She needs a scrupulously clean-cut husband to fit the party of the family image, not some little bastard child that's the result of a frantic fuck on the office floor. She's loaded anyway, and he needs her and her money for his own creature comforts.'

'Jesus, Jamie. Why don't you pitch for the Station soap? You've turned into such a mincing little drama queen. If you could only hear yourself.'

'Stop covering up for him, Michael. Everyone knows you're great buddies with Martin. If he breaks the regulations you'll be incriminated alongside him and you'll go down together. You have to be bloody careful.'

'Are you threatening me?'

'I'm warning you.'

'Listen, Jamie, this may be the first time we've spoken in ten years, but hear this and hear it good. If you so much as progress with this line I'll personally ensure that *Megabrek* does not come to fruition and that Saturn Productions is as good as closed down. I may only be the fucking lawyer round here but that is within my power, I assure you.'

Halley's Comet whooshed past overhead and lit up the starry sky and Michael Farnham's worried face with it. Jamie waited for the comet to pass into oblivion.

'Perhaps Martin Fox is not Basket Case.'

'Oh, I see. We're taking it all back now, are we? Make your fucking mind up, for God's sake. Look. You drop your allegations and I won't mention anything to Martin. If he found out you were touting this theory around London – well, what sort of working relationship would you be able to have?'

'Perhaps Michael Farnham is Basket Case.'

'What?'

'How else would his little boyfriend get into TV so easily working for The Most Difficult Woman, She Who Must Be Obeyed? What deal have Farnham and Myhill struck together? Duncan Cairns will act as go-between and between the lot of them they'll generate a nice little twenty-million-pound illegal earner.'

'Jamie, are you on hallucinatory drugs or something? What you're saying is preposterous. I'm gay, for God's sake. I haven't fucked a women for a decade and a half at least.'

'Not since the seventies, eh? The timing fits . . . Of course, I don't know and I can't prove anything, but it would all come out in the wash.'

'Jamie, I've no idea what your motivation is for all this, but your theories are puerile and childish. They're just plain daft. If you go around saying this sort of thing you can expect to be laughed out of the business. Plus you'll damage old relationships for good and lose your friends. Let's agree to never mention this conversation to anyone.'

'That would suit you, wouldn't it?'

'It would suit everyone, Jamie. Particularly you. Now do as I say or you'll get yourself into serious trouble, big time.'

To phantom music, a menacing and absorbing black hole floated into the ether overhead. Michael Farnham launched himself from his bucket seat and disappeared into it.

60

Orlando held Serena's trembling arm to hold her back on deck. She was whimpering now. Duncan cautiously ventured down the steps into the cabin, followed by Charlotte and Hazel, much as

Carter and Caernarvon must have entered Tutankhamen's tomb. It took a second for their eyes to adjust to the dimness of the cabin's interior after the bright, reflected sunshine on the surface of the sea.

Nigel was lying on the polished wood floor, on his back, his face blue and purple and his eyes bulging.

'Oh my God,' said Duncan. 'He must have had a heart attack.'

Hazel punched the air softly. 'Re-*sult!*' she said.

Duncan was appalled.

'What was she doing to him?' asked Charlotte.

Duncan looked at her askance for her irreverence. He felt sick, though, because he knew the real reason this man lay lifeless in front of him. 'It wasn't Serena,' he said, his voice quivering. 'It was me. I rocked the boat.'

'You can say that again,' said Charlotte. She offered him a manufactured smile of reassurance, but Duncan's gaze was fixed on his prostrate boss.

Meanwhile, Hazel had brusquely pulled Charlotte out of the way and dropped to her knees by Nigel's body. She held her head to his chest and raised a finger for Duncan and Charlotte to shut up. She moved up his body and placed her cheek over his mouth.

'You didn't believe me when I told you I trained as a nurse, did you?' she said. 'Here, Cairns, help me sit him up. He's not dead. Unfortunately.'

They dragged him backwards until they could pull his neck up on to the edge of a low bench. Hazel deliberately let his head fall back on it with a thud.

'That'll knock some sense into him,' she said. 'I think he's asphyxiating due to some blockage. He must have swallowed something when the boat lurched like that.'

She crawled her way round behind Nigel in the cramped surroundings and grinned from ear to ear.

'I'm going to enjoy this!'

She first made a fist with her left hand and next clubbed it together with her right one. She then swung both arms back like a lumberjack and brought the full weight of her body, concentrated in her double fist, down on Nigel's back. He convulsed and hiccupped forward. His head fell limp again over his rotund belly.

Duncan breathed more easily. Hazel's approach was more

violent than the conventional Heimlich manoeuvre, but at least Nigel was alive.

'Won't he get brain damage if no oxygen or whatever gets to his brain?' asked Charlotte.

Hazel was pulling Nigel back into firing position.

'Brain damage? This one? How would they tell?'

She repeated her exercise, walloping him with such ferociousness that a small object cannonballed out of his mouth accompanied by an air-hissing, plopping noise. The object ricocheted off the other side of the cabin and landed between Charlotte's feet.

'Yuk!' she squealed. 'It's kumquat! It's all gungy.'

Nigel was lying gurgling and spluttering on the floor. Hazel pushed two fingers inside his mouth.

'What are you doing, Haze?' asked Charlotte.

'Checking to see he hasn't swallowed his tongue. Oh, look! I've found Serena's!' She threw her head back and roared with laughter, partly at her own joke and partly at Duncan's expression of serious disapproval.

'Shut up, Hazel,' he warned. 'He'll hear you.'

Hazel stood up and picked a paper napkin from the table to wipe her hands.

'He'll be all right,' she said, with a self-satisfied flourish of the serviette.

'Gosh, Hazel,' said Charlotte admiringly. 'You're amazing.'

'Don't sound so surprised. I'm not completely useless, you know.'

The others up on deck heard their voices and Nigel's coughing. They clambered down the stairs and squeezed into the small room. Serena rushed to Nigel's side to comfort him.

'Hello, old girl,' he croaked.

'Oh, Nigel,' she gushed. 'I was so worried.'

'That's what happens when you let a land-lubber man the tiller,' he said, embarrassed by her proximity. 'Some of that champers left, by any chance?'

'It wasn't Duncan's fault,' protested Charlotte.

'What did you choke on, Nigel?' asked Serena. She had completely recovered her composure now. She pushed her hair back into its normal hard-edged bowl shape.

'A kumquat!' Hazel bent over and picked up the evidence in her serviette, holding it aloft.

'Margaret.' Serena's metallic voice grated its way into a complaint. 'It really was thoroughly irresponsible of you to select kumquats for a sailing trip. Small fruit can be a threat. You should have known better.'

Margaret's understandable rage was palpable. 'Don't blame me!' she answered back, in a rare heated response to her superior's face. 'How was I supposed to know he was going to get a kumquat stuck in his great gob! I've a good mind to stuff it back in!'

'*Margaret*!' Serena gave her secretary a severe reprimand.

'Well, honestly,' said Margaret, wounded. There were tears in her eyes. 'I suppose if the yacht runs aground and we all drown that'll no doubt be my fault too!'

They suddenly realised that no one was at the tiller. Duncan and Orlando hurtled back to their posts with the creatives hot on their tracks. Margaret stamped her way up the steps to let the chill breeze blow away the heat of the moment. Meanwhile, Charlotte and Hazel helped themselves to champagne and wandered leisurely up on deck with glasses for the others. Out of earshot of Nigel and Serena, Hazel turned venomously to to her friends.

'I can't fucking believe it,' she said. 'I've just saved that fat bastard's life and he didn't even say thank you. Neither did she. They're unbelievable.'

She downed her champagne in one go. Duncan and Orlando raised their glasses in unison.

Yes. Once again, Nigel and Serena's annual summer outing with the grateful little people had been an unqualified success.

61

'Nigel, lay me on my back and stick your long, slimy pink tongue down my throat.'

'Charlotte Reith, you are path-e-tic!' Hazel roared with laughter and gulped down another half-glass of the agency Pinot Grigio. 'Is that the best you can do?'

'I think that's quite good,' said Charlotte weakly. She blushed, admiring her handiwork, written in thick red Magic Marker pen on Serena's white vinyl noticeboard.

'I feel completely pissed,' she said, emptying the dregs of the second bottle into her glass.

'It's got to be more raunchy,' criticised Hazel.

'But they're not a raunchy couple,' protested Charlotte.

'Well, more sordid, then. Change "tongue" to "penis".'

They both sniggered at their own infantile smut. Charlotte made the change on the vinyl board and stepped back to review it. She read it out aloud:

'Nigel, lay me on my back and stick your long, slimy pink penis down my throat.' They squealed with laughter again.

'Oh my God,' shrieked Hazel, diving off her seat and under the round meeting table. 'Quick! It's Serena!'

Charlotte leapt six inches in the air with fright. Hazel roared again and rolled around on the floor at her own joke, pointing at Charlotte.

'Fooled you! Fooled you! God, girl, you jumped.'

'You frightened the living daylights out of me.'

'The old hag is not going to come back in. She's off at the hospital doing her Florence Nightingale routine.' She jabbed a finger in the direction of Charlotte's sentence. 'Gobble, gobble.' She stood up and dusted herself down. They started sniggering again, this time at nothing.

'He's back tomorrow, is old Fatboy,' said Hazel. 'Yuk.'

'He's only coming back for Duncan's leaving do. He won't be doing any work.'

'Why break the habit of a lifetime? This place is going to be dreadful without Cairns.'

'I know. And not just the atmosphere. He's the only one who really knows the clients. I mean, the number of meetings I've had with Stella Boddington could be counted on the fingers of an amputee. I've no idea what we're really meant to be doing with her. I've never even been to her head office in Yorkshire.'

'That's no loss.'

'Until we saw her this week I'd completely lost track.'

'So had she. I think she's lost interest. But she's approved creative briefs and given the preliminary go-ahead on media.'

'I know, but how are we going to get the work done? And who's going to present it?'

'Sir and Madam.'

'I am worried about Stella. I hardly know her.'

'We'll be fine. As long as she delivers the goods on the budget or else we're in deep schtuck. Look, kiddo. This is getting boring.' Hazel grabbed the pen out of Charlotte's hand. 'My turn now. Rub yours off.'

'Leave it up for a moment. Then we'll compare.'

'I've had a better idea, Charlie,' said Hazel. 'Go and get Margaret's camera off her desk and we'll record these for posterity.'

'D'you think that's wise?'

'No, but it's fun. Go and get it!' Charlotte went off. Hazel spoke out loud to herself. 'All right. Now what would she say? I know.' She read the words out slowly one by one as she wrote them on the noticeboard. 'Nigel, smear taramasalata over my withered, gnarled, droopy tits and lick it off with your pig-like, scabby tongue.'

'That's dreadful,' said Charlotte, returning with the camera. 'It's not even funny. It's just sick.'

'Well, call me madam. Suddenly we're a literary critic, are we?' Hazel was offended that her colleague did not rate her creativity. 'OK, so what's wrong with it?'

'Taramasalata, that's what's wrong with it. It should be aerosol cream or room-temperature custard or something.'

'I'll change it, then.' But there was not enough room to get anything very long in. Hazel turned round with a winning flourish. 'There!'

Charlotte squealed with displeasure. Hazel had replaced 'taramasalata' with 'excrement'.

Charlotte stood up and fiddled with her glass.

'Is that really the last of your wine, Haze?'

'Yup. Where can we get some more?'

'I don't know. I'll go and have a rummage. Better rub that out first, though, in case someone comes.'

'Lighten up, Charlie. It's way gone eight thirty. Who's going to come along?'

Charlotte paid no attention. She picked up a J-cloth from the ledge of the board and started to rub away. To her horror, the red letters rubbed down to pink but did not completely disappear. Instead, every word remained stuck on the board, legible and much of it in her recognisable handwriting.

'Haze! Haze!' she blurted. 'Hazel!'

'Don't make so much noise. You'll wake up Security. What?'

'It won't rub off.' Charlotte was panicking. 'Oh my God, we'll have to rip the board off the wall. We'll have to say some vandals broke in through the window or something.'

'What? On the third floor?'

'Oh, Haze. What'll we do?'

Hazel convulsed in laughter again. 'You should see your face, you great rabbit!' She pointed at a can of aerosol spirit cleaner on the window sill. 'Use that, stupid. The ink is semi-permanent otherwise.'

Relieved, Charlotte sprayed and wiped the board and then left Hazel alone in Serena's room. She knew Steve normally kept a cache of wine and beer in his cupboard. She went downstairs and, as she entered Steve's office, she felt a quiver of pleasure at the familiarity of the surroundings associated in her mind with her boyfriend. She went over to the cupboard and opened it. This was ridiculous, she thought. He really ought to padlock it. Inside hung ten designer suits and jackets. Two Armani, three Woodhouse, a Thierry Mugler, three Paul Smith, one Versace, in pure new wool or linen, some lined in pale-coloured silk. There were bright, hand-made silk ties from Harvey Nichols and Harrods and a host of King's Road and Sloane Street boutiques. Beneath the rail of trousers were two pairs of Church's shoes, one black, one brown, in a monk's buckle design. Stuffed on the top shelf were silk boxer shorts, socks and Clinique Skin Supplies for Men bottles. There was a large oval bottle of Vendetta Pour Homme Eau de Toilette by Valentino. Charlotte did some mental arithmetic. There must be at least five, and probably seven, thousand pounds' worth of clobber in here. She resolved to buy a padlock tomorrow. She pushed around with her foot behind the two pairs of shoes until she located one lone bottle rolling on its side at the back of the cupboard. She bent down and pulled it out. It would be warm, but no matter. Hazel would be too pissed to care. She switched off the light and stepped out into the corridor.

At that moment Steve's telephone rang.

Charlotte slipped back into the office and put the bottle down on the desk in the semi-dark. She picked up the phone and spoke.

'Hello?'

'Who's that?'

'Charlotte Reith. Who's that?'

'Oh, hello, Charlotte. It's Kaisha.'

'Who?'

'Kaisha.'

Charlotte knew the voice but couldn't place it. 'Remind me. Kaisha?'

'You know me. I'm the receptionist.'

Oh, it was the black girl on reception. So that was her name. Kaisha sounded young and girlish and even more drunk than Charlotte.

'Is Steve there?' Kaisha asked.

'No, he's not.' What was she doing ringing up after 9 p.m? 'Can I help? Is there someone here for him?'

'Yeah,' she giggled. 'Me. Where is he?'

'I don't know, but he's not here, Kaisha.'

'Oh, fuck it. That bastard. He promised me it was my turn tonight. I wonder which bitch he's shagging instead, then? Byeee!'

She hung up.

Charlotte put the phone down slowly and gently. She had just discovered the pit of her stomach.

62

Last days in jobs are always an anticlimax. The about-to-depart are yesterday's news, no longer of consequence. Duncan's last day in advertising was no exception.

At around ten o'clock, Stella Boddington phoned to put their evening drink in the diary a few weeks hence. At eleven o'clock, he handed over the keys of his beloved BMW to the car-pool man. He had never actually known the car-pool man's name, but he wished him all the very best in the job he had had already for seventeen years. At twelve o'clock Duncan visited the personnel department and picked up his P45 and more pleasantries. At one o'clock, he, Charlotte and Hazel met up with with Briony for confit of duck with crushed potatoes and ceps at Bistro Bruno in Frith Street. Briony had to leave early to get back for a promotions meeting. The girls were not in the mood to be effervescently funny, as Duncan had hoped. Charlotte seemed subdued and extra quiet. Duncan felt she must be taking his leaving more to heart than he had expected. Meanwhile, Hazel, as usual, helped herself to the vino, which, Duncan noted, was commendably cheap.

'You'll turn into an alcoholic, you know,' he said.

'You bet,' she replied, grinning. 'And twice as fast without your Presbyterian gloom to warn me off. I'll miss you, Cairns. You're not such a bad guy, after all. Out of you, Nigel and Serena I'd pick you as the one I like the best.'

'Thank *you*! I'm deeply touched.' Duncan caught Charlotte looking morose. 'Cheer up, Charlotte. You'll be OK.'

'I'm just a bit down. I had far too much to drink last night. 'Oh,' she said, trying to brighten up, 'did I tell you I met my Terrence Higgins man?'

'No, you didn't,' said Duncan. 'I'd forgotten about that. What's he like?'

'Very nice. Very upmarket. Quite rich, actually.'

'Great!' said Hazel. 'Get in there while there's still time, girl. Where there's a will there's a legacy.'

'Honestly, Hazel,' fired back Charlotte, 'sometimes you can be a real bitch. You've got no feelings. The man is dying, for God's sake.'

'I know that . . .' said Hazel, realising she had misjudged the mood. 'OK. I'm sorry.'

'Well,' said Duncan. 'What can you expect from the descendant of convicts?'

'Piss off, Jocky.'

Lunch had still not got off the ground when they called a halt and went back to the agency for the leaving party.

There was a lot of sniggering behind hands at Nigel's blustering attempt at being funny. As well as the gang, about twenty of the MCN International people had popped up for a once-in-a-lifetime drink in Clancey and Bennett. Nigel's speech came across more as a list of criticisms and complaints. Clearly, he was meant to be reciting a whole series of amusing anecdotes with Duncan as the anti-hero, but generally he lost track halfway through and didn't hit the punchlines. Duncan was annoyed for as long as he cared, which was not for long. He responded with a few spontaneous words and thanked everyone personally for their friendship and support. They then got further into the champagne. Then Orlando and Charlotte interrupted the babble of conversation. Orlando had made a fantastic leaving card, constructed like a photo album, with pictures of Duncan taken over two years, each subtitled with an amusing, vitriolic line from the self-absented Steve da Silva. Orlando, not a public speaker, held it up for all to see and took his audience through it page by page.

'Shame you don't spend as much time on the ads as the leaving cards,' called out one MCN wag. Orlando had the good grace to laugh.

Then Charlotte stepped forward and handed Duncan a large, flattish package. Everyone cheered.

'It's your leaving present,' she said, and pecked him on the cheek.

'Wooah!' someone called out at the back. 'Wait till Steve gets you home!'

Charlotte blushed and pushed her fingers through her blonde hair.

'What is it?' called out Hazel. 'Charlotte bought it. We haven't even seen it.'

Duncan unwrapped the present from its wrapping paper.

'Gosh, it's lovely,' he said. 'It'll go marvellously in my flat. Thank you.' He held up the modern steel mirror in the shape of a flaming sun so that everyone could see just how chic it really was. 'Where did you get it?' he asked.

'I bought it the other day in Heals,' Charlotte replied. 'Thinking ahead . . .'

And that was it. Duncan switched off his office light, pulled on his navy blue three-button pure new wool jacket, clasped his mirror and his album-card under his arm, walked to the lift and waved goodbye for the last time to his colleagues, his friends, and his career in advertising.

'Serena!' It was Margaret calling from among the revellers. 'There's a call for you.'

Serena placed her champagne glass down on Margaret's counter-top and went to take the call.

'It sounded businesslike to me,' said Margaret. 'I wouldn't take it here with that racket going on right behind you.' She saw the look on Serena's face say 'Don't tell me my job.' 'It was just a suggestion, Serena.'

Serena marched into her office and closed the door behind her. The phone rang as Margaret put the call through.

'Hello?'

'Hello, Serena, it's Louise Thurrock of Japanair.'

Serena braced herself for the news.

'I've just come out of a board meeting and thought I would ring you straight away. I'm sorry it's Friday evening. Is it convenient to talk? What's all that noise in the background?'

'Oh, just a leaving party. We've said goodbye to a rather tiresome member of staff and now everyone is celebrating.'

'Well, I have the results of your pitch, Serena.'

Serena bristled with anticipation.

'It's basically good news—'

'Oh!' Serena could not conceal her elation.

'—with one condition. The condition will have to be put into the contract.'

'Sure,' said Serena. 'It depends what it is, but there is actually no reason why we can't make very specific conditions for your business.'

She leant across and prised apart the slats of the Venetian blind on the internal window. She tried excitedly to wave to Nigel, but he appeared to be hopping around on one leg with a basket of Twiglets on his head. Serena spotted Margaret running towards her and gestured, but Margaret was too busy picking up her camera to get a shot of Nigel looking like a dickhead.

'The condition is a very simple one and I'm sure you'll be happy to fulfil it,' continued Louise. 'You've got it in the bag, Serena. Japanair UK will put forward Clancey and Bennett to the Tokyo office as its pan-European advertising agency, provided that the business is co-ordinated by Duncan Cairns, as long as he is in your employ.'

Serena's grip tightened on the receiver so hard she might have crushed it to dust. An involuntary cracking noise emerged from the back of her throat.

'Hello, Serena?' said Louise. 'We seem to have a crackly line.'

'Er, yes . . . we do, don't we? Er, shall I call you back? I need to speak to Nigel.'

'Tell him the good news? I understand. Well, I'm off home now, so call me on Monday morning, to confirm. Good night.'

Serena was left holding the dead receiver in her hand. She replaced it softly and sat down defeated and deflated at her desk. Not yet home from the last day of his career in advertising, Duncan Cairns had already wreaked his revenge.

63

Cindy held the cup with the piggies on it under the running tap and rinsed it out. She placed it on the wire rack to dry and went through into the living room. The Saturday morning sun flooded in past the heavily draped curtains. She plonked herself down on the sofa and returned to Nigel Dempster's column in the *Daily Mail*. She wasn't concentrating on it, though. She went over to the Sony CD player and put on the first disc from a Deutsche Grammophon boxed set of *Eugene Onegin*. She located Lensky's aria, her favourite bit, and hummed along. She went over to the window, stepping over the delivery crate from John Lewis in the middle of the floor, and looked out into the street. This would not make Alan turn up.

He wasn't coming now, not for the entire weekend. A fat lot of use he was sometimes. The minute he was needed he vanished with the excuse of too much work. She turned round and stared at the cans of paint and the rolls of furnishing fabric than she had had delivered.

She was impatient to get going. She wanted to do the whole room in one go, today and tomorrow, but she really needed someone to help move the bigger pieces of furniture. Perhaps she could paint round them. After all, she was going to be doing small areas one at a time. Dragging the walls and distressing the woodwork. A bit of an experiment, but she had nothing to lose. The surveyor who had been round the other week had liked the flat after all, almost as much as he had liked her. It was worth spending a bit of money on it now, staying here for another year or so, and then moving on. Hey. She had an idea. Duncan was between jobs this weekend. He might have nothing better to do. She found the phone hiding under *Harper's and Queen* and *Vogue* on the settee and dialled his number. She got the answering machine.

'Hi, Dunky. It's Cindy here. It's ten forty-five on Saturday morning. If you're around, I thought you might like to come over for lunch. Then in return for my hospitality you could—'

'Hello.' It was Duncan's voice.

'Oh, you're there,' said Cindy, surprised. 'Where have you been? I hope you're not in bed.'

'No. I've been up for ages,' said Duncan. He yawned. 'I'm working.'

'Working? I don't believe you. You're still in bed. You just yawned. Working on what?'

'I've got to come up with a new TV show for Monday morning.'

'That sounds exciting.'

'It is until you try and think of one. It's make or break. It'll make or break my career in TV and it could make or literally break the company that's hired me. They've only taken me on because their back is against the wall.'

'She's put you under a lot of pressure already, that woman. She sounds just as bad as Serena. You're mad.'

'She's fine. But I'm going to a function tomorrow evening so I've got to get a move on.'

'What's the idea?'

'Well, it's a game show.'

'Yuk.'

'I'm trying to do something a bit different. I'm thinking of giving the contestants a ball thing which they throw to each other or bounce around. Anyway, they can only answer a question when they're in possession of this ball. It's a totem. It lights up.'

'That does sound different. It also sounds ghastly. But you should never overestimate the taste of the British public. Andrew Lloyd Webber hasn't and look how successful he is.'

'It's going to take me hours to crack it.'

'Does that mean you're not free for lunch, then?'

''Fraid not. I'll be busy on this the whole weekend. I'd love to come over but I can't. I couldn't anyway, come to think of it, as I've got no car. What *have* I done, Cindy?'

'Made a great move. I'm jealous. I'll give you my ideas for a backhander.'

'It's a deal, but let me get started first.'

'Well, I'll let you get on. Ring me back tomorrow and tell me what your idea is. I'll be your guinea pig.'

'Thanks. Good luck with the painting.'

'Bye, Dunky.'

'Bye, Cindy.'

Cindy put down the receiver, in the process knocking the *Harper's and Queen* on to the floor. It fell on to Alan's copy of *Johansen's Recommended Hotels in Great Britain and Ireland*. She picked it up and ran through it until she found Charingworth Manor in Gloucestershire. In the glossy colour photography it looked everything Alan had said it was. A fifteenth-century manor set in lush gardens with modern indoor tennis courts and pool and spa facilities. Just the place to strike a money-rich deal with your clients. She'd surprise him.

She hit the buttons on the phone.

'Good morning,' said a posh voice. 'Charingworth Manor. How can I help you?'

'Hi. Can I speak to Alan Josling, please.'

'One moment, please.'

Light classical music came down the phone, jarring horribly with the Tchaikovsky in the flat. Cindy felt like some more coffee. She'd put the filter machine on straight after she'd spoken to Alan.

'Hello?' The posh voice was back. 'Is Mr Josling a guest here?'

'Yes. He booked in last night for two nights.'

'One moment, please.'

The music came back and fought with Tchaikovsky again.

'Hello? I'm sorry. We seem to have no one of that name staying here.'

Cindy was taken aback.

'Are you sure? He should be meeting another gentleman there. Perhaps it's under his name.'

'Which is?'

'I'm afraid I don't know. He's from a company called McKinnon's, I think.'

'I'm sorry. I would need to know his actual name. I can keep a lookout for Mr Josling if you like. Perhaps if you call back later . . .'

'Oh, it's OK. It's not important. Thank you.'

She hung up on the posh voice's goodbye. She dropped the phone back on to the settee and walked through to the kitchen. She took the used filter paper from the coffee machine and dropped it into the pedal bin. So where was Alan if he wasn't at Charingworth Manor? Perhaps there had been a mix-up. There always was a mix-up with Alan, that was the trouble. She reached up into the overhead cupboard and brought down a vacuum pack of Sainsbury's Arabica filter coffee. She took a new filter paper out of its packet and placed it in the machine. She tried to pull open the bag of coffee rather than snip it with scissors. She spilt grains all over the counter-top. There were tears in her eyes now. All of a sudden, two days of specialist painting techniques seemed much less attractive than before. Less relaxing, less fun, less worth doing. Instead, Cindy knew she had hours and hours ahead to watch paint dry and churn over suspicions in her mind.

64

'Could you drop us here, please,' called Michael.

The chug of the black cab diminished slightly. It was already stationary, locked in the jam of London taxis and the occasional Daimler and white stretched limousine which filled Tavistock Street and the other narrow lanes of eighteenth-century Covent Garden.

'Why are we getting out here?' asked Duncan, cross that he was not in control.

'A: because we'll never get there at this rate, and B: because it's much more fun to walk up between the crowds.'

He paid the driver and they walked to the end of the street and turned into Catherine Street. The street had been closed off and each pavement was sectioned by portable metal barricades, behind which a good-humoured throng – mainly consisting, it seemed, of middle-aged women and their teenage daughters, with a few foreign tourists thrown in for good measure – made a sartorial contrast with the black-tie and evening-gown parade heading for the porticoed steps of the Theatre Royal.

'You'll be here this time next year collecting an award for your series for The Station.'

'I don't think.'

'Did you get a title for it in the end?'

'I think so.'

'What is it?'

'I can't tell you. I'm too embarrassed.'

'You'll have to tell Karen Myhill tomorrow morning, so tell me now.'

'I can take criticism from her. But not from the man I love.'

'I won't criticise it.'

'I know you won't because I'm not telling you what it is. I'm a bag of nerves as it is. I'll ring you after my meeting and tell you then.'

The theatre was floodlit with television lights, and a wall of TV, video and paparazzi cameras lined up on the opposite side of the street recorded the arrival of the stars. Michael and Duncan, basking in the glamour of the occasion and letting it rub off on them, walked self-consciously up the open street. A helmeted policeman asked to see their gold-edged invitation and they were allowed past.

'You look so handsome in your DJ,' said Michael.

Duncan smiled. 'So do you.'

'Apparently Steven Spielberg is coming.'

'And Kate Capshaw.'

'Apparently.'

A glossy black Rolls-Royce was allowed through. The chauffeur jumped out and opened the passenger door. A flight of golden feathers erupted from the interior of the car and a bronze-haired Shirley Bassey stepped into the glare. Every flashbulb in the street went off. The crowd roared their approval. They lapped up the presence of a star, the genuine article.

'Over here, Shirley.'

'Here, Shirl. Over here.'

'She looks fantastic for her age,' said Michael.

'No, Michael,' said Duncan. 'She just looks fantastic.'

*   *   *

Inside the theatre they sat sweltering in the stalls. Everyone, as they say, was there. Lord and Lady Attenborough. Michael Grade. Melvyn Bragg. Alan Yentob chatting to Joan Bakewell. ITV's Marcus Plantin. The Station's Martin Fox, but representing the Beeb from his previous job. Sir David and the other Lady Attenborough.

The independent producers tended to be seated further back. Michael pointed out Janet Street-Porter talking to Jamie Hirst of Saturn Productions. He was with a slightly built oriental man.

'That's his lover,' said Michael.

The stage had been cleared of the set of *Miss Saigon* and now twinkled with a concoction of rainbow neon and rather tacky glitter.

'Yuk,' said Duncan.

'They never get it quite right, do they?' said Michael.

A polite ripple of applause ran through the audience as Nicky Campbell, host of Scottish Television's *Wheel of Fortune*, appeared on stage, resplendent in black tie and glittering waistcoat.

'Good evening, ladies and gentlemen. Just a few points before we begin. Those of you who win tonight, if you are seated on this side of the theatre, would you please exit off the stage to that same side once you have received your award. And those of you on this side, if you could do the same, exit off to your own side. I've been asked to say, particularly to those of you from the United States, please do not make a speech on receipt of your award unless you feel it absolutely necessary. And if you do, keep it short. You can only make a long speech at these events if your name is Attenborough.'

The audience cheered.

'I hate it when they're not allowed to say anything,' said Michael.

'I know what you mean,' said Duncan. 'But it does get boring otherwise.'

'Nominees, if you don't win, remember there will be a hand-held camera on you, so keep smiling. Don't mutter any four-letter words, either, because there are a lot of lip-readers out there.'

There was not so much laughter for that one.

'It's not live, by the way. It'll be shown on ITV while we're having dinner at the Grosvenor House Hotel. There will be coaches to take you there if you filled in the forms. We'll still pause for the commercial breaks. You won't hear any music at that point but please stay seated.'

He fiddled with his earpiece.

'Apparently, Her Royal Highness is about to arrive, so good luck, everybody. You won't be able to see her come in on the monitors, I'm afraid, because the OB link has gone down. If you cannot see her from where you're seated when she does arrive, don't worry, just stand when the National Anthem begins. Thank you very much.'

He left the stage to polite applause and the house lights dimmed completely. There was a rustle overhead and then the thud and bang of a thousand seats as everyone stood and the small orchestra played the National Anthem. Then the giant screen at the back of the stage began to flash through micro-clips of all the memorable scenes from the previous year's television. A light fanfare rose in a flippant arpeggio and then stopped dead. An ominous drumroll began.

'La-a-a-dies and gentlemen. From the prestigious Theatre Royal in London's Dru-u-u-u-ry Lane and in the gracious presence of Her Royal Highness The Pri-i-i-ncess Royal, comes television's biggest night of the year. The Annual – United – Kingdom – Television – Awards!'

The orchestra belted out the rest of the title music in the usual vulgar, brassy manner and the micro-clips came to a close. A spotlight went up on the centre of the stage.

'And here are your hosts tonight – Nicky Campbell and Carol Smillie!'

'They're both Scottish,' said Duncan with mock pride.

'They have to give everyone a turn eventually,' said Michael. 'Next year it's the Isle of Man.'

Duncan kicked him fondly under the seat.

Nicky Campbell and Carol Smillie were almost at their podium. They turned towards the royal box and he bowed deeply while she curtsied, exposing one long, slender, tanned leg from beneath her split gown.

'I really fancy that Carol Smillie,' said a voice somewhere behind Duncan.

Nicky Campbell went first and read from the autocue.

'Your Royal Highness, my lords, ladies and gentlemen . . .'

'. . . and the winner is . . . Helen Mirren.'

The audience applauded vigorously as Helen Mirren walked up on to the stage and received her horse's-head award.

Another voice behind Duncan spoke.

'She wins every year. Must have a bloody long mantelpiece.'

Helen Mirren stood at the microphone.

'We've been asked to keep it short tonight, so I would just like to say thank you very much. Thank you.' She went to exit stage left but Carol Smillie cleverly rerouted her to the right.

'And now,' said Nicky Campbell, 'the award for Best New Light Entertainment Series of the Year. Well, we're not eligible for that one, Carol, so why don't *you* read out the nominations?'

'Well, not this year at any rate, Nicky! OK. The nominations are – *Brucie's Party*. Executive producer Jeremy Clarke. A BBC production for BBC1.'

Applause.

'*Fish Windows*. Executive producer Jamie Hirst. A Saturn production for Channel Four.'

Applause.

'*Knobs and Knockers*.' Carol blushed. There was a wolf whistle from the back of the stalls followed by much giggling. 'Executive producer Stephen Leahy. An Action Time production for Carlton.'

Applause.

'And *The Danger Game*. Executive producer Karen Myhill. A Myhill production for ITV.'

Applause.

'And before I announce the winner, let's see the clips.'

As the screen ran through the edited sequences the voices behind Duncan struck up again.

'There's Karen Myhill over there. She's looking fancy tonight.'

'Where?'

'See. With the camera rammed down her throat. I've never seen her so tarted up before.'

'Oh yes. She must be a bag of nerves.'

'Well, a bag anyway. Jesus.'

'What?'

'She's brought Mad Max. Look, he's all dressed up like he's the next Lord Grade or something.'

'Well, he is, isn't he? Going to be.'

'Shame he's not going to be the next Lord Lucan. He could do us all a favour and disappear.'

'You know Babs lost her job because of him?'

'I heard. It's not natural. She treats him like he's her husband. Who else is here with a kid?'

'He's the man in her life, all right. You get that with single mothers who have sons. D'you think he'll grow up to be a woofter?'

'Nah. More like Jack the fucking Ripper.'

'Who d'you think it was, then?'

'Who?'

'You know. The father.'

'God knows. For all we know it could be someone on the panel of judges. He could be dishing out a gong to her tonight just to keep her quiet. It's so unfair.'

'I see what you mean. You know who Babs thinks it was?'

'Martin Fox.'

'That's what everyone says. I heard it was a legal beagle.'

'I heard it was the commissionaire and she's had an aversion to gold buttons ever since.'

'You have to hand it to her, though. Keeping it a secret. Oh, here it comes.'

'And the winner is . . . Karen Myhill for *The Danger Game*.'

Karen Myhill threw up her hands, hugged Max, planted a smacking great kiss on his cheek, rose and walked down the right-hand aisle. Those in the audience who knew her gasped. She was a new woman. Her peroxided hair tonight had been lavishly windswept into a spiky nest fit for a royal swan. Her mascaraed eyes, the triumph of a professional makeover, were like black spiders behind her oblong diamante evening glasses. Her breasts, normally sagging prunes, were transformed by a new Playtex Wonderbra into ripe cantaloupes. Her silver dress, previously unnoticed in the dark of the auditorium, shone like red hot baking foil under the television lights. She rose to the stage effortlessly on success's cloud and took her award, clutching it to her engineered bosom. She turned to leave at Nicky Campbell's gesture and then, thinking better of it, strode to the microphone and held aloft the flaring-nostrilled horse's-head trophy.

The *sotto voce* conversation in the audience continued.

'What the hell does she think's she doing?'

'Christ only knows. I'm squirming and she hasn't even started yet.'

'Your Royal Highness, my lords, ladies and gentlemen. The irony of this award is not lost on me tonight. What I know and what you don't know and what I've been asked not to tell you but I'll tell you anyway is that this series has already been cancelled at the end of its first run. There will be no more *Danger Games* from Karen Myhill.'

'I find that hard to believe.'

'ITV will be stark raving furious she's saying all this.'

'Apparently I am too much of a perfectionist for others to stand the pace of working to my exacting standards. So be it. But it is also no irony that tonight I have carried off this glittering prize for a show called *The Danger Game*. Because, as a lone woman in television who set up her own production company and who took the risks almost single-handed, that is the story of my life. It *is* a dangerous game. And I could not have done it by myself. But I do not wish to thank the director . . .'

'Bet he's thrilled to hear that.'

' . . . Nor do I wish to thank my producers, researchers, production managers, camera crew, editors, and so on. After all, they got paid, didn't they? . . .'

There was a titter in the audience. Karen had never quite found the knack of delivering a thumping good punchline.

' . . . I wish instead to thank one young man, who has been my guide and mentor and inspiration and managing partner these last few years . . .'

'I can't believe she's doing this! Look at Carol Smillie's face!'

' . . . Ladies and gentlemen . . . ' She stretched one arm out towards the stalls. 'My son, Max Myhill. Stand up, Max.'

Max sheepishly stood up and grinned, embarrassed, into the aisle camera. He would kill his mother later for this. The audience applause was polite.

'Look at Carol Smillie clapping.'

'She has to. She might need the work later.'

'How embarrassing. In front of royalty too.'

'Thank you, Max,' said Karen. 'Thank you. I'm so proud of you.'

Overwhelmed, Karen Myhill then publicly burst into a flood of tears and ran from the stage, her own flaring nostrils competing with her award.

Oh, no, Mum! thought Max, cringing. You were meant to go off to the right!

'Well,' said Michael. 'What did you make of that?'

'Hmm. I'm glad I came and did all this people-spotting.' Duncan looked across at Max. 'Now I really know who the competition is going to be as of ten o'clock tomorrow morning.'

65

She brushed her nose against his. He opened his eyes. Hers were directly opposite. Her pupils were huge black glossy circles so reflective he could actually see his own looking back at him. He pulled his bare arm from under the duvet and caressed her face. She reached for his shoulder.

'Ow!' he yelled. 'Paws not claws, Pushkin!'

Duncan stretched over her and turned down the alarm-clock radio. For the very first time the *Today* programme seemed all wrong. Duncan no longer needed to know the day's political or business agenda. He was creative now. With one finger he tried to retune the radio to something else, Classic FM, Capital even, but with his short sight that was a task beyond him. He switched it off and lay back with his hands behind his head, his palms flat against the crisp trim hair on the nape of his neck. Pushkin sat on the duvet, treading. They both wondered what unexpected things the day could hold in store for them.

'Miaow!'

Duncan realised he had drifted off. His right arm had gone to sleep from the elbow down. His neck told him it was behind his head. Funny, that, thought Duncan, how your hand talks louder than your neck normally, but when your hand falls asleep your neck speaks quite clearly. With his other hand he reached for his contact lenses and launched himself out of bed and towards the bathroom to pee away his erection.

'Come on, baby. Time to get up,' he said. 'God. What time is it?'

He peered into the alarm-clock radio. It was almost nine. The Spartan in him disapproved of the hour. Almost 9 a.m. – but no need to be in the office until ten. Duncan relaxed. Why should he feel guilty? He could indulge himself. He could live dangerously. He was in TV.

He cruised out of the room. When he came back twenty-five minutes later he had showered, shampooed and shaved. His fairish hair shone with L'Oréal Studio Line Design Gel and his finger- and toenails were freshly clipped. His armpits glistened with fragrance-free roll-on, so as not to clash with the scent of his body spray. His face was lightly moisturised and aglow.

He stepped across the cream carpet to the antiqued pine chest of drawers. From the second-top drawer he selected the usual, a pair of white Calvin Klein trunks. He quickly slipped them on and checked his profile in the mirror. Furtively, Duncan indulged himself and pleasured in his own reflection. Something was not in its place. He slipped his hand inside the pouch of his pants and rearranged his penis so that it hung pointing downwards. Perfect.

He opened the sock drawer and automatically brought out a pair of navy blue cotton ones. He pulled them up over his feet then withdrew them again. He rolled them back into a ball, though not one as neat as that which he had taken out, and swapped them for a pair of white sports socks. These he didn't even put on. Duncan alarmed himself with the realisation that he had no idea what he was going to wear. He settled on beige. Beige was used-to-be-weekend wear and would go with anything.

He opened up two doors of the wardrobe filing system. He pushed all the white shirts, suspended on hangers, to one side.

Pale blue was Duncan's colour and all the blue shirts hung there together in order, next in line. He toyed with a Ralph Lauren Oxford and then settled on a Levi's chambray button-down. It had a classic, worn denim look to it. He had bought it when factory-outlet-shopping in the States. It had cost only nineteen dollars. Just right for TV, thought Duncan. He plucked it out. For some reason it had not been ironed. Yawning and in his underwear, he padded through the hall, through the living room and into the back extension. It was draughty in there. His bare nipples hardened in the cold. He pulled his underpants tighter round his crotch. In front of the ironing board sat the flaming-sun mirror and the photo album that were the souvenirs of his years in advertising. He picked them up to place them to one side. For a moment he dwelt on all the familiar faces, the situations and events, the totally self-obsessed way of life he would never see again. Then he put them down and got on with the rest of his life. He erected the ironing board and made for the kitchen where the iron was. Pushkin was there, rubbing herself on the light switch.

'In a minute, baby,' he said.

He filled the steam iron from the tap and, using a heel to spring open the undersink cupboard, reached down for the can of aerosol starch. He returned to the ironing board and plugged in the iron and waited for the hiss of steam. He laid out the chambray shirt on the metallic-grey cover of the ironing board and, from the correct eight inches away, sprayed it thoroughly all over with a fine mist of starch. He then proceeded to press that shirt with the dedicated attack of a nimble needle-puller who has been a seamstress of little black cocktail dresses for forty years and who is putting the finishing touches to the ultimate achievement of her life's work.

He returned to the bedroom and the mirror. He went to put on the shirt and then had a thought. He dug inside the wardrobe once more and this time drew out a plain white Gap T-shirt. He pulled it over his head and then slipped the pale blue shirt on over it. He buttoned it up two buttons short of the collar, then one, then two again. What was wrong with it? The T-shirt did not show enough and the shirt looked too formal. Duncan never could dress down. Part of the problem was the crease in the sleeves. He yawned. He should not have worked on into the small hours on his presentation, but he had. He realised he had used the starch out of habit and it had been absolutely and utterly and entirely the wrong thing to do on a loose casual shirt. For all the effort he had put into it, in fact precisely because of that effort, he had rendered it unwearable. He admonished himself for trying too hard. He pulled the shirt off over his head, and, with it stuck there, halfway up both arms which were stretched in the air, and with the T-shirt riding up over his flat stomach, he caught sight of the alarm-clock radio. Switched off. He should never have switched the radio off. There were twenty ticking-away minutes left for him to dress, feed Pushkin and *walk* to work. Duncan Cairns was in danger of being late on his first day.

He dropped the shirt where he stood. It lay wrinkled on the floor. He tried the Ralph Lauren Oxford. No. He dumped it on the chambray. Pale pink looked too poofy. It landed with the others. White was too formal. It topped the pile. He settled on inky denim. The red tab on the left breast pocket said it was Levi's. The T-shirt looked good peeking out from underneath. The beige buttons complemented his socks. But it would be too hot, wouldn't it? He abandoned it in favour of something completely different, a thin striped beige and navy polo shirt from Emporio Armani. He eased his backside into a pair of 501s. Too tight, not right. He flung on a pair of chinos. Too heavy. He tried undyed linen trousers. They'd do. They were Armani too. He stuffed them with the tail of his polo shirt but it was fashionable to wear shirts out so he retrieved the ends from inside his trousers. It looked untidy. He looked fat. They hid his bum. He stuffed then back in again and zipped and buttoned up. It needed a belt, this outfit. He tried his dark burgundy belt and the matching loafers by Patrick Cox. Duncan thought it worked. What would they think of this ensemble in TV? That it looked formal? That it looked relaxed? It looked young? It looked middle-aged? It looked expensive? It didn't look expensive enough? Would they notice at all? Duncan had not a clue and not a minute to spare. He pulled on his Cartier watch.

'Come on, baby,' he signalled to Pushkin. 'Foody-woody!'

She jumped down and raced through to the tiny kitchen, anticipating the moistest Select Cuts imaginable. She made do with a clump of Choosy apologetically walloped into her uncleaned bowl from three feet up.

Duncan stood at the edge of the kerb to cross the road and begin the walk into Paddington and his new life. Where his year-old navy blue BMW 3.25 convertible might have sat before there was only an empty space. He walked into it and stood there in the hollow between the other parked cars. This was why he had worked in advertising. For the perks. Duncan had liked Nice Things. Duncan had liked BMW 3.25 convertibles. Oh God. Why had he switched to television? Would there be nice things ever again? He leapt at the hoot of a horn blasting behind him. An angry motorist, gesturing dismissively at Duncan, was trying to reverse-park a sleek Lexus into the space. Clutching the papers on which he had crafted his game-show ideas for Karen Myhill, Duncan stepped back on to the pavement and walked on. He was a pedestrian now, only a pedestrian, a nobody in the eyes of the comfortably wheeled, something to be tooted at and gestured at and made to get out of the way. He would have to get a car somehow.

As he walked he realised how unfamiliar seemed the streets, how individual were the repeating terraced houses, how uneven were the paving stones. He wondered if his soft leather Patrick Cox shoes were the right choice for walking the mile and a half to Myhill Productions. He could feel every line on the pavement through the soles. The buildings that had always rolled past out of the corner of his eye now bumped along. The magnificent white stucco houses of Little Venice did not look quite so pristine close up. There was a thin film of dust on every ledge and every moulding which you didn't see from the car. Paint was peeling on the architraves and columns of the grand doorways. Rows of black cast-iron railings had gaps or even disappeared entirely. He looked into basement flats, voyeuristically. A lot of people obviously did not make their beds when they got up. Basement flats and bedrooms could not be seen by drivers. He hoped people did not look into his.

Sunburnt, dried leaves fluttered past on the breeze. Duncan's lips moved just perceptibly as he rehearsed in his head how he would present his programme. He had worked on it through the night, revising it, rewriting it when he had returned home after the UK TV awards. That would explain his tiredness. His idea was thoroughly thought through from the beginning to the end. Well, not quite the beginning. The show had an opening, an introduction, a middle, a climax and a finish. But it had no title. Duncan struggled. He stuck at it. He sought inspiration in the very streets around him as he traced his new route to work.

And, by the time he arrived in front of the bright blue entrance of the Myhill Productions annexe overlooking the rusty rails of Paddington, by the time he arrived at this new door, inspiration, that most welcome of all visitors, had knocked at his.

66

'So, Duncan, tell us what your idea is.'

Award-winning Karen Myhill sat back in her chair at the end of the long, black ash table, behind her horse's-head prize from the night before. She had allowed quarter of an hour for congratulations and touches of her trophy. Now it was down to business.

A dirty old Philips white plastic table-top electric fan, which had been stretched as far as its mangled lead would allow, was placed beneath her, whirring away noisily and blowing her peroxide hair vertically upwards on one side of her head. She twirled a leadless propelling pencil in her hand.

Duncan sat at the opposite end of the table, shielded by only a plain mug of bitter Kona coffee. In between sat Karen's team of young freelance producers and researchers. What a dishevelled shower. It occurred to Duncan that if the grunge look had never caught on in the besuited world of advertising, it had never been out of fashion in TV production. Lank hair, inconclusive necklines and overwashed mushroom fabric predominated. And just as there was no distinct line in the style stakes, there was no distinct line to the meeting. Karen could hardly complain about staff slackness, thought Duncan, if she herself only managed to roll up at 10.45 for the first meeting of the day. Perhaps she had been out celebrating with Max? It didn't seem likely. There was no agenda in her head, let alone typed out on a piece of paper. It seemed to be the done thing to interrupt with inane remarks and liberal silliness. These were not like the managed creatives of advertising. Here, the lunatics were in charge of the asylum.

Duncan was perspiring, or at least felt he was, his forehead shiny beneath his spiky, gelled hair. He had tried hard to pitch his dress right for the new company and the tropical heat of the hottest July for years. He hadn't quite brought it off. He was a fish out of water. Duncan looked just too smart. He was classic, elegant and in charge, in his thin striped beige and navy polo shirt and undyed linen trousers. His shoes were not the mammoth Timberland hiking boots welded to the feet of even the most stick-like of the girls present with their white, pipe-cleaner legs. Everyone else, other than Karen, was younger than him. Light-years younger. They noticed it too.

'Duncan's a grown-up, isn't he, Karen?' chirped a curly-haired youth, referring to Duncan's maturity of pose rather than his actual age.

'Shut up,' said Karen. 'Listen to Duncan. He has an advertising way of thinking. You might learn something.'

Duncan would have been only too happy just to learn some-body's name. They hadn't done introductions and job labels as he would have done. On the other hand, they didn't seem yet to have acquired a peg on which to hang your jacket two and a half years into the company's existence. Or a telephone list. Anyway, here he was, about to make his first step in television, but feeling as if he were about to step off the edge of a cliff. He spoke without notes.

'Hello, everyone. My name is Duncan Cairns and I'm a pro-gramme development consultant. I've developed an initial pro-posal for a half-hour daily game show to run on The Station – the yet-to-be-launched interactive cable channel – from the begin-ning of next year. There will be an initial pilot test immediately prior to Christmas and the test results will be instantaneous, due to the two-way nature of interactive TV.

'The show is pitched at twenty- to forty-year-olds in socio-economic groups ABC1. They currently enjoy middle-range light entertainment, and game shows which test genuine skills rather than those based on luck. They are medium-weight viewers moving up to heavier viewing, justified by their investment in state-of-the-art telecommunications and home entertainment. We know from research carried out for The Station that they expect and require The Station to innovate in both technological and entertainment terms.

'Any Station programme *must* use interactivity to enhance viewer enjoyment. That is this channel's genuine point of difference from its competition and the principal reason why it will be viewed. Failure to employ interactivity will disappoint viewers and they will reject the channel. The crucial aspect for Myhill Productions is that the client can test our format by every known criteria – ratings, appreciation index levels, viewer participation – as the show is actually broadcast, giving an instant life-or-death judgment capacity that has never existed before. We are walking, therefore, on eggshells.'

Duncan's audience sat silent. They had not heard a case presented like this before. It was not the logic of his background statement but the fact that he had any rationale at all which amazed them. They developed ideas because they – well, just thought of them on a whim. They came up with programmes because they liked them. Now there sat in their midst a scientist, a focused mind, a directionist. Droplets of reason fell from his lips. However, as far as Karen was concerned, Duncan would be judged only on the quality of his idea. He explained it.

A game-show set in a black empty studio. On the ground, a giant playing board of thirty-six squares called the video floor. Each square is a giant flat-screen TV monitor. The celebrity host is the referee. Three tracksuited players in two teams move across the video squares rather like human counters. Each square they land on represents a general knowledge question from one of six categories. To progress one square in any direction, the contestants have to name the person or animal or object or event or whatever appears on the screen on which they stand. The interactivity comes into play as the referee host asks the audience at home to feed in one of the six question categories for each player. So, the audience 'decides' the subject-matter and difficulty of the show. They influence who wins and who loses.

And the *pièce de résistance*: the players do not play in ordered turns but randomly by bouncing an illuminated power-ball between them to pass the play on to the next person. Whoever holds the power-ball has the chance to answer and move on. If they fail to pass the power-ball or it is intercepted by their competitors, the initiative passes to the other team. And, to win a round, they have to reach the final row of squares and throw the power-ball through a neon hoop, an electric version of the basket in basketball. The winning team comes back on to the next show and plays to win an accumulator prize.

'So,' finished Duncan. 'It has a star referee for initial audience appeal. It looks unique and futuristic and technologically stylish. The viewers engage with the players by setting the questions for them. And it combines the general knowledge test of a mid-range game show with some of the ball skills of basketball. It is, in short, a playing-board version of basketball, with questions and answers.'

Duncan made eye contact with each person in the room, one by one, until he met Karen's gaze. There were murmurs of interest and approval and an air of expectancy. Duncan felt it was going well.

'Hmmm,' said Karen. 'What does everyone think?'

'I like it. I think it's really different,' said the curly-haired youth.

'It's better than my idea,' said Karen, generously. She looked to her award. 'We'd obviously have to play it out in practice to see whether it actually works or not.'

'It sounds expensive,' said someone else.

'Not for Martin Fox,' said Karen. 'What were you thinking of calling it, Duncan?'

Duncan leaned forward, both arms on top of the desk, and confidently appraised his captive audience. He looked directly at Karen and smiled. 'Well, because of the sport it's based on and because it's completely mad, really, I thought you could call it *Basket Case*.'

There was an audible group intake of breath around the table and all heads swung swiftly in formation just in time to catch the flaring of the nostrils of The Most Difficult Woman In Television, award-winning. The explosion that then walloped in Duncan's direction nearly killed him. Literally.

67

Piers sat up in bed, propped up by the pillows. He looked gaunt, a hundred years old.

'How are you?' asked Michael.

Piers took a little time to digest the question and respond.

'Fine. I feel very tired.' His voice was faint and he had to concentrate on forming each word. 'I don't know whether it's me or the drugs.'

'I have some good news for you,' said Michael.

'They've found a cure?' Piers went to smile but the strain overcame his feeble attempt.

'I wish they had. The policeman has gone away. Did you notice?'

'No.'

'They're dropping the investigation. Into you, at any rate. That's great, isn't it?'

'Yes.'

Michael was disappointed by Piers's muted reaction. He continued.

'The rent-boy who had your name in his address organiser admitted stealing it. It wasn't *his* personal organiser. So obviously someone who knows you has been screwing around with prostitutes.'

'Knowing the people I know, that could be anybody.'

'Exactly. The boy has made a statement saying he's never met you. They may try and find out whose personal organiser it is, a person common to all the names on his list, but the whole thing is ridiculous. I've persuaded the police to drop it as far as you're concerned anyway, for the time being, as you're not well enough to help them. The boy's having your name on his list doesn't constitute evidence against you. They finally admitted that. Honestly, they're so homophobic. All the so-called boys are over sixteen, just under twenty-one.'

'I thought they changed the age of consent.'

'To eighteen. This kid was seventeen.'

'It's strange to think I'll never have sex again. I'll die in this bed. I'll never go outdoors again.'

Michael didn't know how to respond. 'Oh, Piers, you will. Don't give up.'

'One does give up. There's no quality to life now. I can't control my bowels properly any longer. I'm like a great baby. Why can't they bring in euthanasia on the National Health? I'm surprised the Tories haven't, with all their cost-cutting. One wants to keep one's dignity at the end.'

'Piers, you're just a bit down.'

'Thanks for telling me.'

Michael decided to call it a day and push off back to the office. He gingerly kissed Piers goodbye and left his friend staring into featureless, futureless space.

When Michael walked into his office, Martin Fox and Briony Linden were there, looking out of the window towards the railway tracks that ran into King's Cross.

'What's up?' asked Michael.

Martin and Briony turned round. They were chuckling.

'Britain's newest poster campaign, that's what's up. Look down there,' said Martin, pointing into the street.

'Ta-ra!' said Briony. 'You can't see them from our side of the building.'

Michael crossed the office and looked down. Between the railway tracks and the street was a row of billboards, each of them covered with the same poster, the start of the new poster campaign for The Station. Each was printed in the now familiar metallic mirror typeface that had caused so much comment when it first appeared earlier in the year.

'D'you think anyone will understand it?' asked Michael.

'Don't you start,' said Briony. 'Wasn't it your friend Duncan Cairns who came up with it? Why is everyone so gloomy round here all of a sudden?'

'Because we're into committing money now,' said Martin. 'Until now everything could only go right. Now it can all go wrong and if it does it's our fault.'

'Well, we've gone and done it now, whichever it is,' said

Briony. 'No turning back. You're all right, Martin. You've got a rich wife. I'll just end up on the streets of King's Cross. Still, a girl couldn't be in a better part of London for picking up a quick trick, could she?'

Michael's direct line rang. It was Duncan. He decided to leave the room and take the call by his secretary's desk. Briony fidgeted for a moment, as she always did when she was desperate for a cigarette. Martin went back to the window and looked out at the advertising blitz again. Briony let her eyes meander across the top of Martin's desk as office workers always do when they are inside a colleague's office. Her gaze alighted upon a familiar form.

'Martin, you've got one of those things. Haven't you returned it?'

'What?'

'That research questionnaire. It's a fabulous example of how to put a really illuminating survey together. You ought to return it.'

'I haven't had time. I can't be bothered with those things. Once they've got your name and address on their bloody computer they just pursue you with junk mail even after you've been laid to rest.'

'I don't think so. You really ought to fill in all research surveys and return them. People like me rely on them entirely to make our business decisions. The value of sound statistics to our society cannot be over-valued. They are a good thing.'

'Well, I'm not doing it.'

Michael returned. 'Not doing what?'

'That research survey thing.'

'Oh, yes. I started it but it was so complicated I binned it,' said Michael, bright-eyed.

'Honestly, you two,' said Briony. 'How's Duncan? How's his first day been?' she asked.

'Pretty eventful.'

'That sounds like Myhill Productions to me,' said Martin. 'What's happened? Give us the goss.'

'Well, over the weekend, Duncan devised a new show. He won't tell me what it is, because it's for us.'

'That's unnecessarily discreet of him,' said Martin.

'He thought up a name for it on the walk into work this morning.'

'That sounds pretty standard for our business. Most of the output on British TV looks just like it was thought up in three minutes flat at the bus-stop on the day of broadcast.'

'Yeah, well guess what the title was?'

'I'm no good at guessing-games,' said Martin.

'*Basket Case!*'

Michael's squeal of excitement and Martin's grotesque groan of disbelief surprised Briony. She couldn't interpret them.

'Haven't you ever told him?' asked Martin. His hand was flat on his forehead.

'No.'

'What?' asked Briony, keen to hear a bit of scandal. 'What's the joke?'

'It's no joke,' said Martin. 'Has he still got his job? Has he still got his life?'

'He only just escaped with it. Apparently an air-conditioning fan or some such thing in the office blew up at the precise moment he said the magic words and the propeller came hurtling across the room and nearly took his eye out.'

'Are you sure Karen didn't throw it at him?'

Michael laughed. 'I think it probably diffused the situation and got him off. He doesn't appear to know the sensation he must have caused. He's just been having a lovely day.'

'My God,' said Martin. 'Wait till this one gets out. "Have you heard of Karen Myhill's new show? It's called *Basket Case*. And Martin Fox has commissioned it." God, but it's brilliant.'

Charlotte ran her fingers through her blonde hair and, pushing off her Armani oval metal sunglasses so they dangled on their cord over her breasts, walked into the Soho cappuccino bar. She stood in the queue of streak-haired secretaries and stripy-shirted young clerks, waiting her turn. She thought of the matter in hand: Steve da Silva, her ex-boyfriend, who she now turned corners to avoid in the office. These guys grabbing a lunchtime sandwich were on the young side and not upmarket enough, but they were more Charlotte's type. The thrusting executives of the future with their London uniforms of woollen suits and discreet cuff-links intact, even in this heat. Instead, she had found herself ensnared by the pulsating copywriter, for whose lycra form and muscled charm she had fallen. But that was all over now. Well, almost. She was angry with a deep burning fury. And hell hath no such fury as an ambitious young account executive scorned. She wanted to orchestrate her own finale. First she needed to know the truth, and there was one person who would tell her what it was. She ordered a large espresso and an almond croissant and sat at the back of the small bar on a moulded metal seat by a small round metal table.

Just a few minutes later, the source of all knowledge rushed in. It was Kaisha, the receptionist.

'Hi, Charlie,' she called over the queue. 'What are you having?'

'Just coffee and a croissant,' said Charlotte.

She felt conspicuous announcing her lunch fodder to the crowd in the shop. As far as she was concerned it was not the done thing. Anyway, she was trying to pull off a surreptitious lunchtime rendezvous. But no one here knew them, so she worried for nothing.

Five very long minutes later Kaisha joined her, awkward with her purchases. She plopped a freshly squeezed orange juice and a chicken tikka sandwich on to the table-top.

'I got you a refill,' she said, and handed Charlotte another large espresso.

'My God,' said Charlotte. 'My head will be spinning all afternoon.'

'Go on. Treat yourself,' said the receptionist. 'You work too hard. You're always in before me and, I expect, stay there much later.'

Charlotte felt it a bit of an affront that the teenage receptionist did not appreciate that her management job was also clearly more draining than sitting behind a counter twittering 'Hi' to all and sundry. She restricted her reply to the time reference, however.

'Well, I won't be staying late so much now. Not since I spoke to you the other night.'

'Did you really think you were the only one?'

Charlotte thought carefully before answering. 'I'm afraid I did. I actually did. Do you think me terribly naïve?'

'I'm in no position to make judgments.'

'Oh, come on, Kaisha, tell me. I want to know what other people think. I *need* to know what other people think. Don't hold back just because I'm management and you're the receptionist.'

'*Only* the receptionist, you mean.' Kaisha could detect the class difference just as keenly as Charlotte. 'That's not why I'm holding back. It's just that no one needs to be told she's been a silly bitch.'

Charlotte's eyes pierced what little space there was between them.

'There. I was right,' said Kaisha. 'You didn't want to hear it from me.'

Charlotte chewed her lower lip. She hoped she wasn't going to cry. She hadn't cried yet over Steve and this was not the place to start. She'd just stick to being depressed and humiliated. 'Is everybody talking about me?'

'Only in as much as you're another notch on Steve's bedpost.'

'Who knows?'

'All of MCN. Creative, obviously. Media. Production. Accounts. Audio-visual. The kitchen.'

'Jesus fucking Christ! The kitchen! Why hasn't it come back to me?'

'Because of the unwritten rule in the building. No one tells Clancey and Bennett anything.'

'Why not?'

'Because of Nigel and Serena. They're hated.'

'Why?'

'They treated everyone so badly when they came over here. C&B was a solution to get them out of the way. Apparently.'

'That's nothing to do with me.'

'They hired you, didn't they?'

'So everyone thinks I'm some sort of protégée of theirs, do they? Buggeration.' She bit into her croissant and a splodge of almond filling spurted out, on to her plate. 'You must spend all your time listening at doors.'

'Actually, I can listen in to all the phone conversations in the company on my night switchboard. I don't think the management realises. You'd be surprised who's sleeping with who in this place.'

'Who?'

'You and Steve da Silva, for example. And anything else in a skirt and Steve da Silva.'

'That bastard. I want the details.'

'Well, me, obviously. Carol in Accounts. Rachel in Accounts. Deirdre in Accounts. And that girl, remember, the blonde one that used to wear bows on everything?'

'What? Madeleine Peters? Her too?'

'Yup. Steve said she even had them on her G-string. How can women dress like that? They must walk past racks of magazines and shop windows blind. I mean, she worked in advertising. She should have taste.'

'She was only in finance. That doesn't count.'

'Does reception count?'

'Oh, yes,' fibbed Charlotte. 'That's the public face of the company.' Kaisha looked pleased. 'How many is that so far?'

'That's just the accounts department. Shall I skip media and go straight on to account management?'

'Don't bother.' Charlotte couldn't believe what she was hearing. 'What are we going to do?'

'What d'you mean, "do"?'

'He's not getting away with this. I've been humiliated. Publicly.'

'No you haven't. You got as much out of it as he did.'

'No I bloody well did not. There's a double standard still operating in this society, in case you hadn't noticed.'

'Didn't you enjoy it?'

Charlotte blushed.

Kaisha went on. 'It *is* the biggest you're ever likely to get.'

Charlotte blushed again.

'Damn near choked me, I can tell you.'

Charlotte grimaced. 'For God's sake. I'm eating my lunch.'

Kaisha shrieked with laughter. 'Every girl in the building he's gone down on has had a multiple orgasm. Or so they say. We were thinking of forming a club.'

'Keep your voice down,' said Charlotte. 'People will hear you.'

'I don't care. We were going to call it the Rosebud Club.'

Charlotte's eyes widened in horror that she should somehow have become a part of this. Kaisha continued.

'Good, eh? My last boyfriend thought clitoris was an island off Greece. He had never heard of the word, let alone where to locate it. You have to give Steve his due.'

'I intend to give him something else.'

Kaisha raised her thin, plucked eyebrows.

'I'm a bit loath to do it by myself,' confessed Charlotte.

'Like what?' asked Kaisha, her curiosity kindled at last.

'Well . . .' Charlotte had to decide whether to trust her companion-in-arms.

Kaisha gave her the reason to.

'Charlie, I'm on your side. Steve has treated you badly and, come to think of it, I deserve to be treated with a little more respect myself, even if I didn't expect to be.' She patted Charlotte's forearm and gave her a winky smile. 'Sisters under the skin and all that stuff, eh?'

Charlotte breathed out nervously. 'Steve is going on a shoot next Wednesday.'

'Uh-huh?'

'He won't be back in London until Thursday morning.'

'Uh-huh?'

'What are you doing, say, round eight p.m.?'

'Now let me think,' said Kaisha playfully. 'Why, being your partner in crime, methinks!'

69

The recorded male voice on the tape was American, or possibly fake American.

'Thank you for calling Maletalk, the phone service that puts you in touch with like-minded guys all over Britain. First I need to know that you are using a touch-tone phone. Press "star" to continue.'

'Beep.'

'You're through to the main switchboard. Press "star" to fast-forward at any time. For general information press "one". For the chatline press "two". For mailboxes press "three" . . .'

'Beep.'

'You're through to the chatline. There are . . .'

At this point an incongruous English female voice read out the number 'twelve' much as if she were announcing the platform number of the arrival of the Peterborough train at Reading station. Somehow it just wasn't as sexy as the American voice, which cut back in.

'. . . callers on the line,' it continued. 'Please record your message after the tone. Remember to speak clearly. You have up to two minutes in which to record your message. You may not leave your phone number on this message. Press any key when finished.'

'Hi, guys. My name is Duncan. I'm in London. I'm a good-looking, thirty-two-year-old guy, feeling hot and horny right now and looking for action tonight. I've got fair, spiky hair and blue eyes. I'm five feet ten tall, medium build, got a firm, smooth body and a rock-hard, uncut dick. I'm lying here on my bed with just a white T-shirt and a pair of Calvin Klein briefs on. I'm looking for older, dominant guys into mild discipline and light S&M. You *must* be well hung. Get back to me with a really raunchy message and let's get it together.'

'Beep.'

'For your own personal safety and to comply with regulations,

you must leave your name, age and phone number after the tone.
Press any key when finished.'

'Beep.'

'Duncan Cairns, aged thirty-two, oh one seven one, eight seven
three, six one nine six.'

'Beep.'

'To repeat your message press "one". To send your message
press "two". To re-record your message press "three".'

'Beep.'

'Message sent. You will now hear other callers' descriptions.
Press "star" to fast-forward at any time.'

'Hi, guys. My name is Mike, I'm thirty-five and work in the City.
I live in central London. I'm good-looking with a well-developed
physique, I go to the gym three times a week, I've got brown hair
and brown eyes. I'm active. Leave me a message.'

'To hear the next caller press "one". To reply to this message
press "two". To repeat this message press "three" . . .'

'Beep.'

'Yes. My name is Andy, I'm in the Heathrow area. If you want
to fuck a tight, shaved arse tonight, leave me a message.'

'To hear the next . . .'

'Beep.'

'Hello, I'm a naughty uncle . . .'

'Beep.'

'Yeah, my name is Mark, I'm a skinhead with tattooed forearms
and neck, pierced . . .'

'Beep.'

'Hi, guys. My name is Carl. I'm twenty-three, blond, blue eyes,
seven inches, very thick. I have a smooth body with two shaved
balls filled with spunk and waiting to shoot. Tanned from my
holiday. Not into anything kinky, just good, dirty phone talk,
possibly meet up later. Come on. Don't be shy.'

'Beep.'

'Hello, chaps. My name is Anton. I'm thirty-eight with dark
brown hair and blue eyes, considered good-looking, with a trim
body. I'm well proportioned down below, dominant and active. I
wear pinstripes during the day and in the evening I'm into jocks,
shorts, discipline – caning, spanking, that sort of thing – and mild
bondage. I'm in the South Kensington area of London and can

accommodate. If you like the sound of me, do please send me a message.'

'To hear the next caller press "one". To reply to this message press "two" . . .'

'Beep.'

'Anton, this is Duncan. Send me your number and I promise you, you won't be disappointed. I'm cute. I'm drizzling just thinking of the good spanking you're going to give me. Get back to me, Anton. I'm gagging for it.'

'Beep.'

'Message sent. To hear other callers press "one".'

'Beep.'

'Hi, my name is Trevor. I'm in the Kent area but can travel. I'm twenty-eight, blond, grey eyes, good-looking, good definition and hirsute. I have a hairy chest, hairy stomach, hairy arms and powerful hairy legs. If there's anyone else out there in Kent or in London, let me know.'

'Beep.'

'You have a message.'

'Hello, Duncan. This is Anton. You sound completely delicious. Yes, that all sounds good to me. My number is oh one seven one, seven eight oh, one six one eight. Let me know you've received this message before you come off the line.'

'To hear the next caller press "one". To reply to this message press "two" . . .'

'Beep.'

'Anton, it's Duncan. I got your number and I'll call you in five minutes and arrange to come round. It's looking good, Anton.'

Paul McCarthy replaced the receiver by his bed and pulled more firmly now on his cock. So what if he didn't look like Duncan? It was a great image to use to pick up down the phone. All that pent-up, frustrated sexual energy of Duncan's could be put to use *in absentia*. By the time he got round to Anton's – Anton, what a priceless pseudonym! – Anton wouldn't give a monkey's one way or the other who Paul looked like.

Paul forgot Anton and his call for a moment, put his left arm behind his head and pushed his neck back into the pillow. He thought of Jolyon, beloved, lost, unfaithful, uncalling, *unprotected* Jolyon. He pictured Jolyon in his mind's eye, the romantic plantsman, his shiny body loosely draped in roomy dungarees. He kissed him, licked him, caressed him, worshipped him, while slowly stripping him down to his eager body. He was depressed that he was lying here tossing off rather than enjoying a torrid affair. Masturbation is no substitute for a relationship and no replacement for love.

On the other hand – hand being the operative word – wanking is a surefire way of achieving a really good come every time.

70

'Max, please eat *something*.' Karen wailed in desperation and hurt at being so openly rejected.

'No, Kar, it's all horrible.'

'It's not all horrible, Max, it's actually rather tasty. It's taken me hours to cook, you know.'

'I do know, Kar. It had gone ten o'clock by the time we sat down. Perhaps you should just stick to cooking at weekends when we can afford the time.'

'Don't be rude. It's well worth waiting for, in my opinion.'

'Well, I'm not a vegetarian. It's unnatural and, as a matter of scientific fact, it's almost impossible to balance your diet nutritionally eating just vegetables.'

'It's one vegetarian meal, that's all. I'm not a vegetarian either, as well you know. You're not being asked to subscribe to a whole diet, Max, just one bloody main course. That's all. It's just for a change. Now come on, Max, or there'll be no dessert.' That was always a surefire hit.

'Kar!' whined the teenager.

That pushed Karen over the edge. 'Don't call me that fucking name, Max. It really pisses me off.' She banged her knife and fork down on the kitchen table. 'Honestly! Call me Mum or Mummy or whatever any normal mother round here gets called.'

'You're not a normal mother. If you were a normal mother you'd have microwaved a frozen pizza. We'd have had dinner at six thirty. Any mother who really loved her son would feed him properly. I deserve oven chips not vine leaves stuffed with Brussels sprouts.'

'You get oven chips and pizza every other night of the week. Now just bloody well eat it.' She moistened her palate with a swig of water from her glass, then said apologetically, 'It's not vine leaves anyway. It's blanched lettuce.'

'Bleeugh,' responded Max.

Karen gave up. She got up and whisked the plate away from him, scraped it into the bin and whammed it and all the other dishes into the dishwasher. She didn't turn it on yet. She knew there would be hell to pay if Max did not get his sweetener. She raided the freezer and produced a tub of Ben and Jerry's Rainforest Crunch ice-cream. Unaware she was being secretly scanned by Max's radar vision, she scooped two dollops out into each of two bowls, topped them with voluminous scooshes of aerosol cream, and finished them off with a sprinkling of crushed nuts.

'Hey, Kar?' said Max, suddenly brightening up.

'What?'

'There's this man who goes into an ice-cream parlour and he orders an ice-cream sundae in a very high voice.' Max did the voice. '"I'd like an ice-cream sundae, please," he says.'

'Yes?'

'"Whipped cream?" asks the lady serving. "Yes please."' Max did the voice again. '"Crushed nuts?" says the lady. And he goes: "No. I've always talked like this."' Max dissolved into silly sniggers as only teenage boys can.

Karen laughed too. These days she missed the little boy in Max more and more and adored it when he returned for fleeting funny moments.

'This is more like it,' grinned Max, clearing his rainforest landscape with one sweep of his spoon.

Karen picked up the bowls and things and bunged them in the dishwasher and turned it on. It whirred into action, not quite as silent as the advertising had suggested. Max had gone through into the living room and was scanning the *Radio Times*.

'God. There's nothing on,' he said. 'As usual. Make some decent programmes, Kar, ones I want to watch. I'm going upstairs.'

'Max,' said Karen, pleased that at least one evening had returned to a semblance of the old normality. 'I've had a thought. Stay there.'

She returned from her study with Duncan's proposal for *Basket Case*.

'Read that and tell me if it will work. It's for The Station. Remember, it's meant to be interactive. You know what it means?'

'Kar, I'm not a child,' her business partner reminded her.

Karen finished clearing up in the kitchen, then fixed herself a small cafetière of coffee. She popped her head back into the living room. Max was lying reading on the settee.

'Would you like a Tango or a Coke or something?'

'Nope,' said Max, engrossed.

She came back in with her coffee and squeezed in beside him at the end of the settee.

'Well?'

'Love it. It'll work.'

Karen was excited. She bumped along the settee towards her son as he swung his legs on to the floor and sat upright. 'Ooh. D'you think so?'

'Yup. I need to know more about the video floor. Are they moving pictures or stills? They should move. Who wrote it?'

'What makes you think I didn't write it?'

'It's too rational for you, that bit at the beginning. It *is* a bit boring at the start, mind you.'

'I'll fix that. I'm going to work on it tonight.'

'Who's going to present it?'

'I thought John Fashanu. He's sporty and experienced. And black – that always helps these days to make the sale.'

'Wrong sport. Anyway, it should be a comedian.'

'A comedian?' Karen instantly dropped John Fashanu straight out of her mental card index. 'That's interesting. Why?'

'To make it mad and zany. To go with the title.'

Karen paused. 'Actually, I was thinking of dropping the title.'

'*Basket Case*? It's brilliant. Sometimes, Kar, your judgment is lousy. *Basket Case* is catchy. People will think it's funny.'

That's what I was afraid of, thought Karen. Max, like Duncan, had never heard the story. No one, including his mother, had dared tell him.

They chatted about the idea a bit more, after which Max went off to his room. Karen finished her coffee and then later, in her study, settled down at her word processor to hone Duncan's proposal to her exact liking. Max was probably right about the title. But how could she ever deliver that to Martin Fox? How could she produce a show called *Basket Case*? It would make them both the laughing-stock of British television. She put the thought out of her mind for a moment and typed her way into the night.

71

The pilot's voice came over the loudspeaker system.

'Ladies and gentlemen, I am sorry to have to tell you that Leeds Bradford airport is still experiencing high winds and that they remain too fierce for us to attempt a safe landing there. So, we will now divert to Teeside. I hope this will not add too much time to your journey. Should you require it, there will be a coach waiting to take you from Teeside back to Leeds Bradford. May I take this opportunity to again apologise for any inconvenience which has been caused by today's bad weather and to remind you that this is beyond our control. Your personal safety is of paramount importance to us at all times. Thank you for your co-operation and patience in this matter.'

'I wish they made these seats wider,' said Nigel, trying to stretch out in the cramped space. 'Where is Teeside, exactly?'

'God only knows,' said Serena, at snapping point. 'Even further north and even further away.' She dropped her hand below the edge of her seat and slipped a finger in between her heel and the cutting edge of a sparkling new pair of black patent stiletto shoes. 'I'm going to get Margaret to take these back to Harvey Nichols first thing tomorrow morning,' she rasped.

'Are they hurting your feet, old girl?'

'Killing them. Every time I put my foot down it's like running my heel over a bacon slicer.'

'I think the air hostess would like your coffee cup, Serena,' Hazel pointed out.

'I've a good mind to give her more than my coffee cup. This whole trip is a complete farce from beginning to end. It is simply impertinence on Stella Boddington's part to expect us to come running at the drop of a hat all the way up to Yorkshire when she keeps an office in Knightsbridge.'

'She's been ill. She gave us a week's notice,' Hazel pointed out.

'If you had been more thoughtful, Hazel, you would have used what powers of persuasion you have to make Stella come to the agency. Nigel and I are very preoccupied with strategic development and can ill afford a day out in a provincial backwater. I appreciate the fact that you are junior and may not have been able to talk her round, but you only had to ask and I would have stepped in and sorted it out.'

'Margaret booked the meeting, not me,' Hazel pointed out.

'Don't blame Margaret. People who always blame their secretaries are poor managers in my book. It was your responsibility. Although why that girl didn't check the weather forecast and switch us to the train – well, it beggars belief. What else does she have to do all day?'

'You did say you weren't prepared to train it all this way,' Hazel pointed out.

'Hazel, if you point out one more thing to me I shall scream. It's like travelling with a Linguaphone repeating tape. No doubt this is all a lark to you, but it is not to me.'

Had they landed at Leeds Bradford there would have been a waiting car laid on by the Carpets Company to whisk them straight to Stella's door. As it was, they had to race all the other exasperated executives for the limited supply of taxis queuing to serve two airports' worth of business travellers instead of the usual one. Sulphuric Serena was slowed by her cutting stilettos. Roly-poly Nigel was slowed by middle-age spread. Harassed Hazel was slowed by a giant black plastic eight-foot-square art bag containing their latest creative proposals in the form of huge layouts. Nigel ran forward into it and tripped and stumbled.

'Careful what you're doing with that ruddy great thing, you stupid girl.'

'I can't help it!' retorted Hazel. 'This bag is longer than the space left in between the end of my arm hanging down and the floor.'

'Well, grow a shorter arm next time, then,' complained Nigel. Hazel scowled.

They were all extremely stressed, extremely irritable and extremely unsure of what to do next.

'Will a taxi take us all the way back to near Leeds?' asked Hazel.

'I have absolutely no idea,' said Serena. 'You'd think there would be some form of reception committee to advise one on what to do. He didn't tell us how far away we are. I hope we're not expected to go out there with all those other people into the driving rain to wait for a taxi. That really is a disgrace. We'll be soaked.'

Nigel looked at Serena. Serena looked at Nigel. They both looked at Hazel.

'I'm not standing out there on my own in the pouring rain,' she protested.

'Hazel. You poor thing. You're drenched. You're soaked through.' As she joined her agency team in the Carpets Company board-room, Stella Boddington roared with laughter. 'I've never seen three such bedraggled travellers in all my life. You look as if you've spent a night on the moors.'

'As good as,' said Serena humourlessly. She reached across the boardroom table and poured just herself a coffee from a thermos jug. She screwed the cap back down extremely tightly. 'Really, Stella, we just haven't earned enough money from your business this year to justify the expense of three senior managers coming all this way.'

Hazel smirked at how she appeared to have been promoted from the junior capacity referred to on the flight.

'I pay all your travelling expenses.'

'I was talking about our time, not the cost of the travel.'

'Yes. You really are very late, aren't you?' said Stella, trying to smooth over Serena's lack of diplomacy. 'I wondered where you'd all got to.'

'My mobile phone wouldn't work in your dales or whatever they're called.'

'I don't own them personally. I knew you'd been diverted when the driver returned without you. But I didn't think it would take another two hours plus for you to get here.'

'We were last in the line for cabs,' explained Hazel. 'We had to get the courtesy coach.'

'Oh dear,' said Stella. 'You'll have to run a bit faster next time, won't you, Nigel?'

'Nothing to do with me. I'm a sailor. As fit as a fiddle.'

'Didn't you nearly die on your last outing?'

'That was Duncan's fault,' said Serena. Behind her, Hazel shook her head disbelievingly in full view of Stella.

'Ah, yes, Duncan. How is he? I miss him.'

'We've not heard from him. We don't miss him. I don't know how he filled his time, that boy. We've got some of the best work we've seen for years out of Orlando and the creatives. I really don't think we'd have got it with him still here. We'll take you through it in a minute.'

'This is the campaign that Duncan briefed in?'

'That's not the difficult part, Stella. It's judging it against the brief.'

'Well, I'm not going to argue about it. There's no point.'

'Exactly.'

'Because there's not going to be any campaign.'

Serena choked on her own next sentence. Nigel was winded. Hazel pulled her chair up for a ringside seat.

'Sorry. I put that too bluntly, didn't I? There will be a campaign, I assure you, eventually, but not this year.'

'I don't believe it,' gasped Serena.

'You'd better believe it! Fibrella have got a serious production capacity problem with their new wonder fibre. They just can't manufacture it in bulk at speed and maintain the quality. With any form of nylon nowadays it is crucial that the structure is light-absorbent to reduce the nylony sheen that we hate so much in Britain. Their only solution is to put a chalky sort of substance into it, but while this dulls the shine it also dulls the colour. Well, that's not good enough. Purity of colour is a key purchasing discriminator. There's no way I can order the new range of carpets until it gets sorted out.'

'Well, this is a sorry state you seem to have got yourself into.'

A rather arch comment from Serena, that one, thought Hazel.

'If I hadn't had that time off when I was ill I might have kept more on top of things,' said Stella. 'Then again, what could I have done?'

Serena's experienced brain picked up speed. 'We'll just have to advertise something else. There must be another storyline we can work up. New designs. Or a service story. A price promotion. Free fitting.'

'I will be taking about ten per cent of the budget and using it to drop the prices for a six-week promotion, but we'll handle that with an in-store makeover with new point-of-sale banners and ticketing. I've found a perfect little company to do it for me. They've come up with some very good creative work.'

'You've briefed them already? I hope you haven't gone behind our back.'

'They're below-the-line. I thought you were too grand for the trimmings. Didn't you tell me that once?'

'We're full service. We can do anything.'

'I don't think you could match them on price.'

'You haven't asked us. Are they local?'

'No, London-based. I think you know them. Thurrock and Josling.'

'*Alan Josling*! He's a complete crook!'

Stella was taken aback by Serena's snarling ferocity. 'He speaks very highly of you. Said you had a reputation going way, *way* back.'

'Now look here, Stella. This just isn't on. You may have had an unfortunate experience with your fibre development and we're totally sympathetic and all that, but you're asking us to carry your loss. You promised us three point three million pounds billings this year. That's four hundred and ten thousand pounds in income for us, not to put too fine a point on it. So far we've had nothing.'

'Zero.'

'Thank you, Nigel. OK. So we may lose ten per cent to Alan Josling. So be it. That leaves ninety per cent to spend elsewhere. It has to come through Clancey and Bennett.'

'Serena, I never promised anyone anything. And I do intend to spend the money. Next year. In the spring. We'll launch then. So everything will be all right, apart from the ten per cent reduction, of course. I accept your disappointment about that.'

'It most certainly will not be all right. You will have to pay us a cancellation fee.'

'What for? I haven't cancelled anything.'

'You've cancelled your entire annual spend with us.'

'I haven't. Perhaps I didn't spell it out clearly enough. There will be a launch. There will be a campaign. There will be a budget. It has not been cancelled. It has been put back six months. That's all. Got it?'

'But will there be a Clancey and Bennett? We cannot continue to keep going without that income.'

'Don't be ridiculous. You're a worldwide international advertising agency. You have twenty-pound notes on the floor instead of carpet tiles.'

'We'll make it easy for you. We can pre-bill the production and media.'

'I'm not putting three point three million pounds into your bank account for six months!'

'You'll get the interest.'

'I'll get the sack. There is no point in discussing this any further.'

Serena stood up sharply and was ambushed by her stilettos. She took it out on her client. 'Stella Boddington. This morning we flew here at your request, at the risk, I might add, of life and limb, in good faith and with good intentions, to present to you the very highest standard of creative advertising on which we have been working night and day for six months. You didn't even have the common courtesy to ask to see it. More than that, you didn't even have the courage to come down to London and face us on our own patch and tell us earlier that there was trouble brewing. You just pulled the rug from under our feet!'

Hazel smirked at the unfortunate pun.

'Calm down, Serena. You're overreacting. The money will be there. You can tell your board to hang on for a few months.'

'I can tell *your* board a thing or two about you, and that's what I intend to do. I'm staggered at your lack of professionalism. Then again, I'm not.'

Stella stood up too. 'There's no point in continuing this conversation. I'm sorry it's bad news but I really think you're making a mountain out of a molehill. You should not have counted your chickens before they hatched. As for speaking to my board, well, I'll cross that bridge when I come to it. Oh, for God's sake, Serena. You've got me trotting out bloody mottoes like a box of Christmas crackers.' She flashed an angry smile but Serena remained steely. 'I'll leave you here to calm down. If you want me to come back in, I will.'

'We won't be here if you do.'

'Please yourself, then.' Stella sighed and left the room. She had never, ever had a meeting like it.

'Well, you've done it now, old girl,' murmured Nigel.

'I can't believe I've lugged this great big stupid art bag all the way from London to Teeside to here and we didn't even open it.' Hazel was speaking out loud to herself.

'Thank you, you two. Thank you very much. Thank you very much indeed.' Serena Sark knew she had stood her ground and stood it alone. While her shoes had stabbed her in the back.

72

'Look at you!' said Hazel. 'Beavering away.'

'It's only seven,' said Charlotte. She gave Hazel a weary smile.

'Why bother? I'm doing less without Cairns here to crack the whip. Well, not less exactly, but there are a few corners which can be cut. And fewer meetings. I'd have thought you wouldn't have had so much to do. Since we didn't get that airline thing and now The Station campaign is up—'

'Only phase one, Haze. The rest is still in production. And there's the Carpets stuff to get going with.'

'That's all off now.'

'Serena doesn't seem to think so. Anyway, I'm doing the billing on The Station posters. If I get these invoices up to Accounts tomorrow morning we'll get the income in a month early. That'll impress Nigel.'

'Impress Fatboy? He won't even know, stupid. Come on. Let's go for a drink.'

'He will know. I'll get Accounts to memo Nigel and copy Serena. That way I'll get a bit of credit.'

'Have they got a replacement for Cairns yet, d'you think?'

'God knows. We'll be the last to be told, I expect. Margaret is keeping an ear to the ground.' Charlotte pushed back her hair and smiled again. 'Apparently, they've not even alerted headhunters – well, not Audrey Goldberg, anyway.'

'Have you been talking to her?'

'Only socially. Don't worry. I'm not leaving. Yet. I've only just got here, remember.'

'Yeah, well, it seems like a lifetime. So, no chance of a drink, then? It's my shout.'

'Sorry, Haze. How about tomorrow after work?' Charlotte picked up her diary from beneath the computer print-outs of invoices. She made a show of checking. 'I'm free then.'

'Yeah, sure.'

There was another awkward pause. All this seemed artificial. Pleasantries. Hazel couldn't understand why Charlotte was intent on hanging around. Although they had not discussed it, she was sure the thing with Steve da Silva was over. If Ben in Production was saying it was, it followed that it must be. So that wasn't the reason. It made Hazel feel bad that she always left the agency first. Well, sod it. That was Charlotte's problem, not hers. She said good night and departed.

Charlotte sat punching in numbers on her calculator, transfer-ring misallocated costs and adding expenses to specific jobs to be invoiced to her client. Half an hour went by. Her office had no window on the outside world and her eyes had to peer at the faint print-outs under her Anglepoise lamp. Billing was the account managers' most loathed job, but on the other hand there was a certain satisfaction to be had from settling up all the numbers, making a profit and putting a completed job finally to bed.

'Pssst!'

Charlotte looked up. It was Kaisha, bang on the appointed hour.

'Hi!'

The two girls automatically giggled mischievously. Charlotte was reminded of midnight capers in the dorm at school when all the staff and prefects were asleep. Although, come to think of it, there had been no girls quite like Kaisha at her school.

'Ready to go?' asked Kaisha. 'The coast is clear, to coin a phrase.'

'All set,' said Charlotte. She got up and pushed her fingers through her hair. She made a face. 'Oh, Kaisha . . .'

'What?' Kaisha looked concerned.

'I thought we'd agreed we'd wear black.'

'Sorry. I didn't realise you were serious.'

'I was. I am. Tonight is a big night. Still, no matter. Have you got everything?'

'What d'you think?' Kaisha came further into the office and laid out on the desk a black bin liner and a pair of dressmaker's scissors. Charlotte picked up the scissors and turned them over in her palms.

'Where did you get these, Kaisha? They're fantastic. They weigh a ton.'

'My mum. She makes all her own clothes.'

'Brilliant. But we need more than one pair.'

'What about those?' asked Kaisha, pointing to a small steel pair in Charlotte's desk-tidy.

'They're no use. They can barely manage paper. I know. Orlando has a big pair he uses for putting together presentation material. I'll go and get those. Meanwhile you get us the wine.'

'The wine?'

'Yes. It isn't champagne, I'm afraid.' Charlotte led Kaisha into Hazel's office and located the duplicate key to Serena's fridge.

'Go into Serena's office and you'll find the fridge under her desk. Get us a bottle of Pinot Grigio. Then drop the key back in Hazel's drawer.'

They rendezvoused by Margaret's desk a few minutes later. Then, armed with glasses, wine, bin liner, the two pairs of sharp scissors and a little black rucksack of Charlotte's, they nervously giggled their way down one soft step at a time, one full floor to Steve da Silva's office. While Kaisha stood in the corridor and checked her sightlines to assure herself they were alone, Charlotte adeptly brushed open the door and crept inside. Kaisha followed and snapped the door shut behind her.

'Fuck!' she hissed, bringing herself up short. 'Look at that.' She pointed ahead to Steve's wardrobe. A small blue padlock and chain hung across the metal handles of the doors. 'That's new. Fuck.' She was already resigned to defeat.

Charlotte laughed wickedly. 'It's part of the plan,' she explained. 'I wanted it as a demonstration of my hold over him. I bought it after you and I met for lunch. I told him it was to keep his personal possessions protected and that I was keeping the spare key for emergencies!' She dangled it like a live mouse in front of Kaisha's nose.

'Jesus, Charlie, that's mean. Is there anything in this building you don't hold the key to?'

'No. At least nothing of any importance.'

'I can't believe I got you so wrong. There was me all the time thinking you were Miss Goody Two Shoes.'

Charlotte grinned like a keyboard from ear to ear. She unpadlocked the wardrobe and opened both its doors wide. Then she helped herself to Steve's corkscrew, uncorked the wine, poured them each a large glass and sat down cross-legged on the floor opposite Kaisha. She took a mouthful of the Pinot.

'Mmm. It's so good when it's this cold.'

She unbuckled the large compartment of the rucksack and produced something tubular wrapped in tissue paper.

'What's that?' asked Kaisha, curious.

'Candles. Black ones.'

'What for?'

'I'm a witch. Didn't you know?'

Kaisha moved her head backwards ever so slightly. 'You're weird,' she said.

'I'm not the girl next door, that's for sure. Not any more.' Charlotte unwrapped the two long black candles and laid them on the floor. 'They're just for atmosphere, stupid. I like a sense of occasion.'

She fumbled within the rucksack again and now produced two sleek spiral silver candlesticks and a box of long matches. She inserted the candles in the sticks and placed them to either side of herself. She took another mouthful of wine and ceremoniously lit first one candle and then the other.

'What d'you think? Am I the High Priestess or the Low Sneak?' she asked her bemused audience of one. 'The candles don't make as much difference as I thought they might. They'll get better as the light drops outside. More wine?'

Kaisha nodded and Charlotte refilled both glasses.

'OK, time to start the production line. Hand me the Thierry Mugler first. The jacket.'

Kaisha took the impeccably cut suit from the wardrobe and kept back the trousers and the hanger. Charlotte carefully took the left lapel of the designer jacket between the thumb and forefinger of her left hand.

'Too late to go back now,' she said. She sang a line from a stage song. 'Past the point of no-o-o return—'

Kaisha giggled. 'Get a move on. I'm terrified we'll get caught.'

Charlotte looked down and decisively snipped the dressmaker's scissors into the fabric of the Thierry Mugler and carefully cut the bottom half of the lapel off the jacket. It was very neatly and precisely done and not instantly noticeable, but her alteration made the jacket unwearable. She took the amputated lapel and dropped it into the bin liner.

'OK. You do the navy Armani. I'll have a go on the Thierry Mugler trousers.'

For the next half an hour, the two girls sat cross-legged on the floor, concentrating, dedicated and silent. They ritually dismembered the bottom section of each lapel of each jacket and cut out the crotch of each pair of trousers. Excising the fly panel and zip section was tough and fell exclusively to the dressmaker's scissors, which were the only ones able to do the job slickly. Each remnant of material was carefully gathered up and deposited in the bin liner, while each suit was carefully placed back on its hanger and relocated in its original place in the wardrobe. They worked with all the attention to detail of the best bespoke Savile Row tailor.

'There! All done,' said Kaisha, with a drunken flourish of her mum's scissors. 'I ought to take up dressmaking. I'm better than I thought. Jesus. I've had more to drink than I realised.'

'Not quite finished yet,' said Charlotte.

While Kaisha sat sipping the dregs of the warming wine, Charlotte completed their task by speedily slicing off the double cuff of one sleeve of each of Steve's shirts, then shortening each tie by a blunt-edged three inches. Lastly, she padlocked the wardrobe, its contents apparently pristine and undisturbed. Steve would only notice, surely, when he had fully slipped on his first pair of trousers, to discover his massive genitals hanging out, wayward, guilty and exposed for all to see. Charlotte emptied the remainder of the wine into each of their glasses and raised hers in a toast.

'To the biggest shit in the company,' she said. 'Make that "bastard".'

Kaisha laughed.

'To the biggest prick, anyway. Aren't you taking all this a bit seriously, Charlotte? I thought we'd go wild and just shred away. You're a touch of the controlled psychopath, aren't you?'

'Absolutely. We should have had a nice Chianti.' She made a gobbling noise at the back of her throat, like Anthony Hopkins in *The Silence of the Lambs*. 'I feel like Hannibal the Cannibal, cutting up my victim in the most painful and hurtful and calculated way. God, but I enjoyed that.' For some reason it came out sounding hollow. 'I can't wait to hear the reaction tomorrow.'

'I can.'

'Having second thoughts?'

'Not really. Will we get caught, d'you think? This is criminal damage.'

'Well, it's too late now. Could have been one of a hundred women round here anyway, couldn't it?' To Charlotte's ears her own words lacked the smack of conviction.

With that they snuck off into the night like cat burglars, glasses, bottle, cork, scissors, rucksack and bulging bin liner in hand, no pointing finger of evidence left to convict them.

But Steve will know I did it, thought Charlotte. And she felt a sadness creeping over her. She wasn't triumphant as she had hoped. Nor revenged as she had planned. She felt self-conscious, she felt let-down. Already she was a bit ashamed. She had a dull headache from the chill of the wine. She had done it now. Only she could have done it, only she *would* have done it. Everyone in the office would soon know that she *must* have done it, and what would they think of her then? All of a sudden Charlotte Reith felt much too old to be carrying on like this.

73

Martin Fox studied Karen Myhill across his desk. She had never looked a particularly healthy woman, but right now she looked downright sick. As if she was about to up-chuck over his office settee.

'Karen, I'll tell it to you straight, like I did on the breakfast show.'

'Aw, fuck, you haven't bought it—' She looked near collapse now.

'On the contrary, Karen, I love it. I'm formally commissioning you to make a pilot of *Basket Case*.'

'Really!' Karen's recovery was immediate, if not miraculous. Big black clouds of helpless uncertainty visibly floated off her wine-bottle shoulders. She was evidently thrilled beyond her wildest dreams and didn't bother to hide it. 'Brilliant! Brilliant! Brilliant! Brilliant!' She had nearly gone hurtling over a cliff and at the last minute had been pushed back from the precipice with a helping hand from an old friend. So saved, she got straight down to business. 'Tell me more. The huge start-up costs of creating the video floor mean we can't fund just a pilot and leave it at that.'

'Well, although I don't say this to many of your competitors, money is not something The Station has to worry about in the short term.' Martin flicked through his copy of Karen's proposal. 'The important thing is to get it right. I'm confident the game will work with a few amendments. We need to discuss the level of difficulty of the questions as well. Who did you have in mind as a presenter?'

'No one yet.'

'We'll make it a joint decision. The Station wants stars and personalities to help us make our mark. Nothing too idiosyncratic, you know.'

They both knew that Karen's one – only – weakness was her inability to cast well.

'You're not worried that basketball is too American?' she asked.

'No, I don't think so. It's not a game very many people play, but everyone understands about bouncing the ball around and popping it in the net.' He paused and, sitting back, changed to a lower, wrier tone. 'Er . . . This is the difficult one . . . How do you feel about the . . . the . . . you know, the name? I couldn't believe it when I saw it.'

For once in her life Karen Myhill let rip and roared freely with uncontrolled laughter. 'It came with the idea. It comes from a staff member.'

'Let me guess. Duncan Cairns, Michael Farnham's friend.'

'That's the one. He obviously didn't understand its implication. Sweet, really.'

'You're going soft in your old age. Will you stick with it, then?'

'Will you let me?'

'I'll leave it to you.'

'Well, it's not a problem for me if it's not a problem for you.'

'Why should it be a problem for me?'

'Martin!'

'What?'

'Martin, you know as well as I do that people speculate about us.'

'Hmm. Well, what will we do? I know. Let's use it for the moment as a working title and see what happens. I might as well take a leaf out of everybody else in television's book and put off making a decision.'

'Working titles grow on people,' warned Karen. 'It's not easy to drop them later.'

Martin put the proposal back down on the desk. 'Actually, I think it's very appropriate. You know, you'll probably find that the name exorcises the old rumours. People will sit up and notice and think we couldn't have run with it unless all those stories were definitely untrue. We wouldn't have dared.'

'Unless people think we're more Machiavellian than that. Which, of course, they will do.'

They both laughed awkwardly at the prospect of renewed gossip.

'When do you plan to air the pilot?' asked Karen.

'Well, *Megabrek* will launch the channel and its first quarter. I'd like to use this show to inject fresh interest, as if we'll need any, at the beginning of the New Year. So if we put the pilot out at the start of December, we'll give ourselves four to six weeks to go into production on the full show. But we'll assume from today that the series will run for proper and that the pilot is a technical run-through.'

'Budgets?'

'To be confirmed. Submit me a budget outline as soon as you can.'

'And the rights?'

'The Station will hold them worldwide in perpetuity. The usual thing.'

'That's not the usual thing for me, Martin.'

'Well, you try and sell an interactive show on this scale to anyone else. There's no other channel capable of broadcasting such a programme.'

'Not this year, perhaps—'

'Karen, you can't have everything. I haven't made you compete for this project. You've got it on a plate. That was, to say the least, a very dangerous thing for me to do. Quit while you're ahead.'

Karen decided not to push further until she had sight of a contract.

'Did Max see this one?' asked Martin.

'Of course. You know he's my right-hand man.'

'And?'

'Well, you wouldn't have seen it if he hadn't gone for it.'

'Still the most important teenager in TV.'

'And why not?'

'Just be careful, Karen. Your own judgment has always served you best. Sometimes, you over-compensate with Max because he has no father. You should be firm with him, not indulge him. How is he anyway?'

'Oh, he's fine. He's wonderful in every way. I love him more than ever.' She looked him in the eye. 'You're right, though. I have been over-protective, I suppose. He does miss the father thing.'

'Do you mind if I ask? Are you going to tell him?'

'Yes, Martin. I am going to tell him.'

'Oh,' said Martin Fox, ever so quietly. He didn't know what more to say.

74

'Cooeee! You two!'

Although Duncan sat with his back to the door, he instantly recognised the unique shriek of Paul McCarthy. He rippled with embarrassment, dreading his friend's camp and showy entrance to the rooftop garden of Daphne's, a small Greek restaurant in Camden Town. They had agreed on it over the phone as a sort of North London compromise that Michael, Duncan and Paul could each reach and park at easily after work. The tiny terrace was a triumph of ingenuity over reality, carved out of the second-floor grime at the back of a busy, nondescript street. Trellis and trailing plants hid the diners from the adjacent unpleasantness of the area. There were nine full tables crammed on to the terrace and,

Duncan was acutely aware, conversations overlapped easily in the confined space. Paul had better be on good behaviour. Michael waved him over. A young, good-looking Greek waiter, with tanned, chiselled features and wet-look jet-black hair, approached their table, while Paul attempted to stuff his bulky shoulder bag underneath it. He looked up, his face at the level of the waiter's crotch.

'Oh, hello,' he said, in an insinuating manner that would not have disgraced Kenneth Williams.

'You like a drink, sir?'

'He's asking for trouble!' Paul joked, his head bobbing at fly level. He made a sideways wink at Michael.

'What have you got on offer, Big Boy?' asked Michael, wickedly.

Duncan squirmed and scowled at him across the table.

'Don't you start,' he warned. Michael made a face.

'Now stop quarrelling, you two. Oh, I don't know what to have. I'm all in a tizzy,' said Paul, unintentionally attracting the attention of the entire terrace. 'I can't reverse yet, so I couldn't park for miles. I thought I was going to be ever so late. I was crying over my Gorecki tape, which didn't help.'

'It's wonderful, isn't it?' said Michael.

'Isn't it? I luxuriate in it. It's like lying in a bath of Fenjal and drinking Amaretto. You just have to let it wash over you. What are you two having?'

'Diet Coke,' they replied.

'How boring. I think I'll have a Campari and lemonade.'

'Two Diet Cokes and a Campari and lemonade,' noted the waiter. He left.

'Isn't he gorgeous?' lushed Michael across the table.

'To die for. Like one of the models in my granny's knitting patterns when I was a child. There was one I always fancied in a Fair Isle.'

'Look at that arse.'

'Stop it,' said Duncan. 'People will hear.'

They already had.

'How long have you been driving now?' Duncan asked Paul as they tucked into the olives and pickled vegetables on the table.

'I passed my test when I was eighteen. But I can't reverse.

You have to do everything the wrong way round. Left is right and right is left and backwards is forwards. You can't tell your front from your rear bottom. I can't bear it. It's too much of an ordeal. Especially when you've taken an E. Here, have you tried anti-depressants?'

'Of course not,' tutted Duncan.

'What d'you mean, of course not? Loosen up, for God's sake. It's just that I read this thing in the paper today that five per cent of people who're on this anti-depressant – I've forgotten which one – have an orgasm when they sneeze. There was this woman—'

'Don't be ridiculous!'

'It's true! They had a man in the article who caught a really bad cold in the office and he'd had to go out and buy a packet of condoms with his Night Nurse.'

Even Duncan laughed. The glossy-haired waiter returned and brought their drinks. Michael's eyes raided his young body as before.

'Very Greek. They all like it, of course, the Greeks.'

'Like what?' asked Duncan, glaring, knowing full well what the answer was going to be.

'You know the expression – "a bit of Greek".'

Paul thought aloud: 'What is "Greek"? A blow-job? No, that's French. Anything to do with the tongue is French. Greek is up the bum, isn't it?'

A young couple next to them momentarily hesitated with their perfectly matched rising spoons of cold soup.

'It's that old joke, isn't it, about dropping the soap in the shower.' Paul turned to talk directly to Duncan who he thought might not understand. 'In front of a Greek. You know, bending over—'

'I know what it means!' Duncan stated it as emphatically as possible.

Paul carried on regardless. 'All that old gay lingo is very fascinating. You can get a book of it now.'

'Who wants one?' asked Duncan.

'Anyone relaxed with their sexuality, darling, which you are obviously not. Speaking of which, did I tell you I met someone new through an ad?'

'Not more ads?' asked Michael. 'What perversion were you after this time?'

'God, Michael, what's up with you tonight?' Duncan was getting snarly. 'Don't encourage him.'

'He's called Anton.'

'Anton?'

'Lives in South Kensington. Loaded, judging by the size of the house. Has a dungeon. All fitted out. The works.'

'A dungeon?' Michael was surprised. 'Have you seen it?'

'Have I?' shrieked Paul, rising audibly in pitch. 'It's a black-painted basement throbbing with kinkiness. It's got a pillar and manacles and inflatables for opening up your back passage.' If that wasn't bad enough, Duncan nearly died at what came next, the words wafted round the terrace by the back of Paul's flapping hand. 'The stupid bugger trussed me up terribly tight in the sling and fisted me so bloody hard for an hour that I've been walking round for the last two days like a hip replacement victim.'

As far as Duncan was concerned, the word "fisted" might as well have launched itself into the air over the other diners and hung there, suspended and lit up in fireworks. He wondered why only he appeared to hear the silent scream of universal disapproval.

'Anton? What a hoot! It's so old-fashioned it makes him sound about sixty. How old is he?' asked a thoroughly amused Michael.

The young couple with the cold soup and synchronised spoons looked up, equally interested.

' . . . difficult to say.'

'Good-looking?'

Paul failed to notice that the black-haired Greek waiter had returned and was also all ears.

'. . . difficult to say.'

'Well, what does he look like?'

'It's too . . . difficult to say. The thing is, he *was* nude but he was wearing an executioner's mask when he answered the door.'

Michael applauded gleefully.

'You know,' continued Paul, oblivious, fingers drawing the details in front of his face, 'one of those black leather ones with only a slit for each eye and a zipper over the mouth. I've no idea what he looks like, actually!'

'Perhaps he's somebody famous,' suggested Duncan. 'Or like the Elephant Man. Someone hideously malformed.'

'Oh my God!' howled Paul. 'He's deformed! I've had my internal organs rearranged by a leper!'

They laughed at their own light-heartedness.

'Have you chosen?' asked the sultry waiter, as Paul drew breath for the first time.

'I'm not ready yet,' he wailed.

'Don't believe him,' mugged Michael. 'He's always ready for it. And, obviously, not the least fussy.'

The cold-soup couple sniggered at the remark. Their menu floated off their table on to the floor and the firm-arsed waiter bent over at the waist to retrieve it.

'Oh, look,' observed Paul gaily. 'Grecian Two Thousand's gone and dropped his soap.'

Oh dear, thought Duncan. It's going to be one of those evenings.

75

Rik pulled back from his patient's mouth.

'Everything seems to be ship-shape and Bristol fashion,' he said, putting his steel implements down and pulling a wrinkle out of one of his protective gloves. 'But you're lucky. Try not to leave it so long until the next visit. Rinse out, please.'

'Oh, good. More Mateus Rosé!'

'How long will you be away on holiday?'

'It isn't really a holiday.'

'Oh, I misunderstood. On business, then.'

'It's not business either. It's an escape.'

'An escape? My God, you've robbed the bank!'

'How else do you think I can afford your prices?'

'Don't be cheeky. Today will be reasonable. I'll finish up by giving you a polish.'

'I wish you could polish up more than just my teeth, Rik. I need my whole life brightened up.'

Cindy smiled, seeking sympathy.

'My dear, what *is* the problem?' asked her dentist.

'Oh, I've just had London up to here,' she said, with conviction. 'I can't stand it any longer. I hate my life. I hate living in Haringey. I hate my flat. Every two years or so I get like this, it seems. I go home to see my mother. I hate Britain. I hate British men.'

'Not all of them, surely?'

'No, not all of them, but some of them. I hate the surveyor who made a pass at me. I hate the VAT man breathing down my neck. I hate that spineless John Major. Why can't we have a woman back running the country and doing the job properly?'

'We couldn't stand the pace, I seem to remember.'

Cindy didn't hear him. She was into her rant.

'And London is just unbelievable. You can't drive or park anywhere in this city. The tube never works and if it does they close it down for security reasons because some old dear's left her handbag on the platform. The trains are on strike every week. The standard of living is so low, I can barely afford a cup of coffee let alone go to the opera any more. The weather is freezing cold and wet for nine months of the year and then we have a smelly, sweaty, body-odour-laden heatwave and the pollution just about suffocates you. I can't sleep in this heat but there's no such thing as air-conditioning in this country. The British are ugly and unsophisticated and unpleasant. And badly dressed. If I see another unattractive, middle-aged, size-twenty-four woman in a skinny-rib T-shirt with yellow bra-straps hanging out who's squashed her pear-shaped bottom into lycra cycling shorts with cellulite thighs bursting to get out, I'll scream. I just want to get away. So I'm going home.'

'To Australia?'

'You bet.'

'And never coming back?'

'I don't know.'

Rik laughed. 'What will you do?'

'Have a ball. See my mother. She's got a farm outside Sydney, near the Blue Mountains. There's space to think. I might look for a job out there. Not on the farm, I mean in Sydney. It's a lovely city. You should see the houses. You can buy a beautiful home with real wood floors and harbour views for the price of a crappy old hovel in London.'

'Still?'

'The standard of living in Australia is so much higher than here. You can eat out in the best restaurants for half the price. No, a third of the price. It's very cosmopolitan. Lots of Italians and Greeks and Vietnamese and Chinese and all the best things from their culture. It's not like here, where everyone hates each other. Cars cost a bit more, mind you, but you earn more. And the weather! There's no comparison, needless to say. You should go some time.'

'I'd love to. You're making me want to pack it in and leave.'

'Why don't you? You'd love it. You'd probably prefer Sydney. More of your sort there.'

'Gay, you mean.'

'Yeah. Good luck to them. You could be a dentist there with no trouble.'

'Would they let me in? I'm not whiter than white.'

'Sure you are. You're loaded. Anyone with money and they're glad to see you. Why not take a break and spend some time out there? Hey, Rik?'

Cindy sat up, bounding forward in the reclining seat.

'What?'

'You should really go to Australia!'

'To Australia?'

'Yeah. My travel agent could get you a really good deal on flights.'

'Money's no problem . . . I've never been there—'

'All the more reason to go now.'

'I need to think about it.' He pursed his lips and made a chirping sound. 'I don't know, but something you've said—'

'Has struck a chord?' Cindy turned on the seat, pleased. 'Really?'

'Yes, actually. If I went away for a few weeks none of my patients would run off in the short term.'

'There. You see?'

'I could just rearrange the appointments for six weeks or so. Or get a substitute to stand in for a while.'

'Terrific.'

'I think I'll make some enquiries.'

'Fantastic. We could have a great time. All those restaurants. You look like you could do with fattening up.'

'Oh, I'm just like everyone else in London. Thin and run-down. Worn out by the strain of it all.'

'Leave it behind. It's not running away, Rik. It's taking hold of life. I've thought it out as far as that for myself. Recently I told a friend life was all about compromising, but I've change my mind. It's not. It's about grabbing it by the scruff of the neck and shaking the living daylights out of it.'

She smiled.

'A smile at last. Time to polish it up, I think.'

That evening Michael took a call from Rik. He asked about Piers. Michael filled him in on the details.

'If I sent him a card could he still read it?'

'I think so. Or the nurse will read it to him. Oh, Rik. That would mean so much to him. And to me. You're so sweet. Why don't you pop in and see him?' asked Michael.

'That's just it. I'm going away for a while.'

'Are you? That's a shame. Anywhere nice?'

'Australia.'

'Brilliant. On business?'

'No, of course not. I'm a dentist. My patients come from godawful spots like Haringey, not Sydney. I'll be away for a while.'

'Lucky you. Isn't it winter over there at the moment?'

'It's spring, I think. I'll be there for some time. Don't be worried if you hear nothing from me. I don't send postcards.'

'What about . . . you know, when . . . if something happens to Piers? He's on his last legs.'

'I'm so sorry, Michael. There's someone at the door. I have to go. I'm so sorry. Don't forget about me, will you?'

'You sound as if you're never coming back.'

'I just want to disappear for a while, that's all,' said Rik. 'Goodbye. Love to everybody.'

The phone went dead. He was gone.

76

Charlotte pulled the files off Hazel's shelves one by one and raked through them. All she wanted was a hard copy of one of the original creative briefs for the first Station radio campaign. She knew she could write the new ones for the follow-up campaign herself, but she had got it into her head that it would be quicker to paraphrase the last set. Forlornly, she looked out of Hazel's office door at Margaret's desk. Margaret was having a day off, spending it with her sister. This was a state-of-the-art office and only Margaret had the word-processing skills to switch on the computer, let alone get into File Manager and retrieve old literature. Charlotte was just thinking how much less fun there was without Margaret's constant caustic slur on the goings-on in the agency when she heard the phone ring in her office. She popped back. It was Hazel.

'Thank God it's you, Haze. I've got to do those new radio briefs for The Station. I was looking in your files to find the old ones but I couldn't see any.'

'I don't think I have any. I didn't write them. Duncan did. They were never even shown to me, I don't think.'

'Bugger.'

'Can't Margaret find them?'

'She's got today off.'

'Oh, yeah. I forgot.'

'Why did you ring?'

'Because recastings are always boring, as you know. Once the client has rejected your first choices no one else ever looks right. I thought we could chat. I've a great story to tell you.'

'Are you still at the casting? Is Steve with you?'

'Steve who?'

'Da Silva, stupid.'

'Name rings a bell. Give me a clue.'

Charlotte realised Hazel was taking the piss. 'Stop it. Don't be mean.'

'Only teasing. You're the agency heroine. At least to us girlies. He didn't show up. He's ill or something.'

'Didn't show up?'

'Well, it's no loss. Why we need a copywriter on a casting in the first place beats me. I thought the art director did that. Or have I been working under a misapprehension for the last eight years?'

'I hope he's all right.'

'No you don't. You hope he's having a very hard time right now. And you hope he's not out buying a huge axe to come and chop you up into minute pieces for revenge.'

'He's already got a huge chopper, as half the little bitches in this place know.' They laughed.

'Which reminds me. You know this casting I'm doing for Bencelor.'

'How's it going?'

'Well, that's my great story. The male model in the poster is in swimming trunks. Remember the layout? I showed it to you.'

'I do. It's quite funny.'

'Not as funny as what happened here. That proper little madam in the art buying department who set up the casting didn't tell any of the models' agents that it was an all-boys swimsuit parade. I mean, it is only professional to ask them to disrobe.'

'Oh, my God!'

'So I've been eyeing up all these absolutely gorgeous men in their weeny underpants all morning. Some of them could run Steve da Silva a close second. At least from what I hear. But you know what Bencelor are like. They're so clean-cut, we have to make sure that no detectable bulge of boys' bits and/or pubic bush appears in the finished ad. By the time that's blown up on a poster it'll look like Sherwood Forest growing on the upper slopes of the Matterhorn.'

'That's dead funny, Haze. You can always take it out in retouching.'

'Interfere with their bits after the event? D'you know how much that much retouching would cost? I haven't finished. The last guy walks in. Name of Rock. Rock? Tee hee. Mr To Die For Drop Dead Beautiful Marry Me On The Spot Gorgissmo in both the face and body departments. You know, Gillette man with added hormones. Expression changes on being told it's a swimsuit parade. He hasn't got his little trunkies with him. Do we have a spare pair? "Nope," says Miss Australian Outback here, in her normal helpful manner. So he takes off his shirt and shoes and socks and stands there looking every inch as lickable as a tub of Häagen-Dazs melt-in-the-mouth and I say, "What's with the trousers, matey?" and he says, "I'm not wearing anything underneath," and I say, brazen Jezebel that I am, "We need to see your legs and, ahem, groin area, for this particular advertisement, so if you would like to be considered for the role I'm sure we can all be very grown-up and professional about this," and I'm about to suggest perhaps his going into the changing room and donning a carrier bag or something over his boy's bits when, fuck me, he calls my bluff and unbuttons his 501s and drops 'em on the spot.'

Charlotte giggled. 'And?'

'And we're going to the theatre tonight.'

'What?'

'Yeah. Hazel's got herself a hot date.'

'Oh, Hazel. You can't have!'

'What d'you mean, you can't have?'

'I mean, well, he's a male model—'

'And I'm not exactly an oil painting unless you include those two-faced ugly Picasso bitches, is that it?'

'No. I mean, the theatre . . . The theatre!'

'That was my idea. This is London, you know.'

'He's probably gay or something. He's a model, after all.'

'Listen to you. You're jealous. Well, fuck you!'

'I am not jealous. I'm really pleased for you.'

'My arse. Shall I shag him?'

'No, of course not. Not on the first date. You'll only regret it. You need to keep your self-respect intact.'

'Hmmmm. You'll make some girl a regular old battle-axe of a mother. Keep my self-respect intact or keep my hymen intact? Fuck it. I'd rather have the shag.'

Oh, for God's sake, Charlotte thought, after she'd put the phone down. I forgot to ask Hazel where else I could find one of the old briefs. She could not get into Duncan's old office. It was locked. Nigel and Serena were off out somewhere and Orlando never kept briefs. There was only one other person who would have copies. Steve. But . . . no, she didn't dare – or was it couldn't bear? – to go down there. Steve had an immaculate filing system. Not just his clothes had been kept well tended in his office, but all the briefs and memos he received. Well, it was perfectly safe. Steve was ill at home. Hazel had only just told her.

Despite the fact that she knew Steve was not in the building, Charlotte's heart was racing as she treaded each careful step to the floor below and entered the creative corridor. No one seemed to be around. They must all have gone off for an early lunch. She brought herself up short in front of his office door. This was stupid. He might be sitting on the other side. Her hand trembled on the door handle. She backed off, and retraced her steps back past the row of empty meeting rooms until she was by the MCN creative secretary's desk. She picked up the phone and let Steve's number ring for ten bells. Satisfied, she returned and ever so gently pushed open the door. He was not inside.

She closed the door behind her. She made a point of looking at nothing other than what she had come in for. She crossed the room until she stood behind the desk and opened the hanging file in the bottom left-hand drawer. Frightened fingers all afumble, she flicked through the little labels until she found one marked 'Radio Briefs'. She pulled out a sheaf of paper and, still bent over and looking away from the door, she began the last stretch of her search.

Suddenly, she heard the door swing wide open behind her. Her racing heart stopped dead and she almost choked with fear. The hand clutching the papers went into cramp and her whole body juddered in a spasm of unpleasant muscle movement. A familiar deep voice boomed out.

'What are you doing in here?'

It was one of the account managers from MCN International. She thought his name was Mark.

'My God. You terrified the living daylights out of me.'

'Sorry. I was looking for Mr da Silva. Is he in today, do you know?'

'No. I mean I do know that he's not.'

'I suppose I'll catch him later, then.' He turned and left and then immediately returned. 'Hey, Charlotte.'

'What?'

'Well done on the old snip-snip.' He made an accompanying scissors gesture with the fore and middle fingers of his right hand and winked.

'Fuck off,' she mouthed as he closed the door. 'And don't close the fucking door.'

A moment later she found The Station radio brief and returned the file to the drawer. She shut the drawer and pulled herself out from behind the desk. Her mission accomplished, she opened the door. The corridor was clear. She turned into it and saw that, at the end, the MCN creative secretary had returned to her desk and was chatting to Mark. So perhaps they weren't all out at a lunch somewhere. She would have to walk past them. No doubt he was already regaling her with the latest gossip: Charlotte Reith caught yet again in lover-boy's office. One of the dispatch boys came running round the corner towards her and then, checking an envelope in his hand, turned and attempted to run off back where he had come from. Charlotte, her ordeal over, laughed aloud as he bumped into a big guy with a shaved head and dark glasses, striding up the corridor in baggy jeans and T-shirt. The boy recovered his balance and ran on. Charlotte smiled to herself as she thought that she could knock these radio briefs off very quickly now and—

She was thrown sideways. Literally and metaphorically. With genuine violence, he shoulder-charged her through the loose-latched door of the empty meeting room and threw her on to the table-top. With the back of his boot he kicked the door shut hard while he used his full body weight to pin her shoulders down. It was the man in the baggy jeans and T-shirt. It was the man with the shaved head in dark glasses. It was Steve da Silva.

Charlotte was so overtaken by events she could barely speak. She could breathe but only in fierce, fast little gasps that did not fill her lungs.

'What happened to your hair?' she croaked. She remembered

the perfectly formed outline of his skull from their times in the shower, when his long wet hair draped it like black silk.

'I don't believe it. After all you've put me through, you care,' he snarled. 'Well, babe, it got cut. This morning.'

The burn of his eyes behind his shades and the curl of his lip, combined with the click of his teeth on the T of the word 'cut', terrified her. She remembered Hazel's jest about his having a huge axe to chop her up into little pieces. It seemed to be coming true.

'You've shaved your head.'

'It's my new image. I can't think why but I've decided to buy a whole new wardrobe all at once.' His voice sang with the sarcasm. 'And because that is one huge fucking expensive outlay, babe, I thought I'd go casual for a while rather than formal because I can't afford it.'

'It suits you. You have such a nicely shaped head.'

It was such an inopportune and completely stupid thing for her to say that they both immediately started to laugh uncontrollably. The tense nervousness on both sides eased and evaporated. His aggression subsided, her defences came down. The empty space that had been between them was filled once more. Filled with what they felt for each other, which was not something as great nor as intense as it once had been but which was still something worth having, nonetheless. Charlotte wondered if Steve might impulsively kiss her. Wondered? Or hoped? She was confused. She didn't know, but she didn't need to because he didn't kiss her. Instead, she felt his hands leave her shoulders and she relaxed her back on the table and giggled merrily away, much as she had done with him in midnight pranks in bed. When he fell silent she did so too, and after a moment of uncertainty looked up. He was standing over her. Tears ran from beneath his sunglasses and streaked his face.

He looked so completely different. Shorn of his glorious mane, his face looked thinner and more lined. The blue stubble that ran over the dome of his head hurried down and round and under his chin. It underlined his convict, hangdog appearance. His body looked weakened in these bigger, baggier clothes which did not mould themselves to his powerful outline.

'You hurt me, babe. You really hurt me.'

For the first time Charlotte saw Steve look vulnerable. She saw in him the afraid, crying little boy who lurks in all men. She saw the man, the real person she had had feelings for, and not just the image, the flash copywriter she had had the hots for. Yet she realised she didn't want to reach out and love him again or kiss him or help him. Rather, she wanted to talk to him and to take the opportunity of his guard being down to tell him for once what was really going through her mind. She realised she hadn't been able to do that before and that told her something about him and her and their relationship.

'You hurt me, Steve. I thought you thought I was different from all those other girls.'

'You are. I just fucked them. But I felt something for you. I did feel something for you.'

'Well, it wasn't love. You might think it was love but it wasn't. Two lines of Elizabeth Barrett Browning was on the right track but the quick screw on the photocopier with Madeleine Peters in the accounts department was, shall we say, more than a slight detour off the path of fidelity. Not to mention Kaisha and . . . what's the use? No wonder half the technology in this place doesn't work, when it's had the life banged out of it by Big Boy Bare Arse here.'

Steve grinned sheepishly and changed tack. 'I never said I loved you. I didn't send you flowers. You wouldn't let me buy you dinner unless you bought the next one back.'

'This is not the Stone Age, Conan, in case you hadn't noticed.'

'We never got romantic. You were free to go off and do what you liked. Wasn't that what we had together? Just a fun friendship?'

'No. It was not what we had together. You cheated on me, Steve. That's it plain and simple. In my book you don't do that. Finish with one before you start with the next. That's fair.'

'They call that serial monogamy. I call it serious monogamy. Too serious for me. I'm a fun boy.'

The great copywriter had run out of great lines. Steve was only making excuses, only giving weak answers. Now Charlotte was disappointed, saddened by the fun boy.

'Stop crying, then.'

'I have. I had something in my eye.'

'Designed by Jean-Paul Gaultier, by the looks of it. Take those shades off so I can see you.'

He did. He was red-eyed. 'Is that better?'

'Yes it is. And, Steve, as for not saying you loved me, what the hell was all that crap that drivelled out of your mouth at my dinner party in front of half my friends?'

Steve looked down, guilty. Then he smirked.

'Where did all that spring from, eh?'

'It won a gold in New York a few years ago.'

'What?'

'It was a campaign I wrote once.'

Charlotte raised her eyebrows and her volume. *'What?'*

'For Kaspian the jewellers. You know, they make all that high-class stuff that duchesses wear.'

'You bastard!' She wasn't annoyed with Steve. She was annoyed with herself.

'Come on, Charlie. It was a late-night game. I was stoned out of my mind. You just say whatever comes into your head. Anyway, Miss Brain of Bloody British Advertising, you should know your ads better. If you were good at your job you'd have recognised the lines. One lot are even in the D&AD book.'

'I'm crushed,' said Charlotte, dispassionately. His words were getting lamer by the line.

'Is that emotionally or professionally?'

'Both.'

'Are you?' It was tender the way he said it.

'No, Steve, I'm not. You were right. It was a laugh, a fling. It was one of the many little goings-on between people in advertising agencies. Half of this place has screwed the other half. I don't know how they all manage to look each other in the eye but they do. I did feel affection for you but the truth is you are not the right man for me. I don't know what my type is but you're not it. From the minute I met you in the lift I was drawn to you. Not because I loved you or thought I could, but because I fancied you. I live dangerously and God knows, you're the dangerous type. I couldn't take a black man home to my mother.'

'Half black.'

'You're the full ace of spades as far as she's concerned. You won't remember but on my first day here you laughed at my getting a job at C&B. Well, you were right. Everything about this place has been a colossal mistake. And, I can't believe I'm saying this, great fun too. I've enjoyed it but none of it is going anywhere. I don't know what to do.'

'Why did you cut up my clothes?'

'You won't prove that was me.'

'I don't want to prove anything. I want to know why.'

'You must be joking! It would be obvious to anyone else. Because, Steve, you humiliated me behind my back. Everyone in this building is talking about me.'

'They were talking about you, babe, the minute you rode over the threshold on a Harley Davidson.'

'Ducati 748sp, if you don't mind.'

'If you had real style you'd have a Harley.'

'If you had real style you'd have a wardrobe that's not in tatters.'

'Why, Charlie?' He had the face of a choirboy now.

'I wanted to get my revenge. As far as I'm concerned we're quits.' She stood up and they looked at each other for an eternity.

'Are you going to leave the agency, then?' he asked at last.

'Yes. Eventually. I don't know. We'll see.'

'I am. Well, maybe. I've been for an interview this morning.'

'So that's where you were.'

'Do you forgive me?'

'No. But I don't hate you either. I'm afraid I can't be bothered trying to. You're not worth it. The whole thing just seems so silly now.' She sighed. 'I wish I was more mature sometimes.'

'Friends, then?'

'Steve, you and I have nothing in common.'

'Great sex.'

'Of which there seems to be an inexhaustible supply available in this building from the front door reception onwards.'

'Charlie, I'm sorry if I hurt you.'

She knew that it was very big of him indeed to have said that. 'I'm sorry if I hurt you too, Steve. I'm actually more sorry about that haircut, Samson.'

'You love it.' He fielded his lupine grin. 'Delilah.'

She pushed her hand through her blonde hair and then let it

hang loose and spare by her side. She blushed. He stepped back from her path to the door and let her walk to it. She opened it and stepped out into the corridor.

'Charlie.'

She looked back and smiled. 'What?'

His tongue lazily lolled out of his mouth and hung suggestively low then retracted. 'I suppose a fuck is out of the question?'

Her smile broadened. 'You cheeky bastard. I think you'll find the photocopier is out of order. By the way . . .'

'What?'

'I *always* have the last word. See ya.'

On the other side of the door Charlotte shivered with the aftershock of a near-miss.

'An Extremely Close Shave,' she whispered to herself and then ran off into self-assuring giggles at her hopeless pun.

77

'Why do we love this sort of food so much, do you think?' Duncan asked Michael, sucking up the last of a coconut milk shake through a twisty straw, with all the spluttering noise and none of the sophistication of a cappuccino-maker.

'People are looking at you,' laughed Michael. 'You're behaving like a big child.'

'I am a big child,' retorted Duncan, using his mouth to pull the straw from the glass and point it at his lover. 'Well, I am when I eat a Friday burger and French fries. It really is comfort food for adults, isn't it? It's a substitute for childhood.'

'It's a substitute for sex, you mean,' said Michael.

'Then what are *we* doing eating in TGI Fridays? We ought to be on a starvation diet.' Duncan was, of course, being cruelly sarcastic.

'Don't get cynical,' said Michael dryly. 'We've had our big set-piece argument for this year.'

'Do you think all couples have less sex as they get older? Or is it just us?'

'They undoubtedly have less, but they don't all stop completely like we have.'

'Don't exaggerate.'

'Well, when did we last have sex?' Michael managed to make a serious point with humour.

'God. Do you know, I can't remember. It was definitely this year, though. What month was the last one without an "R" in it?' Duncan smiled saccharine-sweetly.

'There. See what I mean. Other people aren't as bad as that.'

'Who knows? Everyone exaggerates about sex.'

'Except Paul McCarthy.'

'True. No one could make those stories up.'

'Have you ever been unfaithful to me, Duncan?'

'No.'

'Would you lie to me, Dunky? Don't ever lie to me. I couldn't bear it.'

'You'd like it less if I was unfaithful and told you about it afterwards. I don't expect I ever will be, but if I am, you'll be the last to know.'

Michael was stung. 'That's a really hurtful thing to say.'

'Well, it's the truth,' said Duncan, almost flippantly. 'What's that saying? What the eye doesn't see, the heart cannot grieve over. Something like that.'

'I've been faithful to *you*.'

'That's reassuring to know. Shall we get the bill?' Duncan picked up his milk-shake glass and peered into it, as if it might be magically refilled.

'Would you like another?' asked Michael.

'Absolutely not. I'll be sick. As well as get fat. Did I tell you there was a message on the answerphone from Cindy? I won't see her for at least another six weeks. She's going home to Australia.'

'Really? So is Rik. You know, the dentist, Piers's friend. Says he's run-down and needs a good holiday. I'd like to go to Australia.'

They paid a young waiter in a red and white striped shirt pressed tight to his body by elasticated red braces covered in slogan badges. They left, declining the camp offer of a helium-filled balloon.

'D'you think he's gay?' asked Michael. 'Perhaps we could take him home with us instead.'

'Now who's being childish?' said Duncan.

They stepped out into Bedford Street and crossed over the road towards the stucco-fronted building housing *The Lady* magazine. Michael's pewter-grey Mercedes was parked in front of it.

'Cute, eh?' Michael nodded towards a young, obviously American tourist peering into a street map, on the mismatched corner of Bedford Street and Maiden Lane. 'Shall we offer him some advice?' he asked wickedly.

'My advice would be "Don't talk to a dirty old man like my lover here."'

Michael walked over to the tourist. He was too short to be a male model, but had the shiny looks of a 1930s matinée idol. His hair was immaculately slicked back from his tanned face with wet-look gel. He was wearing a wine-coloured polo shirt, longish khaki shorts and suede deck shoes. Duncan watched from the side of the car and eyed up the boy and his muscular, tanned calves. He wondered what happened to his legs where they disappeared into his shorts. He wanted to rummage in them and find out. The young man looked up at Michael and flashed him a dazzling, chorus-boy smile of perfect American teeth. They chatted out of earshot and then came towards the car.

What's he up to? thought Duncan.

'Hi, I'm Bobby.' His voice was surprisingly deep and, to the two Londoners, he appeared to pronounce his name 'Barbee'. He extended a tanned forearm and shook Duncan's hand.

And so they went for an unplanned evening tour of London's major attractions. The Strand. Fleet Street. St Paul's Cathedral. Tower Bridge. The South Bank. Lambeth Palace. The Houses of Parliament. The Mall. Buckingham Palace. Hyde Park Corner. Knightsbridge. Chelsea.

'We find it very warm here at the moment,' said Duncan over his shoulder to their passenger. 'It's not normally so hot and sweaty as this.'

'It's cool compared to New Orleans,' said Bobby. His Southern accent skipped through syllables that would have tripped them up.

'We were there a couple of years ago,' said Duncan. 'You know, in the French Quarter and on the Mississippi. Tourist stuff, really, I suppose.'

'The two of you went together?'

'Yes,' said Duncan, matter-of-factly and rather proudly. He turned and over his shoulder caught Bobby's twinkling eye. There was a time when young Mr Cairns would have bottled up that sort of thing, but though the thirtysomething Duncan might still have one heel trapped in the door of the closet, he could at least now manage to take a stranger head-on. Anyway, Bobby had been checking out their relationship discreetly and had not yet batted an eyelid. He was definitely here on his own.

'Did you guys have a hot time?'

'We thought so.' Duncan surreptitiously nudged Michael.

'New Orleans is like Sodom and Gomorrah compared to London,' said Bobby, casually looking out at the boutiques on the King's Road. 'It gets real quiet here at night.'

'Not having enough fun?' asked Michael.

'I'd have thought it would be more kinda, you know, wild, I guess. D'you know what I mean, gentlemen?'

'I think we know exactly what you mean, Bobby,' said Michael.

Now, thought Duncan, reassessing his own level of confidence, would I have answered that brazenly?

'Would you two gentlemen care to come back to my hotel for a drink?' Bobby's deep voice drawled like molasses off a spoon. 'That way I could get a lift home from you guys and sort of pay you back for your kindness.'

Michael winked across the front of the car.

'What do you think, Duncan?'

'Oh, I'm up for it if you are,' replied Duncan.

'I'm up for it.'

Their young passenger leant forward.

'Good, gentlemen. Perhaps you'll allow me to show you some real Southern hospitality.'

Under Michael's enthusiastic control the car accelerated, though not quite as much as Duncan's heartbeat.

Bobby was staying off Gloucester Road in a Victorian house which had been massively extended into an international hotel with several modern wings at the back. He walked them straight past reception and straight past the bar.

'I've got some bourbon in my room, if you guys want that. I got it duty-free.'

They took the lift to the third floor of the modern wing. They didn't speak. They walked down a long, soulless corridor and into Bobby's tiny room. It was somewhere between smart and sparse. His things were laid out very neatly on a single bed and on the floor. While the two Londoners hovered, he painstakingly cleared the bed of its neatly arranged piles and then brought the bottle of bourbon over from an occasional table.

'There's only one glass, I'm afraid.' He sat down on the bed and kicked off his shoes. 'Obviously, you English don't expect your guests to entertain in their rooms.'

'Well, not in groups of three,' said Michael.

They laughed. It was enough to break the ice and Michael leaned over and kissed Bobby salaciously on the mouth. He hadn't come up for air before Duncan was unhitching the young American's waistband and slipping a pair of hands beneath the boy's chunky buttocks to relieve him of his fetching shorts. The tanned, athletic, furry legs were revealed in full. Running slim and brown-skinned all the way up into grey-marled crotch-hugging trunks – themselves wrapped around their own surprise – those thighs were everything Duncan had fantasised they would be. They pulled up and parted and Duncan dived in.

'Jesus, it's twenty to three,' said Michael, looking at the Mercedes clock. The car swung round Hyde Park Corner and into Park Lane. 'Well, that was a helluvan evening.'

Duncan beamed in the dark.

'He really was game for it,' continued Michael.

'He was lovely. Lovely as a milk shake,' said Duncan. 'Thick and creamy and fulfilling.'

'Wasn't it you who had just said of himself that he liked American fast food?'

'It was. And boy did I binge tonight.'

'He was so hungry for sex.'

'Starving. I realise how my body's no longer youthful compared to his.'

'You have a great body. Bobby liked it. You certainly got his seal of approval.'

'He was a very thorough examiner. No inch left untested. His stomach was as hard as a washboard.'

'It was as hard as his cock,' said Michael. 'Americans are always circumcised, aren't they?'

'I liked his voice. He was charming. Beautifully spoken.'

'He's probably the local slut back home.'

'No doubt he'll speak equally highly of us,' said Duncan.

'Us "gentlemen". Will it change our relationship, Dunky?'

'What's your opinion?'

'It was just a bit of fun. Nothing more, nothing less.'

Duncan thought in the dark for a moment. 'When you began to kiss him it wasn't as I had expected. I thought it might be a real turn-on in a dirty sort of a way. I thought I might feel uneasy or self-conscious or something. But, actually, it was beautiful to watch.'

'Because he was so attractive?'

'Because you looked so happy. It was quite a thrill to see you pleasuring yourself that way. It was rather loving, loving between you and me, not between you and him. I allowed you to do it and you allowed me. I liked it.'

Michael began to laugh. 'I can't believe we did do it now, can you?'

'No. Not really.'

'D'you think'll he ring us?'

'No,' said Duncan wistfully. 'We'll never see him again. That's the beauty of it.'

Michael took his hand from the steering wheel and placed it on Duncan's thigh and squeezed hard.

'God, Duncan. My balls really hurt. I don't normally come three times in one evening.'

Duncan grinned. 'You certainly know how to spin a poetic line, don't you?'

Michael grinned too and swept the car up Edgware Road. He switched on the radio. An old fifties hit was playing.

'I wanna be Bobby's girl . . .'

They were laughing so hard they missed the gleaming parade of metallic Station posters running the length of the street.

78

Cindy made her way slowly up the left-hand aisle of the 747.

'Good evening,' said the air stewardess.

'Hi,' said Cindy. That was the fifth one. 'Hi' would suffice. She was bored with saying 'Good evening' back. Qantas were overdoing it.

She found row forty-eight and put her fake Louis Vuitton bags on to the aisle seat while squashing in to let a large man past. Then she packed her things into the overhead locker, carefully at first, and then just pushing them in any old how. She sat back down in the aisleside seat but didn't fasten the safety belt as she would have to get up to allow her companions in to the remaining two seats by the window. Cindy hoped they would be an interesting couple. As it turned out, they weren't a couple at all.

First, a rotund middle-aged businessman took the window seat, eyeing Cindy up on the way in, and using the battery hen dimensions of economy class to squeeze uncomfortably close past her thinly clad body. She felt like slapping his face. The whole point of this trip was to fly away from men like that, not to get landed with them.

'Excuse me, please. Could I get in here?'

Cindy looked up to see a younger woman. Her Australian accent gave her away as someone else on her way home. Cindy got up again to let her new neighbour take her seat. They smiled at each other.

'Now,' said the friendly woman, snapping her seat-belt firmly shut. 'Exactly how long do you think it's going to take the drinks trolley to put in an appearance?'

The plane was still heading upwards when the stewardesses began to wheel their solid metal loads up and down the aisles.

'Come on. Come on,' said the woman. 'Push harder, for God's sake.'

'You sound desperate,' said Cindy, laughing.

'Yup. I need a good stiff snorter to cheer me up.'

'Cheer you up? Oh dear. Have you been in London on holiday?' asked Cindy.

'Sort of. Well, no, really. I came out to work here nearly a year ago, but I found it very difficult to get the sort of job I was after. I did get one in the end, but . . .' She shrugged her shoulders.

'It didn't work out?'

'I've just been fired from it, to tell you the honest truth.'

'Oh, I'm sorry to hear that.'

'I'm not. They were complete bastards.'

The stewardess got to them sooner than they had expected. They both ordered double vodkas and tonics, the sisterhood drink of spurned women everywhere.

'Cheers,' toasted Cindy.

'Cheers,' replied her new friend, putting the plastic cocktail stirrer on to her pop-down table.

'Here's to happier times, then. For both of us.'

'You too, eh? What does that signify?'

'Nothing.'

'Are you getting away from something too?'

'Not really. I've just had London up to here. I usually visit my mother round about this time of year. I leave my boyfriend behind for about a month or so and get some time to myself.'

'Recharge your batteries.'

'Yeah. Alan recharges his too while I'm away. We get on top

of each other too much after a while. It really helps to be apart for a period every so often, believe it or not.'

'Absence makes the heart grow fonder.'

'It gives you time for some of the hairline cracks to heal over, I suppose.'

'Speaking of recharging batteries, grab the air hostess, will you? It's time for a refill.'

'I've come to the conclusion,' said the woman, when she had finished her second vodka and a humorous story about a hot date in London's theatreland, 'that all men are complete bastards. Even the one who got me this job in London, or at least helped me – the minute things went badly and I ran back to him for advice, he tried to make a pass at me. Can you believe that?'

'I can believe anything. What business were you in?'

'Advertising.'

'Really? How interesting. I used to work in advertising. Which agency?'

'MCN International. Do you know it?' asked the woman.

Cindy latched on immediately. 'Did you work for Clancey and Bennett?'

'Oh my God, yes. Does it show *that* bad?'

''Fraid so. Is your name – let's see – Hazel Green-something?'

'Yes, yes. Greenslade. How do you know?'

'You worked for Duncan Cairns. He's a very good friend of mine.'

'Wow!' shrieked Hazel. 'It's a small world.'

'Even if it takes a whole day to cross it. So what happened to you? Didn't you save Nigel Thingummyjig's life?'

'Yeah. That was my big mistake.'

'Does your departure have anything to do with Duncan leaving? Don't answer that if you don't want to. It's none of my business, really.'

'Oh, don't worry about that. Yes . . . indirectly. You know they have the Carpets Company account there?'

'Uh-huh.'

'Well, the client got way behind with the launch of a new range and the advertising budget went out the window and when we went to the client to talk about it Serena Sark got on her high horse and fucked the whole thing up and the client refused to put any money through us in the current financial year. I lost my job as a result. They didn't blame me or anything. Nigel just said they couldn't afford me any longer.'

'That's appalling. Something should be done about that man. He's a legend in his own lunchtime.'

'D'you know, if they fired him, they could employ ten people at my level for the same money. The nice thing is that Stella, my client, felt terrible about the whole thing and offered me a job as her assistant.'

'What did you say?'

'Well, I was chuffed and all that. But I don't want to work in carpets, thank you very much. And I don't want to work in Yorkshire either. Everyone in London said it was a terrible place. I've been there but I don't even know where it is. How d'you get a refill round here?'

Cindy remembered something Hazel had said earlier.

'Who did you say it was who made a pass at you?'

'Oh, not Duncan, if that's what you're worried about.'

Cindy laughed. Hazel obviously didn't know Duncan's not-so-secret secret.

'Not Duncan. But who?'

'Someone else in advertising. By coincidence he got the only money going out of the Carpets Company this year. I was telling him all about that piece of business over dinner when I met him – he was no doubt milking me for information for his own ends. Probably I should blame him for my getting fired. If I find out he went behind my back . . . What am I saying? You wouldn't know him.'

'Actually, I think I do. Tell me.'

'Alan . . . Josling.' Hazel's jaw dropped as she herself spotted the coincidence. 'Jesus. Not the same Alan as your boyfriend?'

'Too bloody right he's the same Alan!' Cindy was smarting, suspicions confirmed.

'Oh, I'm so sorry, Cindy. I wouldn't have said if I'd known.'

'I'm glad you did,' said Cindy, finding it hard to believe that she could not escape that bastard's infidelity even halfway towards the other side of the world.

Charlotte was at the reception desk of St Mary's hospital in Paddington.

'Do I have to be out of here by a certain time?' she asked rather impatiently. She hated hospitals normally anyway, and this was much more serious than anything she had faced before. She was going to need all her Terrence Higgins training sooner than she had realised.

The receptionist told her she had only fifteen minutes of the official visiting time left. Perhaps she would like to come back tomorrow if she felt it was not long enough. Charlotte decided to ignore that remark and hurried off down the corridor.

Outside the room a young Asian doctor, with heavy five o'clock shadow, gave her some more details.

'I would have expected to see someone in your role earlier,' he said.

'I didn't know he was here,' she answered breathlessly. 'He's very discreet about the whole thing. He wouldn't even let me have all his contact numbers so it was nothing unusual not to get hold of him.'

'Yes, well—'

'We didn't know until today he'd been brought in. I had no idea he was anything like this ill. The last time I saw him he was fine. Absolutely A-OK.'

'No one's blaming you. As I'm sure you're well aware, one of the truisms about AIDS is you can't tell just by looking.'

'How is he?'

'He's anything but fine. The main problem is with his digestive system. You'll see he's on a drip. And he has no immunity left. His T-cell count is almost non-existent. I think you should prepare yourself for the worst quite soon.'

Charlotte's feelings were anaesthetised with shock. Her heart fell; it sank; it plummeted. She knew it was inevitable that he would die but somehow, on hearing the doctor tell her, for the first time the enormity of the whole thing hit her dead-on, like a huge oncoming, rolling bowling-ball scattering the skittles every which way. She was suddenly acutely aware that her only previous experience of losing someone close – of putting Timmy, her childhood Jack Russell, to sleep – was a complete irrelevance and deeply patronising to the situation of her friend. The doctor gave her a reassuring pat on the back and was gone, distracted by a wan-faced nurse with a clipboard and an urgent look about her.

Charlotte straightened out her rushed appearance and pushed open the door. She was nauseous with anticipation, but there he lay, propped up in bed and spotlit by an overhead Anglepoise lamp. His hair, as ever, was neat and tidy. He had been placed on a drip and there was a plastic tube inserted into his nose. He appeared to be wearing silk pyjamas. That, at least, gladdened her. He was hanging on to his dapper style against the odds.

'Very Noël Coward,' she said. She leant over and kissed him on the forehead. 'But I think you were taking *Private Lives* a bit too literally, not telling me.'

She sat down by the bed on the standard-issue visitors' chair. It wobbled on uneven legs.

'Thank you for coming,' he said softly. 'You never miss an opportunity for wit, do you?'

'Sorry.'

'No. I like that about you. You're bearing up well. I'm proud of you.'

'I'm supposed to say that to you.'

He smiled without parting his lips.

'I'm sorry I didn't come sooner, but that's your fault, not mine. It was difficult to track down via the Trust what had happened to you.'

He nodded understandingly.

'Why didn't you get the hospital to contact them or let me know directly you were in here?'

'I didn't care for the design of their "At Home" stationery. Don't give me a hard time.'

'I'm not. I just need to know, that's all. The least I could have done would have been to have brought you some fruit or flowers or a good book or something to cheer you up.'

'So where are they?'

'I didn't have time.'

'You're always so busy.'

He'd apologised for her. She didn't know whether to laugh or weep. He had caught her out. Almost. She pushed her fingers through her hair and struggled to act as normally as possible.

'I *have* brought this for you.' She forced a smile to her lips and from deep inside her miniature rucksack she produced a half-bottle of Bollinger champagne, capped by two paper cups.

'My word. That's against the rules.'

'I thought we could celebrate our knowing each other. Will you be able to manage it?'

'I think so. You can always pour it in my drip if I get stuck.'

Charlotte's practised fingers popped the cork with only a bass thud and she poured him out a taste and kept the rest back for herself. She swallowed fast and hard while he sipped slowly. They sat quietly until they had finished and Charlotte had stuffed the empty bottle back into her bag. She would keep it for years. The champagne bottle chinked on something as it went in.

'There isn't a phone in here, is there?'

'No, there's not.'

Now she pulled out an MCN International mobile phone from the clever little rucksack and pressed it into the palm of his hand.

'I've pinched it from the company for a few days. Not all hospitals allow the use of mobiles, so check with the nurse.'

'Thank you.'

'I'll need it back.'

'I'll leave it to you in my will.'

'Don't. You'll make me cry. How do you feel?'

'As if I'm dying. Don't look so alarmed. I'm resigned to it, even if you aren't.'

'Oh.'

'I am. I am resigned to it. As long as it is not painful.'

'They have all the latest stuff here . . . Have you had many visitors?'

'Enough.'

'Who knows you're here?'

'Those that matter. Family. A few old friends. You. I don't need anyone else. Charlotte, we did all my funeral arrangements and the will and everything too soon. It's boring lying here. It would have given us something to do here now.'

'I have my notebook. We can still change anything you'd like to.'

'No. It's all fine. Don't let's talk about it. Tell me what's going on in the outside world. How is The Station campaign and all that?'

'You don't want to hear all about that, do you?'

'I do.'

'Well, the campaign is fine. But they fired my best friend there, we've lost our second-biggest client, failed to win a brilliant airline account, and my immediate boss left not long ago. What a catalogue of disasters. What a mistake to leave Saatchi's. It's ghastly now. I hate it.'

'I thought you had your boyfriend there. Can't he comfort you?'

'Oh, him. We've split up. He wasn't a boyfriend, he was a mistake. In fact, since you ask, he was a complete bastard.'

'All men are.'

'Why are they?'

'Because their cocks are normally bigger than their hearts. It means nothing to us, screwing around. If you remember only one thing I've told you, remember that and you'll do all right.'

'I'll remember everything you've told me. You're the only person I can talk to about Steve. You're the only person who can understand. No one else knows, really.'

'Really?'

'Yes.'

'That's nice to know.'

'I got my revenge, though.'

'How?'

'Another girl he had a fling with and I cut up his suits and shirts and ties. Thousands of pounds' worth.'

'My God.'

'It was a great feeling. Well, it was at the time. I admit it was immature.'

'You'll end up in prison.'

'No way. We covered our tracks. Steve knows it was me but not the board. They're not sure who did it. If they fired me, they'd have to fire half the girls in the agency. He's had them all. They've all got the motivation.'

'Did he have a big one?'

She was taken aback. Gay men were always so mechanically straightforward about sex, it seemed.

'Well, he did, as it happens,' she said quietly. 'Enormous, if you must know.' She blushed.

'Fantastic. I like my boys bigger and beefier where it counts.'

Charlotte was horrified, almost sickened. How could a man virtually dead of AIDS be chatting away about the size of someone else's penis?

'I've offended you, haven't I?' he said. 'You're wondering how I can talk about sex when it's almost killed me. I don't regret it at all for a moment, my promiscuity. I've had a great life. I'd do it all again.'

'You wouldn't if you knew the consequences, I'm sure. Or at least, you'd do it more safely.'

'Did you come here on your bike?'

'Yes. Why?'

'No reason. It's nicer to talk about you. You're such a lovely young girl. I like to hear about you, and the things you do. You do everything with such verve. I'm glad I got you. Not some mincing little queen. I wouldn't have cared for that. But you have class and manners and genuine style.'

Charlotte gave him a fleeting smile. She looked down and smoothed out the creased top sheet at the edge of the bed, a minor distraction for her to attend to.

'So do you. I admire you. You're very brave, the way you've handled everything, quietly and discreetly.'

'It's called cowardice. I wanted to keep on working as long as possible. Even loyal clients would have abandoned me. And friends too. This just seemed the best way to avoid confrontation.'

The wan-faced nurse, her eye on the clock, popped her head round the door.

'How are we doing in here?'

'I'm just leaving,' said Charlotte over her shoulder. She turned back round. 'I'll be back tomorrow evening.'

She stood up.
'Don't worry,' he said. 'I'm not going anywhere.'

80

It was five past nine on Friday, 1 September and Briony Linden could hardly wipe the smile off her face. Everyone on every TV channel was talking about The Station and *Megabrek* and The Launch. And if they weren't talking about it on terrestrial television, they were writing about it in the newspapers. And if they weren't writing about it in both the broadsheets and the tabloids, they were singing its praises on radio. And if they weren't singing about it there, then they must be either appearing on it or watching it. Or doing both, because that was the beauty of the world's most technologically advanced interactive cable television station.

Briony had spent the last three weeks slogging her guts out, but with every scrap of available paid-for and unpaid-for media saturated with write-ups, reviews, advertisements, competitions, announcements and analyses, it had been worth it. Amid the stacks of newsprint cuttings and TV broadcast transcripts, she lit up a well-deserved if illegal Camel Light, but could barely purse her laughing lips to puff on it properly. This was it. The Station was up and running and part and parcel of the culture of Britain and nobody could say she hadn't done her bit. OK. With a little help from the advertising agency. And the PR consultancy. And the promotions people. And the sponsorship lot. And the press office. And the presentation department. And the research boys. And the programme team. And a husband to die for who stayed at home and looked after the kids. Briony wanted to dance around the office and sing, but before this most sensible of women could abandon herself to the wind of change and go stark raving mad with delight, the telephone rang.

Cigarette in hand, she clutched her forehead. She'd completely forgotten the launch party in the restaurant downstairs.

It wasn't downstairs though. It was Martin Fox.

'Hi, Briony.'

'Martin!' she squealed, and burst into peals of laughter.

'How d'you feel this morning?' he asked.

'Ten feet tall! You must too.'

'Absolutely. Did you watch the show?'

'Don't be stupid, Martin! Of course I did! I'm still watching the TV now, actually. Everyone else has buggered off downstairs, I suppose.'

'So . . . ?'

'Oh, I loved the bit where George Michael and Lulu sang a cappella with those six housewives in their kitchens. The one who burnt the toast and then scraped it to the beat as George did that wobbly bit was just brilliant. This interactivity thing is fab. Just fab. We'll take over the world!'

'I'm glad you loved the show. Jamie Hirst and his team came up trumps.'

'Absolutely.'

'Oh, there were a few fluffs.'

'Not so's you'd notice.'

'Oh, I did. But I was after the ratings. You know. Instant access?'

Briony screamed.

'Jesus fucking Christ! I forgot all about them. Fuck. Fuck. Fuck. Hang on!'

She swung round to her desk terminal and battered away with Gatling rapidity at the keyboard. She screamed again.

'My God, what's going on there?' Martin shouted down the phone.

'I must have done it wrong. This is telling me that – well, guess what percentage of homes available to view tuned in? Three-minute ratings, of course.'

'Just tell me, Briony.'

'Guess. Guess. You've got to guess!'

'Have you been drinking? I don't know. Thirty-five per cent.'

'*Sixty*-five per cent!'

'You've done it wrong!'

'I haven't! It really is sixty-five per cent. Whippee!'

The line crackled and broke up for a second.

'Hello? Still there?' she asked quickly.

'Still here. I went under a bridge.'

'Are you on a mobile?'

'Yes.'

'Where are you? I thought you were watching from home.'

'I was. But I'm cabbing it now to the *Megabrek* opening party. It's at Jamie's house in Islington. Why don't you come?'

'He hasn't invited me.'

'Don't let that stop you. It'll be much more fun than the office one. And all the press will be there.'

'Oh, well, if it's a professional requirement . . .'

Jamie's very cute Chinese boyfriend led Briony through the great double doors and into the thick of the party on the opened-up first floor. Karen Myhill, The Most Difficult Woman In Television, was standing in the corner, her back pressed hard against a nineteenth-century oriental tapestry, her Bucks Fizz flattening further with every ghastly second. She knew she shouldn't have come. It was Max's fault. She knew she shouldn't have come and he had persuaded her at the last moment. She could rip the shimmering, starry wallpaper off the walls with her bare teeth, she was so jealous. Her thoughts seethed in the pit of her mind. Duncan's *Basket Case* had better be this good or instead of chestnuts this Christmas, she'd be roasting his testicles, still in the bag. There was a time when she could have chewed up Jamie Hirst and spat his bones out for breakfast. But from now on breakfast was his fiefdom, over which the little queen would reign until some jolly jubilee in the future. God's death! An ugly thought sprang up on her and mugged her from behind. Posterity would record *Megabrek* as the show that launched The Station. *Basket Case* would always come second. She had only herself and Max to blame.

'Karen Myhill, is it?'

She looked up.

'Which crummy little tabloid are you from?' she croaked at the short, balding journalist.

'*TV Times*, actually, love,' and he wagged a chewed half-pencil as proof. 'Did you enjoy *Megabrek*? Give us a good quote, love, and I can guarantee you at least a quarter-para.'

'On the record, I thought it was fabulous.' Karen spat the words out reluctantly. 'I'd give back *both* my BAFTA awards to come up with an idea *that* good.'

'That's the spirit, love. I understand that you were the first one to spot Jamie's potential?'

'The first one who wasn't fidgeting beside him in some urinal somewhere.'

'Ooh, we are being bitchy this morning, aren't we? Who do you think *Megabrek* is going to appeal to?'

'The very juvenile.'

'Eh?'

'Well, don't you think the effete homosexual has always had a way with children?'

She haughtily pushed past the journalist and made her way back into the crowd. She was behaving badly and well she knew it. But she couldn't stop herself.

''Scuse me, love!' the journalist called out after her in vain. 'We're not allowed to use words like "effete" on *TV Times*.'

Karen was sickening to leave. The noise of the chattering classes and the clacking hangers on, not to mention the twittering sycophants, gave her a headache that not even a long pee could subdue. You'd think a couple of wealthy queenie types would have more than one lavatory. She came back from the half-landing, down the elegant Regency staircase, and swept through the throng to find Martin. She would say goodbye to him and then push off back to Paddington. In the crush, however, she found herself wedged against the toast-and-croissant end of what her family would once have called 'the spread'. Why was the food at these bashes always so poor? Look at that! BLT sandwiches of white bread and anaemic bacon with its rubber-band rind still on. Plastic catering mini-packs of synthetic jam and no-brand low-fat spread. And Nutella. *Nutella*! What adults ate Nutella? Not even Max would touch it.

The thought of Machiavellian Max suddenly inspired in Karen

an idea for which she genuinely *would* give back both her BAFTAs. She sidled over to the edge of the long table. She covertly investigated the hazelnut and chocolate spread further. Nutella. Europack size. Eighteen grams. Small enough to conceal in one's palm.

She made her way to the great double doors and gave a paper-thin smile to Wung Fu, or whatever his name was. Oh, Derek, that was it. Wung Fu was Max's name for him. Unnoticed – now she was thankful not to be noticed – she made her way out to the stairs. Instead of heading down and out, she crept upwards, as if to revisit the tiny loo on the half-landing. Only, this time she kept on going and carried on to the next floor.

She pushed open a mahogany door. Was this Jamie's bedroom? It was certainly queenie enough, with a four-poster bed draped in crimson silk and golden tassels. Looks like a camp hairdresser's idea of a good night out, she thought. The hubbub from downstairs bubbled up from below. No one knew she was up here. She tiptoed across the shag-pile carpet. Between the pair of long, thin windows stood a tallboy, mahogany again. She stood in front of it, her bird's eyes beady behind their bejewelled frames. She ever so slowly turned her head and checked her back. She heard gales of collective laughter waft upwards from beyond the landing. She was safe. She pulled open the top left-hand drawer. Cuff-links and things. No good. She pushed it back in again but it went in squint and stuck halfway so she left it. She pulled open the top right-hand drawer. Socks. No good. This time she left the drawer drooping out like a thirsty tongue. With both hands, she pulled open the first of the big drawers. Underpants, Calvin Klein, traditional, white, pouch-fronted underpants. Karen Myhill, big on behaving badly, was back in business.

She selected the whitest pair and brought them to the surface of the pile. She turned the pants inside out and pushed her clenched fist into the crotch. She pulled them round a bit, so that her fist was more towards the rear. Then, using her other hand and her teeth, she peeled away the metallic top of the catering pack of Nutella, then purposefully pressed the luxurious, thick, brown, creamy contents into the absorbent cotton crotch of the Calvins.

Karen Myhill let herself out quietly from the party that morning. And left behind, in the corner of the half-landing by the little loo, the pair of Jamie's soiled underpants for all the world to see. Well, not quite all the world, but absolutely everyone in it who mattered.

81

'Duncan Cairns? Is there a Duncan Cairns here?'

The teenaged runner with the shaved head stood with his back to the black-painted brick wall at the edge of the hangar-like studio. He put a hand over his eyes to shield them and peered across the flickering brilliance of the giant video floor into the glare of banked arc lamps and the neon set.

'That's me,' called back Duncan.

'Call for you in the production office.'

'Why did he come in person?' asked Duncan of the director. 'Why didn't he call me on talkback?'

'Not enough headsets to go round, Duncan,' replied the director. 'Karen Myhill's scrimping on the pilot, as per the usual.'

Duncan left the director to carry on briefing the sparks and padded back over the flat screens of the video floor in his socks. He took off his talkback headphones, placed them by the console that controlled the video floor and slipped into his loafers. He walked briskly along the thin edge of the set floorline and the backdrop.

'Duncan?' asked the wardrobe lady he met on the way. 'What do I do with this?' She waved a multi-coloured silk shirt at him.

'No idea,' he shrugged. 'Ask one of the contestant researchers. They'll help you.' Under his breath he muttered, 'There's no bloody organisation in this place. The left hand doesn't even know there *is* a right hand . . .'

He left the stage and trailed for ever through the labyrinthine corridors until he eventually came to the production office. What a tip, he thought. This is all too chaotic for me. He picked up the telephone the shaved-head youth was pointing at. The runner offered him some Orbit sugar-free gum. Duncan looked down his nose at it and then thought again and pulled a stick from the proffered pack. He unpeeled it as he spoke.

'Hello?'

'Hi, Duncan. It's Briony. How are you?'

'Briony! Hello. This is a surprise.'

'Well, I thought I'd better get in touch since we haven't spoken in yonks. Is it all right to call you at work?'

'No problem. Most of the day is spent waiting for nothing much to happen later.'

'How is everything going in the glamorous world of television production?'

'Glamorous? Whatever gave you that idea? Advertising is glamorous. Television is *not* glamorous.'

'Oh dear.'

'But it's much more fun.' He popped the stick of chewing gum into his mouth and bit into it. Duncan had been brought up to think that chewing in public was common. Actually, he rather liked it. 'I feel ten years younger. I'm enjoying working on this show and zooming up the learning curve. At least, I think I am.'

'You'll be running the place before you know it.'

'I wish!'

'Your organisational skills – well, let's just say I'm missing them.'

'Yeah, the thing that's really surprised me is that it's not my idea-generating ability that sets me apart here, but all the basic, rudimentary things I learned in agencies.'

The surrounding researchers, runners and PAs in the office 'woohed' in a mock chorus.

'This place is like a creative department with no account management. Very simple management skills impress the researchers and producers no end.' He played to the audience in the office. 'I think they're all a bit in awe of me.'

He ducked to avoid a screwed-up paper missile thrown by one of the researchers.

'Hey, man, get real,' called someone.

'I suspect they are,' said Briony. 'Sounds as if you're enjoying it, anyway.'

'Tremendously. What's your news, Briony?'

'Well, the reason I rang, or rather the excuse, was to tell you the latest omnibus research results on the launch advertising.'

'Go on.'

'We got the highest recall *ever* of any media launch in the last five years.'

'That's brilliant.'

'The metallic posters were particularly well recalled. And the figures were even higher among the core target. Not only all that, but the propensity to view and to have The Station installed was higher than for any other cable or satellite service, including Sky.'

'God, that's amazing! Congratulations!'

Duncan enthused but he was well aware that that was all behind him now, and the way ad people went on about their research scores seemed a bit silly to him these days. On the cusp of two careers, he recognised that commercial people can never start telling and can never stop selling.

'Well done you, is what I rang to say, Duncan. You put the whole thing to bed before you left Clancey and Bennett.'

'Well done you, really, Briony. Have they got a replacement for me?'

'Don't! There's been absolutely no sign yet. You know that Hazel got fired? They didn't tell me that until after the event or I'd have put a stop to it.'

'Charlotte rang and told me.'

'Charlotte is fine on her own. To be honest, with the success we're having I think we'll probably hold back some of the funds now. There's no point in wasting too much money. We can't keep up with demand.'

'I hope you're going to advertise *Basket Case*.'

'Oh, we'll see. How's it going? How is The Most Difficult Woman In Television?'

'I like the way everyone started using that expression *after* I'd agreed to come and work for her. Why didn't I hear it before? Actually, we're getting along all right.'

'Good. You're very diplomatic.'

Duncan dropped his voice right down. 'The thing with Karen is to understand how she operates. I think that title is just a hangover from the seventies when men were not so used to working with women in high positions.'

'They're used to it now? I don't think so!'

'You just have to go to her with solutions, not problems. In the end, she is rational and you just have to persuade her. I've had more difficult clients in the past.'

'I hope you're not referring to me.'

'No, of course not!'

'How is *Basket Case*, then? I hope it's going to be good. I'm sure it will be.'

'I don't know. It's very difficult to tell with your own idea. You get so close to it you end up being unable to judge. The main problem is simulating the interactivity. You know it has a video floor and all that?'

'Vaguely.'

'Well, all the complicated technical bits you can always sort out in the end. It's the human, emotional bits you have to take a risk on. We have no idea whether people are going to play along on their responders at home.'

'Well, believe you me,' said Briony 'they're playing with them and buzzing in and singing along on *Megabrek*, every morning. In Station homes it's wiped out the opposition.'

'Has it? What's the secret?'

'Viewers love having a say in the programmes. Until now, television has been a feudal society with the viewers as the serfs. They had to live with what they were given. Now it's a democracy in which they can take a fully fledged role.'

'Don't you think you're getting carried away with the metaphors? It's still only telly!'

Briony chuckled. 'You're right. It's all pap! How is Michael?'

'You probably see him more than I do.'

'Oh, I don't know. Duncan, I must go. Someone from the agency is in reception.'

'Who's that?'

'The Most Difficult Woman In Advertising!'

* * *

The Most Difficult Woman In Television could be unpleasantly aggressive when she wished.

'No, Duncan! No! No! Fucking no!'

'But—'

'Don't even think of starting that fucking sentence. If I say no then there is no argument. Whose company is this?'

'Whose idea is it?'

'Don't be selfish.'

'Me? *Me*?'

'Jesus! It's not for you to answer back.'

'But it *is* my idea.'

'It's mine as far as the fucking contract is concerned.' Karen jabbed the air with her finger. '*You* work for *me*. That means your ideas are one hundred per cent mine throughout the universe and in perpetuity or whatever the small print says.'

'Not the small print in *my* contract. The universe doesn't enter into it – it's not that big a deal. I'm self-employed. I have moral rights. It says we negotiate a separate contract for each idea as and when we take it up.'

'That's meant to be a reference to money, not to ownership. You get a royalty if and when anything hits the air. That's what that is meant to be about. God, Duncan, I've argued with some stubborn buggers in my time, but you take the biscuit.'

Good, thought Duncan. About time someone answered back. Someone rational, articulate and right. But he had let off enough steam by now. In all his ten years handling clients no one had ever managed to frustrate him as much as Karen Myhill had done in the last ten minutes. He had never, ever shouted in his agency years. He lowered the volume of his response.

'Do we have to discuss the precise nature of my contract in front of the rest of your staff?'

They were in the production office with the junior members of the team.

'Yeah, why not? Are you ashamed of being overpaid?'

'Hardly. That's not what I meant, anyway.'

'I didn't bring this subject up, Duncan, you did,' said Karen. 'The point is, even with me as executive producer, you cannot produce *Basket Case*. It's not a slur on you. I don't doubt your potential. I don't doubt your ability. But you are completely new to television. You have no production experience. You don't know how anything is done. I simply can't take the risk on someone who's never done it before.'

'I've—'

'Don't interrupt! There's a multi-million-pound commission riding on it. If we pull this off it can bankroll the company for years and then all our jobs will be safe. And you'll be well in pocket, Duncan. If we don't pull it off, the company could well go down the plughole and we'll be out on the streets. And you'll be out of a job in television, with not enough experience to get you back in. We can't treat one of the biggest potential commissions we'll ever get as a test ground just for you. You can go up the learning curve on the back of another producer, but not on your own.'

Duncan didn't reply. Irritatingly, she was making sense, even if it had to be made in front of the other agog people. He would never have been inconsiderate enough to take a staff member to task in front of another. Yet they obviously did that in TV. Amazingly, everyone seemed to know what everyone else earned. Duncan knew there was a lot he didn't know. Karen went on.

'Don't worry. You won't be excluded. I'll take into account your comments and observations. That is, after all, why I brought you in.'

'It doesn't seem that way at the moment.'

'Well, it is, so don't knock it.'

'I'm not—' Oh, what's the use, he thought. He had to admit to himself that despite the pressure she placed on her staff, despite the emotional blackmail and despite the unpleasantness, Karen Myhill was being fair. She was always fair in the end. She just had a very unfair way of arriving there.

He watched fascinated as she manically polished her trademark spectacles with a tissue pulled from her bag. In the argument, a bead of sweat had dropped from her forehead on to her lens and clouded her sight, though not her judgment. He knew Karen was under intense pressure and intense self-scrutiny, which is what had raised both her heated temperature and her heated temper. And she was deliberately piling as much again of it on herself as circumstances had created naturally. Perhaps she had to do this to make things work in her own mind.

Duncan personally felt that Karen approached her business in a lunatic, serial-killer, scatter-gun approach that defied all logic and made mincemeat of other people, let alone timetables and schedules. But, try as he might to fault her unsystematic style, he had to hand it to Karen Myhill. She might have no method in her methodology but she was some kind of genius. Around her things happened. She was a catalyst for creativity, a lightning conductor for inspiration, a source from which new life bubbled up. Duncan admired her. He was in awe of her. He was not sure what he would learn from Karen Myhill, but Duncan knew he would learn a lot.

He watched Karen replace her glasses and mindlessly scrunch up her tissue into a loose ball. She plonked it in an ashtray on the Fablon-topped table and immediately it sprang back larger and even more out of shape than before. It popped up and fell out of its container. She half-heartedly knocked it back in, but all that happened was that stale cigarette ash scattered in a light, wide cloud over the surface of the table. Karen let it be. It would have been unbearable for Duncan to have done the same. His fingers itched to clean up. He did not want to sit among the mess. But he hung loose, or at least as loose as Duncan Cairns could yet get. Perhaps, after all, his own itemised, detailed plotting of life was not the only way to be. Karen Myhill, for one, had another formula for success.

'Who do you intend to get to be producer?' he asked.

'I haven't made my mind up,' said Karen. She was hit by a lightning bolt of inspiration. 'Perhaps I should just produce it myself. I need to get back on the shop floor again. Hand-crafting this my own way could pay off handsomely.'

An air of panic blew round the table. The rest of the team spontaneously conjured up a collective image of Max operating the strings of his puppet mother. Mad Max. Mad Max von Stroheim, the tyrant teenage director/producer and the fastest firer in the business. Karen's brainwave had to be extinguished before it ignited any further. They would not get their fingers burnt. Nothing so slight. No, to the last man they would be incinerated to a crisp. But before anyone had thought of the right formula of words, Karen could tell trouble was up.

'Well, don't all jump in and say what a terrific idea the whole thing is.'

'It isn't,' said one brave soul. 'We need you aloof from the day-to-day production, Karen, to take a bigger view on the structure and writing of the show. Not to waste your time selecting contestants and getting bogged down in the technical development of the video floor. You can't be both executive and day-to-day producer on a massive series of this scale. It's a conflict of interest.'

Karen indulged in a spot of teeth-grinding for a moment. She sighed.

'You're probably right,' she said. 'I need to sit down with Duncan and work out the whole interactivity element. Things like that I do need to concentrate on.'

'The more cerebral things,' said the chirpy, curly-haired youth who always piped up in these meetings.

'OK, OK,' said Karen. 'I've got the message. Get Max on the phone for me, will you? I need a word.'

An hour later she and Duncan sat in her office over a plastic cup each of Lanson champagne.

'I'm sorry I shouted at you, Duncan,' said Karen.

'I shouldn't have answered back. It was my fault.'

She nodded and turned her lips out like a monkey for a moment.

'I think we'll get on well,' she said. 'I need someone to shout at me occasionally. As long as they're shouting sense and not the usual verbal diarrhoea that flows like milk in this business. The trouble with telly people is they don't think things through enough. You do. Because you're from a different discipline. You keep rationalising everything. I like that.'

'You make me sound like a robot.'

'More like that man with the pointed ears. No. He's Max if he's anybody.'

'Well, it's a good partnership so far.'

'Let's keep it that way, then, shall we?'

She raised her plastic cup in a toast.

'Cheers,' she said. 'Congratulations.'

'Cheers. Thank you.'

'To the very good health of Karen Myhill's new baby.'

Only this time, she thought, everyone will know precisely who its father is. She smiled warmly at Duncan.

Basket Case was on its way.

82

Piers was not sure how long he had been awake, if that was what the state that he was now in was. He was not sure. It dawned on him that he had no idea what day it was. Or what week. It was unimportant.

Everything sounded strange. Fuzzy. He could not hear at all on one side. And the light was blinding. Everything was blurred and out of focus when he looked. He could barely feel someone squeezing his hand, it was so numb. But someone was squeezing his hand. He had not the energy to wonder who.

His mouth was dry. His lips must have become sealed up. He tried to part them and wet them with his tongue, but it felt no different. Perhaps he had not done it properly. Should he feel hungry? He did not feel hungry. Should he call a nurse to help him relieve himself? He was not sure if he needed to go just yet. Was this what AIDS did to you? Or was it only the National Health Service painkillers? Was it . . . ? What? What was he thinking? Was he thinking? He was no longer sure. He drifted gently away.

Later he was aware that someone was saying his name softly in his working ear.

'Piers. Piers. Piers.'

He liked his name. He had always liked his name. How kind of someone to recite it. It was like a poem, a lovely-sounding, one-syllable poem. He tried to turn his head to see who might be saying the lovely poem, but he could not manage the effort.

There *was* someone there. He could feel it. Not a nurse or a doctor. Whoever it was, they were not doing anything or going anywhere, just sitting there. Being with him. Being a comfort. It wasn't Mother or Father, as they were always there together, paired, one on either side. No. This was a single person. The person held his hand and called his name again softly.

'Piers. Piers. Piers.'

His own mind's eye made easier viewing than the haze of the hospital room. In it, the grass was greener than ever now. The wild flowers were sprinkled all over the ground in pretty pastel shades. The oak trees were neatly arranged in a random pattern over the rolling English landscape. And there were the sheep, round, fluffy white sheep, tripping over their suckling lambs as they trotted round. Some of them were in the sky, swapping places with the clouds. There was no atmosphere or disturbing wind in Piers's picture. Just a perfect memory of a perfect day out. He didn't know why this image was fixed in his mind. It was always there now. Perhaps it was a preview of heaven. Perhaps it was a souvenir of the past. Whichever it was, it was unimportant. He drifted gently away once more.

Michael had sat patiently for over an hour and a half. He was unable to tell whether Piers knew he was there or not. He had called his name peacefully into the ear Dr Barani had said was not yet completely deaf, but he had got no discernible reaction. So he just sat holding his friend's thin, twiggy hand in his own and looked at him.

In his opinion, Piers's father's phrase was not quite right. The old gentleman had said that Piers was now a shadow of his former self. Instead, Michael felt that the Piers he had known had just slowly, painfully, imperceptibly drained away, leaving behind only a hint of the person, a residue. Intently studying Piers's haunting face, Michael felt he was looking at a preparatory sketch of a subject he had once known as a richly toned oil painting, which, for whatever reason, was now lost to the world. Oh yes, you recognised all the elements. All the lines and the features were there, but you missed the roundness and the fullness and the colour and the reward of the finished work, and you could never get those back however hard you wished or tried. All that effort, all that attention to detail, all that talent were gone for ever.

Michael did not speak out loud but thought of all the things they had ever done together over more than twenty years. The room parties at Oxford. The dressing up for finals. That wild trip to California in the heyday of the seventies and the previous one round Scotland in the rain, when they had no money. No, when Michael had no money, before his trust fund matured. Piers had always had money, even if he never spent it. There was the journey home to South Africa where Piers had charmed all Michael's family as the perfect English gentleman, which he was, while calling them provincial Boers behind their backs, which they were not. There were all those trips to the theatre and to the concerts and to the cinema and out to dinner. There were Piers's own perfect dinner parties, where Michael had ascended into the 'A-list'. There were the arguments – about what? Piers used to get terribly angry about the issues of the day, but frustrate himself by never truly having it out, because it was not polite to do so. There were the legions of lovely, but unloved, young men. There were always the unfinished interior design plans. The little piles of carpet swatches or wallpaper samples that never turned into anything. There were mornings spent drinking coffee and reading to a background of Radio 3. All these things now fell into place behind him, in Michael's personal history of Piers. It was all relegated to the past. Michael realised that he would never get to see Piers's fabulous flat again. And with that he realised that Piers would never get to go back home. Poor Piers. Michael lifted his palm one more time.

'Piers. Piers. Piers,' he tried again.

But he could not tell whether or not Piers could hear him. He squeezed his hand again, but only ever so gently. It was so fragile and so full of veins he was frightened it might hurt him, frightened it might crumple to the dust of old, dried parchment.

'Oh, Piers. I can't say goodbye to you.'

Michael wiped away the tears to no avail. He leaned over and slowly kissed Piers sweetly, chastely. The salt water flowed freely from his eyes and poured down and over his own lips to rest upon those of his friend and to lie there with his loving last kiss.

'You're my friend. Thank you.'

Much later, before he slipped away, he was able to say just one final whispered word, caught for ever at the back of his throat. 'Bye.'
He could not bear to look back as he left.

83

Cindy was dreading being back in London in more ways than one. At least the queue for passport control was manageable, even if they did seem to have to walk five and a half miles the wrong way round Heathrow airport in a refugee snake just to get there. Whoever had chosen these lurid carpet tiles should be taken out at dawn and shot. Cindy was prepared to do it herself. After all, she was here, wasn't she, and it was the right time of day? And it would put off confronting Alan about making a pass at Hazel Greenslade for another five minutes.

She was able to join the fast lane through the European Union gate, having lived in London on an Irish passport gained through a grandmother from Cork on her mother's side. But for once she'd rather have had the twenty extra minutes or even half an hour it takes to get through immigration into the United Kingdom, even for white citizens from one of its former loyal colonies and from a country that is a principal member of the Commonwealth.

She walked on and stood in front of a bank of overhead TV monitors until her flight number appeared. She took the escalator to the baggage reclaim floor and found her carousel. She waited for the luggage to come round. Everyone looked so crumpled and bedraggled, so tired and wiped out. So British. The luggage came in fits and starts. Cindy went off and came back with a trolley and when her two matching fake Louis Vuitton cases, once bought on the cheap in Singapore, appeared, she lugged them off the moving platform in a clumsy panic and then staggered with them to the metal trolley. She wheeled herself and her bags past the luggage carousel, across the marble floor and through the green channel. The irony of the Nothing to Declare sign was not lost on her. Because she had something very big to say to Alan Josling and she was going to have to say it in the arrivals hall of Terminal 3 at Heathrow airport right here and right now.

Alan was standing rigid, looking bored among the animated crowd behind the barrier. He carried a rolled-up tabloid newspaper which had obviously served its purpose hours back. It had failed to kill time. Everyone seemed to be soaking wet. Alan looked particularly bedraggled. Cindy had arrived back on one of the wettest days of the year.

'Hello, sweetheart. What took you so long?'

'I'm not a fast operator, unlike you,' was her answer.

Alan leant forward to kiss her but Cindy bent back.

'Hey. What's up? Was the flight that lousy?'

'Not this one – but the last time I was on a plane I sat next to a woman who said you'd made a pass at her.'

Alan looked at her, first bemused and then gobsmacked. He said nothing.

'Hazel Greenslade. Ring any bells? You pinched some Carpets Company business off her and lost her her job into the bargain. Apparently. And you pinched her fucking bottom, you bastard.'

'Hush, hush!'

'Don't hush-hush me! I'm not a dog! Please don't treat me like one!'

'For God's sake, Cindy, keep your voice down. It's six o'clock in the bloody morning. I've no idea what you're talking about.'

'You made a pass at Hazel Greenslade under Tower Bridge. It's that big one on the Thames that opens up in the middle, in case you need a reminder.'

'I did not! Let's go to the car park and get out of here. I've time to take you home and then I have to go on to a new business presentation in North London. It's pissing buckets outside.'

'Don't ignore me! I don't believe you. She said you made a pass at her.'

'Well, she's wrong. I didn't.'

'Well, she says you did. So one of you must be lying.'

'Is this the thanks I get for turfing out of bed at five a.m. to come and meet you at frigging Heathrow airport? Cindy, for the final time, I did not make a pass at her.' Alan realised he had raised his voice to Cindy's public level. He quietened down. 'I think I may have put my arm round her to comfort her. Maybe. I don't know.'

'She said you squeezed her bottom.'

'She imagined that.'

'She didn't look the vivid type to me.'

'Well, she is. She'd been hitting the bottle all evening. She was drunk and stumbled. I tried to keep up with her, that's all. Nothing happened. I can't believe you're bringing this up here. I haven't seen you for the best part of five weeks. I have a busy day ahead of me. I'm not on holiday.'

'All right. Try this one. Where were you when you were meant to be in the Cotswolds that weekend?'

'What weekend? What d'you mean?'

'It's a simple question. Where were you that Saturday?'

Actually, Alan had no trouble recalling that Saturday, the day he had telephoned Serena Sark and had heard the bad news that he was fifty thousand pounds lighter than he had hoped to be. He answered Cindy's question with an irritable sigh.

'That place in Gloucestershire. Charing Cross Manor.'

'Charing*worth*. You don't even know the name.'

'It was ages ago. What d'you expect? Cindy, you're overreacting. Over nothing, I might add.'

'I have reason to believe you were not in that hotel.'

'Oh, you rang up, did you? And I wasn't there, I suppose?'

'Too right you weren't fucking there.'

'This has happened before, sweetheart. The room wasn't in my name. It was in Gilbert's name.'

'Who's Gilbert?'

'My client.'

'Mr Gilbert or would that be Miss Gilbert, by any chance?'

'Gilbert Patterson, if you must know.'

'Yes! I must know!'

'I should have given you his name as well. And I should have rung and told you. I'm sorry. Is that what's bugging you? I know it's a big empty desert-strewn country and there's not a great deal to do in Australia, but surely you haven't been brooding on that for a month and a half? I can't believe this. I just can't believe it. How's your mother?'

'Leave my mother out of it. I don't believe you.' Acid tears poured out of Cindy's eyes. 'I don't believe you, you lying bastard. I've given you my best years. You've ruined everything for me, you know.'

'Sweetheart, sweetheart.' He moved towards her.

'*Don't touch me!*' Some of their audience looked away, embarrassed at her sudden outburst. Others did precisely the opposite.

'Cindy,' whispered Alan sharply, 'don't cause a scene. You're completely overreacting. Stop it!'

'I am not. *I am not!!*'

Cindy Barratt lifted her two fake Louis Vuitton cases from their trolley and dragged them off across the marble floor under the sign marked Underground, their little plastic wheels scraping and squeaking in protest.

The rain pressed Cindy's matted hair on to her forehead and over her eyes. She was crying so hard she couldn't see clearly anyway. She bent the key into the lock and twisted it with such force that she had no idea whether she just let herself in or broke her way into her own home. She struggled with each case left on the doorstep by the cabbie and brought them in individually. The insides of her hands were striped red and white and sore where the cheaply seamed handles had cut in. As she stopped for breath at the living-room door, she pushed it open and looked through into the room. The air was stale. She could still smell the paint from the redecorating. The antique French clock that Alan had once given her stood dead on the mantelpiece, wound down and stopped weeks before when its energy was spent.

Blundering on into the bedroom, she abandoned the suitcases on the floor. She went straight to the wardrobe and pulled out all of Alan's things. She threw them on to the ground beyond the suitcases. She went into the living room and dug out his CDs and the few books of his she had on the shelves. She piled them on top of his clothes. She went down into the bathroom and trawled through the cabinet for Alan's toiletries. She went upstairs and added those to the pile. Was that all he had? Apparently it was.

Using his coat as a carry-all, she dragged the large mound out of the flat, down the entrance hall, through the front door and along the soaking garden path at the front. She swung open the gate and then dragged the bundle on to the pavement. There she kicked and kicked and kicked at it until it fell off the kerb, between two parked cars and into the stream of dirty water running along the gutter. Her shoe fell off and in with Alan's things. Cindy stepped back on the pavement on her bare foot, making it grimy and gritty. But she did not notice, nor did she care.

'I hope I never see you again, you bastard,' she said, turning her back on Alan Josling and all his personal possessions. 'That's where you belong. In a heap in the gutter.'

The morning wore on and the downpour became tropical in proportions. Alan could barely see through the sheet water on the low windscreen of the lovely little red TVR as he shot through the dingy and depressing streets of North London.

Cindy was being ridiculous. She would have to stop these histrionics. He thought they had been through bad patches before, but this one put all the others in the shade. OK. So he wasn't without sin, but his heart was in the right place. He loved Cindy. He'd indulged her financially to prove it. And now he'd walked out early on Colin Thurrock and his lousy new business rehearsal to prove it. What else did a man have to do?

He checked the car clock. This was crazy. He didn't have enough time to stop off in Haringey, but Cindy was refusing to answer the telephone. Well, fuck it, Cindy, you'll just have to grow up and open the door. You'll only be cutting off your own beautiful nose to spite your lovely face. She would have half an hour of his time in which to sort this out and then he would have to be on his way again.

Damn! There was no parking. Fuck London. He would have to park at the bottom of the road and run up in the rain. He wished he had packed his umbrella for the airport. He would have had it in the rain there, and he would have had it to protect his suit now. He neatly slipped the TVR into a space by the kerb, then he swung open the door and lurched out into the rain.

He ran faster than he had for years. God, this was terrible. The dirt on the ground splattered up round his trousers, the ends of which were soon wringing wet. He came up to the little gate outside Cindy's flat. His face was creased with the effort of running. He caught his breath. For God's sake, don't drop dead of a heart attack in the pouring rain, man. He spotted something at the edge of the pavement, lying sodden between two cars. For a moment he thought a tramp had fallen over in the gutter and was lying there slumped. Then he realised it was his coat. And his Armani suit! For fuck's sake, you stupid bitch. What the hell d'you think you've done? Oh, Cindy! Please don't do this to me. He crouched over his things. They'd obviously been there for hours. His Peter Gabriel CD was filled with water and grains of dirt. His ties were ruined. He fumbled through them. Oh, Cindy, please don't do this to me. Don't leave me. Don't throw me out.

He dropped his valued possessions back into the water running down to the drains and stumbled through the rusty gate and up the flowing garden path to the front door. He stabbed his key into the lock but it went half in and buckled. Cindy had locked the door and left her own key in the lock on the inside. He couldn't unlock it. He rang the bell. She didn't answer. He rang again. Harder. She didn't answer. He held the buzzer longer this time. But there was no reply. He stepped off the path on to the mud in front of the ground-floor bay window. It squelched over the top of his slip-on shoes and on to his socks. He beat on the side pane of glass.

'Cindy! It's me, Cindy!'

The curtains were drawn tight.

'*Cindy!* It's Alan! *Cindy!*'

He was almost weeping with frustration. Rivulets of water were running down inside his collar, long, cold, wet fingers of discomforting unpleasantness on his back.

'*Cindy!* Don't throw me out! *Cindy! I love you Cindy!*'

He was sobbing aloud and beating on the glass with both fists, when the sash window of the second floor shot up and a man's face appeared.

'*Oi, you!* Shut the fuck up or I'm calling the police. Got the message, mate? Now clear off!'

He was doing sixty swerving miles per hour within a few minutes of hitting the dual carriageway of the busy North Circular Road. His clothes were dirty and wet through. He was shivering. He couldn't see through the driving rain, or through his tears. He had picked up his belongings and bundled them into the boot of his lovely little red TVR Griffith. What he couldn't get in there had gone on the passenger seat. But everything was ruined. His clothes. His CDs. His relationship with Cindy. His new business prospects.

'Cindy. You've got it all wrong. I've never lied to you. Not really. I love you, Cindy. I loved you the moment I saw you. I still love you. I'll always love you.'

He sniffed and wiped his tears on the back of his cuff. He had to get over this. He had missed Cindy when she was in Australia. He always missed Cindy when she was in Australia. He had been so looking forward to getting her back. He must pull himself together. Look at the time! He pushed his foot to the floor and the lovely little red TVR Griffith soared past seventy miles per hour on the speedometer. The damp was seeping through his shoes. He realised that the rainwater on the dumped clothes in the passenger seat was also running off on to his new business charts, which he need for his meeting. He took his left hand off the wheel, just for a moment, to pull his business papers out from below the other things.

Uh. They were farther over than he thought. If he just leaned across—

The offside wheel must have hit the kerb of the central reservation. The lovely little red TVR Griffith bounced high into the air, rolled over and landed on its side. It continued to skid forward at over seventy-five miles per hour, its roof scraping along the central reservation barrier, before it ripped it open like a can-opener and the car somersaulted over the barrier on to the opposite lane of the dual carriageway and into the path of a great Bedford pantechnicon truck carrying steel girders.

The lovely little red TVR Griffith, so serene and sensuous of shape, was crushed completely flat and was no more. The severed letterhead of the Josling and Thurrock new business presentation, still carrying its neatly labelled title, 'Our Future Together', fanned out across the unyielding surface of the road and was pounded and pounded into the tarmac until it was pulped by three lanes of ceaseless, sightless, unconcerned London-bound traffic.

Cindy stood plank-erect in her pew, her eyes reddened by crying, her hair pulled back severely from her face, her black coat buttoned to the throat. Her hat was an old wide-brimmed black straw thing she had dug out. It had originally come with a multi-coloured ribbon, but, suddenly inspired at the last minute, she had cut it off this morning with the kitchen scissors, before sealing her hands in skin-tight black leather gloves. It was the perfect outfit for the funeral.

She clutched on tightly to her father's unopened Roman Catholic prayer book. This wasn't a funeral Mass, so she knew she could not use it, but she had brought it for her own comfort. It reminded her of her father and happier times when life seemed simpler. She had been thinking of her father a lot since Alan's accident, and of how he too had lain in hospital, hovering between life and death. She had completely lost the place in the service. In fact she had had no idea what was going on from the moment it started. Neither had Duncan.

Duncan stood immediately to her right, dressed in a black double-breasted wool suit. He felt awkward in it now. Just a few months working in casual clothes had rendered his old daily uniform foreign to him. It was restricting and uncomfortable. Perhaps that was just the Golders Green chapel of rest atmosphere. Like everyone else he stared straight ahead and tried to join in at what seemed the most appropriate moments. But it was a bizarre one-way service with most of the assembled mourners left as passive uncomprehending spectators.

At last, the old bearded priest ceased chanting and, sprinkling petals over the coffin, appeared to wave it on into the next world. The conveyor belt wobbled into motion and the coffin slid backwards between two bunched-up red velvet curtains, accompanied on its way to the furnace by unrecognised, recorded music of stringed instruments and controlled sniffing from the lines of pews.

Outside under umbrellas in the rain, Cindy, Duncan and Michael chatted with relief that the ordeal was ended.

'That was even worse than I could ever have imagined,' said Cindy, dabbing her eyes with a too-thin embroidered handkerchief.

'I'm sorry, but I thought I was going to laugh at one point,' said Michael. 'I had no idea *what* was going on and neither had anyone else.'

Duncan smiled. 'What was he?'

'A Zoroastrian,' said Michael.

'I've heard of those,' said Cindy. 'Wasn't Freddie Mercury one?'

'Oh, yes he was,' said Duncan. 'I suppose Rik was a little bit like Freddie Mercury in some ways.' The others looked at him. 'OK. Perhaps not.'

'I thought he was in Australia,' said Michael. 'He deliberately misled us. I had no idea he was even HIV-positive.'

'You can't tell by looking,' said Duncan. 'You can't tell anything about anyone just by looking. Not these days.'

'I think I must have put that Australia idea into his head,' said Cindy. 'Apparently he used his holidays as a cover for when he disappeared into hospital. It was his way of keeping it secret. It's in the *Daily Mail* today. Have you seen it?'

'No,' said Duncan. 'We don't read the *Mail*.'

'Don't be such a snob. It's amazing. My dentist in the *Mail*. It's caused a big stink for the local health authority, the fact that he continued to practise when he was HIV-positive. Apparently there are patients up in arms about it. They seem not to care that a man has died.'

'How do you feel about it, Cindy?' asked Duncan.

'That he went on practising? I'm not bothered. He took all the correct precautions. I mean, what patients of his could be complaining? He wasn't exactly conventional, asking you to rinse out with Mateus Rosé!'

They were warmed by this affectionate thought and laughed a little together, until a new, quiet, small voice caught them unawares.

'Duncan.'

Duncan turned and was taken aback to see Charlotte, her face streaked with tears from earlier on. For once, she was soberly dressed in a charcoal coat over a black suit and a skirt bang on the knee. Without an umbrella, she was soaked through, and her hair was plastered to her head. She half stood back from the private little group, unable to sense whether she could join it or not. This was Charlotte's first funeral.

'Charlotte! What are you doing here?' said Duncan. He was pleased to see her again but felt he should show it rather than say it. 'I didn't know you knew Rik.'

'I was his Buddy. He was my friend. He was my Terrence Higgins Trust man. Oh, Duncan . . .' She burst into tears. Duncan put his arms around her.

'Charlotte, Charlotte.' Duncan had little idea of what to say to comfort her.

'I feel so awful about it. I feel I failed him.'

'No, no. You did what you could.'

'I don't know. I didn't know he was in hospital until it was nearly too late.'

'Nobody knew, Charlotte.'

'I was meant to be a friend and a comfort to him. If I wasn't so caught up in my job and launching The Station and Hazel getting fired—'

She broke down.

Cindy spoke sweetly to Duncan's friend: 'The Terrence Higgins Trust wouldn't have taken you on unless they were convinced you would do a first-class job. I'm sure you did a lot more than you realise.'

They allowed time for Charlotte to compose herself.

'I wrote down what he wanted for the order of service. It was beautiful, wasn't it?'

'It was moving,' answered Cindy.

'It was dignified,' said Duncan.

'It was the perfect send-off,' reassured Michael.

'He went downhill very quickly, you know. He never lost his looks although he became so thin. He didn't have time to. It all happened so quickly.'

'Perhaps that was for the best,' said Michael, thinking of Piers.

Charlotte ran her hand through her soaking hair. She made it look worse than it was before.

Cindy took Duncan's arm. 'What are you doing now?' she asked.

'Nothing. Going for a drink, I suppose. What would you like to do?'

'I'm going to the hospital. Alan should be having his plaster cast removed today.'

'Give him our love, won't you?'

'I should give him a slap across the face with what he's put me through.'

'Well, at least he's going to be all right.'

'He's more concerned about his car being a write-off! Honestly, he's such a materialist. I don't know what I see in him.'

Just that, thought Duncan.

Cindy gently touched Charlotte's arm, pecked each of Duncan and Michael on the cheek, and left. Charlotte quietly slipped away and followed her down the path a short while later. She wanted to cry her heart out alone at home.

'Is Paul here?' Duncan asked Michael. 'I would have thought that he would be.'

'Obviously not. I left a message on his answering machine. Perhaps he didn't get it . . .' His voice trailed off.

'What is it, Michael?'

'I've just had a thought. I don't know.'

'What? Tell me.'

'Did you notice who was at Rik's funeral?'

'Not really. I was too frightened to look around in case I started to laugh or cry. It was a bizarre service.'

'Well, there were four distinct groups of people. Obviously some relatives.'

'Yes.'

'Then patients. Then the A-list gay set. And then that little group of young men at the back.'

'I thought you'd spot them. They were all very good-looking.'

'I think they were rent-boys.'

'Michael!'

'Don't look so shocked. I mean upper-class ones.'

'Oh, does that make it all right?'

'It makes sense. That teenage sex-ring thing that Piers got dragged into – well, Piers's name would be in Rik's "gay"

address book as well as half the names from the congregation
this morning. And those young boys. They were there as a group
on their own. That could be it. Rik was always with beautiful
young escorts. You saw them once and then that was it.'

'Could be. They wouldn't come to his funeral, though, would
they? Who knows?'

'Exactly. You know people and then you don't know them at
all, it turns out.'

'We'll never discover the truth, I suppose. Shall we go for our
drink now?'

'Yes, Dunky.'

'What about Charlotte?' Duncan had just noticed than she was
no longer among the mourners.

'The girl you worked with? She was very beautiful. And so
loving towards Rik. That was sweet.'

'Will you stay here a minute?' asked Duncan. He didn't wait for
an answer, but dashed off down the path and through the rusting
wrought-iron gate. Something told him Charlotte had not come
by her normal mode of transport. He supposed it must have been
the unprecedented length of her coat and skirt. He sped up and ran
along the pavement scattered with puddles. Past a block of grimy
nineteenth century shops and flats, looking the worse for wear
and the wet, he saw Charlotte around the first corner, heading
back to town. He came up behind her.

'Charlotte.'

She turned. Her face had the grey look of loss; her eyes were
lined in red. She pulled her fingers through her damp hair,
drawing dark furrows in it.

'I thought I'd rather walk. Well, some of the way at least. It's
difficult to get a cab round here anyway.'

'We can give you a lift if you'd like.'

'No, thank you.'

Duncan could barely hear her. He smiled but it made them both
sadder.

'Was that your friend, Duncan?'

Duncan blinked and looked down for a moment and then
up again.

'Yes.'

'What's his name?'

'Michael.'

'Did he know Rik?'

'Yes. They were old friends. I knew him a little.'

'That's a coincidence.'

'Yes.'

'Funny how we never spotted it.'

'Well, not really.'

'He seemed nice – Michael.'

'Yes,' answered Duncan. 'Yes, he is nice.'

'You're lucky to have someone, Duncan. I wish I had someone at the moment. I wish Rik had had someone.'

'Thank you for looking after him.'

Charlotte's expression collapsed again under a wave of tears. She fell into Duncan's arms.

'It's so sad, Duncan. There was no one there when he died. Not even me.'

'I'm very proud of you, Charlotte. I couldn't do what you did.'

'You were my referee. You helped me. I didn't do anything really. I just visited him.'

'You did a lot.'

She sniffed. 'We used to talk about things. He made me feel really grown up.'

'It's funny. He was childish usually. He misbehaved with most people.'

'Not with me. We were a serious pair.'

'Well, that says a lot, doesn't it?'

'He told me things he said he'd never told anyone.'

'He was lucky to get you.'

Charlotte looked up right into Duncan's eyes.

'Why are you all so secretive, Duncan?'

He pulled back from her and sighed.

'I don't know. I'm trying not to be.' It was his apology. He thought hard about what she had said. 'I did know once, but I can't remember why now.'

'Can I go out with you and Michael some time?'

'Yeah.'

'Sure?'

'Yeah. I'd like to.'

'Where is he?'

'Still outside the crematorium.'

'You'd better go back to him. I'll be all right.'

'Are you sure?'

'Yes, Duncan. I'd like to walk on my own for a bit.'

She sniffed and her hand made more tramlines in her hair. Her eyes were pinky-blue now and her skin had regained a little of its bloom.

She and Duncan hugged each other for a minute more and then he pulled his arms apart and let her turn inside them and walk away. She didn't look round but gave a slender wave with one hand over her shoulder. He returned slowly to the corner of the street and, when he turned to watch her, she was far away, an older, greyer figure failing to negotiate all the pot-holes and the puddles in her path.

85

In London when it rains it pours. Stay-dry strategies vary.

One type stays put. They burrow deep indoors to work snugly through the lunch hour, or they retreat into shops or stores and meander through unexplored departments examining objects that harbour only novelty appeal.

Another type leaves the bus queues to hail cabs which arrive like earthworms on a shiny lawn, glistening and wriggling through the lanes of traffic chaos. Invariably this type throws good money after bad as the rush to four wheels locks the arteries of the city. Their only consolation is to view through waterfall windows the slower members of their own species clinging to the kerb and signalling in error to taxis already taken. They are regularly rewarded with a drenching when spurned double-decker buses drive their huge tyres through brown puddles and splash-stain their coats in a way that no amount of dry cleaning will expunge.

A third and introspective type doesn't get out of its car but turns on the windscreen wipers, turns on the heater and turns on the radio and talks back to it. This is a cousin of the breed that takes long journeys on the Underground, deep in tunnel, deep in book, deep in thought, and deeply unaware that the drains are overflowing above them.

The fourth type does not live in London. It lives only in commercials or television thrillers or American films set in London. This fourth type is always male. With vertical rain, warmed by heater and coloured blue, falling like clear plastic curtain rods into the lake, he stands, summer T-shirt jet-sprayed on to his body, on tourist bateau in the middle of the Serpentine, Mediterranean bronzed arms outstretched and very un-English regularised teeth synching to a hollered 'Yes!' Superimposed in the bottom right-hand corner of this picture is an ovulation predictor test packet or the rather more restrained logo of an insurance company whose lump sums never mature for such immature people.

The last type is the very British type that keeps the country going by buying railway season tickets and writing letters of complaint to the proper authorities. This type, which is the only type that can remember anything at all of last night's BBC weather forecast the minute it has finished, already knows it is going to rain and delves into bag or briefcase and produces a sheathed black telescopic umbrella, unpeels it and fires it into the sky. Like marching black mushrooms they continue to walk briskly in padded flat formal shoes and to make their appointments on time.

Under one such baby black brolly, arm in arm and looking every inch the backbone of Britain, walked a loving couple, reverting to type except that they strolled uncaring in the downpour. On other days driven and determined, they had marked out today as the first day of the rest of their lives, and they were slow-pacing it deliberately. For this pair had travelled to the peak of crisis and survived. And after that, nothing requires the same momentum as before.

When Alan had come to, Cindy had been by his bedside. Cindy

was always by his side at crucial moments and, despite everything, here she was again, supporting him as he strolled back slowly through the hospital car park towards his lunchtime appointment to have the plaster cast on his right arm removed.

'It's as wet today as it was the day of my accident. We didn't have to come out in this rain, you know.'

'Yes we did, Alan. You needed some fresh air and we needed to talk, and not in there with all the other patients listening. Anyway, apart from your arm there's nothing wrong with you. I don't know why they've kept you in for so long. They could have let you home a week ago.'

'I have two broken ribs. And a cut eye.'

'Fractured ribs caused by your seat-belt and a bruise on your eyebrow. Don't exaggerate. Why do men always exaggerate about illness? Women don't.'

'Did you have to don the widow's weeds? Are you intending to hound me into my grave?'

'Don't. My dentist died when I was in Australia. I only found out from Duncan this morning. That's where I've been. At his funeral.'

'Really? That funny one with the sparkling wine?'

'Mateus Rosé.'

'That was sudden. Was he in an accident too?'

'He had AIDS and nobody knew. Isn't that dreadful?'

Alan's pale face turned even more ashen.

'Alan! I know *exactly* what you're thinking. Well, don't. *You* haven't got it. He took all the correct precautions.'

'Have you heard from the car insurance people yet?'

'Alan, I've been at a funeral all morning. I'll chase it up this afternoon. But you know what they're like. We won't hear for ages.'

'You said "we".'

'Don't read anything into it.'

They went inside and up the staircase of too-small steps to Alan's grey-green ward. Both of them felt self-conscious and stared-at. He took off his outer clothes and sat down on his bed. They ceased conversing for a while, then Alan spoke quietly.

'It smells in here.'

'Yes. Hospitals always do, don't they? It's ghastly.'

'Cindy?'

'What?'

'Why did you not open the door? Why did you throw my things out? After all the years I've spent with you . . .'

'Don't, Alan. Now is not the time or the place. I hate hospitals. It reminds me of Mum and me sitting with Dad's body.'

'That girl Hazel Greenslade. She made a mistake.'

'Alan, I just don't know whether to believe you or not.'

The way she said it he could tell it was from the heart.

'Phone her and ask her.'

'I don't want to. If she made a mistake she wouldn't know, so what's the point?'

'My ribs hurt.'

'I know.'

'They'll heal, though. That's the main thing.'

'Concentrate on the right arm first. I need it for signing cheques.'

Alan managed a smile. Her joke was actually a self-criticism, a sort of acknowledgement of her own imperfections.

'You're a little vixen,' he said, affectionately.

'A Cunning Little Vixen, please. I suppose that's wasted on you. It's an opera by Janacek, whom *you've* never heard of.'

'I'm very proud of you.'

'Yeah?'

'Yes. You've taught yourself all these things. You're so knowledgeable.'

'Not really. I can say all these things but I don't *know* anything. I'm a groupie, not a true believer.'

'Why didn't you open the door?' he persisted.

'You wouldn't believe me.'

'Try me.'

'Because while I was in Australia some awful fucker moved in upstairs. I felt really hurt when I saw you at the airport and I threw all your junk in the street.'

'An Armani suit is not junk.'

'I know I shouldn't have. I was just very frustrated. I regretted it as soon as I'd done it. So I cheered myself up with my favourite Marilyn Horne at full volume and this guy, who looks like a Rottweiler, starts hammering on the door saying, "Keep the noise down." So I put on the headphones. I never heard you. I had no idea you were there.'

'You had the curtains closed.'

'I was jet-lagged. I closed them so I could have a lie-down on the settee. Well, I didn't know you were going to drive off at one hundred and twenty miles an hour and try and kill yourself.'

'That wasn't the intention.'

'Well, you did a good impression of it. If you hadn't landed in the mud, but had gone over to the other side, the police said they wouldn't have needed a coffin for your funeral. An envelope would have done nicely. You must learn to control yourself more.'

Alan laughed again. 'I'm not the melodramatic one in this relationship.' He stopped laughing. 'Can I call what we have a relationship?'

'Don't push it. Here, eat your grapes. I've got to go now. I suppose that nurse'll come back and tell you what to do now.'

She got up. Alan laughed.

'I love you, Cindy. I do love you.'

'More than your lovely little red car?'

'More than the car, sweetheart.'

'Well. I suppose that *is* true love in your book.'

She bent over the bed and kissed him on the cheek. She tapped his plaster cast lightly and then impulsively dived into her clutch-bag and produced a fountain pen with which she scrawled something on the white plaster encasing Alan's bent arm.

'I'll pop back in a couple of hours, OK? Don't check yourself out before I get back, even if you get bored waiting.'

'I love your hair pulled back tight like that,' he said. 'It really shows off your bone structure. You're still a very beautiful woman, you know, Cindy.'

'Yeah,' she mugged. 'Eat your heart out, Joanie!'

Alan watched her spin round and click her way across the linoleum, her lovely black-stockinged legs raised up on spiky black stilettos. He looked down at his plaster cast and saw that she had drawn a shaky, incomplete heart around the message C.B.L.A.J. His head shot up in acknowledgment of this touching little gesture, but she had made her exit and left the double doors swinging in her wake.

'You were magnificent, Michael.' Duncan embraced his lover and clasped him close. 'I'm so proud of you,' he whispered.

Michael released the pent-up emotion of the gruelling day and burst into tears. Duncan held him tight and let him sob his heart out.

'Oh, Dunky. Two funerals in one week. You've missed two whole days of production now.'

'They can manage without me. You did Piers proud.'

'He deserved it.'

'Your oration was superb.'

'You helped me write it.'

'I only listened. You wrote it. It was very special. Everyone's talking about it.'

'Several people have asked me for a copy.'

'I know.'

'I did want to do my best for Piers.'

'You did.'

'Oh, Dunky, I'm so glad I've got you. But I'll miss Piers.'

'I know.'

'When I saw him in his coffin . . . he was so thin and vulnerable . . .' He cried some more. 'You don't really realise they're dead until you see them in their coffin. His skin was so cold when I kissed him.'

'I know,' whispered Duncan.

Michael took a little while to recover.

'What do you call this nowadays?' He asked. 'A wake?'

'A bash, I suppose. I don't know.'

'His parents are magnificent, aren't they?' he said. 'Look at them. They haven't lost their composure once today, between them.'

'I know. His mother is very distinguished-looking. Still tall for her age and everything.'

'You can see where Piers got his looks from.'

'She must be on Valium.'

'I don't see why. The English upper class still do it better than anyone, don't they?'

'I suppose they do.'

'All that stoic stuff. It must be hard on them. Knowing their only son has died of AIDS and carrying on serving tea and cucumber sandwiches to all the fags weeping into their queenie handkerchiefs. We must all let the side down terribly as far as the MacLelland Whites are concerned.'

'Well, you haven't, Michael. Later on they'll look back and thank you for your speech. You did it with great eloquence and dignity.'

'Did you see our flowers?' asked Michael. He knew Duncan had. He just wanted to talk over all the details to reassure his memory and calm his mind.

'Yes, they were beautiful.'

'They had put them at the front. Everyone could see ours.'

'I know.'

'And the BrAIDS wreath.'

'It really stood out.'

'I didn't really like it myself. It was too red.'

'They must give them all one of those.'

'There're none of the originals left now. They're all gone.'

'The new people will carry it on. Absolutely everyone's wearing their braided ribbons.'

'Mr MacLelland White says they're getting half his money in his will.'

'Who? His parents?'

'No. BrAIDS.'

'Well, I suppose that's to be expected.'

'The BrAIDS people are trying to get his obituary in one of the papers. You know, for setting up a national charity.'

'Oh, that would be brilliant.'

'I hope they do. He never came out of the coma after I left him.'

'I know, Michael. Don't dwell on it.'

'I'm not dwelling on it. He's not even spent his first night in his grave yet.' He started to cry again.

'He wasn't on his own, Michael. His mother and father were

with him. That's as it should have been. You were his closest friend and other than them you were that last to see him.'

'Poor Piers. He never really had anyone close. Not really.'

'That's not true, Michael. He was wealthy and educated and lived the high life in London. He was happy enough. He was luckier than most.'

'He wasn't very old when he died.'

'No. I didn't really know Rik, but I feel sorrier for him. Most of the people at his funeral were his patients. He needed a Buddy to arrange it. There are virtually no work people here. These are all friends.'

Piers's mother came over to them carrying with regal poise a Royal Doulton china teapot.

'Could I possibly offer you some more tea?' she asked.

'Thank you,' said Duncan, offering her his cup.

It was all Michael could do to keep his composure.

Duncan attempted polite conversation.

'What kind of tea is this? It's very distinctive. Sort of fragrant or perfumed.'

'I can't remember the name. Piers bought it for us when we were on holiday in Morocco.'

'You went to Marrakesh, didn't you?'

'Yes, we did. Did he tell you?'

'Piers brought back a lovely rug from the souk. When we saw it we thought it was very Piers.'

'How sweet. No. I can't quite recall the exact name of this tea. How annoying. I must ask Piers. He'll remember, of course.'

She moved away in her trance, following the lead of the teapot's spout.

From the corner of his eye Duncan caught Michael's pang of heartache and took his hand to comfort him.

'Hiya, buster! Guess who this is!'

Charlotte squealed with delight. She pushed her blonde hair back from her face.

'Hazel! Where are you?' Hazel did not reply immediately. 'What brings this—'

'I'm in Sydney – hang on, there's a fractional delay. Give me time to answer, Charlie!'

'Where are you?'

'Sydney. Guess what?'

'What? What?'

'I'm working for your old agency.'

'Who?'

'Saatchi's, you great fool! I've got a job at Saatchi and Saatchi, Sydney.'

'Hazel! That's terrific! I'm so pleased for you.'

'You haven't heard the best bit yet.'

'They're all alcoholics too?'

'Piss off, kiddo!'

'Well, what? What? Tell me!'

'I'm going to be an account director!'

'Oh, Hazel. That *is* fantastic! Oh, I'm so pleased for you.'

'Haven't started yet, of course. I'm starting after Christmas.'

'What accounts?'

'Don't know yet. Who cares? Sydney here I come! Tell that to Fatboy Gainsborough and Serena Sack! How are they all, anyway?'

'Don't ask.'

'Haven't those two been fired yet?'

'They'll never, ever get fired, Haze. Whatever we think. We do all the work and they take all the credit. I spent today with Margaret, typing up my c.v. for Audrey Goldberg. As of January one, I'm out there knocking on doors.'

'How's The Station? It's even been in the press over here.'

'It's doing incredibly well. The posters got the highest something or other in research. Briony Linden was pleased, anyway.'

'Good for you!'

'Nigel and Serena have gone round blowing their own trumpets, needless to say. The campaign's up for awards, as you can imagine.'

'Great!'

'But the agency is hell. There's only Orlando left now to talk to, really.'

'What about Mr Lycra Lover-Boy?'

Charlotte screamed: 'Aaaaaaagh!!!'

'What?' came back Hazel, her ear hanging off.

'I've just realised something. I know something you don't know!'

'What?'

'He's resigned.'

'He hasn't?'

'He has!'

'Has he?'

'And guess where he's going?'

'Where?'

'*Saatchi and Saatchi, Sydney, Australia!* He's going to be a group head or something. Orlando told me.'

'*Aaaaaaagh!!!*'

'You'd better warn the girlies on Bondi Beach to padlock their panties because Super-Sausage is on his way!'

'Oh, that's it. I resign. I can't bear it!'

'Oh, Hazel. Fuck! Look at the time! It's Duncan's programme's pilot tonight. I'm going round to Orlando's to watch it over dinner.'

'Orlando, eh?'

'He can get The Station in his flat, so we thought we'd watch it together. Oh. Thank you for calling. I'm *really, really, really* pleased to hear your news. Congratulations. And happy Christmas when it comes.'

'I'll be surfing in my bikini. Think of me. I take it there's an agency party?'

'An MCN International one out at Shepperton Studios. Pretty

lavish, I expect. It'll be ghastly. It's fancy dress.'

'What are Godzilla and Dracula going as? Don't tell me, themselves?'

'Oh, don't, Haze.'

'What are you doing for New Year?'

'Daddy and I are skiing in Val d'Isère. I was a chalet girl there when I was nineteen. I suppose I'll have to behave a bit better this time!'

'Listen to you! I'll call you from Saatchi's on their bill when I start. Happy Christmas!'

'Happy Christmas, Haze.'

'Byeee!'

'Bye, Haze. Bye.'

Charlotte threw the receiver back on to its base and ran into her tiny bathroom. She checked her lip gloss in the mirror and smoothed down the front panel of her lycra top. The stitched and wired half-cups gave her more of a bust. She hesitated for just a moment and wondered how old she looked. Her hair fell forward. She pulled it up into a tight bunch on her head. What would she look like with a really short crop? Not as short as Steve's, of course.

'I didn't tell her my Buddy died,' she said out loud. Her eyes moistened. Since that day when she had first met Duncan Cairns there had been a run on time. She'd met and lost Duncan. She'd met and lost Hazel. She'd met and lost Steve. She'd met and lost Rik. She rearranged her hair and sighed.

'Next year,' she promised the golden girl in the mirror. 'Next year.' She turned sideways and, caressing her hips, posed and pouted at her image. 'Girls just wanna have fun,' she half sang. She remembered the time.

She popped into the kitchen and grabbed the Moët from the fridge and then ran through the living room with it, pulling on her leather jacket, her scarf and gloves. She unsnibbed the lock on the inside of the door and then as an afterthought ran back to the bathroom. There she picked up her little overnight toiletries bag and marched back to the front door. Well, you never knew. It could be a long night.

Downstairs, outside in the freezing street, she pushed back her flighty blonde hair and thrust her head back into her crash helmet. With that, Charlotte Reith jumped on to her Ducati 748sp and roared off into the London night.

88

Duncan sat on the edge of the bed staring intently at the TV screen.

'I'm sick with nerves.'

He placed a tray of tortilla chips covered in melted cheese down on the floor. Perhaps it was these he was sick with. They were congealed and revolting enough.

'I can't believe I'm eating this crap. That's what telly does to you.'

'What?'

'It doesn't lower your standards. It erases them. God, my stomach.'

'Don't be nervous, Dunky,' said Michael. 'It'll be a great success.'

'Do you think it's peculiar of me to watch it from here rather than see it in the studio?'

'That's up to you. There wasn't any more you could do, was there?'

'No. Anyway, they've got my number here and my mobile number, so if they need to call, they will.'

'Sure they will.'

'I've rehearsed all the contestants. I've set up all the final options on the video floor questions. I've rewritten the script and the opening gags. They won't stick to it anyway.'

'Why not?'

'Karen's dreadful. You can hear her redirecting the director down the talkback. She constantly overrules him and everyone can hear it on their cans. She treats him like a doormat with the word "welcome" scuffed off it.'

'Who's the director?'

'You wouldn't know him.'

'Well, there you are. No one's heard of him, but everyone's heard of Karen Myhill, the Most Difficult Woman In Television. That's because she *is* the best. She's not really difficult. She's just a perfectionist.'

'*You* don't have to work with her.'

'I have done. At Trafalgar Television.'

'Yes, but—'

'Yes, but I only do the boring legal bits. Is that what you were going to say?'

'Not those exact words. Don't be so sensitive.'

'Look who's talking. Mr Don't Tell Anyone I'm Gay.'

'I tell everyone I'm gay now. It goes with being in TV.'

'The hell you do.'

'Anyway, I think I was right to stay at home. I need to play the game on the responder and see if you really can play along with it at home and get hooked on it. That's the crucial test of the pilot. They never found a convincing way of mocking up the interactive element of the game in rehearsals. If this were advertising, we'd have found a way of doing it before going public. Sometimes television is really crappy compared to advertising.'

'Only sometimes?'

'No. Always.'

'So, are you sorry you gave it up, then?'

'Are you kidding? I wouldn't swap this for the world.'

'Do you get a credit at the end?'

'I most certainly do. I wanted "Created by" but for some reason they wouldn't allow that. So I've got "Associate Producer: Duncan Cairns". Then the producer's name. Then "Executive Producer: Karen Myhill", or "Max Myhill" if the boys play this trick they're promising to do. Then the director's name. Then "A Myhill Production For The Station".'

Graphics appeared on the TV screen and flashed through the silver and new-look gold metallic imagery based on Orlando's corporate advertising. The Station had decided to adopt it full-time for its on-screen logo after the success of the launch.

Then the heavy electronic beat started and the screen went black. The title music fanfared over a flying camera 'buzzing' over the studio floor in swoops and swirls. One by one, the squares of the video floor began to light up with fabulously colourful sequences of film all heavily art-directed in an animated version of Andy Warhol-style pop prints. One square showed Hillary on Everest; another, Pelé scoring his World Cup goal; next there was Marilyn Monroe blowing a kiss from a window, morphing into *Henry VIII* by Holbein. A killer whale plunged into slow-motion foam and was superseded by a nuclear mushroom. Meanwhile, a flying neon power-ball graphic and pink and orange question marks flashed on and off on all the screens.

Then everything, even the music, stopped.

One giant message took over the video floor: 'Press Your Responders Now!' Then the theme tune went in for one last burst and two large multi-coloured words filled the screen.

Basket Case.

Michael applauded with excitement.

'Oh, look! Oh, Duncan, it's your programme!'

Duncan beamed angelically. He was in heaven.

'A Myhill Production for The Station.'

Duncan zapped the television off smartly, while Michael popped open the champagne. He filled two glasses and handed one to Duncan, who looked at him quizzically.

'Well?'

'It's certainly different. They all seemed to be playing it at home on the transponders.'

'*Re*-sponders.'

'That power-ball thing works,' said Michael. 'They got lots of goals. It's not just about general knowledge, then. It's more like tennis or something, where there's different pressure on different points. It's quite clever, really.'

'Only quite clever?'

'Dunky, I'm biased. There's no point in asking me.'

'Well, come on, then. We should go.'

'Do you really want me to come too?'

'Of course. You're the company lawyer, aren't you? And you're my lover. I want you to meet everyone at the party.'

'What happened to the old Duncan who could never take me to the office party?'

'Who? Oh, him. He's wrapped up in a tartan blanket somewhere and doesn't ever show his face. Everyone knows I'm gay. I'm too old to hide it or to want to hide it or to care any more.'

The mobile phone by the bed rang.

'Hi, Duncan. It's Briony.'

'Oh, my God. What did you think?'

'Terrific. Congratulations.'

'Are you just saying that?'

'Would I have telephoned otherwise?'

'Thank you. Will you commission it, then?'

'You'll have to ask Martin Fox. I can't help you there. But I can tell you the ratings and appreciation indices. It's so fantastic having instant access on every programme. You know the minute it's over what it's done.'

'Are you in the office, then?'

"Fraid so.'

Duncan heard her tapping into her keyboard.

'Wow. I'm not allowed to tell you the figures, OK? They're confidential.'

'But . . . ?'

'But you should be very pleased. The rating is *higher* than anything we've yet had on in the evening. Oh, Duncan, the figures *are* good. And the appreciation index is off the bloody graph! Woo-oo-ooh!'

Duncan blushed with modesty.

'Remember I told you none of this, OK?' said Briony. A siren went off in the background. 'Fuck!'

'What's all that noise?' asked Duncan.

'I've set off the bloody smoke alarms with my cigarette.'

'You're not smoking in the office!'

'Give me a break! I'm all on my own. I'll get hell for this! I'd better go! Give my love to Michael.'

Duncan laughed and put down the receiver.

Michael could tell it was good news.

'Dunky—'

This time the bedside phone rang. Duncan snapped, 'Who's that this time? We need to get changed for the party.'

'Hello, sweetiekins, it's me!' It was Paul McCarthy.

'Have you been watching my show?' asked Duncan, surprised.

'Was it tonight?'

'Something tells me you didn't watch it.'

'No, I didn't, so there!' said Paul. 'They won't cable us round here for years. We're too poor in this part of London. Bloody fascists. I just rang to say I've been away in Ireland on a job, directing, and I only just got your message about Rik. I read it in the papers, actually.'

'Oh, no.'

'It *is* sad, isn't it? Thank you for trying to contact me. I was surprised to hear Michael's voice among all the dirty messages on my answering machine. I thought I was in luck, at first, then I realised it was him! How's your sex life?'

'We're just going off to the pilot party for *Basket Case.*'

'I can't believe you used that title. That's my invention. I should sue you.'

'Shame there's no copyright on titles, then, isn't it?'

'Smartarse! So? How did it go?'

'Very well, I think.'

'God, you're so self-effacing, aren't you! What are you doing at home, then, if your show is going out tonight? It's live, isn't it?'

'Someone needed to play the game on the responders.'

'The what?'

'Responders. They're a two-way interactive responsive device allowing dual input into your programme.'

'Oh dear, she's off. You've lost me already, darling.' Paul laughed. 'Make a show about tapestry, then we can chinwag.'

'You're very up tonight,' said Duncan.

'I've taken lots of drugs, that's why. E, E, E!'

'Well, you shouldn't.'

'Oh, don't be so miserable. I've been in Ireland, for God's sake. All the boys wear tweed knickers there. I needed cheering up. And, hey presto, it's worked.'

'Well, don't do it again. Sorry, Paul, I must go. I'll talk to you soon.'

'All right. Byeeee!'

'Oh, Paul. Paul!'

'Yes?'

'Think about Christmas. We'll be at the cottage. Why don't you join us? It'll be fun.'

'Can't, darling. I'm going to be – how shall I say? – rather tied up this Christmas.'

'Doing what?'

'Being rather tied up, of course! Anton's having me, in more ways than one, if you catch my drift. We're spending a black Christmas together.'

'God. What's that?'

'Use your imagination. You're supposed to be in entertainment, aren't you? Leatherwear. Rubberwear. Chain-mail. Bonding in bondage.'

'You're becoming degenerate. It's disgusting.'

'I know. Isn't it just fabulous? Bye, then, darling.'

'Bye, Paul.'

'Michael dragged himself over the bed again and kissed the back of Duncan's neck.

'Here's your champagne. Congratulations.'

'Thank you.' With his head over the edge of the bed and Michael stretched on top of him, Duncan was face to the floor.

'Michael?'

'What?'

'Why did you never tell me the Basket Case story?'

Michael pulled away from him, allowing Duncan to turn over.

'It happened years before I met you.'

'But you didn't even mention it when I was being interviewed by Karen. Why?'

'You'd never have gone to work for her if I'd told you.' Duncan looked at him quizzically. 'Well, you wouldn't, would you? I even got Paul to promise not to mention it to you.'

'Really? But why on earth did you let me walk in there on my first day and present this show to her and her assembled throng? It must have looked like a one-man Charge of the Light Brigade to all of them.'

'You only thought up the title on the walk into work, remember? I had no idea you were going to call it *Basket Case*.'

'I'd forgotten that. Nonetheless you should have told me. It was reckless of you not to.'

'Don't start. I did think about it. I know I did the right thing because look how it's worked out. Brilliantly, even if I say it myself.'

'That's your opinion . . . Michael?'

'What?'

'Who is Basket Case?'

'Nobody knows.'

'Somebody must know.'

'Karen Myhill does. I don't even think Max knows.'

'You don't know?'

'Why would I know?'

'Because . . . it's not you, is it?'

Michael separated from Duncan and lay back on the bed and began to laugh, a little at first, then more and more until he was guffawing. Duncan flushed. He was bemused.

'What's so funny? It's a reasonable question, isn't it?'

Michael stopped laughing. 'Oh, Duncan. Sometimes I think we don't know each other at all.'

'Don't say that. And don't answer it. I don't really want to know. I don't want to have to share you with anybody . . . Michael?'

'*What?*'

'Nothing.' He found Michael's hand with his own and clasped it. 'Just thank you for helping me and encouraging me.'

'Did I do that?'

'I couldn't do it without you.'

'Oh, Dunky. Will you still love me when you're rich and famous? Or will you run off with some younger boy, who's very good-looking?'

'I won't run off with him. I'll share him with you, like Bobby!'

They giggled naughtily.

'Come on, Dunky. Let's get ready.'

They were about to get off the bed when their little friend shot into the room, jumped up on to the covers and dropped a large, thick, wriggling pink earthworm on to the fresh white pillowcase between them.

'*Eeeugh!*' said Michael. 'Pushkin!' He threw the worm on to the carpet.

'Don't be cross, Michael. It's a present,' said Duncan. 'You have to say "thank you" or you'll offend her.' He pulled the beautiful sorrel-coloured Somali into his arms and spoke to her. 'Thank you, Pushkin. What a lovely wormy.' She pressed her button nose to his.

Duncan turned to Michael, who had started to laugh again. 'Just think of it as an early Christmas present.'

Then he joined in with Michael and laughed too.

89

The elderly lady stood, arms folded over her white nylon coat, face a picture of disapproval behind large plastic bifocal spectacles and tone of North London voice decidedly unimpressed. Through the plate-glass window, and in between the reversed writing on it advertising her services, she picked out the odd couple walking away from her florist's shop. She talked to her colleague over her shoulder without turning round.

'Look at them. Nutters.'

Her colleague looked up from behind the counter and for a moment stopped wiring leftover sprigs of spiky greenery into a traditional holly wreath for her own front door.

'It takes all sorts, Betty.'

'Don't I know it. You meet the whole of mankind in Golders Green. But in all my years, I've never had a request like that.'

'It wasn't so difficult.'

'Well, I mean, this is the thing. I'm a floral artist. I'm certificated from the Royal Horticultural. One of the old school. I take pride in a job of work. I do try to keep up with the trends as long as they're appropriate. But I don't like to have them taking the Michael.'

Her colleague yawned.

'Well, she paid up for it, so it's no skin off our nose. Come on, Betty. It's five to one. Let's shut up now and have our sherry and mince pie. I got Marks's.'

She stepped forward, swung the door sign round so that on the inside it read 'Interflora. Open', and shut up shop for Christmas.

Karen and Max walked along the meandering path, her head twitching from side to side trying to spot the location, Max tied down to the ground by the weight of the floral contrivance.

'I think it's over there,' she said.

'Think. You think,' said Max, 'But you don't know.'

'Max, be pleasant. There's still time to hold back on the presents tomorrow, you know.'

'Come on, Kar. That old chestnut hasn't worked for ten years.'

'Please be nice, Max. This is important to me.'

'It's important to me too. It's more important to me.'

She stopped, stood at arms' length in front of Max and placed her hands on her son's shoulders. Behind her bejewelled spectacles, there were tears in the corners of her eyes.

'I know, Max. I do realise. I may not have done the right thing.'

'May not?'

'I did try to. I'm not sure now, but I wanted to do what was right for you. I think that I may have done entirely the wrong thing.'

'I'm not going to disagree about that.'

'Oh, Max, please don't hate me. You're my precious baby.'

'Yuk.'

'I've always meant the best for you.'

Max gave his mother a rare affectionate smile.

'I know, Mum. That's the problem.'

They walked on and wandered criss-cross over the wet grass, between the headstones, one here adorned with a pot of fresh red roses, another there with faded plastic tulips leaning against it.

'Max!'

Karen had stopped in front of a squat, thick granite block. Max caught up with her and stood at the edge of his father's grave.

'It's a bit small, that thing,' said Max. A lot of the others were much larger and showier.

'It *is* small, isn't it? He was cremated. Then they buried the ashes, I suppose. Are you disappointed?' Karen was.

'Makes no difference, really.'

'No. I suppose this is the style they go in for nowadays. Minimalist. Everything today is so . . . so nothing,' said Karen. She wiped away a small tear with the back of her woolly gloved hand. 'So, there he is. It *is* sad. If he had lived a bit longer I'm sure you would have met him.'

'How can you say that? You did everything in your power to stop us meeting.'

'Only because you were a child, darling.'

'I'm not a child.'

'Not now, but you were.'

'You would never have allowed it, Mum. You would have always found some excuse to put it off, to deny me.'

'Oh, no, Max, no.'

'Oh, yes, Mum, yes. Oh yes, oh yes, oh yes.'

'I'm sorry, Max.'

'I'm sorry too . . .'

'What, Max?'

'Nothing.'

'Don't clam up, darling. I can't bear it when you stare me out like that. What are you thinking?'

'Only that it's all just so you.' He guffawed. It was really a cry of agony and hurt and frustration, albeit dressed up as a response to farce. Max brooded for five minutes and Karen let him. Eventually, she cleared the air.

'It's my fault, Max. Blame me. I thought you were too young to understand.'

'I don't blame you, Mum. Not deep down. I resent it, yeah, but I don't blame you. I can't. You're lucky, you know.'

'Lucky?'

'Yeah. Now I'm grown up at last you've got somebody to save

you from yourself. I don't begrudge your not having someone to save me from you when I was younger.'

Karen wept.

'Don't cry. I thought you said he meant nothing to you. Why are you crying?'

'Oh, Max. I wish I was crying for you, or for him, but I'm not. I'm crying for myself. I don't know. I'm just crying because I'm fifty, I suppose, and he was part of long ago and that was when I was a lot younger and I was a success and you're no longer my baby any more and I've spoiled your formative years and you'll grow up soon and leave me and I'll be on my own and I'm frightened of being old and lonely and I can't change anything now and your life just goes on day to day and then you realise it's all gone past you and that's it. Sorry, Max. Mummy is becoming an old sentimentalist.'

Max continued to study the headstone.

'And I'm crying because everyone thinks your father was somebody in TV and that Mummy couldn't have done it on her own and isn't a very nice person and I've done everything all by myself and had lots of bad luck that people don't know about as well as all the awards that they do know about and I've tried to bring you up on my own which was much, much more difficult than I could ever have imagined and I try to be a nice person and help other people only sometimes it gets very trying and very difficult and it doesn't help if everyone imagines you're somebody you're not.' She stopped and sniffed back her grief. 'Or your son's father is somebody he's not.'

Max read aloud the name on the headstone.

'Piers MacLelland White. I could have been called Max MacLelland White. I quite like that.'

'I'm not sure Piers would have approved.'

'Why not?'

'Perhaps I mean *I* wouldn't have approved.'

'Why?'

'Because he was nothing to do with me, really. Or you. He was literally your father but nothing more than that. You were *my* baby. I wanted you. I wanted you all to myself. I wanted to bring you up on my own. I wanted you to be my friend. I never had any friends before you, Max. Any other woman in my position would have had an abortion. I was the feminist type, but a different sort. Well, at least I think I was. I don't know what I was.'

'Did he ever come to see me when I was little?'

'No.'

'You prevented it.'

'No! No. We agreed you were my baby and that was it. The thing was, that, as you know, Piers was gay, and when he was younger, like a lot of gay men, he experimented a bit with women. He'd not had a relationship with a woman for years when, one day, he came into Trafalgar Television to a research meeting and he met me. I didn't get on very well with a lot of the men around me at that time because they were not used to a woman being in charge.'

'Blimey, the Stone Age.'

'Well, this was before Mrs Thatcher, even. A lot of men at work in those days were threatening and overpowering. They were sexist, or even sexual. Piers wasn't like that because he was gay or at least gayish and . . . well, we went for an early drink in the bar and then I wanted to show him a tape or something, I can't remember why, and we went off to a quiet spot somewhere and I, well, I suppose I took advantage of him. It was my decision. I was in control. It was one of my five-minute ideas. I was just being silly for a moment and threw caution to the winds.'

'And you had me.'

'Yes, darling. I had you.'

They stood in silent tribute, Karen sniffing, Max sulking.

'Somebody spotted us doing it, Max. Can you imagine how awful that was?'

'No.'

'But I had you, darling, and it was all worth it.'

'Was it because he was gay that you didn't want me to meet him?'

Karen paused and struggled to find the answer.

'It's half the reason, I suppose. I was embarrassed that anyone, even you, would find out. I'm so hideous-looking. Not conventionally beautiful, Grandma would have said. Men never fancied me. I thought they'd all laugh at me. Or pity me. I didn't know which was worse. I only spoke to Piers once on the phone afterwards and he said the experience had cured him of any wayward heterosexuality. Well! Think how I must have felt. He didn't mean it the way I took it, I imagine, but I was pretty insulted, I can tell you. And I thought if you knew and the other children at school found out and the neighbours and everything—'

Max laughed coldly. 'Since when did you care about the neighbours?'

'Society disapproves, Max, even now. I didn't want you to have a cross to bear. The plan was for me to tell you who he was when you were eighteen and then you could decide if you wanted to meet him or not. But it was not to be. He had developed full-blown AIDS when I next heard what he was up to. I thought that would attach even more stigma to you, so I didn't contact him. I don't know if I did the right thing. I'm sorry if I didn't.'

'Why didn't he come and see me? Why didn't he ring me or even send me anonymous Christmas cards? You didn't tell him about me, did you?'

'I most certainly did.'

'He did know I had come into the world? He did know I existed?'

'Oh yes, he did. But . . . Max, you'll just have to accept it. It's the truth. He made no effort to ask to see you, so . . .'

Max sighed determinedly through gritted teeth.

'That's it, Max. The story of your father.' Karen had long since stopped crying. 'He's left you some money in a trust fund.'

'He hasn't?'

'He has. I'm barred from telling you the details. In fact, I don't actually know them, but I think you can only get it when you are twenty-five.'

'Twenty-five! That's ancient. I'll be too old to do anything with it when I'm twenty-five. I can handle money now. I'm good with it. You know that. How much?'

'I don't know, actually. It sounds like a lot, though.'

Max hopped from one leg to the other in the cold. He was still holding the flowers.

'Mum?'

'What, darling?'

'Who does MF stand for?'

'MF?' Karen looked around at the names and initials on the surrounding gravestones. 'Where do you see that, Max?'

'In your diary.'

'In my diary?'

'Yes. One day when you were out I found an old diary and I guessed the day that I was conceived and you had written in MF and gone over it and over it again. I thought it was my father's initials.'

Karen thought for a moment. It was over fifteen years ago. 'Oh. I remember. God, I was a stupid cow sometimes. I can't tell you.'

'Mum! You've got to!'

'I can't.'

'Just tell me, Mum. You owe it to me to tell me, especially now after what's happened.'

'I'm embarrassed.'

'I won't tell anyone.'

'It's not someone's name.'

Max winced. 'Oh no. What is it, then?'

Karen exhaled and told her son. 'Mad Fuck. That's what it was. One crazy moment.'

Max laughed. 'Mum?'

'What?'

'You really are funny sometimes, you know that?'

'Have I ruined your life?'

'Ask me when it's over.'

'Can you forgive me?'

Max did not reply.

'The truth is, Max, that I wanted you for me. You're my own precious baby.'

'Yeah, well, don't go around saying it out loud to everybody. I have no credibility as it is.'

Karen smiled at him. 'Come on, darling. It's freezing out here. Let's go and have a slap-up lunch somewhere. Your choice. Put the flowers down in front of the little stone.'

Max did as he was told and the two stepped back and stood for a moment and then, arm in arm, they slowly sauntered off down the winding path back to the car, the drive into central London and the Christmas Eve queue at the Hard Rock Café.

In front of Piers's headstone they left behind their tribute. Sixteen large, pure white lilies, one for each year of Max's life if you counted next birthday, a magnificent and striking display arranged in a traditional cane wastepaper basket.